KATZENJAMMER

A shot of romance

Eve Upshall

Copyright © 2025 Eve Upshall

First published by Eve Upshall 2025.
This Paperback Edition 1/2025

Eve Upshall reserves the moral right to be identified as the author of this work in accordance with the Copyright, Designs and Patents Act 1988

A catalogue record for this book is available from the British Library

Ebook ASIN: B0FCFLDTF6
Paperback ISBN: 9798285755746
Hardback ISBN: 9798287201517

This novel is entirely a work of fiction. The names, characters and incidents portrayed in it are the work of the author's imagination. Any resemblance to actual persons, living or dead, events or localities is entirely coincidental. All rights reserved.

No part of this publication may be reproduced, stored in a retrieval system, or transmitted, in any form or by any means, electronic, mechanical, photocopying, recording or otherwise, without the prior permission of the publisher.

Cover Design by Eve Upshall & Henri
Artwork by Eve Upshall & Henri

For Ann France

*And to anyone who has ever woken up with
mascara smudged, dignity slightly misplaced,
and a katzenjammer of a thousand wailing
cats stuck in your head - this one is for you.*

ONE

Double Orgasm

When I make a cocktail, it must be perfect. Just one wrong ingredient ruins the whole thing. The wrong spirit. A missing garnish. Chipped glass. Too much ice. Easily fixed? Just start right over. If the correct flavours are on hand, you can mix them again and enjoy. But not everything works that way. Some things, some experiences, do not get a do-over. These canon events leave a lasting scar, unrepairable, leaving you changed forever.

What happened to me today is, without a doubt, a bad mix. Like when a taste so bad contorts your expression into something so tragic that strangers comment, 'cheer up love, no one died'. It annoys me when people say that. Sometimes I'm tempted to say 'yes they have', just to see the look on their face. But not today, although it comes in a close second on the enshittification scale.

The day started well—the best, with all the flavours in the right order. For starters, I made it to work on time, which is a huge win, as that almost always never happens. I should get an accolade, even though the credit belongs to another. My boyfriend, Hugo, is the spirit to my mixer, mixing things up when life gets boring. Today, in a rather unprecedented move, he pushed me out of bed when it was time for work.

Yes, I feel a little rejected. But it is not a disaster. A light splash of responsibility creates a big impact. We are now in a serious relationship, heading for the ultimate flavour pairing: marriage.

Things get better when I walk through the door and am

personally greeted by the head of human resources, inviting me for a chat.

I'm going to get promoted. Nerves take over, and I'm either going to be sick with excitement or wet myself. This is the moment I have been waiting for. All my hard work has paid off. Finally, something good is happening.

"Kat James. I find you guilty of gross misconduct, unbefitting an employee here at Artisanal Delight." Dextra Dominica, small head, large hair, long nailed monocratic bitch, delivers the news with sour notes.

This seems unfair.

Dextra Dominica teases the ends of her elbow-length curls before smoothing the ruffles on her red bodycon dress.

"Gross Misconduct?" My voice is diluted by a click clicking on the mouse that wakes the wall-to-wall video screen.

I am a model employee, on paper anyway. Uma clocks in for me, so my tardiness goes undetected. Never late and always willing to please, she is the modifier to my professional life. We had an agreement. Uma would never betray me.

But human resources found out somehow.

It can't be the security cameras. I always stay off the radar when sneaking in. Regardless, the quality of recordings will be substandard. I've been in the security office, and the monitors resemble water added to ouzo, snowy pixels of a system installed about a hundred years ago.

But I am looking at images. Lots of images. Images of me. Clear. High definition. In colour. The only thing missing from the photo montage of my 'best bits' is music. An Artisanal Delight reality show where I, the evictee, watch career highs and lows. Pictures of me enjoying my role as Entertainment Executive. Here's one of me downing a few cheeky shots 'paid for' by clients. Another depicts me clearing up, tucking a half-empty bottle of Anejo Tequila in the back of my trousers. To keep my hands free, of course. Technically, it's not stealing as I had charged it to a client who drank what they wanted before leaving. It's not theft, it's gifting, which Dextra Dominica reminds me is not actually a thing.

Frame follows frame until we reach the finale, filmed late

last night in the private members lounge. Sultry lighting from chrome ceiling chandeliers provides just enough illumination to make out two persons entering the room via the staff entrance.

The video cuts to the deep-seated velvet Chesterfield sofa. Handmade and newly installed, I selected it myself from the company catalogue. It was above budget, but the ochre shade complements the nubuck eco-leather of the industrial armchairs. The acts of last night would have been impossible if not for the Chesterfield. Hugo bends me backwards over the low rolled back and I hook my fingers into the plunging recesses. My head on the seat, the luxurious velvet caresses my cheek as he lifts my left leg over and I straddle the firm, curved back. Hands brush up my leg, fingers tease to the thigh-length slit in my black midaxi dress. The sweetheart neckline reveals a hint of cleavage.

Wait, Dextra may have a point. This does look bad. My twelve-hole platform boots graze the fabric. That is going to mark. I should have asked him to remove them as I'd been on shooter duty when Hugo pulled me from the dance pit with promises to give me a Double Orgasm. A Double Orgasm is messy and ignores the restraints of a cocktail shaker and glassware. Hugo slides crushed ice over my body, then pours the Amaretto, Irish cream liqueur and Kahlua straight into my mouth, at the same time as giving me an actual orgasm. If your mind is boggled, you are halfway to appreciating Hugo's talents.

Dextra Dominica pauses the movie, Hugo frozen at the point of sliding my knickers midway down my thigh. The familiar curve to the edge of his mouth, eyes looking into the lens of the camera.

Eyes.
Looking.
Into.
The.
Lens.
Of.
The.
Camera.

But there are no video cameras on that wall. Only the new art deco framed mirror was fitted last week. It must have a hidden camera. The room is nothing more than a honeypot. I'm such a fool.

Although my face is masked, it is quite clearly me. The parting in my dress reveals my tattoo, a floral tribute running from hip to mid-thigh. The same thigh is currently visible through the slashes in my washed black jeans. Dextra taps the glass table, her Curacao blue acrylics follow my tattoo as I cross my legs, my hands add an extra shield, but it's too late.

This is revenge porn at its finest, only it's not Hugo's fault. Dextra is the one to blame, watching enough to rule it unacceptable. Or watching it all, including when Hugo followed the path of the flowers up my thigh, tasting the sweetest bloom at the top. Jealous at viewing the pleasure he delivered using only his tongue, wishing someone, anyone, would eat her out and give her a double orgasm. If anything, it's her behaviour that's inappropriate.

"As of this moment, you are no longer an employee of Artisanal Delight."

This is a mistake.

"Please submit your pass and collect your things from your locker on your way out."

So that is what gross misconduct means.

I am fired.

Pressure builds in my throat, tongue paralysed. Chest heavy, I pull at my jacket, but the compression grows, inversely proportional to my efforts. Something slams into my ribcage, the air sucked out. Breath shallow, worthless, every drop drained from the bottle.

Small head, large hair, long nails, tap, tap, taps the table, pace quickening. I close my eyes. This has happened before.

Break, twist, tumble, then shattered glass. Trapped. Helpless.

Darling, these three steps will help. Your body will automatically know what to do with practice.

The meditation, I cannot remember. I am no good at this. Did not practice enough.

Something about feeling the emotion. But this is a problem for me right now as emotion equals crying, and I am not about to blub in front of human resources. Any sign of weakness and they win. Stay strong and show resolve.

Hands caress my face, offering comfort. Dextra Dominica's? No. Mine. A grounding essence of compassion. My palms press into the table, fingers spread so each knuckle makes contact. Feet flat on the floor. Stability. That was step one. I remembered. I have done well.

Next, observe my surroundings. I am in the boardroom, a three-meter square out-of-the-box cube. The antithesis of bespoke craftsmanship. Sterile papered wall panels joined with plastic strips, monotone grey carpet squares, oval glass table set on steel arches. Four charcoal fabric chairs of hessian quality, rough to the touch. All ugly. No help here.

Visible through the table are Dextra Dominica's shoes. Animal print pony skin toe cap set into a chunky one-and-a-half-inch black heel, which supports a sturdy ankle strap. Pretty. The orange tipping on the toe panel mismatches her dress. The curve of her calves, red hem kissing her knees. Perched on the chair, back poker straight, narrow waistline, gentle curves up to shoulders.

Don't rush. I got this.

"Your pass." Dextra Dominica holds out her hand, elbows resting on the glass, talons lengthen to snatch the lanyard off my neck. Head nods in encouragement. She is enjoying this.

Meditation interrupted, I stand on shaky legs. My palms press so hard on the table that my knuckles whiten. As I release my hands, I stumble back. Part from shock and part to clear her field of reach. The badge knocks against my shoe as the cord falls to the ground and rests against my black lace ankle boots.

"Shit." My heel slips as I stoop to gather up the ribbon. A sharp tug and OUCH! The split ring hooks into my shoe, tearing my skin and drawing blood.

Dextra Dominica sighs. I am taking too long.

I toss the pass onto the table and grab my bag, which catches the leg of the chair. I just want to leave, but the components are all wrong. Dextra, the sour faced bitch, prolongs the agony.

"Wait."

She's changed her mind. It's all a big candid camera moment, and Hugo is in on it. Last night was a scene in an elaborate plan, and any moment he will walk through the door with a ring and a proposal. I turn to look, but nothing.

"As your apartment is leased to you by Artisanal Delight by nature of you being an employee, your contact also terminates at midnight. An agent is waiting at the property to oversee the close down of your tenancy." Dominica pauses, expecting me to have something to say. "Sign this before you go." She waves a document.

"What is it?"

"Formalities. Sign by the 'X' to confirm you accept the cost of the cleaning bill for the private members lounge. Artisanal Delight's clients expect the highest standards and your little stunt necessitates an extra deep cleanse."

Dextra Dominica does have a point. Hugo's double orgasm was messy to the highest high, he insisted on a freestyle pour, despite my plea to use precise measurements. In my upturned position, half landed in my nose, the rest spluttered over the Chesterfield as I choked on the steady stream.

The top left corner of the paper tears as I extract it from her grip, removing the 'Artis' from 'Artisanal Delight'. The company strapline stays intact: 'Experience the finest pleasure'. If only she knew. Oh wait, she saw the video. She knows.

So, I'm out of a job. Unemployed. Unemployable? A failure. I take one last glance at the screen before I escape. No, not a complete failure. There is talent in performing those acts so masterfully. Hugo prides himself on proficiency, each time modified to keep the passion alive. What if? Yes. He would love to see a semi-professional reportage-style erotic movie of us doing what we do best. Hugo often begs to record our passion, and this fulfils his desires. Legally, I'm entitled to see the personal data Artisanal Delight keeps on me. And it doesn't get more personal than this. It may help to divert his frustrations at being evicted.

"Can you pop a copy of the footage onto a USB for me? I have one in my bag."

Dextra Dominica's eyes fix on her laptop, tap, tap, tap on the keyboard. "Just get out."

"Only it's just, under the rules of GDPR. I think I'm entitled–"

"You are 'entitled' to prosecution for theft of company property. But we are letting you go without ruining your future career. If you think we are giving you a copy of your pornographic behaviour in the workplace, you are more stupid than I thought."

"Well, how about–"

"And, before you ask, if we find your knickers, we will not be returning them."

In her haste to end the meeting, Dominica slams her laptop shut, catching the play button with her thumb. Three incorrect passwords later, a hurried call to the support team for resolution and my 'best bits' pause on a close-up of my face. Drunk on passion, ready to experience my Double Orgasm.

TWO

Whisky Sours

Everything will be okay once I get home. Hugo will understand about my job and the privacy infringement, although he will be annoyed at the lack of a personal copy. I can only hope he's being nice to whoever they sent over to kick us out of the flat. I don't know where we will go tonight, maybe nowhere. We could just stay up all night and hit the independent agents tomorrow to find a new place. Money is no immediate worry, I have savings to bridge the gap, but it won't be easy. I'm effectively blacklisted. Artisanal Delight holds a monopoly in Tilly Gate, buying up successful clubs whilst destroying those who refuse to submit. I knew of their reputation before taking the job, so I shouldn't be surprised they turned against me.

After leaving the boardroom, I change into my black sequin sneakers and clear my locker to walk home past one of Artisanal Delight's newest acquisitions, The Arches. A bunch of run-down old lockups beneath the railway line, currently mid-conversion into pop-up style bars. This was my idea, which I shared with the CEO at the Christmas Party. The perfect solution to an inclusive Artisanal Delight experience; from bar to club in a few hundred meters. Careful promotion and digital algorithms feed an app. Notifications and incentives direct punters where we want them. All the company needs now is a post club coffee bar, but I keep that to myself. They don't deserve any more of my genius.

Only one venue in Tilly Gate remains self-governed. The Lock Wheel. The last stand in independent entertainment, kept on the fringe by cunning building development and underhand planning. When finished, the pop-up bars will form an impenetrable barrier, the communal beer garden surrounded by a twelve-foot wall blocking the shortcut to the Lock Wheel from Tilly Gate. Anyone attempting to visit the Lock Wheel will need to walk past the entrance to the tempting pop-up bars and will no doubt nip in for a drink, or two, or three, until they abandon all plans of moving on. Once the Lock Wheel is weakened into a position of surrender, Artisanal Delight will force a sale and cut an archway in the wall, bringing it into the fold.

The door to the apartment is open, Artisanal Delight moves fast. Hugo must have let the agent in, which is odd because knowing him, he'd protect our home for as long as possible.

"Honey, I'm home." No reply. I've been gone less than an hour. Not normally long enough for Hugo to make it out of bed. "I really need a hug right now."

The place is a mess. My laptop is missing, and the TV is missing from the bedroom wall. Hugo must be grabbing anything he knows we need and is taking it somewhere. Anywhere. The covers on the bed ruffled and still warm to the touch, his punchy floral scent diluted as I smooth the duvet. I crawl in to soak up his essence and forget the world for a few minutes.

There is movement in the hall. Hugo is back! Thank God.

"Hugo, you will never guess what they did to us."

"Hello. Miss James?" That is not Hugo.

"Who is it?" Hopefully, it's not one of Hugo's ready mixes, I'm in the middle of a crisis.

"Quinn Moore, Tyler Estate Agents. Out of hours support. In other words, your landlord." Words tumble out of my mouth. I can't help it, she seems harmless, like a little Pink Squirrel. Sweet like White Crème de Cacao, and slightly nutty like Amaretto, I figure if she knows what happened, she may give me more time. I tell her everything. Well, almost everything. Not the part where my sex life was recorded without my knowledge and shown to security, the head of human resources and a member of the helpdesk. But I do make one slip, one wrong ingredient. I forget Hugo is not registered to live here.

"Miss James. Kat, I have the greatest sympathy for your traumatic day, I really do. However, considering the information you gave me, harbouring an illegal tenant whose actions led to the criminal damage of this property," Quinn Moore from Tyler's references the hole in the wall where the bracket for the television used to hang, "only adds to the long list of reasons you no longer have tenancy of this apartment. You have until midnight to gather your possessions and leave."

"What do you mean? Hugo is helping us move out. Right?"

"I have not seen this person. The apartment was empty and in this state that you see when I got here." Quinn seems nice. She must be able to help me.

"But my stuff is gone. What happened?"

"Miss James. I can only tell you what I know, which is not very much."

"Where can I go?"

"That is not something I can help with. We only deal with Artisanal Delight properties. Perhaps family or friends may be able to help you?"

"I need to find Hugo first."

But he's not in the living room, and neither is the television, my laptop, or the games console. The contents of my desk litters the floor, keepsakes brushed off shelves, cushions ripped off the sofa, the foam syphoned over every surface. It didn't even look this bad the time we planned a small soiree that 'found' its way onto social media. At least that's what Hugo said. Within an hour, we had over a hundred people crammed in and a onslaught of neighbour complaints. We escaped eviction with a written warning from the landlord. If only Artisanal Delight were that kind.

Wait, I run back to the bedroom. My jewellery box is missing. A vintage cigar box, the print on the lid faded from years of use. Instead of rings and necklaces, it holds my passport, emergency credit cards and lists of bank details and passwords not stored on my laptop. A sort of portable unlocked safe.

The mobile banking app confirms my fears. There is no money in my account, current or savings. And there is nothing I can do. Not because I left my details lying around the flat, but because last week I set up a joint account with Hugo. An obvious cocktail for disaster, but I did it anyway. The statement shows I transferred money into our joint account and then to a random un-numbered account.

"I think we've been robbed." This just adds more shit to the dung pile that is shaping up to be my life.

"Miss James, the clock is ticking. I am required to collect the key and secure the property. I suggest you collect what you need and find your errant boyfriend once you have somewhere to stay. It doesn't look as if he is coming back anytime soon."

"What do you mean? About Hugo?"

"This looks like a classic case of abandonment with a side of treachery. There is no note taped to the fridge or any indication he knew of your circumstances this evening. Therefore, I would suggest he is to blame for the state of the apartment. Which, unfortunately, comes out of your bond."

"That can't be true, he would never do this."

"Miss James, Kat." Quinn's voice softens. "I've seen enough apartments and watched enough true crime series to know the boyfriend did it. Trust me. He is not coming back."

Thick air sticks in my throat. I wretch, fighting the urge to be sick, my heart zooming into overdrive. Can she be right? Was I so stupid to trust him? Such an idiot to think he cared? If this is the case, he never did want me. Instead, he was just biding his time to get money... and brandy. The drinks cabinet is empty. He took the booze as well. I don't want much, but a heavy swig would help calm my panic.

I don't have any fight left. Dextra Dominica did too good a job. I grab at clothes, thrusting them into my large tote, too shabby for Hugo to see the value. But it means the world to me and is a symbol of my independence, bought at the vintage market with my first paycheque. Proof that I can achieve what I want all on my own. The brown crocodile leather, soft to the touch, lost its new glow years ago, but I recognised the dependable quality the minute I saw it.

There is only one place to go when I have nothing. So, with my dependable leather tote on one shoulder and a crunchy oversized bag for life on the other, I step out into the night rocking a new trend called blended reality.

Walking back along the canal path, the air is cool. Moisture hangs thick as droplets from weeping willows hit the back of my neck. Building pace, it morphs into rain. Turning towards town, the avenue of trees do nothing to buffer the elements. A taxi is off limits, so I face into the rain wholeheartedly. I need to feel this. I deserve it. A shot of snot hits my mouth. Sweet, warm, and strangely comforting. My tongue reaches over putty-textured lips to lick as much mucus as possible. Useless. I would sniff, but my nose is blocked. Pathetic. I can't even walk across town without turning into a drowned mess.

The bags weigh more by the second, soaked by the rain. Too heavy for my shoulders, the straps cut into my hands. Steps to the right and a mountain climb to the paved courtyard of the ruined castle. In the path across the old dining hall, uneven slabs disguise sinkholes of water. One pivots, soaking my sequined sneaker and half my leg. I should wear sensible shoes. Something warmer. Something waterproof. My choices are poor.

Onto the main road, Victorian street lamps illuminate my reflection in office windows. The wind has sculpted my hair into a crazed jumble. Rain soaks through my clothes into every crevice from the base of my neck down my back into my jeans into my knickers. No one hears my shouts of frustration. No one comes to my rescue.

Unable to defend myself, Dextra Dominica took my voice. I am – was – the top-earning Artisanal Experience Executive in the company. Month after month, I smashed targets. The clients love me. I should have said this when the big haired, long nailed, sour bitch was turning my moment of tenderness with Hugo into the bitterest kind of vengeance.

And Hugo. He knew about the cameras. He looked into the lens. It was a game. Hugo only ever does things by design.

I let this happen. Completely delulu that this could be my life. Too weak to fight back. I deserve this. Choked up. Forgot what to do. Unable to stay true to myself. Intimidated, I allowed Whisky Sours to control my life.

That's it. That's what I should have remembered. That was step two. Make a drink.

As I breathe in, I select a sours glass. Wider lip, tulip curve down to narrow stem. High shine, no blemish, smooth, confident, impactful. Chilled.

I breathe out and make a Whiskey Sour: 2 shots bourbon, ¾ shot fresh lemon juice, ½ shot syrup. Vigorously shaken over ice.

Then, I take another breath in as I strain into the sours glass and garnish with a lemon slice.

No, that doesn't fit. Dextra Dominica is not garnished with a lemon slice.

Go back one stage and breathe in. Strain into sours glass. Garnish with a lemon spiral tumbling over the edge of the glass.

Finally, I breathe out to the count of ten.

I didn't remember that when I needed it because I'm too lazy to practice. Rubbish at working through the steps. It's too difficult to remember. Too hard to stick to the rules. I can't do this anymore.

THREE

Brandy Alexander

These last few steps feel like miles as my mind goes into overdrive, the meditation forgotten so quickly. What did I do to deserve this? They must hate me so much that they want to ruin my life. The sinking in my chest deepens as the buildings on the side of the path close in. Walls crumbling, burying me. It's all my fault. I should never have trusted them, not after the last time.

I believed all my friends and family when they said they cared, but the messages of comfort were empty offers to be by my side. When I was at my lowest, when I needed them most, they were nowhere to be seen. This is why I make my own way and decide my fate.

What happened today is a reminder to never let down my guard. Faith in Artisanal Delight, conviction in Hugo's devotion all misplaced. It must not happen again.

❋ ❋ ❋

It's been eight years, ten months and nine days. There was nothing I could do but walk away from those who betrayed me. The feelings are just as strong today as back then. The exam hall: students, people who said they were my friend, scribbled away as if nothing had happened. Acting as though things were normal, they crushed what was left of my heart. What little memories I had were locked away so no one could take them. With my shaking hands and tightness in my throat, I tore the booklet open, and there it stayed, lying on the desk as empty as the day it was printed. Even if I could remember the answers to the questions, it was pointless, my future was already destroyed.

So I pushed back my chair, stood up and left the building.

* * *

The cobbles of Castle Walk slip under my feet as my legs tire. Just a few more steps until I reach the Vanilla Pod. Until I am safe. After all that's taken place today, I'm counting on Ethan being here.

All the people look as I open the door, the cold breeze announcing my arrival. They feel sorry for me; I can see it in their eyes. A poor helpless swamp beast. I can't see him. It takes all my strength not to lie prone on the floor, masking my face and troubles. If no one can see me, perhaps it did not happen. My legs buckle, and I use any shred of energy left to give this one final try, but it is not easy to focus on the room when things are starting to wobble. There is no need to go through the whole meditation. I don't have time before the world will go black and I faint, falling to the floor in an overdramatic fashion. The half-pint version will be good enough, this is the one I practiced over and over with Ethan. The one he taught me when I had nothing.

Step one is to get grounded. I plant my feet on the refurbished wooden floorboard and take a slow, deep sip. Step two means viewing my surroundings. I am in The Vanilla Pod, comforting and sensual. This is Ethan's bar, where twinkling tea lights line the walls. It feels intimate, like home. Step three is to make a drink.

Everything about Ethan screams Brandy Alexander. He laughed when I told him, but accepted he embodies the comforting taste, the welcoming aura and the satisfying feeling that only Ethan gives. This is a friendship like no other. First, the brandy, unparalleled in its restorative nature.

Then add Crème de Cacao, velvety smooth, a mood elevator. And finally, vanilla ice cream, cool, delicious, and indulgent with real vanilla bean pieces. Blend the flavours until smooth and pour into a cocktail glass. I like to rim the edge first with finely ground dark chocolate, but Ethan prefers vanilla essence for his signature cocktail. The final touch is freshly grated nutmeg, each stroke against the fine steel releases a soothing, warm fragrance.

With my focus recovered, I search again for my Brandy Alexander.

To the right, the snug, reserved for a party. To the left, the fireplace and leather tub chairs with at least two clients per chair, soaking up heat from the open flames. A central aisle leads to the bar, and I bump through the maze of wooden tables and chairs. Most of them are empty as they are too far from the fire on such a chilly night.

"Darling!" Ethan's at the bar polishing glasses. "You look like a drowned rat. What happened?" he thinks I look hideous. "Bad day?" He doesn't know the half of it. "You're dripping on my vintage boards, and I just had them steam cleaned. Leave your bags here and dry off in the bathroom."

Set free, my arms are fluffy and out of control like a newborn. I swipe away the rain-filled tears on my cheeks.

"Quick! Before I have to fetch a mop or heaven forbid an ugly yellow hazard sign."

This is the welcome I needed. My slug lips soften enough to form a small, grateful smile as I obey with a squelch.

Things are worse than I suspected. My hair is matted, and tendrils forge sideburns on my cheeks. There is a crusty snot moustache lining my upper lip, and my bloodshot eyes are framed by streaky mascara. No wonder people stopped drinking when I walked through the door. I put them off their cocktails and destroyed the ambiance of Ethan's eclectic bar. At least my clothes are black. The sheen could pass as coated jeans rather than extreme soaking.

My jacket peels off like citrus skin, revealing a thousand cold pimples on my arms. Shivering, I search for something to help me dry off and fix my new romantic eighties makeup.

Bugger, there are no paper towels. After many years of nagging Ethan to improve sustainability in the workplace, he has developed an ecological conscience. Just when I need a mountain of warm fluffy hand towels or a hand dryer with a rotating nozzle thingy, all I have to work with is a slim slotted dryer.

There may be a slim chance of hope in the pile of tissue paper brimming over the top of the rubbish bin. Clearly, people have used the toilet roll to dry their hands, so it must be reasonably clean as they would have washed their hands first. Almost brand new. As I pull out a clump, the relative dryness is a sign I hit the jackpot. One or two is enough for my snot moustache. The rest of the tissues seem a little more stuck together, so I rip them apart and something cold and wet runs through my fingers. As the smell hits me, I know what it is. I'm going to be sick and instinctively lean over the sink, only to make things worse. An unknotted rubber taunts me as it nestles in the plughole. The tissues were wrapped around a condom. Retching, I step back into the cubicle to hunt for toilet paper to clean the sink. Why did I not use this to start with? I am not thinking clearly. Lesson learned. Never snuffle through a pub toilet bin.

There is not enough soap and water in the world to remove the smell of stale cum from my hands. I wash them three times, but I can still smell the funk. Oh no! My face. I used the tissues on my face. No wonder the stink is still potent. Sperm facials are not alien to me, but always direct from the source. Fresh is best and I usually know the supplier by name, but this particular brand is one I could never go for.

The new fancy ecological hand dryer taunts me from its position of hygienic earth-saving capability. Designed to dry hands and only hands, it's impossible to fit any other part of your body into the small slots. And I try. My arms and legs won't squeeze in, no matter what angle I try. Maybe hair will work better. The drier leaps into action as I reverse limbo and lay my head on the top. But it's neither warm nor drying. The burst of crisp air whips the strands up out of the slot, slapping the cold dripping tresses back onto my cheeks, streaking what little mascara remains. This is too hard. All I want is to dry off and look normal. Nothing is working. I feel wetter now than when I got to the bar.

With hair in a messy bun, I squelch back into the bar and pretend to be a regular person celebrating the weekend. There is no better place to do this than the Vanilla Pod. Candles line narrow shelves on the wall behind the bar, and the scent of vanilla soothes me, enveloping my senses. The soft glow is kind enough to mask the truth of my ordeal.

Ethan slides over a drink as I perch on a stool. My jeans are too wet to allow a full knee bend.

"This should warm your cockles. You look half drowned to death."

So, it appears my labours in the restroom were fruitless, but the insult is worth it. The drink, Cognac, is nectar from the heavens, and I gulp it down before the realisation hits me. I have no money to pay, so I smile to hide the truth.

"Well, that's halfway there." Ethan grins back. He always gives the most contagious beams. "Want to talk? Darling, my bartender senses tell me you've had more than just a bad day."

Ethan leans over the deep bar to give my arm a comforting rub. As usual, I cry when anyone shows me sympathy. This is pure weakness. I was fine when I left the toilet, but all it takes to reduce me to a blubbering mess is a head tilt and a gentle touch. I'm not a regular person. Regular people don't cry in bars. The brandy is not working.

"Oh, Ethan, I don't know where to start. My life is one big dumpster fire."

"Try and start at the very beginning." Ethan lays out shot glasses for a stag do that he's expecting. "It's a very good place to start."

But I don't know how.

"How is work?"

"I got sacked." If I look up to the ceiling, I won't cry. That's the trick, but my eyes swell, ready to burst. This is a sure sign I need more brandy.

"What the buggery for?" Ethan abandons the shot glasses.

"I mean... They said I turned up drunk too many times."

It's the closest to the truth without revealing too much and is believable, knowing my history. But that won't stop Ethan from being disappointed in me.

When I was little and this sort of thing used to happen, I would hide behind my palms pretending they were invisibility shields. Just so my parents would not be ashamed of me. With this type of protection, I never needed to disclose the true disgrace of my misdemeanours.

"Darling, life's a bitch sometimes." Ethan moves to pour another Cognac, but real paying customers divert his mission. Someone worthy of his hospitality.

He deserves the truth, but I need to survive. Need alcohol, my medicine, my life saving treatment. Just one glass to numb the pain, another to add a rosy glow, and a third to bring joy. Ethan says there are other ways but right now is no place for reflection and meditation, that can wait. A few drinks will work. It's not something I do regularly, only when things are really bad, were really bad. Can someone please call the National Health Service to pay my tab, or at least appeal to the Chief Medical Officer to handwrite me a prescription for medicinal brandy to cure my stupidity.

Ethan returns, his eyes full of sympathy. "Kat, your dream job. How did it get so out of control?" His voice softens. I'm beyond chastisement.

Inside, I know where the fault lies, only I can control the situation. My hands fail to gain superhero invisibility powers, and my glass is unequivocally not large enough to hide behind.

"Things got out of hand."

"What? Being more pissed than your clients. Hahaha!" Ethan's big belly laugh is as infectious as his smile, but not tonight. Tonight, I am immune and deserve to suffer. "A party planner sacked for partying too hard, now that is funny."

"Well, if it's any consolation, I feel terrible. I never want to drink again." That said, I do all but lick the glass to eke out the last drop of brandy. Ethan replaced the empty snifter before I have the chance to blink. "Oh Ethan, you're so good to me. Thank you."

"Darling, you know what they say?" Ethan leans in, brown eyes twinkling in the candlelight. "If you go through life looking in the rear-view mirror, you may miss that rainbow up ahead."

"Rainbow?"

"Yes, rainbow. Colourful thing in the sky, with a pot of gold at one end. What's done is done. There's no treasure found moping in the past, you must look forward, then you won't miss any opportunity waiting for you." Ethan talks shit sometimes.

A group bundles in from the storm, talking all over each other. Six guys in their mid to late twenties, I guess. Oh, that one's cute. Ethan jostles them into the snug with promises to return with drinks. The stag do, and no doubt the cute one is the stag. It's typical, all the good-looking ones get snapped up. Oh, hold on, here are two more. The tall one wearing light-up antlers must be the groom. Three shuffle out to let him sit at the head of the table. The cute one relegated to the end closest to the door.

Ethan continues our conversation as he makes the drinks.

"So, what did Hugo say?" His words sting my eyes. "Oh, Kat, the bags! Did you have a fight?"

"Fight? No. Not a fight. Much, much worse." Fighting was not Hugo's way. "He... he cleared me out." Tightness constricts my throat at the fear that once spoken, the words become reality. My agony is prolonged by Ethan's silence. "After I lost my job, I..." a sip of Cognac loosens the tension a little, "I came home to find the flat gutted and everything gone."

"Gone?"

"Taken. Everything taken. Except what's in my bags."

"The snake! What did he take?"

"Everything. Anything of value, at least. All my jewellery, money, laptop. Whatever he could sell for drugs, no doubt. The place was destroyed. The agent thought Hugo did it"

"Scum. You're better off without him. What matters is you're safe." Ethan moves with ninja stealth and his powerful arms surround me like armour. "You're with me now. Everything will be okay, well apart from the fact my polo shirt has soaked up half the water from your top like a failed entry in a wet t-shirt contest. Who would have thought that flimsy, pretty much see-through lace thing capable of holding so much water? Darling, did you forget to put a top on? It barely covers your middle bit."

"It's a bralette."

"It's a bra-that-lets everyone see your nipples and areolas. Give me a second." Ethan disappears into the storage cupboard. "Here." He tosses a branded polo shirt over the bar. "Put this on before you catch your death or another undesirable leech. Now, where were we? Ah, yes, it's all over now."

"But... that's not all, it gets worse."

"How? How can it get any worse than losing your job, your house and your boyfriend all in one day?"

"Hugo emptied my accounts, bank accounts. He took every penny." All hope is lost for Ethan's t-shirt as my tears flow. "I literally have nothing to my name, just a few clothes and the jewellery I'm wearing. Thank God, Grans' diamond ring never leaves my finger."

"But, your savings?"

"Gone."

How long will it be before Ethan realises I'm stealing from him, sip by sip, drink by drink? I'm such a shitty friend. The worst.

"What? How?" Ethan runs his hands through his cropped hair before curling his fingers into fists. Solid and dependable, my unfazeable buddy looks different. Angry. Hugo brings out the worst in everyone. "The robbing bastard! If I ever get hold of him, I–"

"Ethan, it's not worth it. He's not worth it."

"Are you kidding? Nothing would give me greater pleasure."

More customers approach, and Ethan exhales as he returns to the business side of the bar.

I am in his way, an inconvenience, so I drain my glass.

"But how did he know the codes?"

"Codes? Oh, yeah, I'm such an idiot. They were saved on my laptop."

"What, all of them?"

"Yes." I'm not going to tell him about the cigar box. "It's confusing, what with every website demanding complicated passwords with symbols and numbers and stuff. My computer offered to remember them for me, which is so helpful, but so easy for someone to hack in and steal them. Hugo learnt the password to my laptop, which gave him access to my entire existence."

"Darling, I wish I could help and give you a place to stay tonight." He shrugs. "But Laura has vetoed guests until baby Oscar has settled. He's not sleeping well after the move."

Ethan lived in the flat above the Vanilla Pod until Laura, his wife, insisted they could no longer stay there. A responsible father must provide a decent base for his family. An apartment above a public house is not a suitable place to bring up a child. Plus, the entrance is at the top of an old Victorian wrought iron staircase. It's tricky to negotiate at the best of times as it's open to the elements. In the wet, carrying Oscar, his bags, buggy and the many things that babies need, it is a disaster waiting to happen. Ethan agreed to move, conceding that the bar is too noisy. His reward; a happier Laura, a new build in Newtown Tilly with a garden, much closer to their new baby friends.

Laura wasn't always this way. Before they had Oscar, she rivalled me for turning any small gathering of acquaintances into a full-blown party. Bold and potent, it is easy to see what attracted Ethan to Laura. A Naked Martini, garnished with a green olive and the purest cocktail. One sip and he was intoxicated. Only now she's transformed into the first pathetic alco-free variety. All the taste but none of the fun. Inevitable when kids come on the scene, I guess.

"We leased the apartment, otherwise, I'd give you the keys. Where will you go? Back to your parents?"

"Home? No way! I mean, I can't let slip to Father about the money. He's always telling me I must grow up and stand on my own two feet. The last time I saw him, he told me *Life is not a continuous party, Kat. One day, you will wake up and realise you have wasted half your innings drunk.*" Despite the cricket metaphor, I'm beginning to think he's right.

"So, what will you do?"

In truth, I don't know. I only planned making it to the Vanilla Pod. Ethan has saved me before, and he's right. I should know what I want to do. But all I know is I can't go back now.

FOUR

Climax

Cynthia and Gordon, my mother and father, don't live in Tilly. The distance shields them against any displeasure of me. But now, with nowhere to go, it would be better if they were closer. Close enough for me to walk and knock on the door. Close enough to show them I have failed all over again.

My glass is empty. I have nothing.

Nothing but the single most precious thing Hugo didn't take.

That's it! The answer is staring me in the face.

No, not the brandy glass, but the antique ring. Grans' ring.

Grans lives in a big house on Kingsgate in Tilly Brook, to the south of the park. Almost village-like but still close enough to feel like part of town. She is always telling me to visit more, so why not now? If Grans were a drink, she'd be a Champagne cocktail. Energetic, bubbly, hedonistic, the perfect blend of fragrant freshness. Cooler than Cynthia and Gordon, who are tap water by comparison.

Grans will welcome me with open arms any time of day or night, I am sure. And she won't judge me for what's happened, instead, my turbulence will remind her of an exciting calamity in her own misspent youth. The day will end in triumph, and I will take inspiration from her guidance.

"I'll go to Grans'." The one thing I hate more than bastarding, robbing ex-boyfriends is taking advantage of people. I've accepted Ethan's hospitality for too long and it is

time to come clean, even if it risks the only friendship I have.
"Ethan, I have no money. I can't pay for the drinks... sorry."
"Darling, maybe your dad's right. The party must end. Has ended. Your so-called friends completely screwed you." Ethan's right, and so is Gordon. The party has ended. But it was good while it lasted.

❋ ❋ ❋

After leaving home, I slipped into a student-type lifestyle, only better. With no exams and a regular wage, I was not weighed down by enormous debt and crippling anxiety. I found a job way beyond my wildest dreams, paid to party each night with a new circle of friends. Only they were not really friends, and I had no intention of letting them get close. It is not worth the pain, so I kept them at a distance, as acquaintances.

The people I knew at school graduated from university and moved on to bigger, more boring things in the city. But I had the best role. Soon promoted to manage the VIP Champagne receptions, I mixed with genuine celebrities, not just people who pay to sit in the fake VIP section. I worked hard, much harder than anyone else, only it didn't feel like work. It was a simple existence fuelled by an everlasting party.

I never took drugs, but others did. Hugo did. Tall, dark, devilishly spiced Hugo. Potent, addictive and hard hitting. A cut-to-the-chase shooter. A climax in a shot glass.

Life went from Prosecco to Champagne the moment we met. A natural charmer, life and money came easy to him. So enchanting that everybody fell under his spell, including me. Always craving another taste, he was my world, my everything. I was drunk on love.

I met Hugo whilst working a gig for a prestigious athlete. It was the end of the night and I was handing out the gift bags. A disaster in a fancy pouch, I'd mis-ordered the contents and neglected to check the invoice until the afternoon of the event. All my meticulous research of local artisan goods was ruined because of one little error. Next time, I will stick to party poppers, plastic glow rings, jelly shots, and tickets to future events. But an attitude like that didn't get me my dream job.

The problem would have been averted had I selected gender neutral packs, but I was swayed by one of our main sponsors for the evening, who insisted on supplying monthly hygiene products. Only, instead of an even split by gender, I opened the third box to find all the bags overflowing with moon cups. No matter, I hear you say, every day we take one step further into a gender-neutral society. If they can't find a use for it as a novelty shot glass, they can give it to their mum, sister or aunty, or any friend who needs them. Now I know that gendered gift packs are not okay. Such a stupid move.

Basically, I spent the evening apologising to angry egotistical sportsmen, unaccustomed to rejection from a party bag. Their surgically enhanced arm candy followed suit, not in solidarity with their narcissistic dates, but because they were hoping for more from the sponsors.

The company is called Replay and they specialise in innovative natural plastics for intimate use. I think my clients were hoping for panties (crotchless or edible). Anything would have been fine other than the ReplayF-Kup (the aforementioned menstrual cup). When I insisted Replay exchange them for a ReplayDigi-Rib (a textured finger sleeve) or the ReplayMko-Kup (a cock ring), they told me it was too late. A recent unprecedented demand for sexual pleasure has drained all their stock. What a F-Kup!

Hugo was amongst the last to leave, something I soon learned was a habit to ensure he played the entire party to the last drop.

"Here's your gift bag, Sir. It's the last. Alongside the products from our key sponsors, it holds makeup, lingerie, chocolate, oh and monthly hygiene products."

Hugo stood, brooding dark pupils, seductive pools of cocoa sweetness. Lips pursed, sucking the last drops of a Rum Cooler. Oh, to be that straw, stretching from the bottom of the Collins glass to his plump lips. Eyes magnetised, he leant over the table, drawing me in closer with his invisible force.

Bodies mirrored in movement, heads tilted, my ear near his mouth, his breath stirred the hairs on the back of my neck. Seconds later, and I'm left hanging.

Silence.

He grabbed my face in his hands, mouth meeting mouth. This was not an innocent romantic peck from old movies where the leading couple lock lips, staying motionless for a few moments. No, this was a 'get a room', French-style, tonsil tickling snog. One hundred percent proof, forceful flavours promising more. Intense, Amaretto eyes, so strong a little goes a long way. His natural perfume, Cointreau, has sweet, intoxicating herbal notes. Heavy on the charm, an acquired Crème de Banane taste. His power was undetectable, like vodka, hitting straight to the heart, he was Crème de Cacao in human form, alcoholic chocolate, guaranteed to please. The kiss was decedent, like heavy cream, a luxury distracting me from the painstaking act of living.

And then he was leaving, bag in hand.

"I'll be outside. You can show me how disappointed I will be with the contents of this bag. And I will show you how wrong you are."

Never have I ever finished up an event so quickly. What normally took an hour, I achieved in fifteen minutes. I liked what I tasted and craved more, a double shot. I opened the door to rain. Typical! No one would ever wait for me in the downpour on a kiss promise. Not when there are plenty of other girls to share his party bag.

I saw movement in the shadows. Burnt almond eyes glisten through the drops. It is him. Rain soaked down his bare, toned arms, and his t-shirt clung to his lean frame. Hugo waited for me and was true to his word in every sense. He made full use of the makeup, hair scrunchie, vodka shot and F-Kup in a way the manufacturers could never envisage. This was the future. Hugo was adventurous, with a no limit approach to both life and sex in equal measure.

❋ ❋ ❋

"That's more like it. Stop drowning in self-pity." Ethan spots me smiling. "So… hold on," he pauses, reaching to find his vibrating phone. The eye roll signals a no-show from a member of his team. "Miss James, I get it. You're penniless for a while, but there are no handouts in this bar. Turns out I need help, too. So, rather than worry how to pay for your drinks, you can work off your bill instead."

He's not angry with me. This is amazing! I knew all along that Ethan would make things right.

"I mean, okay, when do you need me?"

"Now actually. Annelie just messaged. She can't make it tonight."

"Tonight? Oh, Ethan, I'm not really in the mood."

"Nonsense, Darling. Now that you've had a few drinks, it's just like any normal working night. Come on, show some of that party atmosphere you're famed for."

A generous offer, but after the day I've had, wallowing in my misfortune far outweighs donning my professional host face. But Ethan needs me. Only a rubbish friend would say no, and I am champion quality in that area.

"Okay."

"Great! But… no more drinking on the job. I mean it, I can't afford to give you a second chance if you fuck up. Laura watches my every move and if anything happens, she'll never let me forget it."

"Agreed, but we should drink to that. To seal the contract." It's worth a shot; no pun intended. "One last drink to put this nightmare behind me."

"Not a chance in hell. From now on, you're back on the wagon and–" Ethan's hand moves to his pocket again. The phone. "Laura." Ethan disappears into the back room.

The bar is busier by the minute and for good reason. Ethan created the Vanilla Pod to welcome all who cross the threshold. He sourced interiors from a reclamation yard, including the waxed floorboards and deep bar set on sculpted panels the colour of Blue Margarita. Shelves painted the same, displaying his signature bottles. Vanilla Pod Vodka, syrup, dark rum, gin. Straight up or in a cocktail, they keep the punters coming back for more.

In my favourite bay window is the snug and the stag do, who seem far too sober for my liking. This is nothing to worry about as I am quite capable of turning harmless, quiet introverts into wild exhibitionists.

To the right, the fire reduced to embers, which is nothing to worry about as there are now plenty of bodies to generate warmth. Down the middle, the labyrinth of small wooden tables are now full of couples. People are high on the thrill of finishing work for the week, dressed up and out for a good time. For some, it is Friday night date night. I see a blind date, uncertain of how it will end. A set up, wishing they had enquired about more than eye colour before they met. A long-term relationship engrossed in their not-so-smart phones, communicate through occasional grunts, showing screens when something is share-worthy on unsocial media. Best friends laugh about failed hookups, eyes scour for the next opportunity. Shared moments. Laughter. Happiness. Time. All the things I lacked with Hugo. Sure, before him I tried, but it never worked out. Then came a busy work schedule with no opportunity for romantic dinners or polite exchanges over drinks. The closest I achieved was drunken fumbling at after-parties with randoms, although that ended when I met Hugo. He was my final drunken fumble. It never occurred to me, until now, that we missed a whole stage in our relationship. We went from strangers to lovers in minutes, without one single date. Instead of eating out, Hugo preferred to eat me out. From the moment I invited him into my flat, on that first night, he never left.

Despite my unconventional start with Hugo, and after eighteen months together, I'm proud that the relationship never reached the depressing depths of sitting in a bar on a Friday night staring at phones because life is too dull at home. No, we were too busy partying. Unsociable hours and perma-hangovers are not conducive to forming relationships, so I made no real connections, links, or followers. Instead, I let whatever ready-mix entourage Hugo selected stand in for my social support network. The ever-changing group of people never became my real friends, although they enjoyed the hospitality of my apartment most evenings. Fresh and simple on the outside, they were easily consumed and slotted into our life, all innocent looking but dangerously potent. When I was at work, they drank my booze and ate my food. If I was lucky, Hugo kicked them out when he came to meet me in whatever club I was hosting. On the times that didn't happen, they were my welcome party when I returned home, still raving in the morning. At times, it felt wonderful to be popular, surrounded by people who wanted to be with me. But I was a means to an end. The end being the wonderfully alluring, addictively fuckable, bastarding Hugo.

FIVE

Black and Tan

Ethan returns, phone slipped back into his pocket. "I imagine you want to start so you can pay for those drinks?" Tension in his temples, frowns around his eyes.

"I'd prefer to nurse my sorrows in a bottle of vodka and stuff my face with your finest Vanilla Pod Ice Cream, but you need help. Is that a stag do?" I say, pointing to the booth.

"Yes, correct-a-mondo on both counts. Help is welcome, even if it is from someone so sad." He is a fine one to talk.

"First though, I require a drink."

"Kat, we just–"

"No, dumbass! I've learnt my lesson. A coffee. To aid sobriety."

Ethan laughs, his spirits lifted... oooh spirits. Oh, no! Maybe Ethan is right, and I do have alcohol on the brain.

"Agreed. Go put on an apron and I will pour you a fresh cup."

Suited and booted, but still soggy, Ethan tasks me with the stag do. With a list of bars to crawl, I must keep them here as long as possible. Stag dos equal money and although these guys are starting to show signs of warming up, they are still a long way from making legendary memories. The cute one on the end has brought the storm in with him, which is really bringing the mood down. He holds the essence of darkness and misery and is difficult to read. Whilst his liquid blue eyes and dirty blond hair signify a fresh clean light, his unshaven face and unkempt hair hang over him like a cloud of depression. Heavy, dark in colour and bitter to taste, he is a half-and-half, the stout overshadows the lightness of the pale ale in this Black and Tan. This is a shame, if it weren't for the gloomy face, I could go for his type next time. Not that there will be a next time. Not after Hugo. I have learned my lesson.

I hope I don't look that bad, but if I do, there is good reason. Nevertheless, I hide my 'World's Worst Day' trophy from my clients. I am the life and soul of this party and there is no way I'm giving up my accolade to Mr Black and Tan without a fight.

Ethan, ever prepared at the bar, hands me a tray loaded with Tequila shots, salt, lemon and lime and a Pink Panther cocktail. The vibrant liquid is a beacon in the pink sugar-rimmed hurricane glass. The garnish of bright pink dianthus flower, a pink umbrella, and a cube of pineapple complete the look. With drinks held high, I weave in and out of the weekend party people, the tunes working their magic to improve my disposition one step at a time.

"Hi guys, welcome to the Vanilla Pod. I'm your host, and here are some shots to get you in the mood. First some Tequila, then a round of sambuca, then I think you will be ready to handle the big guns... jelly shots." With the tray safely on the table, I get to work. "I assume this belongs to you." Handing the Pink Panther Cocktail to the antlers, now decorated with a pink feather boa.

"Stag! Stag! Stag! Stag! Christian, get it down you!" A Blue Shark and a Tequila Ghost chant.

"Christian, congratulations! When's the big day?"

Christian is like the island of Capri. Warm and inviting. "Oh, um, in a week... on Saturday." He replies with the usual nerves of a man about to commit to a life with one person.

With the shots distributed, I place the salt, lemon and lime in the centre of the table. "I see you're making the most of your final few nights of freedom."

Christian downs the shot without hesitation but shows more reserve when faced with the cocktail.

"And who is the best man?"

"My baby brother, Sid." Christian points to the silent guy,

lost in a vacuum of hopelessness. The choice must be misguided pressure from parents. It's obvious he prefers his own company.

"Yeh! Sid." A harmonious chorus of Tequila-fuelled energy. The Black and Tan turns and nods. He is so pathetic; he is crying out for my help. Apart from benefitting his older brother, the longer he plays this game, the higher the chance my reign is in jeopardy. Plus, he is too pretty to look this sad.

I squeeze in next to him. "Hard day?"

"Hard month." He disregards my flirty wink.

"You know, it's better with salt and lemon. Here, I'll show you."

"Sure. But life's sour enough." He doesn't look up but reaches for another drink.

This guy's funny despite his melodramatic mood. No one gets depressed at their own brother's stag do, especially when you are the best man.

"Well, it can only get sweeter, what with your brother's wedding in a few days."

The silence conceals a thousand words. Now is not the time to press for answers. Sid will tell me when he is ready.

We do the shot together. The Reposado Tequila is rich and warm, but the honeyed vanilla undertones do nothing to shift the cloud. Yes, life deals shitty cards, I'm proof of that. But not horrendous enough to ruin his brother's fun. Not bad enough to spoil a once-in-a-lifetime wedding. He needs reforming and I'm up for the challenge, it will be my pleasure.

SIX

Bloody Mary

Hangovers are the devil's arsehole. The gentle knocking of my brain against the side of my skull resembles a muddler mashing up memories, crushing all ecstasy, leaving only bitterness and vacuum.

Where am I?

The gentle knocking continues. My eyes feel dry and so does my mouth. The bedside table feels empty as I reach out, eyes sealed. Wait, a bottle. But it's vodka, I can tell from the shape. Familiar mouldings and etches of the label give it away. Narrow at the bottom, gently increasing upwardly, my fingers glide over the ribs.

Grans' favourite.

The knocking ends.

"Tea is better for you, my dear. It's peppermint and will ease that throbbing head." Grans stands at the bedroom door, holding a tray.

The floral duvet muffles my groans.

"What happened?" That was a strong storm last night.

"I'm not entirely sure. You told me you lost your keys, but it looks more serious. Is everything okay?"

"Umm, I don't know." Meaning I'm not ready to say. "How did I get here?"

"I can't tell you. Not a taxi."

"Never."

"Do you remember anything?" Grans sits on the edge of the bed.

"Not much. Only that I walked from my place to the Vanilla

Pod and after that... nothing."

"Well, it is too far to walk here from there with two heavy, waterlogged bags."

"Thanks for letting me in, Grans."

"Well, I didn't need to. You found the spare key and had it all under control."

My hand shakes as I reach for the cup.

"Grans..." Words stick in my throat. I'm not sure how or why she's the only family member who believes in me. If I were at home, at my parents, the spot lamp would be poised, Cynthia leading the relentless grilling until I relinquish the answers.

"No need to explain." Grans pats the duvet, releasing a lavender scent. "Plenty of time. Stay here as long as you need. Your clothes are washed, they'll dry before you know it."

"But... how?"

"My dear, you've slept the day away."

Nothing new there, I'm stuck in reverse. Awake at night. Asleep all day.

"Drink your tea, dear. One sip at a time and I will come back with a pick-me-up."

Grans returns carrying two highballs and hands me the one with the larger stick of celery. The scent of lemon on the rim of the glass kisses my lips before the thick red liquid. No shortcuts here, Grans made the perfect hangover cure. Tomato juice, packed with both vitamin C and potassium, fresh lemon juice, and less than subtle spices of horseradish, Tabasco and Worcestershire sauce.

"Grans. You forgot the vodka."

"Oh ho! Yours is a Virgin Mary, my dear. Mine is the real deal." Sipping away at the good stuff. "Hair of the Dog never helps in the long run."

"Oh, Grans, I'm so sorry." I should explain.

"Whatever is the matter?" The Bloody Mary has relaxed all but her concern.

"Everything's gone wrong. I've lost it all, everything."

"Everything?"

"Everything." I take a big gulp of Virgin Mary. "It got too crazy and Hugo... aarrgghh, there is no more Hugo..."

"Killed?" Grans reaches a new level of seriousness.

"No! No, no. Grans, chill. He's not dead, not that I know."

"Only I know someone. Very discrete. You would never know." She's joking, right?

"I mean he, um... we broke up and... he did the dirty and ran off with all my stuff."

"Mmmnn, maybe he would be better off dead." Grans looks thoughtful, she really feels my pain.

"I have nothing left, nothing. Well, apart from the wet bags I carried here and the loose change I earned helping my friend Ethan. He owns the Vanilla Pod, that's why I was late getting to you."

"Oh yes, I remember Ethan, lovely lad. You are always so kind, dear, thinking of others during your hour of desperation. But your flat, your job. What will you do?"

"No job. No Boyfriend. Nowhere to live." My words cast a shadow over her bright disposition. "Don't worry, Grans. Lesson learnt. Men are complete shits, and I'm not trusting anyone again. Ever!" I finish the mocktail. If only it were real. "Thanks for looking after me, Grans. You're the best."

"Get some more rest, dear and let the Virgin Mary work its magic. Things may not be as dire as you fear. During times of stress, sleep is the answer."

"How can I, when I have so much... so much..."

A gentle pat and the emotional turmoil overwhelms my senses and a dreamless slumber engulfs me in my fluffy cocoon.

A dull buzz. Rhythmic and circular, builds higher and higher to a crescendo. Hugo's up to his old tricks with my vibrator and it sounds like my favourite setting. Guaranteed to hit the mark every time, the pulse swells over and over, bringing waves of sensuous gratification.

Not better than the real thing. And lucky for me, I have both to bring me hap-penis. I reach over eager to join the fun. Hangover sex is the best. Forget the hair of the dog, I prefer a real cocktail, one I can get my lips around. A Cold Comfortable Screw doggie style. The first touch of pleasure after the hedonism of the night before chimes the nerve endings back into a state of arousal. Stripped back and overcome with exhaustion the instinct to fuck brings satisfaction.

But the bed is empty. No Hugo and no vibrator. This is not even my bed. The duvet releases a scent of lavender as I return to a curled-up position and remember.

Hugo is gone.

I will never trust again.

It is hard enough to lose someone without this.

There it is again. Buzzing. Quiet at first, then louder and louder until a short break in the vibrations before starting again.

Not an alarm.

Never.

Possibly a ringtone.

But few people phone. Well, not me anyway. Hugo used my phone, running up huge bills, never concerned about the cost. Often, I'd leave for work without it. But not this time. This time I took my phone with me.

The vibrations return. I find it on the nightstand.

"Ethan." Caller ID.

"Darling, how are you? Still licking those wounds?"

"You woke me. I'm trying not to mope." But it's hard, too hard.

"Kat, today is numero uno without that scumbag. There's nothing wrong with staying in bed to recover after the shock, so long as you don't go full goblin mode on me. Anyway darling, I have a message for you. The guy you adopted last night popped into the bar. You offered to help him next weekend, only he doesn't have your number."

"Adopted?"

"You took him home with you."

But the bed is empty. Ethan is mistaken.

"Home?"

"Well, back to Grans' anyway."

Yes – the familiar lavender-scented bedding. This is Grans' house. I remember now. She brought me tea earlier. If I did try to bring a man back, doing it in a grandparent's house is a guaranteed cock-block, it is no wonder he did not stay the night.

"There was no way you could carry those bags on your own. The guy looked pretty chipper for a heavy night. Your legendary status is intact. You certainly cheered him up since I last saw him."

So much for Hugo being my final drunken fumble. But I don't feel like I had a heavy night of passion.

"Did he leave his name?" He left no clues here.

"Yup, I'll message it." Ethan is being deliberately elusive.

My brain is hazy, currently resembling a bunch of jumbled puzzle pieces. Even if I could link them together, most of them are missing.

He's gorgeous go 4 it 4get bastarding Hugo choose Sid.

A number follows and no more. My mind remains blank, the vodka is to blame. Ethan's message is no help. He should have asked this Sid person more questions. Whoever he is, Sid must be desperate to think I can help him. I was a mess last night and in no state to believe in myself, let alone persuade anyone else to have confidence in me. I have nothing and no one, unless you count Ethan welcoming me in, giving me a job. Oh, and I forgot Grans' generosity.

I'm sure when I hear his voice, it will all come flooding back. I dial, but the phone rings and rings with no answer from this mystery man. I hang up and call straight back, only to hear it ring three... four... five... six times. There is no point if he is going to—

"Sid speaking." The voice is unfamiliar. So much for an epiphany.

"This is Kat James. You left your details with Ethan at the Vanilla Pod. How can I help?"

"Um... well... it's a little awkward," hesitation. "Last night, between the excessive shots and pole dancing, you introduced your business."

Shots. Pole dancing?

We went stripping.

"Err, yes. Sorry about that. Antihistamine sometimes affects my... doesn't mix with the ... well..." Think fast,

Kat. "Yes. That's right. My amazing business. My memory is slightly hazy regarding your exact requirements due to the…" Help! I don't have a business. I don't even have a job. All I know is this man took me home. But it can't have been great, or he'd still be here. "What was I saying? Antihistamine. Yes. Umm. Do you have something in mind?"

"Sure," clearing his throat. "I have a wedding next weekend and need a plus one. How does it work… this whole arrangement? I'm sorry I dismissed your suggestion when you offered to help me."

This is awesome! And such a great idea. He thinks I run a plus-one service. I can charge him lots of money to be his plus one at this wedding. This is the perfect revenge after being taken for a ride with Hugo. A momentous turn of the tables and the opportunity to screw a man for money, instead of the other way round. Wait! Not a great idea. What if he thinks I'm an escort? I would never offer that. It must be a mistake. Ladies and Gentlemen, may I present Tilly's first accidental prostitute.

"Let me check my availability for you, Sid." Hopefully, a pause presents the illusion of checking a busy schedule. What a joke. My diary is completely clear for the rest of eternity. "Yes, I have an opeee… ahem, I'm available next weekend." I nearly said opening. I need to get better at this. So stupid. Embarrassing innuendos cement any suspicions that my work is wanton, willing to supply a happy ending. "With the wedding so soon, I suggest we meet at once to discuss plans and confirm payment." Then I can see what he looks like and remember what happened.

"Sure, absolutely… payment." There is silence on the line.

A Boston Shaker in the centre of my chest fills the void as I fill up with nerves.

"How much will it be?" He speaks cautiously.

This is such a good question, I wish I'd thought of it myself. If I say too much, I fail before I even start. Too little, and he will know I am making it up as I go along.

"The preliminary planning meetings are free of charge. There is zero obligation to continue with the booking if you are not satisfied with all elements. Charges only apply to the event itself. The hourly rate is fifty pounds." I hold my breath.

"That sounds a lot for a whole day at a wedding." Sid immediately rejects my opening gambit.

Of course it does. Stupid me. Why did I think I could bluff my way through this instead of coming clean? "You are absolutely right, which... is... why... I cap the rate for assignments longer than five hours. The day rate is two hundred and fifty pounds." I went too high. I should have prepared more. Hung up and called him back, giving me time to think. I was stupid to think I could do this.

More silence. The ice clacks in my chest.

"Okay. How do I pay?" He said yes!

Yesterday I was homeless and destitute, screwed over by the love of my life. Today, I'm reversing my fortunes and fleecing the first gullible man foolish enough to give me his number. I need to sound blasé. He can't suspect this is my debut assignment.

"Oh, the usual. Bank transfer or cash is good. When are you free to meet?"

"Tomorrow?" He is keen.

"Perfect. Vanilla Pod, two pm?" I hope returning to the scene of the crime will prompt memories.

"Sounds good."

I clutch the phone tightly and cream into the pillows before I hang up.

"Baaaaaaaaaa!!!!" This can't be real, I must be dreaming. A stranger just agreed to pay me TWO HUNDRED AND FIFTY POUNDS to go to a poxy wedding with them.

And it was so easy. I must have been on fire last night and really sold this fake business of mine. Plus, he must be a hottie, or I would never take him home for mind-blowing sex. This is a win-win situation. There is only one problem: now he is paying me a repeat fuck is off the table. Not to worry. It will keep my mind clear, and for once I won't screw up by screwing him.

Grans bursts through the door dressed in a tiered skirt, ruched off the shoulder button through blouse, and a multi-patterned head scarf adorned with flat silver beads.

"Goodness, my dear. What happened?" She is holding

her phone, which gives out a digital chirp, momentarily diverting her urgency.

"Grans, what are you wearing?"

"I'm channelling my inner Roma. My father was a quarter gypsy which means an eighth of my blood is of the line. Enough to provide me with talent beyond the world you experience, my dear. Sadly, your blood is too diluted."

"But why are you wearing those clothes and what is that smell?" Like a roast, it must be for dinner.

"My vardo arrived this afternoon and it needs some work. I wanted to cleanse the aura with some burnt sage and it does wonders for removing negative energy." She should bring some in here and cleanse my aura.

"A caravan?"

"To you, yes. For the back garden. A dedicated space to expand my palm reading circle and branch out into new things like tarot cards or jewellery reading."

"Grans, I have a new job as well. It's my own company." The words sound odd.

Like a crazy person, I phoned a stranger and offered to be this date for money. This is sounding dodgier by the minute. How stupid, and despite what people think of me, it is completely out of character. I'm not a high-powered businesswoman, I'm Kat James, hiding from the world. Lying in bed nursing my heartache.

"Grans, I need your help. The meeting is tomorrow afternoon. To present a fictional business born during my drunken ramblings last night." I'm as clear as glass, but Grans looks confused. "I told a guy I run a business and he has made a booking."

"How exciting, like a date?" That's something Cynthia, my mother, would say.

"No!" I told her this was business. "To accompany him to a wedding. Why did you say date?"

"Oh, I misheard you, my dear. My mind is fogged by the burnt sage."

"So, he asked me to accompany him to a wedding and will pay two hundred and fifty pounds."

"Money?" Grans is still confused.

"Well, yes. That's how commerce works." Or it's not business.

"Oh! And how much did he agree to pay?" Grans sounds worried.

"Grans, are you okay? You seem distracted."

"Yes, yes. All fine. You said two hundred and…"

"Fifty Pounds. Isn't that great? Just for going to a wedding with someone."

"Yes, to be a plus one. So much money. And he agreed?"

"Well yes, he agreed."

"So, it's not a date." Grans looks disappointed. "Are you pretending to be in a relationship with him?"

"I guess."

"Then people will think you are together."

"I hadn't really thought." There's no time after the phone call to get things straight in my head about what this means.

"Looks like a relationship."

"Yes."

"Like a Bloody Mary?"

"No thanks, Grans." Typical Grans, to get diverted in the middle of my exciting news. "I'm still not done with talking about this plus one idea." Ooh, that is a good name. Plus-One: for all your companionship needs. Well, not all. You know what I mean.

"I know, dear. I should have said Virgin Mary. Your new business looks like the real thing, smells like the real thing, feels like the real thing,"

"There will be no feelings here, Grans." Never again.

"Tastes like the real thing."

"And definitely no tasting. I don't even remember the guy."

"Oh, he's lovely. Sounds lovely, I mean."

"Some guy rings me up offering money in exchange for a plus one and who knows what else. And you think that sounds lovely?"

"HE offered you money?" Grans still has trouble understanding.

"Well, no. Actually, he seemed as surprised as you when I mentioned payment."

"I mean, if Ethan approved of this, he must be okay." Now

Grans is confusing me.

"How do you know Ethan approves?" I didn't mention Ethan.

"Didn't you say?"

"I don't think so."

"Well, you were at the Vanilla Pod with him last night, so he must agree. Or knowing Ethan, he would have put a stop to it straight away."

"True. And he said the guy helped me home last night, so he must be half decent."

"And attractive."

"Did you see him, Grans?"

"Oh! No. Like I said earlier, you let yourself in. You were all alone when I found you. All alone. Definitely not with someone. I simply mean... he must be attractive for you to bring him home. And ever so decent if he didn't force himself on you in your inebriated state."

"No one should do that, Grans. It's called rape. Anyway, how is my idea like the Virgin Mary? I have no intention of getting impregnated, immaculate or not."

"Let me explain. To the non-expert eye, your new enterprise looks, smells, feels, and tastes like the real thing." Grans goes full circle back to this again.

"With no touching or tasting." Or smelling. That's just creepy.

"Yes. But it will seem real. And have all the trappings of a real relationship."

"But none of the side effects. Like a hangover."

"Like a mocktail. Oh-ho! That's it. You should call it Mocktail."

"Mocktail? Sounds like an escort girl." Granted, I am being paid to escort someone, but only as a platonic plus one and nothing more. "I was thinking of calling it Plus-One."

"How common. Everyone uses that." Grans is unusually dismissive.

"What about Platonic?"

"Sounds like a companionship app for the sexually incontinent." Grans could be right there. "No. Mocktail sounds refined, the ultimate charade. A Mocktail is more than fizzy water and fruit juice. It's the perfect combination of textures, flavours, and imagery, which contain all the essence of a cocktail, carefully orchestrated by a mixologist. The untrained eye would not know the difference unless they tasted it. And even then, it can fool some."

"Like I said, no tasting will be happening in this business contract."

"So Mocktail it is."

"Well, I hadn't confirmed–"

"Now pop in the shower and get dressed." Grans is in a bossy mood. "You've rotted long enough."

"All my clothes. Soaked from the storm."

"Borrow from me, dear. I've popped something on the chair that's perfect."

"You don't own anything that would suit me, Grans. I only wear black." A broderie skirt and ruched blouse is not my style.

"You're selling a dating experience, dear, not a funeral service. My wardrobe contains a few things that may work for you. Shower first, then dinner. You look like you are ready to eat after your overindulgence." The items Grans selected are black and look suspiciously like yoga gear.

"Overindulgence! Oh ho! Mocktail is such a good name."

SEVEN

Perry

The time on my watch says twelve, which to me is still early. I've just enjoyed the best sleep of my life after the first home-cooked meal in years.

"Ah, you're awake, my dear. I've been hard at it all morning."

Grans is in her dressing room playing stylist, the walls an array of outfits.

"How about this?" Grans holds a floral tea dress. Made in chiffon, the dress has a tiered skirt and a light frill on the capped sleeves.

"Err, no thanks Grans, far too fussy." Not to mention the large-scale flowers on the lemon ground, which making me feel nauseous.

"Don't pull that face dear, it's ideal for a garden party. But yes, a bit fancy for today." She moves on to the next wardrobe.

"Grans, what are you doing?"

"Selecting you an outfit for your date." Moving along the rail.

"Grans, it's a business arrangement," I explain again. "A planning meeting, scoping out the needs of my client."

"And you need to be properly attired to command respect."

Grans waves a few more choices at me, but nothing tempts me. Until she finds a little black crêpe dress.

"This is perfect." Nineteen-sixties in styling and sleeveless with a few delicate front pleats, it's smarter than I usually wear but the perfect colour.

"Oh ho, my dear. Such a wonderful ensemble." Grans' eyes

mist over. "Did you know? I wore that dress on Abbey Road, I had a sheer white blouse underneath and bare legs."

"What? No tights?" The dress is cheek-grazingly short.

"Oh ho, yes dear. It was the trend. There was some sort of fuss happening at the zebra crossing. All the traffic had stopped, so I thought I'd make a dash for it. I remember a man with long hair, white suit walking towards me with a strange look in his eye and I thought my luck was in. Then, all of a sudden, I'm bundled off the pavement and into someone's front garden. At first, I thought I was being kidnapped, but apparently, they were modelling a photo shoot."

"What year was this?"

"Oh, around the late sixties."

"Grans, are you telling me you were–"

"Oh no, no, no. They are NPC's."

"What's an NPC?"

"Nameless persons for confidentiality. To protect their anonymity. Anyway, as I was saying, I remember the boys joining us in the garden after they finished. The one in navy had no shoes. So bohemian. Such a lovely group of boys." Grans blushes. "The one in denim winked at me, he was such a good-looking man I nearly lost all composure. No doubt I caught their attention because the dress was so mini. It's hard not to flash your knickers every time the wind takes flight."

"Grans!" I don't want a dress that reminds me of Grans' knickers.

"Oh ho! I was nearly an extra on the shoot, but in the end, they just went with the four of them." The faraway look returns. "Still, the afterparty was lots of fun. Oh ho." Grans chuckles.

The black dress is super short, no wonder Grans attracted attention. As I'm a few inches taller, there's no way I can go bare-legged to my meeting. Flashing my knickers will only land me a client base interested in getting inside them. For this, I need the thickest opaque tights and a smart white shirt. I threw some leggings into the bag during operation evacuate the flat, but they will be ruined in the storm.

"Grans, I need something under this. Did the rain trash all my stuff?"

"Don't worry, dear. I sorted your clothes yesterday. They're drying in the utility room."

"You're amazing! How do you do it?" My grateful hug knocks her off balance.

"Oh ho, I don't know." Grans looks at the clock. "My dear, you must be quick. Not much time until you leave."

Thirty minutes until my appointment at the Vanilla Pod. Getting ready never takes me long and is a natural fallout from spending days hungover in bed, only to sleep far too much and wake up late for work once again. The quickest of quick rush jobs sorts my face. No matter what the result, it's an improvement on Friday night. A bit of eyeliner and a sweep of mascara, and I'm fixed. No time for foundation, the fresh natural look will rule the day. Not that it matters, this mystery man obviously fancies me as he made the effort to help me home.

"Grans, I'm off now. Wish me luck."

Grans is in the study, hovering over the printer.

"Just one more minute, dear. Come here and pick your logo."

The printer launches into life, and the cartridge zooms back and forth before a few credit card-sized templates fall to the floor.

"I've designed some business cards and am working on a web design. What do you think? Black and cloud, or cloud and anthracite?"

"Cloud? Looks white to me." They are both the same.

"Details are everything. I favour the cloud and anthracite. It smacks of sophistication."

Grans slips the business cards and a proforma into my vintage tote, along with a contract ~~in case~~ for when Sid confirms our agreement.

"Nothing anyone can't learn at the local library."

"Well, your internet sorcery is impressive."

"As is your resilience to pick yourself up and start again."

Not resilient but very kind of Grans to say.

"Thanks, Grans. Got to go, or I'll be late."

"My car keys are in the top drawer of the credenza. I added you to the insurance while you were getting ready."

"Grans, you're fantastic! Is there no end to your amazing support?"

"Oh ho, I'm sure there is, my dear. I'm sure there is."

The keys to Grans' Mini fit perfectly in my hand, like they belong there.

"Not got a new one yet? It's gotta be twenty-five years old." It will never get there in one piece.

"I just had it refurbished." Grans reads my face. "Found a place in Tilly that does electric conversions. All the style of a classic without the emissions."

I should never doubt Grans. She is so generous to let me borrow it and knows it is too far to walk given the time, and the bus is a definite no-no.

PRIVATE NO PARKING. The space lies empty in the service yard of the Vanilla Pod. Ethan won't mind me using his spot, he doesn't drive to work as Laura 'needs' their car for the baby.

This is a make-or-break moment and I have no idea what to say. I'm going to look ridiculous and Sid will tell everyone I'm an escort, a common whore. Not even one of those high-class call girls but one that propositions men in bars. Not that I have anything more to lose. No job, no home, no relationship. Staying in bed is easier, on my own of course, even if a lover makes it more fun.

At least the Vanilla Pod is a safe zone. If I am making a mistake, Ethan will protect me.

The bar looks different in the daylight, less opulent, more continental cafe. Gone are the late-night beats, instead, the warming sun dapples on the tables to a soft acoustic vibe. Candles still burn, but the air is lighter, fresh and mindful. The place is quiet as it's still too early for Sunday afternoon meet-ups, the tables house the tail end of brunchers seeking the elusive hangover cure.

Rich, soothing vanilla drifts out as I open the door like a mild sedative, bringing with it a sense of familiarity. I have planned a thousand parties and events, so I'm not sure why I feel so scared. This is simply a smaller, more personal version and should be easy. I am dignified and risk-free, supplying all the colour of a relationship but none of the grief. I have my proforma if my mind goes blank, thanks to Grans writing down a list of requirements to help design the event. Where, when, how, time, key people, etc, etc. So much to remember, but all at my fingertips in my trusted vintage tote.

The fun of a blind date is not knowing what your partner looks like. Old, young, fat, thin, dark, fair, but for me, there is no fun in meeting someone without these clues. I should have asked Sid to sit at a specific table. But then, it may not have been available and I would approach the wrong person, asking them for two hundred and fifty pounds to accompany them to a wedding. That would not go well and is definitely prostitute territory.

There are two lone men. One at the bar with Ethan, and one lingering in the doorway. I catch the eye of the guy in the doorway, a Picasso Martini, hips rocking back and forth. Nervous. He could be Sid.

Surely, I'd remember if I took a distinctive Picasso Martini home. But there is nothing familiar about him. I make my way closer, my sparkly pumps squeaking on the clean scrubbed floorboard. But he escapes before I can take more than three steps. Not Sid. Or maybe Sid with a garnish of regret. The man waves to the street and is joined by who I like to think of as his mum and dad. Not Sid. No regrets. Unlike me. I have that feeling of dread soaking over my body. Tension builds in my throat. I should never have pretended to know what we agreed. I should have been honest and fessed up.

"Kat, Darling. How are you today?" Ethan halts his conversation with the man at the bar. Definitely tense enough to be Sid, and attractive enough for me to take him home. There is something about him. If only I could remember what happened on Friday night. It must have been good, or he would not have sought me out. I blame the shots, I should have stopped drinking when Ethan told me to. There's no déjà vu moment, no eureka event, only emptiness. He has a fresh but sensitive vibe, dressed in mid-blue jeans and a white t-shirt. Clean living. The opposite of Hugo. Deep blue eyes hold a familiar sadness, reflecting my pain. That must be the something that we have a connection.

He stares.

It's my hair, something is wrong. I check the ends, smoothing any frizz.

No, stop! This is a business meeting, not a date. It doesn't matter if I have a few strands out of place.

"Great thanks, Ethan." I should have rehearsed my professional smile. All I have is flirty, which is not suitable. Ethan giggles behind his bar towel.

"Kat, this is Sid." Even after Ethan confirms this is the man, there is still nothing.

"I'm Kat. Owner of Mocktail." Sid, who grows taller the closer I get, accepts my outstretched hand. A kiss is too intimate, but tempting. Not on the mouth, of course, a cheek-to-cheek kiss. His smooth, shaved skin is begging to be embraced.

"Mocktail?" He smiles. "I mean Sid." His grip is warm and firm and strong, really strong. I should have practised my handshake. Too soft and I am powerless in negotiations, too firm will intimidate.

Hand to hand, his touch comforts.

And not for the first time.

Friday night.

There was more.

I wish I could remember.

Sid's hand lingers on mine, all smooth, with a hint of callus on the tips of his digits.

When I awoke, I was in my underwear. He used these fingers to remove my clothes. Stroke the skin on my arms, examining every miniature mole, kissing the scars earned learning to ride a bike as a child. His hands lifted off my t-shirt, still damp from my stormy walk. Tracing the shape of my curves starting at my throat, stroking the ridge of my clavicle, along the peaks of my breast and the sides of my waist. Pausing to kiss my décolletage before moving to undo the top of my jeans, peeling them over my hips, sliding to the floor. His strong arms, carrying me to bed.

Sounds good. But it's wishful thinking.

I need to find out what happened, but I need this job more.

"Sid, how are you today? It looked as though a heavy night was on the cards when we met." For both of us. My overly cheery, sing-song tone masks my misdemeanours.

Sid clears his throat. "Surprisingly good, thanks. But then you know how it was. I wasn't in the mood for drinking too much. I'm a little nervous now, though. It's best to be honest in an awkward situation." Awkward. Something did happen between us.

"Well, that's perfectly normal for my clients," and here starts the web of lies shrouded as strategic thinking on my feet. Sid values honesty, but opening myself up to ridicule will never happen. He won't sign up to be my first client if he knows the truth, that I am a fraud, as nervous and uncomfortable as he is. "Let's get straight down to business. Minimise this awkward tension." I hope my legacy smile is not morphing into a grimace.

"Sure. I was just ordering. Do you want one? Vodka, right?"

A man is offering to buy me a drink, this is the closest I've ever come to an actual date. Fortunately, before I make a fool of myself, Ethan comes to the rescue.

"Darling, grab a table and I'll bring them over."

"Thanks, Ethan, perfect as always. Let's use the snug, it's my favourite spot."

"And where we first met." Sid remembers. Well, it was only two days ago.

"Yes, of course." Still nothing.

Sid leads the way. I should be doing that, this is my meeting. As he moves, a faint essence of citrus, not overly sweet, awakens the possibilities.

The snug is reserved for us. Ethan knows what I like. Sid gestures for me to sit. This feels like wooing, but it should feel like work. Whatever happened between us, it must have gone wrong, or he would have stayed. So much for being a strong single businesswoman. I don't remember if I slept with my first client. Mega fail. And he is fuckable. His attractiveness is not helping me to focus.

So, I ground my feet and control my breathing. I close my

eyes and imagine meeting Sid for the first time. An aroma, like cider, but not cider. He has a natural sweetness, strong and dry. A Perry, fresh, sensitive face, clear eyes, deep golden hair. Solid shoulders, strong, supportive, lean toned body. Mouth-watering presentation. A tall pint glass, solid base, straight sides dripping with condensation, and I want to drink him up, savouring every mouthful.

After a deep breath in, I open my eyes to find Sid still standing, waiting for me to sit first.

"Thanks. I wasn't expecting that."

Sid laughs. "There are still a few gentlemen left in the world."

Perhaps that's why I can't remember. He was the perfect gentleman. Not allowing me even one sip of his refreshing essence.

"Welcome to our first meeting of Mocktail. I'm Kat." He knows that. I must try to sound less amateurish and not get distracted by his cocktail. "I set up my business to help people, people just like you. People who receive an invitation for an event but—

"Kat, I know, remember? You don't have to pretend with me."

"Sorry to interrupt, Darling, I hope you're hungry." Ethan delivers a pint of cider for Sid and tea for me. He leaves after a kiss on the cheek (mine, not Sid's). On his way back to the bar, he stops to pick up empty glasses and pivots to send a cheeky wink back my way. Ethan, of all people, can see right through my facade. He knows I'd rather be getting down and dirty than getting down to business with my client.

"Oh yes. Of course. I told you all this on Friday night. Sorry." I need to get up to speed. "Could you tell me more about yourself, so I can write it down this time. If you're happy, you can sign up for the booking or walk away with no obligation to continue." And leave me destitute with no future but to work here in the Vanilla Pod, picking up the occasional free shift. Silence. "Can I ask... how long do we have? Are you on lunch?"

"It's fine," Sid looks up from his pint. "You don't know this about me, but I'm self-employed. We have as long as you need."

"Great. Well, if you don't mind, I have a series of questions to set the scene. At Mocktail, we give a personal." Sid's eyebrow lifts again. "Not that personal!" I should have applied foundation to mask my blushes. "An individually tailored package for functions, like a fake girlfriend. For you, perhaps the 'first date' Mocktail package. As we don't know much about each other."

"Nooooo?" Sid's voice softens and lowers in contemplation. He sounds unsure, or he is completely sure, and I do know him intimately. Not that carnal knowledge would help me at the wedding when I meet the bride's ageing grandparents. *'How do you know darling Sid?' 'He gave me multiple orgasms the night we met. He has the best cunnilingus technique I have ever come across.'* That would be enough to set off Grandad's angina.

This is scarier than I anticipated. The muddler bangs against the wall of my chest. My heart rate increases, powering the blood rushing to my cheeks. "Another scenario to consider is the newly formed relationship. You've been dating your Mocktail for a few weeks and are in the first stages of romance." A big sip of tea gives me time to compose myself.

"The second one sounds better, if we need a scenario. Although perhaps we don't need to define it."

"Who's getting married?"

"Christian, my brother. And I'm the best man."

I'm so stupid. I would remember that if we met on Friday night. And with Sid, the best man, I'll not have the luxury of blending into the background, to hide away from inquisitive eyes behind a floral display. I am the floral display.

"Brother's wedding. Of course, I remember you telling me on Friday night." I'm usually so good at remembering details of what happens, even when hammered. I definitely had too much vodka.

"Is that a problem? Me being the best man, I mean. You'll be unaccompanied at the wedding for parts of the day, left to fend on your own."

I feel shaky. Stay calm Kat, and show this is business as

usual. I try another professional smile to fool both of us.

"That's okay. Nothing is a problem at Mocktail. May I ask a sensitive question? Why do you need me to occupy your plus-one space?" I didn't mean to make things awkward again, but Sid avoids my gaze. "I assure you I am sensitive to all issues."

He picks up his pint. A few gulps empty the glass: Dutch courage.

"Okay. I will play along, sure. I confess, I've not told you everything. Once you learn more, you may change your mind about the deal."

EIGHT

Pousse-Café

Sid looks me straight in the eye, face serious.
"My ex-girlfriend is the chief bridesmaid."
Shit. This just got a lot more complicated. Sid seems so calm, sensitive and supportive. Surely any ex-girlfriend of his would be friendly, but when pushed, he says not.

"If what you say is true, it's no surprise you're not jumping for joy at the prospect. Absolutely, you must take someone. Show her you've moved on."

With a face like that, Sid doesn't need to pay for company, so there must be more to it than he's letting on.

"No chance of that. We broke up less than a month ago. I assume you don't eradicate ex-girlfriends."

A joke, I hope. Eradicating ex-girlfriends sounds more than illegal. Grans said she had contacts, but no, even if money is tight, I'm not desperate enough to take up contract killing.

"No. But if that was an option, my ex is top of the list." And just like that, we bond over plans to kill our exes. "Say no more. Believe me, the plan will accommodate this delicate situation. My proposal is this, we've been on a few dates and it is getting serious. You consider it acceptable to bring me to the wedding. Will that rest easily with your ex-girlfriend's feelings?"

"Fuck her feelings!" Sid doesn't hold back. "The story sounds plausible... then again, it's not been long. Our relationship must be very new, is very new."

"Our mock relationship, you mean. We need a meet-cute." Holding back is not my style. By now, even after only two days I would know every layer of his desires and every detail of his body. Instead, he knows all about mine and I remember nothing about his.

"A fake meet-cute, you mean?" Sid inhales deeply. "Kat, I didn't tell you enough on Friday night for you to understand what you're offering to do. I'm not sure it's entirely fair until you know what you are up against."

"Up against? Is it really that bad?" A nervous laugh escapes my mouth.

"Yes, she's quite a handful. What you see is not always what you get." The corner of Sid's mouth lifts, but not from humour. This is an admission of the dark truth. "It is that bad. We were together for five years. Things were serious."

"What happened?"

"After her best friend Jessica got engaged to my brother, she put more and more pressure on me to propose."

"And you didn't want to?"

"No, it's not that. Marriage is a great idea. I'm just not convinced I want to marry her."

"Even after five years, you're not certain?"

"Exactly my point. If she is the one, I should know after all this time. She, Lex, is very sweet when she wants to be. Charming, intelligent, successful. But also, quite domineering and," he gives a little cough, "anyway, it transpires after all her nagging and pushing to commit, she was having serial affairs with anyone she laid her cheating eyes on. I was in the dark until around three weeks ago."

"And…"

"She was fucking the best man."

Not a great moment for me to sip tea. A fountain of chamomile spills over the table. There are times when it is better to swallow instead of spit, and this is one of them.

"The best man at the wedding? But you are the best man?"

"I got promoted when he slept with the chief bridesmaid."

"She sounds like a Pousse-Café."

"What's that?"

"A drink." He doesn't need to know I do this. "She has layers. Some are sweet like raspberry syrup, some dark and bitter like Amaro Averna or spicy like Chartreuse. Pretty on the outside, but you never know what layer you are going to taste next. Sometimes, the unexpected rises to the top. A Pousse-Café is delicately prepared and chilled to perfection."

"Sounds like you've got her measure." Sid jokes. "Just remember, from your point of view, Lex is pure evil. She will not make your life easy, despite what you perceive on the outside. Her behaviour is not as innocent as it appears." No wonder attending the wedding on his own fills him with dread. He stares into his glass, searching.

"Another drink?"

"No. I'm bordering on liver damage after the amount I've drunk over the last few weeks. It's time I face this, which is where you come in." He said come. I can do that for him. "When you explained everything the other night, I figured we should do this. My brother needs to enjoy his wedding and not worry about me."

This time, my smile exudes genuine empathy.

"Okay, let's plan a day you will appreciate, but she will abhor." My words receive a nod. Sid is intrigued. "What kind of date will leave her seething with jealousy?"

"The mere fact that I've found someone else is enough to annoy her... err..." he clears his throat, "even if it is only you."

If it is only you. That sounds like an insult. Let's dial it back a bit. Ethan says Sid helped me home, but he left before morning, and I was still wearing clothes. So, perhaps nothing happened.

"If your looks were more... conventional." More throat clearing. Nerves. If only it was impending sexual nerves, but no, here comes another insult. "I mean, only a glamourous... shit, this is awkward. What I mean to say is... the goth style... Lex thinks I'm worthless. It will be a surprise for her to discover I could mean something to someone, anyone, even you."

Yup. An insult. How stupid I was to think he could fancy me. I was a mess on Friday night, I still am. He took pity on me and nothing else.

"Do you want Lex to regret her choices?"

"Well, yes. But I'll never take her back after what she's done... it was going on for months and months." He runs his hands through his hair, tension in his temples as he glances towards the bar.

I can't concentrate. His words hang in the air. How will we make this work? His ex-girlfriend and family will know I'm not his type just looking at me. We must appear credible, the genuine thing. And yes, my hair is far from the conventional spectrum, I recently added some softer purples, the layered ends showing off the subtle hues. And he noticed, which has to be a good thing. He has an eye for style.

"What do you do for a living?"

"I'm an Artist. I also lecture at the local college in the evening and run a youth rehab group. Sometimes, I exhibit at the Riverside Arts Centre, but not for a few months. Not since things..." He drifts off. The memories are too painful.

"The exhibition sounds like a good opener. When you were last there, I took your card. Then we met for a drink to discuss a piece and you asked me to join you at the wedding. Does that sound credible?"

"I've not exhibited for a while and my studio's been closed. The stag do was the first time I'd been out in weeks, and only because the lads dragged me. Where do you think this greyish pallor comes from? Certainly not leaving the studio for dates." Sid rests his head in his palms, thumbs rubbing his forehead.

"Please, stop worrying." I lean over the table, taking his hands in mine. He hesitates before relaxing into the hold. He has firm, warm, artistic hands. "The wedding day will be without a care in the world, you have my guarantee. You are in safe hands with me. Why don't you tell me about the wedding plans?"

"The rehearsals are, well, I'm supposed to be there now. But I can't bear to look at her, let alone stand next to her."

"Sid! I thought you had nothing planned. Let's wrap up here. What we've discussed will be enough."

"Are you sure you can handle this? It might be too much. You know." Even in his stress, he thinks of me.

"No problem, I assure you. A quick recap, and we are done. First, to settle our history. I saw your work in the window of your gallery. Loved one of your pieces and called you. Sparks flew, we went for a coffee, and you thought what the hell, you'll invite me as your date."

"Sure."

"Great. So, all that's left to say is I'm polite, discrete, and professional. I drive and do not drink. I won't stay much past midnight, owing to a prior commitment on Sunday. You will be amazing, and she'll regret letting you go."

"Sounds so simple. Let's not pretend I want her back, I just…"

"Really, I understand. No one wants to attend a family wedding on their own so soon after a breakup. Where is the venue?"

"Umm, it's posh. Have you ever been to Beachbury Manor?"

"No, I…"

"Um, you may choose to wear something more refined than today. And the jewellery." He points at my piercings. "Look, it's important to know this is a posh affair. Very posh."

Another dig at my appearance. There is nothing I can do, this is me.

"Oh, this," gesturing to my hair. "I… it was for an event last weekend and, err… I was trying it out to see if I liked it. For fun." This is my signature style and I love it.

Sid is amused, his eyes crinkle around the edges.

"Sure." He doesn't believe me. "You said £250 for the whole day."

"Yes, that's right. Expect an email later with my bank details."

"Great. Pick me up at ten-thirty from my studio. That's where I'm staying." He slides his business card across the table and takes mine in return. "Cloud." He nods with approval. "Nice."

I summon a confident smile, pretending I don't feel like a pile of shit he scraped off his shoe after his candid appraisal of my appearance. "Oh, and thanks for the feedback. Don't worry, I will look perfect for you. That's my role." I stand. "Good luck today. See you bright and early next Saturday morning."

NINE

Violet Champagne d'Amour

Grans is in the drawing room, flicking through her copy of New Soul New Life, a magazine for the older generation.

"How was it, dear?" The magazine lays open at an article on the health benefits of power walking for the over-seventies. "He is gorgeous, yes?"

"Grans! This is business." My flaming cheeks reveal too much. "Mocktail just booked a posh wedding next weekend with no time to prepare. First impressions are so important, and he's not enamoured with mine."

"Oh ho, this sounds fun. Don't worry about your looks, we can help with that. You have a natural beauty to uncover behind multiple layers of wallpaper, and he recognises that. Whilst you were out, I finished laundering your clothes and must admit, they are a little too morbid for the socialite you now are. We need to add… how do I put it? Style."

"Like what? Pencil skirts and court shoes. No way, that's far too dull."

"Agreed, but you must acknowledge, some people carry that look well, but no, that's not for you. It's far too corporate. What you need is some natural vintage spritzed into your wardrobe."

Sid's words resonate as I touch my hair.

"He said it was super posh. What if I don't fit in? Maybe I've spent too long in basements living it up with the great unwashed."

Grans leaps up out of the chair animated, the power

walking paying off, beckoning me to the front door.

"Where are we going?"

"I'm taking you to meet the experts in vintage fashion."

Grans slows the Mini to a stop outside an old people's home just off London Road, the main road into Tilly Minster.

"Where are we?"

"Oak Mews. A source of experience and style."

"Looks like a care home to me, Grans." A source of urine and dead bodies.

"Caring is the number one currency here but not in the way you think. The rest home is in the north annex with panoramic views over the lake. The sheltered accommodation is in the east wing, with access to the trim trail. This is the south building, a home for a retired community of friends. Think of it as a centre for wellbeing, where everyone has a lifetime of experience to share."

I follow Grans through the automatic glass doors that look more at home in a hospice. This is where my life will end. Scraping away at the toaster crumb tray of life for stale, mouldy morsels.

Sandy, otherwise known as Death in the Afternoon, greets us at the reception. She wears green nurses scrubs and a pair of indoor welly shoes, proving my point.

"They're waiting for you in studio one. It's all set up." A blend of medicinal herbs and bubbly effervescence, Sandy points through the archway to another door.

"Sounds ominous."

"Nothing to worry about, my dear. Whilst there are plenty of outfits in my wardrobe perfect for a top-quality socialite, I thought you'd appreciate a larger family to support you in your new venture."

The automatic doors fold back to reveal a rush and babble of noise.

"Vera, Corry, Lulah. Give us some space. Don't crowd the girl."

The sea of bodies parts and Grans navigates us into a semicircle of chairs, each placed next to a mannequin or clothes rail.

"Grans, what is this?" The room, clearly an all-purpose studio, has been transformed into a supersized walk-in wardrobe. Yoga mats and watercolour easels are stashed away and it now resembles a television makeover challenge, minus the cameras. Music sings out of a gramophone on the stage at the end of the room. This feels like one of Mother's setups.

"A movie makeover!" The Ballet Russe pink pigment dye shrills from the left.

"Like where the ugly duckling turns into a beautiful princess." A Soixante-Neuf, tall with long blond hair, skips up and down.

So much for this being a centre for caring.

"Gee, thanks. Less of the ugly duckling, if you don't mind." Haven't they heard of #imageshaming?

"Quiet, everyone. Stop your teasing." Grans controls the room. There is a lot of respect here, even if it's not directed at me.

"Too soon?" The Irish Eggnog with a thick fringe offers an apology by way of open palms.

"Yes Vera, too soon." Grans' voice softens as people take their seats. "Kat, you stand by me whilst we work our way around the room. Are there any questions before we begin?"

"After we fix your wardrobe, can we sort your hair?" A henna Cherry Blossom offers.

"Friends, remember to introduce yourselves when you speak, just like we said. Kat is new here."

"What's wrong with my hair? It happens to be trendy in the club scene." I need to give them a lesson on the dangers of #bullying as well.

"And then your piercings." Suggests the Woo Woo Shooter.

Grans clears her throat, commanding authority.

"Kat, I'm Tallulah. I've heard so much about you. I'm only trying to help." The Soixante-Neuf steps in, attempting to calm things.

"This," I gesture up and down, "has taken years to perfect. I get a lot of compliments."

"I am sure you do." Tallulah smiles, her eyes soft and comforting. She stands tall and statuesque next to a rail of sequined outfits. "No man, or in my experience woman, would complain about the pleasures of a tongue piercing."

"Grans!" Help me.

"Thank you, Lulah. It may be too soon for that level of sharing." Grans turns to face me.

"Gran, what are we doing here?" I lower my voice.

"Kat, remember you're not in the club scene now. You are creating an impression that says attractive and successful, confident, in control. But also poise. Today, this urban family will show you some wardrobe ideas for your assignment. Think of them as the glassware and you the cocktail. They will consult on your presentation and supply a touch of elegance appropriate for the occasion."

"What about the garnish?"

"I am in charge of the garnish." Grans brings her hands together and rests her thumb on her sternum. "I've ordered you a new set of lingerie, frills and all, so no need to worry."

"Underwear? I always wear underwear."

Grans ignores me, probably because I have underwear but nothing matching. No one bothers with lingerie sets anymore. Everyone pretends they do, but in reality, we just reach for the most comfortable clean pants we can find.

"Let's start with a drink." Grans knows me too well.

Next to the turntable, Veuve Clicquot sits on ice. Grans' Champagne of choice. Everything about Grans distils Champagne, but it's not just that she's bubbly. She has a unique standing in the world, which is playful, refreshing and envied by many. Yes, Champagne and Grans are premium players, but it does not stop there. She is a cocktail of experiences, each taste bringing something new. More than a simple Royale and not as disruptive as a Dynamite, Grans is Violet Champagne d'Amour. Purple reigns here, and I am not talking about rinse, nothing so transparent. Grans has a Parfait Amour light fragrant joy about her, colourful and unpredictable. I had not expected such planning or to be taken so seriously. The rails of clothes signal a sharp focus, like lemon juice. Then Cointreau, comforting in its brandy base, is trusted to deliver the rich sweet personality every time. The Champagne is poured slowly into the glass, and we are almost there. Just one more thing, the garnish, always important in the theatre of life, and only fresh violets adorn her halo.

"I'm Wendy, and this is my contribution." The Cherry Blossom thrusts a cream silk suit dress with puffy sleeves in my face. "I wore this to the wedding of Princess–"

"No, no, no!" Grans cries.

"NPC!" Everyone screams. The acoustics in the room bounce the chorus off the back wall.

"NPC?"

"Nameless person for confidentiality." A harmony rings out.

"Sometimes I forget." Wendy apologises. "And whilst the name is not important, this is." Wendy slips her hand into the end of the sleeve, adding life to the jacket. "Regardez the shoulder pads, they are to die for." Bright yellow floral embroidery trails up the body of the jacket and over the super padded shoulders. "I partnered it with a cheery yellow hat, pulling the small veil over like this." Wendy puts what looks like a plucked Easter chick on her head. "At the time, I was slightly embarrassed–"

"At the time?"

"You see," Wendy explains. "It was very similar to the outfit that the other Princess was wearing."

"Who?"

A chime of NPC rings out again.

"You know. The sister of the prince."

"It would be easier if you used their name." This code just adds to the chaos.

"It was a nightmare in the photos. I had to duck behind someone so as not to appear like a stalker. Unfortunately, this meant I was merely a floating head in the backdrop. She didn't speak to me for almost a year after the wedding!"

"Complete nightmare." I comfort.

"But good for your date, yes? It is a wedding after all." Wendy finishes her pitch.

"Umm, not right for my date, assignment, errrr booking. Most definitely not a date. Not a date."

"Wendy!" Grans chastises. "You forgot the introduction."

"So sorry. Kat. I'm Wendy. And as you can see by my shapely figure, I am your bandy sniffler. However, as the mannequin shows, I have not always been this round, but I have always been short. But don't let that stop you, we can make all the necessary fittings and alterations." Wendy removes the hat and smooths her grenadine crop, checking the kiss curls are behaving at the nape of her neck.

Brandy, yes. Wendy got that part right, but a Cherry Blossom is served in a chilled cocktail glass. The brandy, Kirsch, Cointreau, fresh lemon and grenadine, all shaken over ice.

"Thanks Wendy, I will remember that."

"Next up is Olive." Grans moves us on to the Ballet Russe heckler complete with pink hair.

"I'm Olive Groves. Think of me as your cocktail glass, delicate, fun and fruity." Olive pirouettes on strong slender legs, the vodka, Crème de Cassis, lime, lemon and simple syrup hitting the spot. "And this is Lucy."

"Who?"

"This." Olive steps sideways to reveal a frothy tulle marshmallow pink dress. "I wore it for a ballet recital at the inauguration of president–"

"NPC!" The room erupts once again.

"I know, I know. I wasn't going to say their name. See, I even held back on the pronoun so you wouldn't know their gender."

"Not too difficult to guess that though, is it? Not when you tell Kat the rumours." Wendy interjects.

"Don't poison my submission, just because your eighties effort was so easily passed over." Olive grins, showing this is all good-humoured fun. "The president had a reputation for beautiful women, and appreciated someone as limber as I. You can pare it down with this silk wrap," also pink, "these ballet flats and select from this set of matching satin wrapped jewellery, or maybe you prefer a string of pearls. With Lucy, I guarantee you will knock his socks off."

"Thanks Olive, but I'd rather he kept his socks on." And I'd rather not wear a dress called Lucy.

"So, he's not attractive?" Olive turns to Grans "I thought

you–"

"Thank you so much Olive. It's time we moved on. And let's not forget people, we are creating the illusion of a perfect relationship. These outfits allow Kat to create her brand."

Grans words make sense. This job requires a polished, stylised approach. But so far, nothing fits the bill.

"Perhaps Lulah will help." Grans hands me over to the tall Soixante-Neuf, wiry with long blond hair which falls in waves over one shoulder like a lemon twist garnish. The gin and lemon juice topped with Champagne never fails to entertain.

"Kat. Lovely to meet you at last. I'm Tallulah. Think of me as your long drink. A Collins glass, tall and straight just like myself." Tallulah winks as she reveals a black tuxedo jacket and knee-length ostrich feather skirt. "This is a wedding ensemble fit for a musical legend, who remains happily married to his husband to this very day. See, I didn't even need to use NPC for my talk."

"What did you wear to his first wedding Lulah?"

"We don't need to talk about that, Olive."

"I heard you were uninvited after he blew you at the stag do."

"Well, I have changed a lot since then. Just like Wendy said. We don't all have the same figure as once we had. Some of us continue to make improvements." Tallulah holds up a pair of four-inch platform patent leather shoes. "And for accessories, you must add more height. You can never be too statuesque."

"And now my turn." Grans whisks me away, placing her Champagne glass on the stage at the far end of the room. She spins a mannequin around to reveal what looks like a navy sheet, embroidered with a large dragon. "I wore this to the NPC garden party. Accessorised with shoes and jewellery. Oh ho! Such fond memories. I was at the cake stand when the duke himself–"

"NCP!"

"Oh ho, how can I forget? And I've given it away, no matter, I will start again. The NPC could hardly take his eyes off me. And I may have let him–"

"Grans!" Too much information. Whatever it is, the dress reeks of Grans getting felt up next to the French Fancies.

"Nothing happened, I assure you. Not that I would have refused a little bite of cream horn, but it is not the done thing. Here, try it on and see what you think."

Goose bumps spread along my arms, partnered with a creeping sensation down my back.

"My dear, you are cold. Let's find you a wrap or a fur to warm you."

The room-length mirror confirms the outfit's individuality. It has a sort of wrap detail, tied at the waist, the fabric cascading in waves. A little like when you wrap a sheet around you after a sex marathon to toddle to the toilet. The other person already knows what you look like naked, but you do your best to keep some dignity. The drop shoulders hang off shoestring straps and support almost kimono-like sleeves. It is unique and difficult to describe but holds a distinctive drape which cuts up to the high thigh. I cannot wear it to this event. Apart from the revealing style, the reflection returns Grans and the Duke in a compromising position.

"Are there any more?"

"Yes, I have saved the best to last. Corrie." Grans introduces me to the final outfit and the owner, the Woo Woo Shooter. A long white dress with a crinkle touch. It is soft and floaty in my hands.

"I am Corinne. And you can tell by the length of the dress, I have never worn it. For I am a shot glass. Small and sturdy, I leave a lasting impression."

"But it is yours?"

"I acquired it, so yes." Fruity notes lead to intrigue.

"Acquired?"

"Yes, from Studio 54 in New York before I emigrated to England. My hair was big, bigger than this. You know how it was back then." Corrine stretches her arms out. "I went out in a sequin playsuit. It had these little hotpants that showed just a tease of cheek. In the club, an NPC model caught my eye. More stunning than any other woman in the room, a hundred men surrounded her. Crowds of men followed her, but somehow, I got close enough to touch her hand." This story could be long. I sit on the window seat overlooking the Japanese gardens. "She was in a playful mood and kissed me hello. Not a peck on the cheek, you know the type, the kind that makes the men's jaws drop to the floor." This sounds more fun than Grans and the Duke at the garden party. Corrine continues. "Well, you know how free and easy those days were. I had the NPC close, whispered in her ear how much I adored her dress. Her response was exquisite. She told me she envied my hotpants. As the night wore on, our paths kept crossing until eventually we decided that we loved each other's outfit so much that we swopped."

"Swopped?"

"Yes, right then and there, on a corner of the dance floor. Just stripped and swopped our clothes. It was so exciting!"

"Corrine! You're outrageous! Did anyone see?" I sound shocked, but it is only to be expected from a short, sharp shot of vodka, peach schnapps and cranberry juice.

"Not that I noticed. Nothing held us back in those days. And don't forget, I got the better deal. It's a beautiful dress, even if it is too long for me. The NPC's so tall, but it was okay as the long flowing maxi trend was in that season. She didn't miss it for long. From what I heard, she received another the next day. She was close to the designer."

As I slip into this infamous dress, it's obvious why it has such an interesting history. It is stunning, more so if that is possible. The mirror returns a deep neckline, with floor-skimming hem full of thousands of pleats of chiffon. No wonder the Ancient Greeks enjoyed mass orgies if they wore these dresses.

"Is it okay for me to choose white for a wedding? Will it upset the bride?"

"Vera, what do you think?" Corrine refers to the Irish Eggnog with a thick fringed grey bob.

"Hi, Kat. I'm Vera, and I like to think of myself as a punch cup, never to be underestimated. Whilst I don't have an outfit, having worn a uniform my whole working life. I can tell you not to worry. It's not completely white. If you look closely here, there are layers of ombre pastels, and it's on trend this season. However, there's no doubt you'll be the only one in a dress with such a tale to tell."

Corrine sets to work on the accessories, trimming it with a thin gold belt and Grecian sandals. For the jewellery, a delicate plaited tri-metal set wraps around my wrist and neck.

"Amazing! This is the dress. Not only is it stylish, it's timeless and drop dead sexy."

Grans moves closer for a celebratory hug but stops short of my outstretched arms.

"Oh no! That will not do. Luckily, I had the foresight to book you into the salon first thing in the morning to work on your hair. I've already briefed them, it's out with multi coloured rubbish and in with dignified and stylish. This Vampire My Little Pony mane kills the aura."

"But what do you think about the dress?" I stroke the bright tips that undercut the bottom of my dark locks, perhaps for the last time.

"My dear, the dress is perfect, but your hair is far too gothic. It's completely wrong. Such a mismatch."

If I'd asked her opinion on my hair, it would be fair to tell me what she thinks. But I didn't and the unwanted criticism cuts deep after years of sculpting my looks to fit into my nightclub role. I don't want to look normal. Normal is boring. Normal conforms to societal constructs that do nothing to help me. Grans just said the appointment was first thing in the morning. This is the bigger challenge.

"But I'm never out of bed before midday!"

"No stressing. Your appointment is at eight a.m.. Plenty of opportunity for beauty sleep. Once you return, we will take afternoon tea and begin the studies."

"Sounds like a plan, apart from the early start."

"Setting up a new business requires hard graft. Success is not found lounging around in bed, well not in the direction you say you want this business to go in."

"Grans, can I ask one more thing?"

"Of course, my dear."

"What's with all the NPC? Why not just say their name?"

"Because _we_ are the headliners in our own story." Corrine

pats her full curls.

"I learnt, long ago, that others' behaviour is out of my control." Tallulah nods, knowingly.

"Their actions are determined by God, or fate, or karma. But never me." Wendy confirms.

"Just like a non-player character. NPC." I offer.

"She gets it!" Vera celebrates by opening another bottle of Champagne.

"Welcome to being the main player in your own story."

But I am not ready. Nothing I have ever done, no decision I have made up to this point in my life has gone well. Why will it be different this time?

TEN

Chambord

The buzzing sound that wakes me is once again not the man of my dreams about to go down on me with a vibro bullet, but a sole destroying alarm for stage two in the grand makeover plan. In a way, it makes sense. Grans is right, the whole point of Mocktail is the pretence of being something else, so it makes sense that the new me goes to bed alone and wakes up alone. I wish it was nice to be anyone else but me, but this part of my life is lacking.

Ali's designer studio is situated in a side alley off the top end of Oxford Street. Sandwiched between a café and a jeweller. The ceilings are low, and the narrow room is decked out in eau de nil washed panelling, making the space cosy and intimate.

I've been double booked, a Scotch Mist waits on the cream leather sofa. I'm not sure I'm ready to share this experience with an audience.

"Come sit down. Let's chat about what we are doing today." He pats the empty seat.

"I'm here for Ali. I'm Kat James." I am not talking to him about my hair. I need a professional.

"Pleased to meet you, Kat. I'm Alfred. Or Ali as I am known at Oak Mews."

"I thought everyone at Oak Mews was retired." Is Alfred the stylist?

"Retired, but not completely out of the game. For you, I made a special appointment."

"How often do you work?"

"Just one day a week. It keeps me out of mischief when I am not invested in other Oak Mews projects."

"Like me?" I am just a project to them.

"Oh no! You are one of us now. We're a family who takes care of each other and supports new ventures. That's why I will also style you on the wedding day as well. My treat."

"But I'm not the one getting married."

"Shush now. It is all settled. You will come back here on Saturday, and nothing more to say. Now your Grans said I was to introduce myself in a particular way. So here goes." Alfred stands. "I'm Alfred. An old-fashioned glass. I don't agree with this description myself, but some people think me short and stocky, with a solid base."

Alfred begins by creating a mood board. Selecting a new hairstyle is not as easy as selecting a dress. There are so many looks, but the cut is the most important. Once cropped, it takes time to grow back. Colour is not up for consideration, Alfred selects a more natural tone that maintains my individual expression but removes the coloured tints. The best colour to suit my skin tone is a modern shade called Autumn Red, a deep auburn hue that shimmers copper tones in the light. The length can stay if I promise to return for an early appointment on Saturday to style it for the wedding.

Grans is footing the bill and that's a good job as I could never afford to get my hair done in such a luxurious salon. I savour every moment of the head massage, the big comfortable chair, the free drink (even if it is a generic-tasting smoothie mocktail with a synthetic bottled taste).

After my initial protests and reservations about changing colour, it looks good. I am now a serious business owner. But it does not look like me. Not like the me I relate to. The mouth is mine, yes. And the eyes, they never lie. But the hair. This is not mine. Not the me I want to be anyway. This is the me of the past. My cover is blown.

"Here you go." Alfred gives a final pat to his masterpiece, checking the bounce in the blowout. "What do you think? It is a better match to your roots, so nice and easy to maintain."

"It looks so different I hardly recognise myself." The first lie.

"So much more natural now. How long did you overdye it

dark?"

"So long I can't remember never doing it." The second lie.

"And now here you are. Back to your natural self. How does it feel?"

"It looks great, thanks so much." Not quite what Alfred asked. But if I told him how I feel, he would take it the wrong way. Pressure builds, heat at the top of my nose, then stinging in the corners of my eyes. I feel anxious. This is the Kat that saw it all. Felt it all. I close my eyes to stop feelings flying out.

※ ※ ※

After it happened, I dyed my hair with a black-blue overdye, which made it easier to talk to the face in the mirror. A mask to camouflage my feelings. Cynthia muttered on about how I looked depressed, so I bleached the lot, adding candy garnish to the ends. Her friends, the Swizzles (on account of them poking a stick in and stirring up any situation), comforted Cynthia's horror with unhelpful musings. *'It is only to be expected.' 'The girl is only expressing her feelings after what happened.' 'Say nothing, and she will grow out of it.'* But it is not something one grows out of. No one understood how I felt, as proven by their presumption that changing my hair was part of a predestined process. Whatever colour I used, blue, red, purple, black, the result was the same. Other people's naïve comments of *'rebelliousness'*, *'attention seeking'*, and *'a cry for help'*, proves how alone I was.

Cynthia and Gordon collected me from the hospital. Once discharged from care, people imagined I was as healed on the inside as I looked on the outside. Assuming there was nothing wrong or afraid to face the horrors of what happened, people stayed away. The Swizzles said, *"why is she not accepting?" "she must be broken" "fix her"*, so Cynthia and Gordon paid for counselling. It was a cold, formulaic process, close the book to the past, it is done. Complete. Finished. Over. Life starts a new chapter, shaped by my actions, defined by my attitude.

* * *

As I drive, each shiny surface returns fresh reminders. Windows, glass-fronted billboards, the rear-view mirror in the car. Closing my eyes helps but has a devastating impact on road safety. After several close shaves with other drivers, a cyclist, a pedestrian crossing, a skip, and wing mirrors on parked cars, I make it to the Vanilla Pod. Ethan saved me the first time. He was the one who taught me how to control the panic, and now I need him more than ever.

The back door is locked. Of course it is, it's before midday. The front entrance is too far to walk for the urgent care I need, so I start pounding on the door. Heavier and heavier until I attract Ethan's attention, but he gestures to go round the front.

"This is the back entrance." He does not recognise me. He never saw this version of me.

"Ethan," I call through the glass, too close to see myself for a second. "Let me in. It's me. Kat."

He moves forward, frown lines covering his forehead.

"This better be an emergency. These doors don't open for anyone before the official time. Of course... if you were Kat, I'd not hesitate. You appear to be Kat, but you can't be for two reasons. Firstly, it's not yet twelve, and the Kat I know will still be in bed. Secondly, Kat has got crazy goth hair. Yours is a beautiful colour that shines brighter than the sun."

He throws the door open and engulfs me in a welcoming bear hug.

"Ha ha Ethan, it wasn't that bad." My armour thickens a little, it is working.

"No, but it's fucking amazing now! You look like you just stepped out of a salon."

"Hilarious, Ethan."

"Darling, are you here to pick up more shifts or use my mirrors to admire your new barnet?"

I'm here for help. Answers.

"What, oh, sorry, no. Here to show you my new hair."

"I love it. But..." Ethan tilts his head, crème de cocoa eyes narrowing. "What's wrong? You don't like it?"

"I feel naked. Exposed. Mocktail is about the charade. Pretending to be something I am not. This is..."

"Change can be tough. You will get used to it."

"No, you don't understand." I close my eyes and expel a wavering breath. "This is me. This is what I looked like when it happened." I need him to see.

Ethan's strong arms steady my pose as my legs wobble.

"Darling, you did the right thing coming here. I've got you. The real Kat, no matter what colour hair, has always been here." Ethan's hand rests on my chest. "Traumatic memories can be triggered at any point. We discussed this. Can you remember what to do?"

"Yes, but I'm not sure it will work any more. I have not tried it like this."

"Let me help you. Only this time, we try something different. I think you are ready for it."

"For what?" There has been enough change today. I'm not ready for more.

"I'm not letting go until you are grounded."

"Ethan, I can't do this." It's too painful. "I'm going back to make it right."

"We are going to breathe in for the count of four." Ethan takes my hands in his. "Keep your eyes closed. Feel the ground beneath your feet, pushing back up, and you push down. Two. Three. Four." He removes his hands, resting them on my upper arms, soothing the uncertainty, gentle pressure moving over my elbows, down to my wrists. "And out for the count of eight. Listen to your inner voice. Be open to what she is telling you. Two. Three. Four. Accept and listen. Really hear what you need." His hand moved again to my heart. "Acknowledge the pain and give yourself the compassion you deserve. That is all you need today. Six. Seven. Eight."

"But what about the drink?"

"Oh, that's easy. You are the real Kat. Super strong, reliable and vibrant."

"I feel weak and vulnerable and broken."

"Darling, give yourself time. You have been through so much, and then the job thing, and Hugo. Only true strength would get through this. Your resolve has held you together for all these years, never letting you down. Never giving in to the darkness. You are lush, sweet, and always bring flavour to sour moments. You are Chambord." Ethan speaks my language.

"But how can I continue with this charade when I feel exposed?"

"This is about moving forwards. Now is the time. You are ready to listen."

"So why do I feel like I'm propelled back? Undoing everything I've worked for?"

"Focus on the now. This minute. This second. Listen to your internal voice. Is it what she wants?"

"I don't know."

"Then, give yourself more time. She will tell you when she is ready."

"Grans has homework for me this afternoon, I have no time."

"None of this can be fixed in an afternoon. It took years for you to reach this place. The journey you are on must be free from expectations, or you restrict where it will take you."

Ethan is right, I do have high expectations. I am just like the Swizzles.

"Nevertheless. I need to go."

"Good, because you drink too much of my profits. It's going okay with Sid then?"

"Why the surprise? I made him an offer he found hard to refuse." My slip of the tongue makes Ethan laugh. "NOT like that. Ahhh! I'm getting out of here, going home. You have been a great help until now."

"Okay darling. Phone me later if you want a shift." Ethan blows a kiss goodbye.

How wonderful it is to call Grans' house home. Well, for the short term, at least. Her Victorian villa nestles amongst hundred-year-old trees on Kingsgate, an original cobbled street in the old part of Tilly Brook. The roads are narrow and bendy but there is less risk of knocking into something when you're small and beautifully designed. Ethan's words echo in my mind. I am strong, like Chambord. Rich in flavour and experiences. The wheels crunch on the drive and I smooth away moisture from my cheeks. 'Thank you for looking after me.' The reflection in the rear-view mirror speaks. 'I am here. It will be okay.'

Grans walks out from the garden. "Go to the vardo, my dear. I have some books for you."

"What do you think?" The sun catches the copper hues as I flick my locks.

"You have lots of studying to do. I'll make fresh tea and sandwiches and we'll get started." Grans walks away, towards the house. She doesn't like my hair. I should not have trusted a stranger to pick the colour. Wait, she's turning back. "Oh, and yes, your hair is delightful, my dear. It's good to have you back."

The caravan at the bottom of the garden contains a huge pile of books. Tempting as it is to take a look, I wait patiently while Grans shares her morning visit to Oak Mews. Today was the debate club, where they conversed about organ donation.

"A little close to the bone, don't you think?"

"Oh no dear, it was ever so interesting. Harold's daughter had a transplant of some sort when she was young. They are logging on to register this afternoon. It was a huge success."

"Logging on? To the internet?"

"They may be older, but they're not incompetent. Believe me, ageing feels no different. Your body reveals the experience of living, but you are still young in your heart and head." Grans pours the tea. "And now, back to work, starting with this one." She holds a book entitled *Etiquette and Relationships* by Lady Rosamond Gifford. "I was at school with Rosie, and she was quite a goer, I tell you. Possessing such a vibrant spirit gave her the drive to succeed, and so can you. This book has proved to be my trusty manual. Read it, and the week ahead will seem less daunting."

I thought this was going to be fun. Whilst I enjoy a good novella, the first book has over eight hundred pages. Every flick of the page reveals an exponential increase in workload as the words decrease in font size. So many rules and so many behaviours to follow in so many social situations. It is impossible to be in the moment with eight hundred and twenty-seven pages of text on social behaviour to absorb.

"But Grans, this is so much reading and Ethan has offered me more shifts. I have no time. It's much quicker if I check out some cheat hacks online." I flip to page five hundred and forty-three. "Surely it's not necessary for me to learn the etiquette of giving birth and the benefits of hiring a doula."

Grans takes the book, marking pages with little arrow shaped pink post-it notes.

"My dear, this is your preparation. There is no shortcut. You must be ready for every possible conversation and this will equip you for success."

"Mocktail is about the bluff, not a study group."

"Darling, life is a study. You make mistakes and keep on learning. You should try to have a growth mindset, not a hack lifestyle. This is very different from nightclub hosting. People are paying you to be perfect, not paying you to be a party animal." Grans continues with her little flags, switching to green ones. "Once you absorb these, we will plan a get out of jail card."

"What do you mean? I can handle myself."

"Yes, dear, but what if it goes wrong? What if it's unenjoyable, or he expects more than just a date for the evening? What will you do? There are no bouncers to remove uncontrollable men." Grans rolls her right hand into a fist, punching her open left palm. Funny, but serious.

She is right, there is risk and no contingency plan. Sid may want more than a platonic relationship. Attractive as he is, I won't whore myself at any cost. On the other hand, if he was not paying me, there would be no hesitation on my side. Not that this is an option, he made his feelings clear at the Vanilla Pod, I'm not his type.

"In my day a friend chaperoned and we had a secret code when we needed rescuing."

"Secret code?"

"Yes, a phrase or a word dropped into conversation."

"Well Grans, in modern times we use mobile phones. We text if things go badly."

"Great idea. Let's think of something you can say. Something not out of place. We don't want to raise suspicion."

"Like, the classic you are in the hospital?"

"There's been an accident." Grans hands me a glass of fizz. Not that I'm complaining, but she kept that hidden whilst we were working. "Oh no, the Champagne's gone flat."

"That's perfect."

"My dear, it's undrinkable."

"No, not the Champagne. I mean, the Champagne is flat, yes. And undrinkable. I meant the phrase."

"It's undrinkable?"

"No. The Champagne's gone flat."

"Hmm, yes, it could work. But with something else. Silver Explorer magazine recently had an article about tracking apps. You can download them on mobile phones. If we set you up with that, I will know your location if you get abducted and murdered."

"Murdered! I hope it won't come to that Grans. He seems nice."

"They always do dear, especially the bad ones."

Don't I know it.

ELEVEN

Poire Prisonnière

The big day arrives. Alfred styles my hair in a cascading one-shoulder tumble of decompressed curls. The colour is still haunting, but I'm getting better at avoiding mirrors.
There is no time to go back home before I pick up Sid, so I change in the rear of Grans' car. This is a risky move as the space is compact and the windows are not tinted enough to act as a screen, but it is a true homage to the legendary history of Corrine's dress, from nightclub corner to the back seat of a car.

Sid's business card lists his studio location as Oxford Street. It sounds close, but Oxford Street is famed for being the longest road in Tilly Minster and part of the tricky one-way system installed to protect the older buildings from polluting cars. If you exit at the wrong point, you face a two-mile round trip to get back to the beginning. Lucky for me, I spy a cut-through called Whatnot Lane. I've not noticed it before. The sign says it's just for service vehicles, but as I am providing a service, that's okay. By my calculation, it should join Oxford Street about halfway up, which should be close to Sid's studio. Yes, I was right at the end of the lane, I see Oxford Street and the Minster, only the way is blocked with bollards and a serious sign. NO MOTOR VEHICLES. The bollards look sturdy but not too narrow for me in Grans' Mini, so I cross my fingers and inch forward, squeaking through within a hair's width. Imagine Grans' horror if I judged it wrong. Thank goodness it is a small car and I make it unscathed.

I pull out into a pedestrianised zone, the sign makes sense now, but not to worry, no one is around yet, so I sneak onto the main road undetected and park up outside Cioccolato, the ice cream parlour opposite Sid's studio. Perfect. I have a few minutes to spare after my clever navigating. I close my eyes, focussing on my breath. One of the books Grans assigned me was on manifestation. The exact words are too complex, so I make it up.

"May today be a success. May Mocktail be a success."

I repeat this for three breaths, and for some reason, I feel calmer. Sure, I still have adrenaline fueling a sort of fizzing in my stomach, but it's the good kind.

The ice cream manager wrestles cast iron tables onto the pavement, the legs scraping on the slabs. It is nearly time. I should have asked Sid what type of art he creates. I'm not ready to face a disembowelled ferret or the contents of a toilet cast in bronze this early in the day. The front windows have the shades closed. He should be showing off his work, not hiding it.

The bell is an old-fashioned twisted iron handle hanging long. I yank with as much spirit as I can muster. It's never good to start a relationship with a feeble pull on someone's bell end. A faint tickle sounds from the other side of the door. I expected more, like so many women before me.

Sid is quick to answer the door. He must have been waiting, eager to set off. Did he see me waiting in the car? Was he watching me, wondering why I was waiting? His clear eyes silently stare, dark blond hair styled by patience and care, each strand in place. The top button of his crisp white shirt is open. A textured blush pink tie knotted loosely at the neck frames his dark stubble. He didn't have that on the weekend. The stubble. He was cleanly shaven. For most people, the initial texture of new beard growth is rough, scruffy and unkempt. On Sid, it adds a distinctive edge, and I imagine it's less scratchy than most when kissing.

Maybe he will ask me to fix his tie, and I will run my hand down the blush silk, the gentle shape of his abs detectable through the fabrics. I will take a silver tie clip from his upper pocket and fasten it in place. Close enough to drink in his intense aroma, he will plant a soft kiss on my lips. All for show and orchestrated to perfection. All part of Mocktail. Apart from the kissing. That was never on the agenda. Not for him anyway. I am not his type.

A French navy suit jacket hooks on his finger, the buttons undone on a matching waistcoat. Flat-front trousers complete the look, with tan leather brogues and a matching belt. All efforts lead to this point. Sid is more than a Perry. I underestimated him. I am losing my touch.

Today, he is the embodiment of a Poire Williams. No. A Prisonnière. Delicate, crisp and clean. The gentle curves of the pear are visible through the bottle, teasing in nature, thought-provoking. Care and attention are paid to each moment leading up to the perfect package, the bottles affixed to the branches, so the fruit grows inside. The observer, that's me, eager to get close to see the splendid wonder and savour the sweet scent.

He is silent and staring. Something is wrong. Sid doesn't like my dress. The hair is the wrong colour. Maybe it's the jewellery. Or, he was not serious about the date, I mean business arrangement. The money was paid into my account yesterday, although it took longer than I thought, but Grans says even internet banking is not always instant. He is thinking about the night we met. The parts I forgot. The taste of my mouth as he kissed me, the smell of my hair as he nuzzled my neck, yearning for more. The feel of my skin as he explored with his hands. All the intimate moments that are withheld from me sit captive in his brain. He should let them out and show me what happened.

Sid looks me up and down, up and down. And I have never felt more like an object to be bought than I do now.

"Good morning." My confident voice attempts to match my bell ringing. "I am here to esssssss…" Eeeek! I nearly said escort, which was stupid. "To accompany you to your brother's wedding."

Nothing but silence.

Lady Rosamond recommends using silence as a powerful tool in the courting arena. Not that this is courting.

"It's me. Kat. Remember? From Mocktail. You made a

booking."

"Sure." Finally, a break in the vacuum as he exhales long and slow, still looking me up and down.

My cheeks flame. I should have worn more foundation. A repeat pattern when it comes to Sid.

"My car is parked nearby... Sid?"

"Sorry, good morning." Why is he laughing?

My underwear must be showing, or my dress is translucent so that I look naked.

"I meant to say good morning. Sure, yes, let's go."

Wait, I'm not ready for this, whatever it is. The atmosphere sours as we walk to the car. All my preparation, all my studying, has been worthless. The bottle has been opened and the wine corked. This is not as easy as the books make it out to be.

Lady Rosamond says the ideal host offers a drink. Yes, I can do that. Drinks come naturally to me.

"The ice cream parlour has just opened." The tables and chairs have been joined by oversized sun umbrellas on the broad pavement.

"Oh, err, no. I'm good, thanks."

"I meant for coffee." I was not clear. "Of course, it's too early for ice cream."

"It's always the right time for ice cream." Sid's eyes narrow, he is teasing. "Depending on who you are with." Flirting? "But also, no to the coffee, thanks. Too much risk of spillage."

True, a coffee stain on my pale chiffon would mar the whole day.

The forty-minute trip can only be described as uncomfortable. Sid remains silent for the first twenty minutes, and the atmosphere reeks of a cloudy bottle of wine, dusty from years of neglect at the back of a drinks cabinet. Perhaps my company is so tedious I lull a grown man to sleep. It is so ridiculous to think one week of reading would be enough. I'm too dull. Too boring to be an artist's muse. Even still-life has more charisma than me. The charcoal stays firmly in its box, there is nothing worth noting here.

At a stop sign on the road, I glance over to Sid, to find he is wide awake and regarding me with the same expression he had at his studio. The silence is unnerving. He is so different from last week. Perhaps he is sketching me in his mind, noting all the flaws and items for improvement.

"Sid, what is it? Is everything okay?"

"Nothing. You–"

"I what?" Something is wrong. I check my hair and makeup in the rear-view mirror. Nothing looks out of place. The colour is... one step at a time.

"You... you... look perfect."

"Perfect?" That can't be right.

"Yes. Different. Almost unrecognisable. Almost. But there is something right about it. About you."

"Oh." A thinly veiled compliment. "Well, thanks. I guess. That was the aim of Sunday's meeting, to... to enable me to fit the part you need me to perform."

"Yes, yes, of course, that's what I meant." He exhales slowly. Back tracking. Embarrassed. "You clearly understand what the plan is. Thank you."

"Shall we review the expectations of the day? List all the important people to know, or those to avoid."

"No, you're going to be just fine."

The edge of his mouth twitches. He's amused. This is not going well.

TWELVE

Sambuca

Once we turn off the main road, I feel no closer to reaching Beachbury Manor House. The drive takes us over a cattle grid, into a world of crunching gravel paths and bluebell-trimmed woods. I drive past fields of deer basking under broad oak trees and sheep roaming through gaps in crumbling dry stone walls. A lake is bound by weeping willows, and on the far side, a lawn sweeps up to the main house, where sandstone walls rise to the sky above fortified turrets. It is a dream castle fit for a wedding princess.

It's not yet midday, which means nothing as I have no idea what time the ceremony starts. Or if there even is a wedding. I feel a sense of panic. This is all a ruse to bring me miles from anywhere to... to murder me and bury my body in the woods.

There is no escape.

No way out.

Any minute he'll grab my key, smash my phone, and I will be history.

"It's quiet. We've a few minutes to kill before the guests arrive." Sid's voice is calm. Calculated. Just like how a psychopath would sound.

Time to kill. For him to... kill me. My mouth goes dry and bile swells in my throat. This is madness and could never end well.

I could scream, but there is no one to hear me.

A crushing, pounding sensation in my chest muddles my brain. If I message Grans, she will send help. But I can't write anything obvious. Nothing with the words 'danger', 'help', or 'frightened'. Sid will see and realise I saw through his efforts. I need to use the code.

Someone knocks on the window. A knight in shining armour come to rescue me? No such luck, it's just Sid, my potential attacker.

"Kat, are you getting out?"

Not to be maimed and murdered. No.

"We need to find the wedding planner. Make sure everything is in order." His hand grips the handle of my door, clicking it open. "Are you okay? You look a little..."

"Yes, fine." A little stage fright and an overactive imagination. "Just looking for my phone."

"It's in your hand. Come on, don't worry, you'll be fine."

Trembling fingers unlock the phone. Grans has already messaged.

```
Pleased you arrived. How is it?
```

The witchcraft of shared locations.

```
                                        Nervous
You got this.
            What if he drags me in the woods 2 murder me
It won't happen.
                                        How do u know?
Trust me.
                                        Trust?
He's a good one.
                                        ??? How do you know?
```

From what you told me. Now go have fun.

Sid walks away in the direction of a split wooden stable door. The top half hangs open and displays the brass Estate Office sign. This is where Sid will chain me up and hold me as a slave until I'm too weak to escape.

"Morning. Anyone home?" Sid calls out to his accomplices.

"Just a minute." Long, fluffy, amber hair on a tweed suit pops her head out from behind a wooden filing cabinet. Bamboo. Not the filing cabinet, the wedding planner. Flat loafers, pop socks, and trousers that graze the ankles. The type with a sharp crease down the front of the beige tweed. One part Sherry, aged and complex in structure, trusted with her knowledge. One part French dry vermouth, providing a delicate edge, slightly nutty in temperament. Finally, a couple of dashes of orange bitters, reflecting her sharp mind, covering all requirements of the big day. Never shaken, staying chilled under all eventualities. A Bamboo Cocktail.

"How can I help? Are you looking for a venue or here for the wedding today?"

"Sid, Sid Richmond, best man at Christian and Jessica's wedding today. Christian asked me to arrive early to support the set-up. If you need me."

The Bamboo cocktail shakes Sid's hand, forming a strong grip, her smile spreading from ear to ear with every vibration.

"Sarah Kennedy. Good to meet you. There's not much. Most things are done, so I'll give you a little tour. Let's start with the ornamental gardens, then walk back via the orangery to the entrance where you will welcome your guests."

Sarah leads us through a side gate, behind the estate office, into a delicate garden. I am no expert but I spot tulips and bluebells without needing to be told their names. Fine gravel paths lead to a maze of rows and rows of five-foot-high topiary. Statues snuggle in corners, some hidden within the plantings. We walk through the middle, so there is no risk of getting lost down any of the side passageways, and exit onto a manicured lawn and miniature lake. Sarah pauses so we can admire the view, but I keep my eyes closed and allow the sunshine to soak my skin, healing the broken cells abused by years of working nights.

Caterers buzz around a gazebo in the courtyard next to the orangery, a glass sided Victorian structure boasting tall arched windows. This must be where Christian is to be married.

"You may as well stay here," Sid says, as the first guests arrive. "No point going through tedious introductions, after all, well, you know what I mean."

He's right, it's hard enough explaining to Grans I'm not an escort, let alone to a hundred guests.

"I'll explore the gardens. Don't worry about me. I will sneak into the back for the ceremony. You have my number if you need me."

If I sit down anywhere, I will mark my dress, so walk into the labyrinth. A narrow archway brings me to the heart of the maze, and a couple cosying up on a bench. Weddings bring out the romance in everyone, and this pair are entwined in such an intimate way that it's impossible to work out where one person ends and the other starts. Arms and legs snake around each other, looping like spirals of peel on the side of a cocktail glass. My shoe crunches on the gravel, and they repel quicker than two like magnetic poles, untangling themselves into a less x-rated position.

"Splendid. Is that the time?" The man smooths his silver hair, straightening his waistcoat. The woman says nothing as she tries to look nonchalant despite her knickers peeking out below the hem of her dress. Both stay seated as I pass. As I leave, I wonder if they will make their way back to the party later or decide to miss the wedding altogether and finish what they started.

The orangery is filled with rows of nutmeg painted chairs. Fresh flowers trim the end of each pew. Sid stands at the front, chatting to a man I assume is his brother, Christian. Solid, like an island and calm in the heat of the occasion, he is rich and smooth. Capri springs to mind, but I don't remember meeting him Friday night. With any luck, the rest of the stag group will also suffer from drunken amnesia. If not, and they recognise me, it will be my own fault. I should have plied them with more booze. I find a seat at the back, and as I catch Sid's gaze, his shoulders relax somewhat. Is he smiling? One corner of his mouth makes a slight move north. No. Nerves. Stress from a day in public with his ex-girlfriend.

Christian traces our line of sight, so I hide behind the order of service, but it makes poor camouflage. I have been seen.

As a harpist weaves a harmony of strings into the air, the room simultaneously holds its breath as Jessica, the embodiment of Venus, enters. In her hands, a large bouquet creates images of gathering armfuls of blooms, grasses and herbs. The dress, a faultless combination of lace and beading, skims curves before it cascades to a floor grazing train.

After the ceremony, I slip out the back, circle round and head for the darkest hole of obscurity. Or I would, if the silver-haired man from the gardens was not blocking my path.

"Good day." A sweaty hand extends in my direction.

"Hello again." Please let him have washed up since the last time our paths crossed. Lady Rosamond says it is rude not to reciprocate when offered a hand, but I guess she didn't contend with stale bodily fluids.

A lady hooks her arm around the crook of his elbow.

"Again?" She is not the same person he fingered in the topiary but clearly staking her claim. "Have we met?"

"No, I don't think so. I lost my bearings earlier. I was in the gardens and spotted your... Husband?" I fumble a guess, crossing my fingers behind my back.

"Yes." The lady nods. "Carry on, you found my husband..."

This could not be more awkward unless I was face-to-face with the gentleman, his wife, and his lover locked in a game of naked Twister. Oh! Naked Twister is one of my favourites and I've not played it for a while. Even if there is an after-party planned later, I have no intention of setting up a game with this couple.

No doubt, his wife would not like the truth, so I dig

deep for a lie. I found him helping another guest with her malfunctioning dress. Or, I found him conducting a routine cervical examination on another woman. Got it, I found him depositing heroin up a mule's ass.

"Husband, walking in from the… the–"

"Carpark." He interjects. "Carpark. I left my wallet in the car by mistake. Remember my love."

"But that is nowhere near the gardens, my love." Her rigid smile says she is not enamoured with him right now.

"I was checking the gardens first. I feared it had fallen out of my pocket when we explored the kitchen gardens earlier." He turns to me. "I have a fondness for home apothecary remedies and heard they have a fine example here of Knobweed, Hyptis Capitata. Quite rare in the United Kingdom. Can be used as a powerful antiseptic, do you know?"

Knobweed! There is no suitable comeback from Lady Rosamond.

"And are you a friend of Jessica's?" The wife is wise to ignore the Knobweed and probably wants to de-capitata her husband. She is full of questions and rightfully so, considering how free her husband is with his affections.

"I'm Kat, a guest of Sid, the best man."

"Oh, Sid." The lady smiles, glad to be talking about anything other than her philandering husband. "A lovely young man. So talented. You've seen his work?"

"Yes, his studio is amazing. Although I've not seen much. We only recently started dating." Stick to the plan, Kat.

"Splendid," said the man, who openly admires my arse. "Just Splendid."

"Kat, this is Sid's Uncle Wilfred, and I'm Nora, his wife."

"How do you do?" I shake Nora's hand, trusting she is free from intimate fluids. "The ceremony was splendid, do you agree?"

"Wilfred. Nora." A bridesmaid looms in on our conversation.

"Oh, just lovely dear. Thank you for asking." But she didn't ask, and neither did they.

"And you are?" The bridesmaid turns her back on Nora,

giving me her full attention.

"How do you do? I'm Kat. The poem you read is a favourite of mine."

"Yes, yes. But who are you?"

"This is Kat." Uncle Wilfred steps in, swerving the professional body block.

"I heard you the first time. Why are you here? I know everyone at this wedding except you."

"Alexandria." Aunty Nora steps in. "Don't you know? Kat is Sid's new girlfriend."

The bridesmaid's eyes grow dark, and she laughs as she slowly looks me up and down. They may have split up, but they still share common habits.

"No." Her eyes narrow. "She is not."

I need to be careful here. "Good to meet you, I'm sure. Sid was kind enough to invite me."

But the bridesmaid swiftly turns, walking off before I finish. I am part amused, part insulted, or would be if this was my fight. If my feelings for Sid were real.

Alexandria. But that's not what Sid called her. Lex, yes, that was it. Definitely a Pousse-Café, but too early to say which, although I get a strong sense of aniseed. The one layer I have seen is distinctive and hard-hitting. The only shot that leaves my mouth contorted in horror. Tongue repelled, seeking relief from the bitter herbal intensity. So possibly sambuca, itself an infusion of witch elder and liquorice. Yes, she has a definite essence of witchiness.

Suddenly, Whisky Sours, Dextra Dominica is relegated to second place on my menu of bitches. Fingers crossed the new champion will not cost me my job this time.

With a fake smile in place, I continue my conversation with Wilfred and Nora. "I take it I have just met the ex-girlfriend?"

"Yes," winks Uncle Wilfred. "You most certainly have."

"But don't mind her, my lovely." Nora consoles. "She's like that with everyone, and you handled that like a professional. You are just what Sid needs to make a new start."

"Please, do not worry. Sid's past does not concern me. Today is for enjoying the celebrations of Christian and Jessica. Nothing will ruin that."

Uncle Wilfred raises his drink. "Splendid."

As our glasses meet, I search for Sid and find him at the lake's edge, taking a verbal beating from Alexandria. He senses my concern and returns my look. I send him a supporting smile and receive a nod in response. His expression remains neutral as Alexandria continues her animated, aggressive monologue.

"Goody," says Uncle Wilfred as a gong sounds for the wedding breakfast. "My favourite bit. The line-up."

Which gives me time to message Grans. Once the other guests are seated, I can sneak in undetected. Although now the multi-layered Alexandria knows my name, my anonymity may not last long.

THIRTEEN

Tequila

The line-up awaits my return. They are fully committed to greeting all the guests, real and fake, which turns this into a gladiatorial event with me, the rank outsider. All eyes of the family lock in. I can't afford to lose. My chest feels tight. No one must discover I am a phony.

Gladiators ready? Contenders ready? Honestly, no. But here goes!

First up are the giggling flower girls, easily distracted with amusing compliments. "Hello, beautiful fairy princesses." I swerve to avoid attacks that may lie behind sweet innocent eyes or sticky fingers on my vintage dress. Fortunately for me, they suffer a sudden onset of shyness and run away, giggling.

Next in the gauntlet of wedding day bliss are the bridesmaids. One at a time I can handle, but I'm facing a triple united foe in what I like to call the Danger Zone. Toe to toe with Alexandria, flanked by her bridesmaid minions who are ready to launch an attack on her signal.

With my eyes locked in, I have the upper hand: Alexandria does not know Sid and I have not slept together. We've not even kissed. At least not to my knowledge. What if I am too sure of myself? Doubt is the ultimate self-sabotage, and the sinking feeling in my stomach tells me I'm headed for a crash. This will be the moment the curtain is pulled back and my cover blown. But in a surprise move, I'm saved by the adjudicator as the move is deemed illegal. Alexandria orders the retreat, chasing after the flower girls.

Elevated to level three, I find an apologetic Sid. This should be easy, but my self-assuredness will be my downfall. I did not anticipate the Earthquake Round, where all things muddle into one.

"Sorry about that." Sid signals a calm before the storm.

I tilt my head, it means nothing; I am a fake guest. My attraction to Sid is just part of the charade, at least, that's what I tell myself when faced with unrequited feelings. It's easy to pretend when you know there is no danger of getting hurt.

"Shall we?" He waits for approval before his warm hand slips into mine. This unexpected touch leaves me defenseless as his fingertips brush my palm and tingles run up my arm. To make matters worse, he plants a tender kiss a breath's width from my cheek, stopping short of contact. The perfect illusion to everyone else and the almost-kiss leaves me wanting more, knocking me off my guard.

"Let me introduce you to the parents." These are dirty tactics. He is supposed to be on my team, but instead, he weakens me with his fresh citrus scent.

This is the Eliminator Round and the final challenge. Whoever survives the ordeal is crowned champion. But as close as I am, Lady Rosamund's etiquette for meeting parents does not include being slightly turned on after having your professional sensibilities compromised. I must be mad. My mind is a vacuum, helpless, naked and unprepared.

"Mum, Dad. This is Kat, who I was telling you about."

"Delighted to meet you." A Royal Smile Cocktail and the original Mrs Richmond leans in with cheek-to-cheek air kisses. "I hope you don't feel abandoned today. It must be tricky dating the best man."

Her initial taste kills with kindness. The welcoming smile, an underlying sweetness. She is too innocent to betray with our charade, but there is no room for compassion in this game.

I have limited experience with this, I never met Hugo's parents. There was no time, not even when I thought we were the real thing, and by that I mean true love. It seemed normal to be independent from his family. Happy to tell myself he didn't have loved ones, but of course he did, he came from somewhere. The real Kat James was not good enough.

With the action replay over, the Mocktail Kat James can make this happen. I dig deep to overcome emotional weakness.

"I am having an amazing time. Thank you so much. Congratulations on such a stunning ceremony, it brought tears to my eyes."

"Good to meet you, Kat." Sid's Father is an older version of Sid, only improved with age, if that is possible. He is a Pear Dream, perfect to complement the sweetness of his wife. With reminiscent flavourings of his son, Mr Richmond has grown into his good looks.

But I don't fancy him. Of course not, that would be weird, although Sid at that age may be a different story.

"We'll catch up later. Looks like you are doing a good job with Sid so far." Mr Richmond knows. "He's not easy to handle, what with his tricky baggage and all."

"Don't be daft, Dad. I'm not that bad." Sid's face betrays nothing. Perhaps it is all in my imagination.

"Well, if not with Sid, Lexie. She's hard work at the best of times." Mrs Richmond laughs.

This is a power-play move to see what my reaction is. I join in the laughter, although I'm not sure what is so funny. I feel tackled from both sides. "And you seem to be breezing along like an expert."

"Well, she seems perfectly pleasant to me, Mrs Richmond, Mr Richmond. Straight up."

"Please. Call me Graham."

Sid keeps hold of my hand until the end of the challenge, I mean the line-up. If he feels guilty for lying to his family, guilty for leaving me to fend for myself earlier with his potent ex-girlfriend, he needn't worry. This is my job. Maybe it's okay for him to touch my hand, almost kiss my cheek. I'm an actor. The intimacy is all part of making it appear legitimate, to make people believe we're in love.

Sid walks me to my table, his hand hovers in the small of

my back, giving the appearance of touch. Although he barely skims the fabric of my dress, I can feel the energy flowing from his palm into my core. I won the Gauntlet, and the best fake boyfriend in the world is my prize.

The table is relatively obscure at the back of the room, the location often reserved for the least important guests, such as the florist or the hairdresser. But the position of girlfriend to the best man means my route is surrounded by whispers. 'Who is she?' 'Why is she with Sid?' 'What happened between Sid and Alexandria?'

The table offers a new challenge. I'm seated opposite the lady from the gardens, the one in flagrante with Uncle Wilfred. Knicker Dropper Glory (as I now call her) avoids eye contact, mitigating the risk of unmasking.

Each side of me are two old fashioned glasses. To my left, a Blue Shark. "Peter, Good to meet you," he says, raising his glass, "this is my wife, Liz." Peter introduces a Little Princess.

The Tequila Ghost to my right joins in. "Brian, cousin of the bride. Over there is my sister Frances, Frannie." He gestures in the direction of a Rose Martini, deep in conversation with Knicker Dropper Glory. "And that's her girlfriend, Imogen."

So, Uncle Wilfred has competition, and her name is Frannie. Beautifully presented in a cocktail glass, the sweet cherry brandy mixed with Cointreau is much to contend with. I would be worried if I were him.

"We have not met before, I think." Brian, the essence of aniseed mixed with Tequila, has a sharp focus.

"No, no, not met. No." I stand strong.

"So, what brings you to Chris and Jessica's wedding?" More prying questions intended to trip me up.

"I'm a guest of Sid, the best man."

"Ah… yes! You are familiar," Peter interrupts. "Have we met? I don't remember Sid introducing anyone."

I knew it! The Blue Shark remembers me from the stag do. My cover is blown, and I'm strapped to a chair, blinded by the interrogation light. Question after question follows in an attempt to wheedle out my secrets, but I will not be sucked in by the Blue Curacao eyes.

"No, I don't think so. I used to be an events manager.

Perhaps you have seen me in one of the clubs along the canal in Tilly Gate?"

"No, that's not it. But I'll keep thinking. I'm sure I've seen you somewhere. Your face looks familiar."

The man is a human lie detector. I can only hope their recollection is as foggy as mine. After all, I am famed for pumping out shots quicker than you can say...

"Tequila!" Peter and Brian cry out in unison.

They steal the words out of my mouth. Why didn't I ply them with more drinks? Of course, they remember, and it is my own fault. I should not have joined them at the stag do, but I hadn't foreseen the loss of memory, getting up to who knows what with the best man, then charging money to be his date at the wedding.

"Fantastic idea. Liven things up a bit. You seem the kind of girl who would kill for Tequila shots." They are testing me.

"Oh, yuck! Not for me, thanks. I'm driving."

"So boring. I was sure you were the type."

"Yes. I swear you ooze Tequila." Brian reaches for a hip flask from the inside of his jacket.

"So much so that when I look at you, I see Tequila." Peter produces a metal canister a few inches high containing a set of stainless steel shot glasses.

"As do I. The taste, I can feel it in my mouth." Brian makes a generous pour.

"The flavour." Peter salivates.

"Lively." Brian finds the table salt.

"Smooth." Peter scoops out the lemon from his water glass.

"But with a vanilla aftertaste." Brian places a shot in front of me, and a few drops spill on the white damask tablecloth.

Tempting, but one sip will spark their memory of countless shots at the stag do. Perhaps I went as far as to do body shots. No. That would have been too much for the Vanilla Pod. Ethan would not allow it. Although there is no doubt in my mind, I did the trick where I line up the shots along my thigh. The stag sits, and I place my leg on his shoulder. He must reverse limbo into a standing position and pivot to take the shot. Sometimes I end up with wet pants and demand the stag sucks up the spillage, but that's another story.

"Well, I don't drink. So, you have me all wrong." Lies upon lies. This one is the most ridiculous yet. Impossible to maintain, but I have no choice.

"No way! I had you pegged for a party girl."

"Yes, Sid needs some fun in his life after Alexandria."

Is that all I am? Fun. This is why Sid asked me.

"Where have I seen you?" Brian comes in from the side, hoping to misstep me.

"Oh!" I say in an overtly *I solve that mystery* style. "Maybe it was at Sid's gallery. I've been popping in for ages to check out his work, hoping he'd notice me."

"I bet you have. Checking out his artistic talent?" Laughs Peter.

"Checking out his large portfolio more like." Adds Brian.

"Yes, something like that." I attempt a fake blush, focusing on my napkin. They are losing the scent.

"So, have you faced the wrath of Lexie yet?"

"We met earlier. She did a fabulous reading during the service."

"A very diplomatic answer. It's never a good idea to go up against my sister. She can be brutal." Peter sighs.

"She seems just lovely to me."

"Are we talking about the same person? I'm not sure even Sid describes her in that generous way. And he, supposedly in love with her, until, well…" Peter, unsure if I know.

"I only talk from experience."

"Yes, and I talk from a lifetime of hell." Peter chuckles, without one kind word to say about his sister.

The speeches finish, glasses run dry, and I feel overwhelmed by the intoxicating flavours at the table. There is only so much Tequila, vodka and Pernod I can take before I lose sobriety. I need fresh air and to stretch my legs.

"Hey." Sid joins me at the table once everyone else leaves. I can't work out if he smiles because he is pleased to see me or because he is relieved that the most nerve-racking part of the day for him is done. Or maybe he knows I've been fighting off the mental attack from his friends for the last hour or so and finds it amusing.

"Great speech, Sid."

"Thanks, it was short and sweet. How are you doing? Did you survive the rite of passage with Christian's friends?"

"Yes, perfectly fine."

"Listen. Sorry I've not spent time with you since the wedding started. It must be tricky not knowing anyone."

"It's fine." I place my hand on Sid's arm. With Hugo, there was sexual tension, desire, and lust, but with Sid, it feels sincere and intimate. Natural, but not completely alien. I have felt this before. A long time ago. I straighten up in my seat. "Do tell me if there's anything you need. Remember, I'm the one that's here for you."

"Sure."

Before I can remove my hand, he rests his on top. Indiscernible at first, eyes searching to find out if it is okay. A subtle nod, and his thumb rubs the back of my hand. He scans my well-being, stripping away the protective layers.

"Come on love birds." Christian's head appears through the ornate doorway, the deep wooden frame hand-carved centuries ago. "Time for photos."

"Okay, Bro. Be there in a few mins."

"If that's all it takes, mate!"

Happy banter between siblings should bring joy, but I don't have this with my brother and sister. Jeremy and Zara have banter, only it is centred around success and money. Jeremy fancies himself a Park Lane cocktail garnished with a maraschino cherry. He is all show and displays great delight in throwing his medical degree around the place and his aims to become the youngest consultant in the shire. Zara, a Flamingo and a little too pretty for her own good, bats this back in his face with her three cookie-cutter children and management of a branch of Father's law firm. Jeremy ups his game to include international aid work, and Zara, sweetened with apricot brandy, retorts with numerous charitable works. High-powered jobs are not for me. Children are my kryptonite. I am the charity case.

"Sid, can I help with the photos?" My speciality is managing groups of people who consume too many drinks. "I need something to do after sitting for so long."

"Sure, why not?" He stands, hand extended. "May as well make this look genuine. If you agree."

It comes easy with Sid, to make it look genuine. If I told him, it would sound wrong. Better to keep this in play.

Easy for me to say as he grips my hand, and something gives in my chest. It's hard to explain, but a little like the loosening of a pressurised bottle of soda. The cap turns a millimetre, giving just enough relief to spark a reaction inside. A few bubbles rise before the lid tightens again, sealing the pressure within. Things are different, but I don't know how.

The room wobbles from left to right with a sort of spinning sensation, like being drunk. Not a massive sway, but enough for me to stop walking. I need to catch my... my... only I am not out of breath but bring my hand to my chest. The ground shifts a little beneath my feet, and there it is. The epicentre. A slight skip in my heart and the world dims as my vision blurs.

"Watch out! You nearly trod on my dress." Snaps Alexandria, her venom sprays as we collide with the group of bridesmaids.

Sid's hand tightens, pulling me out of Alexandria's path.

"I'm so sorry. Let me see if it's okay." I try to smooth things out.

"No need to bother yourself. You have done enough damage." She storms off toward the gardens, followed by her minions.

"Kat, are you alright?" Sid asks.

"Yes, I'm fine."

"But you went a bit–"

"Just lightheaded from sitting down for so long. I feel much better now."

"Sure, only your eyes look a bit tipsy." Sid acts concerned, but of course, he doesn't really care. He needs me to be on top form after paying me so much money.

"Still stone cold sober."

"Okay. That's not what I meant. But. Well, I'm sorry about Lex."

"Please don't apologise, Sid. You are not responsible for

her."

"I guess I'm apologising for myself really, for ever having a relationship with her."

"Don't worry." I squeeze his palm. "Let's get some awesome pictures taken."

It wasn't a lie when I said I had been sitting too long, so the fresh air and purpose restore my energy. The joy of doing what I love with moderately sober people refreshes my vigour. In the dark nightclub, I barely hear words above the loud music as I vertically limbo past punters without knocking their drinks. Today, I casually breeze around. Hold drinks (without taking a sip) and compliment guests on beautiful shoes that would be ruined in a nightclub.

As the final photo is lined up, I take a lingering look at the group before I leave to message Grans with an update. It's wrong to stay for this part. I'm not a real guest. When they look back at the pictures in years to come, they will see me, a stranger. Just some girl Sid found in a bar and brought to his brother's wedding. I don't belong in their book of memories, and they certainly wouldn't want me here if they knew the truth.

"Hey! Where are you going?" The seconds slow as I realise the question is for me. I turn to see that absolutely everyone is looking at me, and just like that, I am no longer incognito. Christian shouts again. "Kat! Stop sneaking off. Get in the photo. There's room for you here."

"Yes, come on Kat." Calls Jessica, and then Graham and Nora and Wilfred. And before I can stop them, the whole group, except Pousse -Café, are waving me in and shouting my name.

If they learned the reality, they would not be so keen for me to join them. Alexandria's eyes burn into me. She would not waste her energy if she knew this is all pretend.

Christian makes a space next to Sid and I squeeze in. I imagine his arm across my back and then feel his hand hook on my waist, pulling me closer. Like a puzzle piece, I fit in the nook, his hold firm and protective. In my dream, I relax into his embrace and pretend I belong here. In this group. In this photo, in his life.

FOURTEEN

Ginger Rogers

Mistakenly, I thought being a fake guest would be easy, however, I had not contended with people's curiosity to interrogate me, question my position here, and call me out to the entire group. This is as far from the anonymity of a nightclub as you can get. There are no shadows to hide in as the toastmaster announces the first dance. The room, lit by the ambient anticipation of the newlyweds sharing their standout strut into married life, holds eyes like spotlights which search the room for seminal moments to capture on camera. I step back to blend into the upholstery but connect with someone, the heat of their body burning into my back.

Trapped, I ground my feet and give a gentle sway back, not enough to touch but a hint that they need to move, but they do not budge.

It is Uncle Wilfred. The strange looks he threw during the photos meant only one thing. A mark on his next prey.

No. It's Alexandria, Pousse-Café. Here to seek me out and publicly knife me in the side. An act of revenge for coming close to her discarded property.

The fabric on the back of my dress stirs. In a club, I would show my condemnation with a signal, a word, or a physical act. In that setting, if this was Uncle Wilfred, I could land a swift kick to the bollocks. If this were Alexandria, the colleagues surrounding me would intervene, offering protection and a warning to stay away.

With eyes closed, I draw a deep breath and bite my lip. A

moment to think. Now is not the occasion to cause a scene. And then I feel familiar pressure in the small of my back, barely making contact. There is no need to look, I know who it is. I lift my head and lean into Sid's hand, savouring the touch as I exhale. Everything is perfect, sweet and clear. A welcome calm as our bodies connect. My heartbeat is strong, quickening with awareness that we breathe the same air.

"See you on the other side." His lips are on my ear. His breath on my neck.

I turn, my head angled to look into his eyes as I sink into the clear blue. I want more. I miss this. Clumsily, I misjudge the distance and my lips brush his cheek, branding him with my lipstick. Now we are face to face, and I wipe away the stain with my thumb, my pulse slowing with every stroke. The pigment lifts off with minimal resistance on the smooth skin high on his cheek, but not so much on the stubble framing his mouth. His lips gently part, the corners lifting as I continue to work on removing the war paint. The effort releases an aggressive citrus aroma, fresh and vibrant like a shot of Limoncello. But that is not Sid. He is not Limoncello. That is his cover, his scent, his aftershave. Closer still, I smell woody undertones, masculine and rugged. As my body connects to his, the bouquet envelops further, and the energy breaks through the light chiffon pleats of my dress. His mouth is just millimetres away. This is a perfect kiss moment. But I cannot. I lean close and hold my breath.

Sid pulls away, and our eyes meet. "Sorry, I–"

"Good luck." I mouth. As no sound comes out. I'm swept away by turquoise eyes, a glow deep in the pit of my gut sucks away my voice. Sid breaks contact and heads onto the dance floor, leaving me cold and alone.

Alexandria, never the type to miss an opportunity to lord it over people, is by his side in seconds. She grabs Sid's outstretched hand as her head follows an elliptical path taking in the room before she settles on me. Her territory marked with a victorious sneer, claiming her prize.

Everyone watches. No one can resist, given her recent betrayal. The whispers start. *'Can it be a reconciliation?' 'An olive leaf to heal the acrimony?' 'No.' 'I think not.' 'But Sid held out his hand.' 'That's his duty as best man.' 'You could see he didn't want to.' 'Oh, he wants to.' 'Yes, just look at them together, they are perfect for each other.' 'There's been no time for him to meet anyone else.'*

The atmosphere is so thick, it could make a six-layer Pousse-Café, but there is no need to worry, their dance is less awkward than feared. The years in a relationship give an automatic synchronicity that outweighs the pain of heartache. The motions are without emotion, at least not the romantic kind. Alexandria whispers into his ear, but Sid's demeanour gives nothing away, responding with a simple nod. Pupils dark and muddy, the blue lagoon has been polluted.

They make an odd couple. Alexandria is so formal and perfect in her presentation, perfect in the dance. Sid is bohemian, his style artisanal, and he looks uncomfortable under the limitations she imposes. She must have a softer side. No one could find her attractive when she's in power play.

"Cosy, aren't they?" The second I take my eye off the ball, Uncle Wilfred makes his move. "They make a beautiful pair." No doubt he would not sense the truth if it were shaped like a twelve inch dildo poking him up the rectum. After all, his whole life is a big sordid lie in which he is comfortable to wallow. "Shall we join them?"

"Nothing would give me greater satisfaction." I'd rather stick pins in my eyes, but I'm not employed to be rude to ageing, sweaty, perverse relatives. With any luck, Sid will cut in, and I will be rescued from the philanderer before he marks my dress with his grubby mitts.

Far from the dignified steps of Sid and Alexandria, Uncle Wilfred leads me in a dance that can only be described as the human gyroscope. With great delight, he spins me around and around until I lose sight of Sid.

"Refreshing, yes? I do love to muddle things up a little on the floor." Like Old Spice, he whiffs of ginger, sickly and sweet like syrup as his body brushes up against mine. "Fred Astaire, eat your heart out. I always fancied getting myself a little Ginger Rogers."

As my stomach moves into high spin, a muddling of mint joins the ginger, crashing up against the side of the glass. Neither settles my constitution. Uncle Wilfred turns and flips the rotation in the opposite direction, the Coriolis effect adding a double shot of gin to the mix. This is the type of intoxication to daze and confuse and sexual harassment of the basest form.

"I do love to add a bit of sparkle to the occasion." Uncle Wilfred tips me over, hand brushing against my breast as he reaches to hold me steady as ginger ale is added to the cocktail of disaster.

The desire to scream 'get off me, you big fat perspiring aged pervert' is too much, but I forbear. There are better reasons to remember a wedding than Uncle Wilfred being outed as a… wait… he just touched my arse. This has gone too far! I will complain to my employer about unfair treatment in the workplace, but no doubt my claim would fail in court. Oh, how the tables have turned with a dash of lemon to sour. Labelled, or libelled even, as a whore I picture the headlines, *'Escort loses in her claim of molestation by sweaty ageing uncle as judge rules: If you are being paid for services, you must deliver on your promise.'*

The spinning continues, and I concentrate on not being sick.

Sid is gone.

He left me under the control of Uncle Wilfred, in a living hell.

Normally, I can look after myself, but here at the wedding, I am unable to give Uncle Wilfred the extreme punishment he deserves.

I shout out, the sound scattering all over the room as the twirling continues. He regards my squeal as delight and swops hands, giving a show tune bow to his fellow guests. His touch slips to my hips, and my stomach lurches, colour draining from my cheeks. If this continues, the wedding breakfast will make an unwelcome return any minute. Someone get help!

Nora glides over to my rescue. She has been too long. Maybe she was in on this all along. Perhaps she gets a thrill from watching him play.

Finally escaping the clutches of Uncle Wilfred, I weave out of the main hall with the appearance of having one too many Ginger Rogers. Tottering from right to left, left to right, my brain thinks I'm stuck on a giant, whirling rollercoaster.

The befuddlement clears somewhere between the chocolate fountain and the ice sculpture. For Sid to abandon me to the come dancing twirling champion of yesteryear, something must have happened. He needs my help.

The building stops cycloning as I enter the library. Sid cradles the tulip-shaped copita glass, the expression on his face shows the pose is not based on a deep connoisseur's appreciation of the amber liquid. In one move, he downs the whisky then reaches to the floor to replenish his glass with a local small batch single malt. He admires the empty bottle before tossing it into the fireplace. Glass shatters over the parquet, reaching as far as the edge of the Axminster rug. He raises the glass to his lips.

"Having fun?"

Sid places the glass on the side table, eyes on the floor, oblivious to the broken shards. "Not really."

"Well, I just escaped from your uncle. The one with the somewhat energetic dancing." And an archaic, inappropriate, disturbing attitude to women.

Sid's eyes return to the glass with a sense of yearning before snapping into consciousness. "Oh. Yeah. Okay. Sorry. Kat, this has not turned out how you planned. And it's a bit of a nightmare, really." He thinks I failed him by getting trapped on the dance floor. "I thought it would help... doing this. But I feel like I'm making things worse. You should go. This is not working. I tried, but I don't think I'm capable right now."

"Listen, I know what happened was not in the plan, but it wasn't that bad. I can stand up for myself." Not true. It was pure sexual assault, and my professional capacity limited my natural response. That is to shrug it off and find someone who I do fancy to brush up against my breasts and fondle my arse.

"What are you talking about?" Sid's tone softens.

"Absolutely, of course. I will go if you want. But it's not

what I promised." Surely a few minutes with Alexandria could not induce depression this severe. "I'm sorry I was too long, but Uncle Will-Fred-Astaire had me locked in high spin."

"Kat, did something happen?" Sid lifts his head, eyes searching.

"Only a non-consensual erotic dance with your ageing uncle... and I'm not convinced Aunty Nora is wholly innocent in the act." She is no Fred to his Ginger, but a Shady Lady.

Sid snaps back into consciousness. "I'm so sorry. For a moment, I got sideswiped by Lexie's emotional power play and took my eye off the ball. It won't happen again, I promise."

"Sid, I'm the one that's sorry. I am here to support you today. I let you down. I should have cut in. Should have done anything to save you from Lex."

"Then let's call it even and get back on track. I'm pleased you survived your *damsel in distress* moment." Sid's lip twitches as he attempts to restrain laughter.

"Is that some effort at Fred Astaire humour?"

"Uh-huh. I hope you're impressed. So, what was he?"

"A maniac, who is lucky to avoid a swift kick to the bollocks, but I was too afraid of bringing on a heart attack. Not quite how your brother would want to remember his wedding."

"No, I mean, did you do that drink thing? I imagine you know all the Fred Astaire-themed cocktails."

"What?" Ethan knows better than to betray my confidence, my coping strategy. We devised it together. "How did you–"

"What drink was he?" Sid sounds innocent enough, but I need to check.

"Drink?"

"Come on. You work in a bar, you must label people as drinks. It's like a vet guessing everyone's spirit animal. You said Lex was a pussy something."

Oh, yes. The planning meeting. I clear my throat before giving away a piece of my armour.

"A Ginger Rogers." I'm not ready for Sid to press me for

more information. Not after all that's happened today.

"Nice. Another Fred Astaire-ism. I like it."

"Hmm."

"Hey. Kat. I meant what I said. I won't leave you again. Come back to the party with me and have some fun. The serious stuff is over." Sid sounds earnest enough.

"Do you honestly think that's possible?" If it is, I want to relive some of the fun from the night we met.

"Of course. Don't forget I have seen you in action before. This should be easy. Nothing like work" Sid would rather give me the money back than a repeat performance. Another hint that it was a disaster in the bedroom.

For a moment, I'd forgotten our business agreement. The Ginger Rogers shook me up.

"Challenge accepted. I've worked hard today and have no intention of quitting now."

Sid downs his drink. He must have drunk the whole bottle. Enough to add a bounce to his stride as he exits the room and weaves through the crowded bar like a pro. Twisting and turning, a nod to his parents, a high-five to the flower girls. A best man with a mission, the pace increases in tune to the sounds of classic disco, and I skip to keep up.

Tunes flow as smooth as Uncle Wilfred's dad dancing, and I slip into the groove. There is something freeing about letting go to the beat. Releasing all the day's tension with a comedy boogie. Lost in music. No turning back. This is disco heaven. We dance and dance until we can dance no more. Until our feet protest and our mouths scream for moisture. We give each other a quick nod, no need for words as we head to the bar.

The utopia lasts a matter of seconds before we run into an irate bridesmaid on a mission to destroy happiness.

"Lex."

Alexandria squirms. She clearly hates the pet name. "It is not acceptable to turn up here with her?"

"Meaning, how dare I enjoy myself at my brother's wedding?"

"You cannot walk out on me and move on this quickly, Sidney."

"Like I said, this is my brother's wedding. And not the time to discuss your infidelities, Lex."

Alexandria turns towards me. Venom hangs from the tip of her tongue. "We have not been properly introduced, what with my duties as head bridesmaid being so full. Alexandria." Her outstretched hand threatens to crush my spirits. A passing glance to Sid. The missile destroys on impact as she emphasises the complete pronunciation of her name.

"We have met. Several times, in fact." My smile does nothing to cool the situation. "And you've done a remarkable job today. Your dress is stunning." My flattery fails. Uncle Wilfred is more likely to give up his philandering ways.

Alexandria leans in close. "Be careful. I will obliterate you, bitch."

This woman is a complete liability. If anything about the day for me was real, like my feelings for Sid, I could be intimidated by her comment.

"This is not over, Sidney." Alexandria seals her status with a parting death stare. On her way out of the bar, she radiates sweetness and light. Grandparents gush. Children dream of being her when they grow up.

"Shit! Kat, that was brutal. Are you okay?" Sid reels in the aftermath of the attack. "I didn't mean for any of that to happen."

"Yes, perfectly fine. I mean, remember I have nothing to be threatened by."

I touch his arm to reassure him, and Sid responds by resting his hand on my shoulder. This act of comfort changes everything, and a crack forms in my armour, allowing part of him to seep in. I have been kidding myself that this is make-believe. It hurts a little that Alexandria is undoubtedly not over Sid, and Sid is not over her.

The barman calls last orders and we are on the home straight.

"Let's finish the night in style. Make new memories." I can prove life carries on after the loss. "They're calling the final song."

A gentle trot and we are by the side of Christian and Jessica. The music slows to an intimate sway. Uncle Wilfred adopts a strictly come dancing stance with Nora, and I shiver at the memory.

"Will you dance with me?" Sid offers his hand.

I accept, giving him the green light to pull me in, but not too close. Now is not the occasion for grinding, although if I had to choose between Uncle Wilfred and Sid, I know whose muscle I would rather rub up against. The pleats of my dress brush against his shirt as my head rests on his chest. Our bodies blend into one with the rhythm, and I breathe in his scent. He smells good, woody, smoky, masculine, and it takes all my effort not to nuzzle his neck. My cheek lifts to meet his with a desire to find out how heavenly he tastes. But I am not supposed to feel this way. I am working. He is my client.

I know what lust feels like. Lust feels like Hugo and a paired ambition to reach climax as quickly as possible. I was blinkered to his intentions to only get into my pants, he was a parasite leeching money. This, right here, is not lust. I don't know what to call it, only that it feels deeper somehow.

As I lift my head, Sid gazes back. Without speaking, I tell him everything. Things I've never told Ethan. Things I'm yet to admit to myself. And he answers with a knowing nod. No one else is in the room. Only him. Only me. I close my eyes, and this unspoken intimacy sparks memories of feelings hidden for so long. The missing half locked away for fear of pain. But there is no pain now, only peace, as familiarity brings a welcome joy. A throwback to when I was whole. If I could kiss him now, I would. His lips are soft at first, then fierce with the urgency of passion.

The end comes too soon and brings with it dramatic harshness. The instant the song finishes, someone switches on the lights. The resulting blindness rips up my memories of a time dead to me now.

We slide into awkwardness as our bodies ease apart. I said too much, I crossed the line.

"Come on love birds, they're leaving." Sid's dad responds to my silent cry for help.

I take Sid's hand, vulnerability exposed by a nervous laugh. His eyes search for answers, but I have none. The moment is over. It was not real.

"Kat, please join us tomorrow. We're having a small gathering at home for Christian and Jessica before they go on honeymoon." Sid's mum wastes no opportunity to matchmake her single son. "I won't take no for an answer. You have proved yourself one of the family today."

"That is very kind of you, Mrs Richmond, but I–"

"Of course she will. Won't you?" Sid interrupts before I can refuse.

He can't have forgotten this is not legitimate, despite the last five minutes. But I can't justifiably refuse the money.

"Well, I need to check the diary. I visit my grandmother on a Sunday morning–"

"Visit?" Sid bears a quizzical look. Of course, he helped me back to Grans the night of the stag. But he doesn't know I live there.

"You can persuade her, Sidney?" Mrs Richmond is all charm in her Royal Smile.

"Sure Mum, I'll do my best." His palms open. "Right then. Kat, time I got you home."

Time I got you home. How I wish I knew, remembered what really happened the last time Sid took me home. Knew if he did obscene things to my body, and I to his.

The car park is deserted. Sid grabs my hand, forgetting this is only for show. This is not a date. This is my job, and he is a client who seems determined to make it difficult for me to stay professional.

"Can I take you home?" A slip of the tongue. "Your home. A lift to your home, Sidney?" Good deflection.

He laughs. "So, now you know. Only my mother calls me that. Um, sure. A lift is great. If you don't mind."

Not just his mother, Alexandria calls him that too.

The acceptance of the lift is a surprise. But the alternative is to return to the party on his own with Alexandria on the prowl. I need him to say yes for selfish reasons. This fake relationship supports my restored faith in men and faith in humanity. A reminder not all men are bastards, like Hugo.

"Despite a few blips, I had a great day. And it's all thanks to your plan. We pulled it off..." Sid stops to check his phone. "Missed calls from Lex." He scratches his head, deep in thought.

I was right, they have unresolved feelings and are unable to let go.

He turns off his phone. "I'd like you to come to brunch tomorrow. Can you rearrange your plans?"

This should be an easy decision. A second booking hails a successful start to Mocktail.

But if I agree, it will be for business reasons only.

"Are you sure you want me there with you? It's quite intimate, being at your parents' house."

"Yes, definitely. Today was the hardest to face up to, and being with you made it, I don't know… bearable, enjoyable even. Without you, who knows if I'd have left the studio this morning."

Sid just confirmed that this is professional.

"Okay then, it will be my pleasure. It is short notice, so we have almost no chance to plan a strategy. Is there a dress code?"

"Something suitable for a garden party, I guess. But, judging how amazing you look, you'll pull it off." He sends images to my head of me pulling him off, and I bite my lip to stop the giggles. "Pick me up at eleven. We can chat in the car. It should be a breeze."

So, he's not coming with me now, he has unfinished business with Alexandria.

"Okay. I'll send the invoice and contract when I get back. That gives you space to confirm you're still happy to continue before the morning."

"Sure, yes. The invoice." Sid clears his throat. He forgot this is business. A paid service.

I am better at this than I thought, or neither of us is good at pretending.

FIFTEEN

Angel Face

"Kat James!"

I feel like I'm back at Artisanal Delight, about to get my marching orders as Grans whips back the curtains in a manner that screams disappointment.

"Kat James. Explain to me why I have three." A low chirp emanates from her pocket. "Not again." Grans sighs after checking the phone. "Kat James. Explain to me why I have four. FOUR! Road traffic violations from Tilly Minster council sitting in my inbox this morning." She pauses for a few seconds, hand poised in case there are more. "Well, I think we can assume that is it for now."

I am confused. Where is the cheery *'how did you sleep my dear?'* Or the *'congratulations at securing another booking so soon'*?

This is not the start of the day I ordered.

"Do you have anything to say?" Grans' exasperation spritzes into the air.

It was all going so well. A repeat booking trumps five-star feedback.

"Nothing went wrong yesterday, Grans. I was not stopped by the Police or caught speeding. I don't know where they've come from."

"If I was up to date with my transport infringement codes, I could tell you. But fortunately, as a law-abiding citizen, I don't need to be."

"It must be a mistake. I was at the wedding all day." And had the car keys with me the whole time.

"Not all day, my dear. You were on Union Street yesterday morning."

"Union Street? Where is that?"

Grans taps furiously into her phone. "According to my Tilly street finder app, it is off Oxford Street. The end by Alfred's design studio."

"I must have parked there for the appointment. It said free parking, so I'm not sure why you've been sent a ticket."

"Let me see if I can fathom out the code." Grans frowns. "What type of 'parking' did you do?" The air quotes tell me this is not a standard parking ticket.

"Why?"

"The offence is coded as indecent exposure."

"What?"

"Kat, what kind of service are you running?"

"Honestly, Grans, nothing happened. I had my hair done, I got back to the car and... oh! There was no time to come back home to get changed, so I did it in the car. I thought the tinted windows would prevent anyone from seeing."

"Well, it seems like nothing gets past the eagle eye of Tilly's security cameras, judging by my emails. Right, let's see what you got up to next." Grans taps the screen, finding the second ticket. "This one says Whatnot Lane. Whatnot Lane? That's not even a road." A frown forms between Grans' eyes.

"Err."

"Yes?"

"I may have taken a shortcut."

"May have?"

"Okay, I took a shortcut at the end of the service road to cut through onto Oxford Street. It said it was not suitable for motor vehicles, but the car fitted easily. So, it was fine. Honestly, there is not a scratch on it."

"Well, it would appear when the sign says *no motor vehicles*, it means you are not authorised to use the road in a car. I see we need to brush up on your highway code. Never mind a scratch, there is a large dent in your finances forming." Grans swipes on her phone screen and shakes her head. "Let me guess. Your entry onto Oxford Street was not ideally placed."

"I had to nip right, on the pedestrian bit for a few metres. It wasn't for long, and no one was about."

"Aha. What you missed here was the fact it was only a part-time pedestrian." Phew, that's a relief. "But full-time one-way."

"Ah, man! There were no signs."

"That tends to be the way when you exit a footpath. No requirement for signs for vehicle users. Only pedestrians."

"So, what was the last one?"

"I'm confused. It has the same location, Oxford Street." Grans switches to search up the code. "Well, what do you know? The timing was such that you also have a ticket for driving in a pedestrian zone."

"That seems a little unfair."

"How so? You drove down a road that is not a road. You exited the wrong way on a one-way system, where shortly after, the part-time pedestrian-only zone kicked in. Ill-judged but not unfair."

"I have some good news that will make up for the tickets, Grans." Surely, this will make it all better. "I have another job. Today, in fact."

"Well, that's amazing, my dear. Well done! Is it enough to pay for the two hundred pounds of fines you incurred yesterday?"

That seems excessive, considering no one got hurt.

"I hope so."

"You hope so? What does that mean?"

"It felt rude to talk about money when the day was such a success."

"You need to make as much money as you can. Who is this assignment with, my dear?"

"The same person as yesterday. His mother invited me to her garden party today, and he wanted me there."

Grans does not look pleased at this. True, I should have checked that Sid was happy with the price. But even if he negotiates a repeat discount, it is still enough to cover the driving offences.

"Did you send your client a contract?"

Oh no! When I got home, I was so tired, I forgot. I failed the first time I went solo and arranged something without

Grans' guidance. "Yeeesss." I never was good at lying to Grans.

"Kat, dear, at this current moment, we are four hundred and fifty pounds in arrears, and that doesn't include the salon costs yet. I need to know how much you are expecting for the work today."

"Grans. I made two hundred and fifty pounds yesterday, minus the driving fines, which means we are still fifty pounds up."

"Oh! Yes, of course. My bad. There was an error on the spreadsheet. Negatives were never my strength."

"So today will make up the shortfall." The words do nothing to change the expression on Grans' face. I have never seen her mad like this.

"Well, you have already charged him so much. Maybe offer a discount." Grans voice softens as she nods to persuade me.

"But a minute ago, you told me to get as much money as I can. Won't a discount have the opposite effect?"

"Quite the opposite, think of it as a reward for his loyalty. You will earn more in the long run if the clients keep coming back for more. New clients, that is." Grans moves towards the door but not before picking up a half-empty bottle of vodka from the bedside table.

I don't know where that came from. There is no way I drank that much after getting back last night. Maybe I had one or two shots, but not enough to make a dent in a bottle.

"Enough talking. We have much to do. You send over the contract to… your client. Put two hundred and twenty-five as the invoice amount." Grans checks her phone. "No, that's too much. Make that two hundred. And I will be in the dressing room selecting an outfit."

I feel so guilty, I put on the dress that Grans lays out. It's the fussy floral chiffon number. Not that I am against tea dresses per se, nor tiers and frilling, but combined with lemon floral, it just seems a little mumsy. Grans said I have an image to keep, but an actual girlfriend of an artist would not turn up in this. Grans even cajoles me into kitten heels, the type that Alexandria would wear, so I guess Sid will like them.

I drive to Sid's studio after Grans makes me promise not to

take any shortcuts. She said another ticket would be taken out of my cut of the profit.

The double yellows outside look so tempting. I'm not staying long, and it's rare to see traffic wardens out at this time, especially on a Sunday. Plus, if a warden does come along, I'll drive off before they get the chance to ticket me.

The door to the studio opens with almost as much gusto as Grans with the curtains this morning. See, I was right. There is no point in finding a parking space when Sid is ready to go.

Only he is not ready. He's not even dressed wearing only thin, fabric-like towel, the type you take camping. His wet hair drips, and his skin glistens as water runs down his neck onto his bare, toned chest.

"Morning." Rivulets travel down to his hand, resting on his firm, glistening abs. The towel flutters in the backdraft of the opened door, and he crosses his legs. "You don't want to park there. This is an automatic penalty zone." Sid points up to the street camera, and his makeshift sarong slips a little. Reaching to protect his modesty, he fumbles to find enough hands for his phone, the door, and the microfibre sheet. "They just email the penalties through. No need for a warden anymore." His eyes crinkle at the edges. He must be sensitive to the morning sun. "I will leave the door open. Come in and look around while I finish getting ready. I won't be long."

Obedient, after Grans' warning, I do as I'm told. Although, by Sid's reckoning, it may be too late and there is nothing I can say that will calm her.

I could tell her that Sid's naked body distracted me. It is certainly not unpleasant, and Grans is not to know I already parked up before I saw it. No, she will see straight through the lie. Of course they have cameras, that's how I was caught yesterday. Ethan calls this repeated destructive behaviour, but I didn't set out on a path of sabotage. Today was supposed to be a good day and I ruined it by not thinking.

"Like what you see?" Sid emerges from the back of the room with no shirt on. His chest bare and smooth all the way down to where the thick belt of his pale jeans rests on his hips. They are at the point, you know, where one slip will give me a glimpse of the top of his— "The painting."

"Yes, I do." Very much. More than I expected, although I am a woman after all and when faced with a body like that. Oh, hold on. "What?"

"You were staring at that painting."

"Was I? I mean I was." Yep, I ruminated in front of a... "It's interesting. I mean I like it."

"It's a type of abstract expressionism. This one's called *matriarchal suffering*. It is an acquired taste."

You're telling me. But I can't insult his life's work. I need his money for my rocketing traffic offences. "I can relate to that." Anyone who's seen Cynthia in action knows the suffering inflicted when she is in full flow. "But I've seen nothing like it before. What was your inspiration?" Fingers crossed I have not subjected myself to the open wounds of a motherly relationship gone bad.

"The power play of relationships. See here the battle between the two styles. Subtle in places, but brutal conflict over here."

"Yes. I see." But I don't see. To me, it is merely a mash-up of colours. Like someone vomited a palette of paints onto the canvas. "So clever. I could stare at it for hours." Meaning I could stare at him for hours.

"Err, listen," he can see through my artistic ignorance. "I should have said this before, well, I have only just realised I have no funds to pay you for the booking today."

"Sorry, what?" My head is jumbled from the naked aperitif.

"Sorry. I don't mean to be a dick. I guess I got carried away with how easy everything was yesterday and, and if you were with me today... err... it would not turn out as fucked as that painting."

"So?"

"I was thinking. You love that painting, and it is the most expensive item in here."

"Really?" I've seen better art in the nightclub toilets after they've been obliterated by tactical chunders.

"Yes, you can have it. And when I get more money, I will pay you. I know it is unorthodox, and you're entitled to tell me where to go. I'm not intentionally being a complete arse."

He disappears before I can explain that my 'really?' was

not through delight that he was gifting me his art, but that anyone would pay money for that. Not just any money. A lot of money.

I should walk out, but that would let him down. A sane person would walk out. A businessperson would honour the agreement, but right now, I'm neither sane nor a businessperson. I'm a failure in my job, a nightmare to Grans, a weak pushover fleeced by a man for the second time in a month.

His body did this. For sure, in any other circumstances when faced with a half-naked man the morning after, there would be no deliberation. No philosophical arty debate on the matriarchal dominance in past relationships, just naked, sated fucking until we… "Gahhhh"

"Everything okay?" Sid calls from the other side of the door. "Sorry it's taking me so long. There's not much room back here, and I'm still living out of boxes. Even my towel is for camping."

"Yes, okay."

"Great. I was convincing myself you'd refuse."

Wait! I meant all was okay, not that I was accepting this crazy offer.

"I mean, it is, as you say, unorthodox, but–"

Sid steps into the studio in a crisp white shirt to complement his light blue jeans. Angel face and blue eyes cut through the misdirection with a familiar fresh honesty, but no longer perfect. Today, he is tempered in a different direction.

What if he planned to distract me with his body so I would accept a painting instead of money? There is the appearance of purity, but beneath it lies a cocktail of personalities. His white shirt, the freshness of Calvados. Most would not waste such fineries in a cocktail, but perhaps it's too harsh to downgrade him to an Applejack.

I didn't think him capable of deviousness. Certainly, an Angel Face is potent in its ability to disarm. With no mixer to dilute the hard-hitting equal measures of brandy and gin, it is a combination of comfort and, some would say, depressant. A medley of desire and despair. He needs me but cannot pay.

The sweet apricot brandy - he deserves the benefit of the doubt after the thoughtful gesture to save me from another fine. The double yellows are potent, but it is too late, the eagle eye already captured the traffic violation.

I can't help but worry that once vigorously shaken, Sid may not be such a good guy after all.

SIXTEEN

Irish Cream Liqueur

Any awkward feelings are concealed by a monologue as we travel to Sid's family home. He tells me of an idyllic childhood spent playing hide and seek in the neighbouring woodland, building dens. Walking miles and worrying you'd never get home again, when in reality they never walked further than the edge of the woods bordering the garden. A promise to show me his favourite tree in the orchard, the one he climbed over and over again.

How easily Sid shares this intimacy after the deception of the studio. It comes naturally for him to trick me, cheat me and is something I should be used to by now.

He talks with delight as though it were yesterday, the magic of time stretching out like there is no tomorrow. Things are different for me. The slowing of time is torture. Unmoving. Since it happened, every minute becomes an hour. Every hour, a day. Separation grows with each breath as distance multiplies exponentially. It is impossible to go back, but the raw feelings remain as if no time has passed. Sometimes, I remember what he looked like. But always at the wrong moment, never when I am desperate to see him.

As we reach the house muffled voices break through the hedge. Only the loudest, the most direct breaks through, thick and creamy. She commands the scene.

"Darling, put the gifts here. The photos of them being unwrapped will be divine with the backdrop. Sweety, put the drinks on that table, the crystal glasses are perfect. The guests sit there, the bride and groom there. What time is..." Alexandria turns, "look who has finally arrived... the lovebirds." Chilled sarcasm accompanies the sickly taste of jealousy. "Sidney, be useful. Move chairs from the garage to the lawn. Kate–"

"It is Kat." Sid deflects the shot, stopping Alexandria in her tracks.

"Bring the wedding gifts from the dining room onto the table over there." Alexandria ignores Sid's correction of my name. Her tone is raw, potent and cutting.

Sid offers me his arm. His touch says, *'I made you a promise not to leave you again. Not after what happened.'* And I believe him.

"Sure, no problem. Always happy to help." I am here to work, after all.

"Wait. Kat. You don't..." As I rest my hand on his, the hold relaxes, and I am free. I don't need him to protect me from Alexandria.

Stepping into Sid's family home is like walking into a hug you didn't know you needed. The door from the garden opens to a boot room. Dried herbs and flowers strung in the bay window release the scent of lavender as I brush past. Into the hallway, the wooden boards creak as I peek into a room. This must be the dining room, the table is full of gifts. Larger boxes cover the floor, even the chairs hold gift bags. Christian and Jessica know lots of people.

I select a few packages, the largest at the bottom acts as a tray to support smaller, lighter boxes on top. I was a two-time record holder at Artisanal Delight for vessel vulnerability. If I can retain the title for breaking the fewest glasses, I can carry this pile of wedding gifts unscathed. With ribbon handles looped over my arms, I hold a couple of gift bags on each side, weight distributed evenly to avoid the tilt of destruction, my hands free to lift the tray. The stack is taller than planned, but I have the skills to succeed. A left turn into the hallway, side-stepping through the door, in a crablike motion.

And then disaster. A kitten heel jams in the floor. The boxes on the makeshift tray slide forward a little, but not enough to fall. Thank goodness. If I break one of the gifts, I will be bankrupt before the company is up to speed. I slip out of both shoes, kicking one to the side, leaving the other wedged in the middle of the hallway.

The step down into the boot room comes out of nowhere. It was definitely not there a few minutes ago. "Help!" The little profit I banked falls, box by box. There goes a salt and pepper shaker. That's another fifty pounds. And that box contains a pair of Champagne saucers. Add another thirty pounds. One more and I can never face Grans again.

"Whoops." Sid's mother swoops in. "Allow me." Both packages are saved from destruction with a swift bend and snap, as Rebecca steadies the stack with the dignity of a Royal Smile.

"Thanks, Mrs Richmond. How did you…?"

"Circus school for the hen do. And call me Rebecca, please. Has Lexie got you slaving away? You are our guest." She takes another gift from the pile. "Now, pass me those and get yourself a glass of summer punch."

"No, no truly Mrs… sorry, Rebecca. I love to help. It's my pleasure, I assure you."

"Yes, but you have a more important job to do." She knows. Sid told her. "It's much better if you spend time with Sidney and do some rescuing of your own." Rebecca takes one more box, revealing the garden and the multi-layered Pousse-Café bossing everyone around. "Tell him I need his help in the morning room. No doubt you need a rest after the drive home late last night, not to mention the early start this morning. Today is for celebrating, not working."

I wish I knew what happened after I left last night. Judging by her comment, Rebecca thinks we went home together. Her head filled with visions of us up half the night shagging. Well, not in that way. She is his mother, but I know if Sid was shagging, it wasn't with me.

Stepping out onto the lawn, Alexandria verbally abuses Sid, eyes blazing. "And you are yet to explain who the little ray of sunshine is that you magicked out of nowhere?" Raw. Cutting the atmosphere like whiskey in a parched throat.

"That's no business of yours, Lex." Sid stays strong.

Lady Rosamond Gifford has something to say about this intimate conversation. For certain, nobody wants to hear

Alexandria in full flow of her overpowering routine. A polite cough will gain their attention and save everyone's pain.

"Ahem," Tentative but successful.

"What?" Sid snaps. His patience is running tight.

"Sorry to interrupt. Sid, your mum requests help in the morning room. My apologies, Alexandria. I appreciate you have plans for him."

"Do not apologise on my account, Katy. You will find out very soon just how much usefulness Sid brings to the party." The words burn as they go down.

"Come on KAT. Let's see what we can do for mum." Mid eye roll, Sid thrusts his hand at me. Gladly I take it, but his hold is rough. The acceleration across the lawn spins me around like a tossed cocktail shaker, performing a show for the thirsty bar with only Sid's arm supporting me. He swops hands, throwing me into the air behind his back catching me deftly on my return to earth. The whole time, Alexandria stares, utterly astonished.

"Sorry about that. I reached my limit and can't ruin Christian's wedding weekend with a big showdown." Sid's pace slows as we reach the house. "I needed to get out of there and wasn't going to leave you alone. Are you okay? I didn't hurt you, did I?"

"No. No." I like that he needs me.

Rebecca waits in the morning room with a tray of tea and crumpets. A large bay window overlooks the driveway, so we are hidden from the chaos of the garden. A tall velvet armchair next to the fireplace calls to me. In cold weather, this room must be super cosy with it lit. As it is, the midday sun pours in, warming the space with a light glow.

"Here you are, my darlings. Put your feet up and relax, enjoy yourselves. Forget Lexie. She's capable of managing on her own, yes?" Rebecca winks before she closes the door behind her. Subtle.

"Your mum is sweet."

"She's trying to ensure our relationship blooms. She worries Lex will poison it."

But it's not real. Maybe this warm, welcoming house and the understanding, supportive Rebecca clouds his mind. Rebecca is so different from Cynthia, my mother. If my family knew I broke up with Hugo, they'd never welcome a stranger into their home so soon. The questions would be in full flow. *'What happened?' 'What did I do?' 'Why do I shut people out?' 'It must be because of your past.'*

But that does not explain why my mother is so distant.

"Tell me more about your art. The studio has some amazing pieces." Of course, I'm lying. Distracted after seeing Sid in his semi-naked state, I have no idea what his work looks like.

"Hmm, not sure about that. Especially the nudes I did of Lex."

The tea catches in my throat, and I cough. This is too much information! All I see is Sid teasing out Lex with his oil paints. A sheet draped over her for modesty, tactfully slipping lower to draw him in and consume her many flavours.

"What a laugh if you were to do an exhibition of those. The original revenge porn." Such toxic words, and so unlike me. I am ruining everything. Today was a mistake. First the parking offences, then the painting instead of payment. Let's not forget the near breaking of the wedding gifts, and now I'm slagging off a client's ex-girlfriend. I pretend I feel nothing, but jealousy does not come from nowhere. "Sorry, that was unprofessional of me. I do not know where that came from. Can we call it a joke gone wrong?"

"Honestly, it was funny." Sid chuckles and leans forward in his chair. "Everything you do makes me laugh, Kat. The way you stand up to Lex like no one else… she doesn't quite know what to make of you, but then again, neither do I." His eyes narrow as he examines me. "Mocktail. Is it going according to plan? I thought this would be harder, the pretending, but it seems to come easily. It's a bit confusing."

An opening to tell him I feel the same. But it is all too soon after Hugo. Too soon to trust another. And even if it wasn't, I am not an escort.

"Am I not delivering what you thought? For your money?"

"Oh, yes. The business. Yes. Almost too good sometimes."

Those pupils. The intensity magnifies as he moves even closer. I cannot trust him or anyone. Sid stares. Looking for something. The emotions of last night are still raw but have been tarnished in light of my failings today.

We return to the garden hand in hand. This is my idea, to create an impression. Alexandria stands, tinkling a Champagne glass with a cake fork. Attention drawn to her once again. As if people have not had enough of being bossed around.

"Ladies and Gentlemen," Slightly formal, but sticky. Alexandria is out to make an impact. "It is my great pleasure to welcome the bride and groom. Mr and Mrs Richmond." Her velvet, almost chocolate tones, hang in the air like Irish cream liqueur. Don't get me wrong, she has not changed. This is another layer to her Pousse-Café, carefully added to the sambuca in a precise, calculated way.

Everyone claps and cheers as loud as an intimate group can, humouring the beast.

"Thanks, guys," Christian doesn't stand. "And thanks to Lexie for that introduction. I'm glad you know who we are now."

"How were the nuptials?" Uncle Wilfred heckles. Trust him to lower the tone.

"All good, thanks, Uncle." The new Mrs Richmond blushes as Christian drags the conversation out of the gutter. "Shall we just relax and open our gifts, babe?"

"Yes." But it's not Jessica who answers. Alexandria diverts the spotlight away from the two most important people here today, thrusting two glasses of Bucks Fizz at them. "Come, sit over here. On some seating I made." Which is about as truthful as the Egyptians claiming they built the pyramids with their own hands.

Sid and I lounge underneath a tree, laughing along with his family as they make jokes and tease each other. I play the part of girlfriend to perfection. The illusion is so seductive, the family so addictive, it is hard to remember this is fake. Seduced by the love of family, resistance is futile. I need this intimacy in my family. Yes, we have family parties, but nothing like this. The James family gatherings, of which there are plenty, are thinly veiled business meetings to advance Gordon's profit line. Long afternoons discussing strategies with associates, planning reward schemes, arguing over who is the highest performer in the team. All under the umbrella of a charity event, giving back to the community. My parents never mingle together, they prefer a divide and conquer technique.

Sid's mum and dad sit united, hand in hand, arm in arm, laughing and chatting. They welcome Jessica and her parents into their house with gusto.

My family is diffused. They have no spark and no true friends.

I want what I have here today, only I don't belong here. This is not what I deserve, this is their time. The Richmond family's intimacy is overwhelmingly good, and as much as they say they want me here and make me feel welcome, I am an observer in the wrong place. I am my parents. I know, I know, everybody turns into their parents but that's not what I mean. I sit here but am not a part of this. I'm not really here.

The laughter is not my happiness. My only friend is Ethan. My 'new' friends are clients. The best thing to happen to me in a long time is this, which is a business arrangement just like my parents taught me. Even their relationships with us children fell into the same pattern. I am so good at pretending, I have betrayed this lovely family. Tricked them into thinking I care for Sid and it is not fair. This is business. I am just like my parents and Sid is a 'pretend' friend, only here to add profit.

"I need to get back." Please understand I cannot stay here any longer. Nausea pushes up from my stomach as emotion burns from behind my eyes. "I've stayed much longer than intended, neglecting Grans, umm, and we had plans."

"Shit, Kat. I'm so sorry. Have I completely ruined your day with my selfishness?" Sid scratches his stubble before pulling on his lip. He's so relaxed, so natural, happy even, and I've ruined it like I ruin everything else.

"I mean, it's fine. Really. I had a good time. Lots of fun. Would you like a lift home?" A false offer. Please say no.

"Sure, but... I'm gonna hang here with the fam. I will walk you to your car though."

We tread in silence, my shoes rescued from the hall on the way. He senses I am out of place here too and it is time he took his family back, they were never mine to usurp. But for a moment they welcomed me in, and it felt good. Good to be loved for who I am or who they think I am.

Sid lingers on the car door. The moment he lets go, it is back to reality and the reminder of failure.

I want to take a piece of today, the emotion, the love and happiness of his family. Like a slice of wedding cake, to savour and enjoy bite after bite whenever I want. I want these feelings of love and friendship to be the truth, to consume at my own discretion.

"Thanks again for everything, Kat. I never thought I'd enjoy myself this weekend, but it's been great. It's been real."

I wish it were real. That he felt the same way I do. I reach out for one last chance to touch him. To see if the connection still exists or if it was all my imagination. Seduced by his family. Erasing the doubt over where he went last night. Burying the deception of the trick to give me a painting instead of money. Burying the feelings like I always do.

But he is gone, and nothing can bring him back.

SEVENTEEN

Fake Orgasm

"Method acting?" Ethan greets me over the Vanilla Pod's trademark soothing scent and live music. "Sunday night, jazz night. You used the wrong door again, so missed the sign out front."

"I thought you could do with a hand." Grans will be less disappointed with this morning's traffic violation if I can earn some extra money.

"True. I'm expecting a full crowd later. This dude is the hottest piano player in town, a big draw. I intend to make him a regular. Give him a residency." Ethan downs tools to give me one of his signature big bear hugs. "So, darling. Why so much chiffon and lace today? Not that you are immune to the style, there is just a little more fabric than I am used to seeing on you."

"The wedding, remember?"

"So, you went through with it?"

"No, I have not 'gone through with it' but conducted my first assignment for my new business venture, Mocktail."

"Was it an overnighter? You dirty dog."

"No!" Punching him on the arm. "This is one hundred percent fake dating, no sleepovers whatsoever."

"That's what they all say." Teasing. "So, tell me about the drinks." Ethan stifles a yawn. "Sorry darling, I've not slept much. The new little dude is keeping me up at night."

"What about Laura? Doesn't she cover the night shifts? She has the day to recover."

"Migraines." Ethan looks beaten. "It gives her migraines to

get up at night, so I do it."

"Seriously? Ethan, you're completely under the thumb. I'm gonna use that line after I give birth, so I get an entire night's sleep while the baby daddy does everything!" Unsurprisingly, Ethan is crestfallen. But before I can apologise, he steers the conversation back on track.

"Darling, this is not about me. And you can't change the topic so easily without me noticing. Back it up, I wanna know. Spill the drinks."

"Too many. Would you believe I woke up again this morning with a half-empty bottle on the bedside table, and I don't even remember drinking it?"

"I meant the people, but–"

"Oh. Yeah. Of course. The people." So stupid. Now he thinks I have a problem. "Um, Sarah Kennedy was a Bamboo. Uncle Wilfred." saying his name makes me shiver. "Was a Ginger Rogers. Alexandria is definitely a Pousse-Café, but difficult to read. It's like every time I meet her, she reveals another layer."

"And Sid?"

"What about Sid?"

"You know… what drink was he?"

"Well, yesterday, he was the perfect Poire Prisonnière, but today, he was completely the opposite. Angel Face."

"Sounds like you're struggling."

"A little. It's almost like he changed his personality overnight. He's just not what I thought he was–"

"No, I meant the empty bottles by your bedside." Ethan never misses a trick.

"Everything is fine." But I cannot look him in the eye.

"How long has it been happening?"

"What?"

"The drinking. Has it been since you split up with Hugo?"

"And lost my job, savings and apartment all in one day?" That stress alone is enough of a reason.

"Kat, I've known you a long time. You are doing amazingly well. But it is worth examining if the empty bottles in the morning are a new thing or if it was happening with Hugo, but–"

"But I didn't notice because of all the other empties lying

around? Is that what you mean?"

"These last few weeks have put more pressure on you. It is easy to reach for a crutch to help you carry on."

"Are you saying I am self-destructive? Ethan, it's not as bad as you imagine. So far, it's not been over one bottle and only at night." I can feel my voice rising. This is not the best conversation to have in public.

"Depends on the bottle."

"Why not just come out and say what you mean?"

"Subconsciously, you feel you don't deserve the success, so you enter into patterns of behaviour that lead to failure."

Ethan thinks I made all these bad things happen. I pushed Hugo away. I acted out in the workplace to deliberately lose my job. I encouraged the late-night parties to enable my drinking to go unchecked. And the driving offences. Inadvertently, I made that happen so my new business would fail.

No. Ethan is wrong. That would suggest everything I have worked for has been only to destroy myself. It can't be right. I won't allow Ethan to fill my head with this negativity.

"Ethan, stop! I don't need psychoanalysing right now. During the assignment, I've had no alcohol and even better surrounded myself with people who don't use drugs for business or pleasure. I experienced it myself. Me. Stone cold sober."

"Sorry, darling. Just looking out for you, that's all. But you just said 'weekend'? The last time I checked, weddings take one day. You said there was no sleepover, but you saw him yesterday and today. The Poire Prisonnière and the Angel Face. Where did you spend last night?"

"In my bed." Time for another punch to the arm.

"You took him home?"

"Oh my God! Ethan, I told you there was no overnighter. Sid slept in his own bed, well, to the best of my knowledge. I left him at the wedding last night and picked him up from his studio this morning. It's as simple as that, nothing else." Apart from the multiple traffic offences, being distracted with his half-naked body and almost bankrupting my new business by trashing the wedding presents.

"Shame, you normally have awesome gossip to spill. I was hoping to live vicariously through you. Late nights in the bar, then back home to a newborn, don't lead to much action."

"You need to make time for action, Ethan. It doesn't just happen."

"Anyway… It sounds like a good little earner for your first job. Two days of money? I am surprised you agreed to help me out tonight if you're so flush."

"Well, he didn't exactly pay me for the second day."

"What? A buy one get one free? Darling, a freebee is not good business." Ethan reaches for a stainless steel cocktail shaker. Flipping it up into the air, he spins and catches it one-handed behind his back. He is in the mood for a show. The display is reminiscent of Sid on the lawn earlier today.

"Not a freebee. He gave me something in return."

"I bet he did." Ethan bends to scoop a generous measure of ice into the shaker.

"No! A painting." I bite my lip, knowing full well this will not disguise my stupidity for allowing my first client to take advantage of me.

"A painting? What's it worth? Is it a lost master's or something?" Ethan pours a shot of espresso over the ice.

"I don't know. I've never been into art." Not until this morning, anyway.

"Ha! Well then, let it serve as a reminder that you should only accept real money next time!" Ethan adds a few drops of almond essence.

"I kinda got swept away by…" Sid's wet torso. An unexpected but familiar connection. "…the romance of the weekend."

"I should say. Let me guess. After a few drinks and a slow dance, you were in that familiar place, wanting to tear his clothes off." Ethan adds one ounce of heavy cream. Luscious, rich, and fulfilling.

The night of the stag do. The feelings I mistook for something else, someone else, were in fact Sid.

"Darling Kat, you never change. What with your habit of thinking someone is your soulmate the minute you meet, this desire to screw every half attractive bloke is just another way of covering up your real feelings." Ethan squirts chocolate syrup into the cocktail shaker, and my mouth waters.

"Sid is more than just half attractive!" I didn't mean to say that aloud. Mortifying. "I mean, there is a connection there. Like something I have not felt since…" My throat constricts.

Gin. London, pink, blackberry, rhubarb and ginger. The bottles behind the bar catch my eye, and I read them to calm my anxiety.

"Kat." Ethan rests his hand on my wrist. "Talking about it is good."

"I have nothing to say."

Vodka. Chocolate, pear drop, raspberry, and of course vanilla.

"Not about what happened but the way it felt. What it means to go through that experience emotionally." Ethan adds a few drops of signature vanilla essence to the mix.

"You wouldn't understand. You were not there." Rum. Dark, spiced, white. "And it's over now. I'm moving onto the next client."

"Client? Is that what you are calling him?" Ethan moves the cocktail shaker with vigour, the ice clacking in rhythm to the jazz.

"It's too soon after my split from Hugo to consider anyone else romantically. Even if I did like Sid in that way," Which I do. "Which I don't. At least this way, I have fun instead of being a bitter twisted old spinster shut away in Grans' house crying myself to sleep every night."

"So, in honour of your next client, let me introduce you to the first of Vanilla Pod's new Mocktails." Ethan rims a chilled martini glass with lime, turns it upside down, and dips it in cocoa powder. "The Fake Orgasm."

EIGHTEEN

Red Silk Panties

A fraudster stares back at me from the bathroom mirror.
"Grans. I don't know how to tell you this." No. Poor start. "Grans. No. I can't do this. Mocktail is a mistake. No. I'm a mistake." Even worse. "Grans, you were right. I screwed up again." This is hopeless. Everything that has happened over the last few weeks is too much to process, and I'm unprepared for these feelings. I don't even know how I got here, in this situation. The change is too much. Change I did not ask for.

It is time I owned up to Grans. This is not working. All her efforts have ended in more anxiety for me and a bunch of traffic fines along with a worthless painting.

Maybe a text.

> Grans.

Delete.

> Firstly, thanks for all your help.

Sounds too much like a farewell message. Delete, delete, delete, delete, delete, delete.

> Sorry.

Delete.

> ...

This is not worse. Not a text. Maybe a letter or email.

No. If I send her an email, she will see the message from the Tilly Minster council even sooner, and I need to get to her before then.

There is no other choice but to face up to the truth.

"Oh, Ooohhh." I hear Grans' disappointment long before I find her. "This is terrible. How could you?" The screams are coming from the library. "I didn't think it was this bad."

I am in serious trouble. Grans has never been this vocal before, even when she discovered the traffic violations. She has had enough and will ask me to leave.

Without Grans, I would have nothing. No home. No love and no support.

"You promised me you would listen. That it would be different this time." A sob eeks through the crack in the doorway. She must have seen the email. I have really messed up.

"Grans, I'm... Grans... what's going on?"

Grans lies face down on a portable massage table, her modesty covered by a square of terry towelling. Straddled and mounted above her, hovers an arse not six inches from the back of her head, dipping up and down. The arse belongs to a therapist stretching out her right leg.

"Oh ho! Good morning, Kat dear. How are you?"

"Worried about you. I heard screaming."

"A by-product of my pole dancing venture, I'm afraid. A few of us clubbed together to pay for some physio. Otherwise, the finale of the cabaret show is at risk."

"Cabaret show?"

"Yes, but never mind about that now. You have a new assignment."

"But I–" How am I going to tell her?

"I know dear. So, I set up a website. And an app. Use my laptop. You have admin access, and the logins are unchanged. If you click into the bookings section, you will see a bio of your next client."

My next client?

MOCKTAIL CLIENT MENU

NAME: Marshall

EVENT: Tossa. Double date with my twin sister Monica. She is looking to meet 'the one' and I want to support her. She is very outgoing, but never met the right person.

BIO: Student, aspiring model.

IF YOU WERE A COCKTAIL WHAT WOULD YOU BE: A slim double.

LOVES: My twin sister Monica. We do everything together, so when she is asked on a date, naturally it becomes a double. But I'm missing the vital component... a date. It is important to us to approve of the choice of the other person. Never been married. Just not met the right person yet.

HATES: To be apart from my twin.

HOW DID YOU HEAR ABOUT MOCKTAIL: Lucky for me, the Mocktail advert popped up in my stream when I was looking for a third person to share the evening with.

This is my next client, and he comes with such a compelling narrative, albeit mostly about his sister and not his own needs. Mocktail has morphed into a humanitarian cause worthy of the United Nations' recognition. Ignoring the fact they will pay me for my part.

"Tossa!" Grans exclaims. "Who could refuse?"

"Errr, me if that is the case." I've had my fill of tossers for a lifetime.

"Oh ho! The restaurant is called Tossa. I am quite jealous. It has been a while since I have been. Not since the opening night if my memory serves."

Tossa, is a new restaurant in Tilly Minster. A hybrid, high-end tapas fused with a Champagne bar, or if you want to be true to the Spanish theme. I've been desperate to visit since it opened last year. The place is so prestigious that tables book up within minutes of release, making it almost impossible to experience.

Marshall sounds like a valuable client if he has a table for four already booked.

"And if you're going Spanish, you wear Spanish. There is only one option." Grans picks up her tablet. "Liv, how are you?"

Olive Groves, hair big and purple pings up on the screen. "Alfred suggested I update my look for the portrait. But I'm not so sure. There was plenty of dye, so we did my head as well. I think pink was better but at least I match. Not that you will see my head. Maybe I will ask S–"

"Olive, I have a favour to ask." Grans changes the subject, but I want to know more. "Kat has a dinner date at Tossa."

"Not a date, Grans. Business."

"Yes, yes. Business, Tossa. What do you need? I am ready for action." Olive leans in.

"The dress."

"The dress? Oh, the dress!" Olive runs off. "Back in two ticks." She shouts as the purple glow gets smaller and smaller. She returns in what can only be described as a few giant bottle tops held together with paper clips. "What do you think?"

"Seems revealing." I see what she meant about the dye. Purple pubes bush out between the gaps in the dress. "Any reason why you are naked beneath?"

Grans offers comforting words. "It's original and looks great with the correct lingerie."

"Like long johns!"

"This is how I modelled it for–"

"NPC, remember?" Grans is always quick to dive in.

"Well, obviously. I was not going to say their name." Olive twists left and then right in an attempt to look at herself. "Strategically placed, you would be fine, as long as you wear knickers and cover your nipples. I have some pasties somewhere."

Grans looks thoughtful. "A simple black slip would be better. I have one the perfect length."

"No, Grans, I have something better in mind."

Marshall shares a flat with Monica in Newtown Tilly, a stone's throw from my old stomping ground and the dominance of Artisanal Delight. The familiar roads guarantee a penalty-free drive, at least for this part.

Mid-thirties, Marshall wears his shoulder-length flaming hair with confidence, his lean frame modelling a slim black shirt with room to spare. He has a clean herbal scent, mixed with the vigour of pomegranate. Marshall is a Maidens Bush, innocent and fresh, his luminescent absinthe green eyes hypnotise me the minute he opens the door.

"Monica is already there. Let's go." It is so sweet that Marshall doesn't want her to be alone for long.

Monica and her date, a Liquid Symphony, sit next to each other, side by side. Pretty impossible to give each other flirty looks as they tuck into their chorizo. Although better placed for flirty whispering or a discrete hand job below the table. Maybe they are on fire with lust. Maybe the date was doomed before we arrived. That's why Marshall is keen to get seated and skip a pre-dinner drink.

Marshall sits opposite his sister, leaving me facing Miller, Monica's date.

"So, how did you meet?" I break the ice before someone gets trapped under and runs out of breath.

"Our mothers. Mine is obsessed with Monica and has a mission to get us together. I guess she's finally done it." Miller, elegant and floral, does not share his mother's aims.

"Mums, hey? Think they know everything." I've said enough. This is not the moment to talk about Cynthia.

"Huh, I suppose. There's something particularly tragic about being so desperately single that you need your mum to plan dates." His laugh lacks humour but remains sweet like honey.

"Shall we toast the night ahead?"

Maybe Miller will relax and enjoy himself if he has a drink.

"Great idea! Let's get this party started. It was super

dull, but now you guys are here, we are certain to liven up." Monica raises her cocktail, as vibrant and red as her cascading corkscrew locks. "Mmmnnnnnnn" She elongates the satisfaction just that little bit too long. "Delicious. Let me order you one, Kat."

"Red Silk Panties? Not tonight, thanks. I'm driving."

"Well then, maybe a sip of mine?" Licking her lips. "Did you recognise it, or did my brother divulge my favourite drink with you?"

"No, Marshall gave nothing away. I enjoy mixology and this venue which is so fabulous and inspiring."

Tossa has a modern aura, with contemporary accents of chrome and gold interwoven together. Chandeliers hang low above every table, cutlery falling fluidly. Almost tempting diners to pick off a fork and use it to eat the food. Beautiful but useless at lighting as they're not connected to power. Instead, we have candles on the table.

Is this how double dating works? Miller is charming and funny, it's impossible not to enjoy spending time with him. Monica is one lucky girl that his mother played matchmaker. I enjoy chatting to Miller, but there is a problem: Marshall is my date, not Miller, and I've not spoken to Marshall since we got here. There is a danger of assignment failure and my first pissed off customer. He is paying me money to join him at dinner, and I rudely spend it with someone else. More importantly, it is the person his sister is dating. This seems fun, but in reality, it is a disaster. I don't need any negative feedback on my new website. *Dating guru???... More like a date snatcher. I paid this woman £150, and all I got was an expensive dinner bill and the humiliation of seeing her leave with my sister's blind date.*

Surely Monica thinks it rude that I have stolen her date for the evening, but she smiles and laughs, unconcerned. Marshall leans over the table, holding her gaze as they share tapas. The closeness I attribute to the fact they're twins. I don't have this level of intimacy with any of my siblings. If we go out to dinner, it ends up in an argument, and we don't talk for a month.

I tap Marshall gently on his arm, releasing notes of

botanicals.

"I'm so sorry, Marshall. I've been neglecting you."

"How so?" He looks blank.

"I mean, we've not spoken since we sat down." This is awkward. "How's the food?"

"Fantastic thanks." Sharp as lemon, he gives nothing away.

"May I try some chorizo?"

"Sure."

"It's so wonderful that you guys are close. I dream of being that close to my brother and sister."

Monica purses her lips, nodding. "Yes, I love him dearly. It's great being so intimate."

Marshall, laughing. "Well, who wouldn't love me, Nic-Nic?"

A pet name. Wow, they really are close. This is how twins are. They shared such a tight space together in the womb, they are literally one person split into two. Monica stretches out her arm, rubbing the back of Marshall's hand. Super close. Perfectly normal.

It's time we put the double in our dating. True, it's easier to chat to Miller, but that's not what I'm paid for. Is it? Both Monica and Marshall make it super easy for me to talk to Miller and difficult to communicate with them. Every time I try to engage them in chat, I interrupt a conversation.

Maybe I got the purpose of this assignment wrong or maybe Marshall took an instant dislike to Miller and wants to keep him apart from Monica, using me as a buffer. Monica knew from the start that Miller was not the one for her. But if that were true, she should message Marshall to let him know, and he would alert me to the change in plan. I am being paid to complete a task after all, it makes no odds to me if I'm here to spend time with Miller or Marshall.

Maybe Grans can help. It's not a complete disaster, so no need to execute our agreed safe word, but she may have advice. I excuse myself and message from the powder room cubicle where no one can see.

```
                Grans all ok but a little odd
```
```
How so?
```

> I'm a 3rd wheel

Last time I checked, double date equals four.

> Exactly

Last time I checked, double date equals four.

Sounds interesting. Stick it out a bit longer. Let me know if you need me.

I open the door and run into Monica waiting for me right outside the cubicle, trapping me with her emerald eyes.

"You didn't flush." Monica purrs, her face inches away from mine, peach schnapps on her breath.

"Turns out it's impossible to pee in this outfit." The slip grans suggested felt too revealing, so I opted for a close-fitting black stretch playsuit. Under normal circumstances, it is easy to slip off and use the toilet, but with a metal chastity dress, I am trapped until Grans can release me.

"I can help you slip off your dress. It's what us girls do to help each other out." Her lips, sweet and crimson as grenadine, turn up at the corners, teasing and moist. "There is room in there for two if you move back a bit."

Is this usual for powder room etiquette?

"Well, the moment has gone, so I'm ok, thanks."

"Sorry sweetie, you don't mind me joining you? I need a girly chat after all the time with the boys."

Boys? But she spent the entire night talking to her brother, who she lives with.

"A girl's cha... I mean, yes, perfect." What do girls talk about? "How are you enjoying tonight?"

"Good thanks. And you? How do you like my brother?" Monica lifts one arm, resting it on the door frame, elongating the gap on one side just big enough for me to escape. "I'm afraid we have spent the whole evening arguing over you."

"Oh, he seems nice." I morph into a bendy snake and squeeze around Monica, making it as far as the sink. So, we're having a boy chat. Now that I can handle. "What do you think of Miller? You must think me rude. I've spent lots of time talking to your date."

"Nonsense." She moves behind me, our eyes meeting in the same mirror. "The more the merrier." Her hand rests on my waist as she leans in, her breath tickling my ear. "Sweetie, this dress is divine."

This must be the part of the powder room chat where we compliment each other on our outfits in the style of mutual girly moral support.

"Thanks. It's vintage. Grans insisted I wore it tonight. Err... you look great too."

"Oh, this old thing." Monica runs her hand down her red bias-cut satin dress that leaves nothing to the imagination. Her frame is as svelte as her brother's. "Matching underwear, of course." Sliding the hem up her thigh. "Perhaps I can tempt you with this kind of Red Silk Panty?"

Her head tilts to the side as she stretches one leg out, releasing the scent of orange citrus.

"Oops, my mistake. I'm not wearing any." Her tinkling laugh fills the room. "But I am as smooth as silk, here," reaching for my hand, pulling it behind my back. "What do you think?"

She places my hand at the top of her thigh and sweeps up. And yes, her skin is impressively smooth. Huge compliments to her waxologist, but to ask would only encourage her. Not that she needs it. She continues to trace my hand over her full Brazilian and down until my fingers rest on her clit.

Monica loosens her hold on my hand, so I turn and face her, my fingers gently teasing as she grows moist. A stray hair on my face catches Monica's attention. As she moves it off my cheek, she delivers a soft kiss on my lips, the hit of vodka, powerful, strong and potent. This is not what girls do in the powder room, but I like it. No questions. No expectations. Just the type of fun I enjoyed with Hugo.

But this is different. This is not a bit of fun in a dark corner of a club. I swore Hugo was the last fumble I would enjoy on a night out after the way it ended. Monica is not my client, but I owe it to Marshall to remain professional and not screw his sister in the middle of our double date although it may already be too late as my fingers slide inside her and she groans, a sort of cross between a tickling laugh and the pleasure you get from that first mouthful of delicious dessert.

"Monica, I..." I want to kiss her, but I pull back, and the satin hem falls over my hand, covering her legs once again. "Marshall must wonder where I am."

"He will assume we are getting to know each other better." And then she laughs that musical tinkling laugh. "Men fantasise about what we get up to in the powder room, but they never dream it this good."

"So... Miller?"

"Oh, he is okay but not my type. Actually, I'm pleased Marshall found you." Monica straightens her dress, and places one hand on my shoulder and the other on my waist. "He told me you were lovely, and he's right."

"I'm needed at the table." Before I do something regretful.

"I mean it. We normally like the same people, so it's no surprise."

I give her one last kiss on the lips, brief but full of meaning, then leave her. I have done well.

Stopping in the corridor, I reach for my phone.

> Grans the champagne's gone flat

Do you need me to send help?

> No I will be fine leaving now

Be safe. I will have help on standby.

"You waited for me!" Monica grabs my hand. "Sorry I took so long. You really turned me on with what you were doing, and this dress is not very forgiving with any form of moisture." She lifts my hand to her lips, sucking them one at a time. "You didn't wash. I like that." And then her hands move, touching my hips, my shoulder, my hair all at the same time.

"My brother is the most gorgeous man. Don't you agree? He's a real sweetie."

Not one that I want to suck on, thanks.

"Yes, but I don't know him that well." I respond.

"We tell each other everything?"

Does she mean what I think? I must ask Grans to add a confidentiality clause into the contract.

"It's great you're so close."

We take our seats back at the table, and I study the dessert menu, wishing it was bigger so I could hide. What happened in the powder room must end here. I have no choice. No matter how much I enjoyed the thrill, it is not good for business or my reputation.

"I love dessert. The naughtier, the better. What's everyone having?" Monica asks, although I know she's not talking about food.

A foot, soft, gentle, rubs against my leg. Not Miller's, he just stood up, and the foot is still there.

"I'm heading off. Early start tomorrow."

Nooooo! Don't leave me. Not only do I want him to stay, but I need him to stay. I don't care if tonight is a write-off for him. He offers limited but vital protection from myself.

"Okay, sweetie," Monica stands, giving Miller a pat on the back. "Have a safe journey home."

"Maybe see you in the Vanilla Pod sometime." I shake Miller's hand, which is comforting like brandy. "Do you know it?"

"I play piano there." Miller pulls a face. "Jazz night?" It all makes sense now. Liquid Symphony. Miller is a musician.

"Oh yes. I thought you looked familiar." I do not recognise him at all. Too busy talking to Ethan about Sid.

Thanks to Monica, that was a whole other kiss ago. Not that I kissed Sid.

I want to leave too, but my assignment is for the entire date or until Marshall says our appointment is over.

We are a party of three. A threesome! Is that what they wanted all this time?

Marshall puts his menu on the table, turning to face me for the first time this evening. His green eyes are hypnotic. "We mostly skip dessert, unless it is back at our place."

"It's so much better snuggled up at home sharing a wicked dessert, don't you think, Kat?" Monica winks at me before reaching to hold Marshall's hand. Tempting. But I cannot.

"I... am... not sure." I need to get out of this as smoothly as Miller. "I'll pass if you don't mind, Marshall, err, Monica." Who exactly is inviting me? It doesn't matter. I cannot accept it, regardless. "I'll be getting back too if that is okay. The double date has come to a natural close."

They can enjoy their closer than close relationship on their own. They don't need my help.

"But Kat, sweetie, you can't leave now. We have a connection. I know you felt it." Monica begs.

I really did.

"Oh... no... I really have to go. I am staying with my grandmother, and she needs me back early. You know how old people are. Can we take a rain check?" Empty offer.

"I'll walk you to your car." Marshall says, leaving no chance to refuse.

"Thanks, that would be nice." But not as nice as the parking space the Mini is conveniently nestled in. Just steps from the door, enabling a swift escape.

"So, Kat." The door handle is millimetres away as Marshall prolongs my stay. "Monica took a big shine to you tonight."

She told him.

"It was good to meet your sister, and such a shame that it didn't go well with Miller."

"Kat. Please reconsider the offer of dessert. Nothing makes me happier than giving Monica pleasure." The glint in Marshall's eye gives away the truth. I should have guessed from his client profile.

"I have to go." His hand rests almost undetectably on my shoulder. His touch is light, and I get flashbacks to the restroom. Monika and Marshall are predatory twins, hunting in a pack. "Marshall, I understand you're just being friendly, but regrettably, this is a business relationship. I have a strict code of conduct that forbids me to take things beyond a professional level."

"That is a shame, sweetie." Monica, once again the expert of surprise. Her deep red lips are moist, pleading to be caressed once more. "But as I've not paid you, there is no strict code of conduct between us. Marshall can just watch if it makes any difference." She laughs. "I'm joking, of course. About my brother watching. Euugh." She shivers. "But you are more my type than his. We agreed at dinner."

Tempting, but not this time. Once maybe, in my previous life, before Hugo and the resulting self-destruction. I feel triumphant to leave with the promise of sexual gratification right before me, which makes this move, right now, opening the car door and driving away, proves I have broken the cycle. I am back in control.

NINETEEN

Absinthe

Cut crystal glasses rest on the table. I count them. One. Two. Three. The cork slides out of the bottle releasing the aniseed aroma. As the vibrant liquid tumbles into each glass, it forms rich emerald pools. Absinthiana is lifted from a pewter tray. First, a triangle-slotted spoon is placed on the rim of the glass. An organic sugar cube sits in the centre of the spoon dissolving drop by drop as a pipette is held above. A teasing foreplay until the ritual is complete.

The liquid burns into the back of my throat. Too much makes my head spin so I focus on the green pupils. Seeing double, I'm sucked into the neck of the bottle, narrow at first, then widening to the deep sumptuous glow.

Monica stands naked. She lifts my red silk dress, slow at first, over my thighs skimming my tattoo with her fingertips. Gentle sweeping strokes lift the satin over my bottom. Marshall joins us, coming in from behind. He strokes my hips, hands rise in time with the dress. He is naked too, I know this because his erection pushes into the small of my back. Monica teases the inside of my thigh, fingers reaching up. I shift my feet a few inches wider and lift my arms, the dress glides higher exposing my breasts. My nipples pinch as Monica slides her hands up to cup them, massaging them in a way only a woman knows how. As she gives each one a flick with her tongue, the heat grows between my legs. The dress slides over my head and my red hair cascades over my shoulders. As Marshall ties the fabric securely around my wrists, Monica squats to tease my red silk panties with her mouth, her fingers sliding under the gusset. My hands fall back over Marshall's head, and my pelvis pushes forward yearning for her tongue. Marshall grips my chest to steady my pose as his erection slides between my buttocks.

I had not intended to join them. Mocktail business ethics held strong as I drove as fast as the speed limit allowed. A diversion in the road took me left, away from the most direct route home. The ring road reduces to a single lane and traffic slows to a standstill. Nose to bumper, cars inch along going nowhere fast. A left turn leads back to the old part of town and another diversion. But it's okay, I know the road. Yes, Union Street. There's the carpark for Alfred's studio, I can find my way from here. Hold up. Another road closure. It's like Tilly Minster council is rerouting traffic for fun. Oh no! The diversion points to Whatnot Lane, the no motor vehicle penalty route leading straight to a fine. There must be an error. Grans will kill me if I get another. The rear-view mirror shows the road behind is clear, so I complete a quick three-point turn but I am still facing Whatnot Lane. I must have done too many turns. When I try again the car still points to Whatnot Lane. There is some master trickery at play.

Maybe it is ok. The bollards at the end of the road have been removed and I cannot see a warning sign, so here goes nothing. Fate tells me to take this path. A hard left at the end will avoid the problematic one-way street. But I am facing away from the Minster. I definitely made a left turn but ended up facing right. On the plus side, it's the quickest way back to Grans' so with the pedal to the metal, I continue up Oxford Street, only slowing outside number 698 and Sid Richmond's studio.

The lights are off and the blinds down. A small splinter of green breaks through the edge. Sid must be having a late dinner or working on a piece at the back of the room. The glass is cold on my face, as I press up against the window and the view turns misty white thanks to my breath. I see two white-robed figures in the doorway to the back room, shadowed by the green glow. Sid has someone in there.

Alexandria.

It must be.

The glass melts away as I rub it clean, and I step into the room.

Sid is with a girl, but to my surprise, it is not Pousse-Café. This woman is slender, with long legs and lean arms. Skin so pure, her makeup-free face glows in the emerald luminescence. Her tousled hair hangs loose, grazing her collarbone. He pulls her in close and wraps her hair around his wrist, giving a little tug to tilt her head back before kissing her. She laughs as he lifts her off her feet with a hug, swinging her around. She is the embodiment of Sex on the Beach. Intoxicating, leaving you wanting more. Cranberry hair, sweet melon liqueur and punchy pineapple. Sid drinks her all up, getting drunk on the vodka and Chambord.

Chambord.

As I step back, I tread on something or someone behind me.

"Sorry." I turn but don't need to look up.

It is him.

His scent.

It has been too long. But I remember.

Eager, I reach out and knock a bottle to the floor. I stoop to pick it up but I am too late.

He is gone.

Always gone before I am ready.

Gone before I can touch him one last time.

The strap tightens on my chest, squeezing the air from my lungs. The force, hard and sudden, comes from the driver's side, pushing the car off the road. My head whips back as the car slides down a steep bank, trees bending in its wake on the soft ground by the river. Nothing to break the momentum, the car sinks and water laps against the window, vibrant and green. The air thickens to a dense white mist.

And then comes the smashing.

Glasses shatter all around me. Shards cover my face and arms as I reach up to shield myself. The force of the blow carries me onto the roll bar and I rebound back, my arms stretch to grab him but strong hands pull me clear before I have the chance.

"You are not supposed to be here." A woman's voice chastises. "You nearly ruined everything, you stupid girl."

"Get him out." My voice is weak.

"Who?"

"Help him. Please." I croak.

"There is no one there."

"No! Please, you have to help him. Help him. You must help him."

"Help who, my dear?" The voice changes. Familiar and comforting.

"You must help to get him out before he dies."

"Kat, are you okay?" Gentle hands on my shoulders, scooping me up.

"Grans? What happened?"

"You were crying out in your sleep." Grans' grip loosens as she turns to the nightstand. "I guess this was to blame."

A bottle of absinthe knocked onto the floor.

"It must have been a dream." But it didn't feel like it. Not the red silk panties with Marshall and Monica. Not Sid kissing the girl. And not the car accident. They all happened.

"Grans. Something odd happened last night."

"Something odd always happens when you flirt with the green fairy, my dear."

"No, I mean with Marshall. The assignment. I thought they were brother and sister. Twins. But they were really close, too close."

"Kat dear, anyone else's siblings will seem close to you. You don't exactly see eye to eye with Zara and Jeremy."

Maybe I did dream it. Not the part with Monica in the powder room. That did happen. But the threesome, going back to their apartment, that must be a dream.

"Shall we see if they posted a review?" Grans waives her tablet in the air. "Your first one."

"What about the wedding? Is there no review?"

"Not yet." Grans holds the tablet at arm's length, turning it one way, tilting her head the other. "But this," turning the tablet upside-down, "this is most interesting."

"How so? Is it a review?"

"No review yet. An email."

"Can we cut and paste that into our reviews section?"

"Hmm. I don't think you want this image on your website."

"Why?" Reaching for the tablet. "Let me see. Grans."

"The email is entitled dessert." She resists handing it over.

"I thought you met up with a man?" Grans flips around the screen. "Maybe this explains the bio."

The image shows Monica enjoying a red silk pantie. Naked. Her face is shielded by a mass of red hair. But I know it's her from the smooth line of her wax.

TWENTY

Volcanic Blast

"Looks fun." Ethan hands me a drink, steam rising from the cup.

"It's from the parents. I have been summoned." A lead lump builds in my throat.

"Summoned? It says 'Jam-Fest'. Like a festival? How can you be summoned to a festival so innocently named as Jam-Fest?"

"Cynthia prints the tickets on super thick embossed cards, designed to impress, awe, and inspire. Ergo, I have been summoned."

"Are you telling me your mum planned a festival?" Ethan is as impressed as Cynthia intended. "Named it after your family, and she sent you a free ticket?"

"Not exactly. Well, yes. Cynthia holds an annual festival, and yes, she sent me a ticket. She always sends me a ticket."

"And you go?"

"Not always." Ethan throws a bartender look that compels his audience to explain further.

"It's not the same on my own."

"Surely you are okay with your parents?"

"You have no concept of what it's like. I've had a few unpleasant experiences in the past." I take a big sip of tea. The camomile hits the spot, with sweet antioxidants offering comfort. Although to be honest, vodka would be a better remedy given the unwanted subpoena. "It's harder than you imagine being single at my parents' house."

"You said 'my parents' house'. Is it not also your home?"

"I think you know the answer to that, Ethan. And the last time I attended Jam-Fest on my own, my mother scheduled a parade of 'esteemed gentlemen' to introduce to me. It was shameful." Not to mention embarrassing. She doesn't understand me. Thinks if I meet someone else, I will forget.

"So, take someone with you."

"Who?"

"Did you ever take Hugo?"

"Yes, last year. He was a nightmare."

"Really?" Ethan reaches out to finger the invitation, he has spotted the handwritten note. "Wait, what's that smell?" Rubbing the card between his thumb and forefinger. "Is that raspberry?"

"Yes." I sigh. "Cynthia sprays each one with her signature scent."

"Don't tell me." Ethan holds the card to his face, first wafting it beneath his nostrils, then sniffing the card up close. He closes his eyes, absorbing the essence. "Something sweet like papaya, with a bitter undertone of coffee. Am I right?"

"Almost. You missed the orange."

"Nice touch." Ethan reads the card again. "So, why does it say please remember to bring your fabulous Hugo? Doesn't sound like a nightmare to me. From the tales you tell, how can they be so in love with him?"

"It was a disaster. He was completely useless when I took him. I realised straight away he'd not stand up to their attempt at conversation, which is a grilling intelligence agencies aspire to. They'd expose his idiocy if I did nothing. However there was nothing I could do, there was not enough time to save the impending disaster."

"So no happy ending."

"Hmm." I ignore the double entendre.

"Kat? What are you hiding?" The restorative notes in his voice comfort as well as tease.

"Well, anyone is better than Hugo. Apart from the sex, he was rather talented in that area." That's why I put up with him for so long.

"You're a Hugo dicksomaniac."

"Do you think my drinking is that bad? Huge seems a bit much. I am, after all, drinking camomile tea right now."

"Not a huge dipsomaniac. I said a Hugo dicksomaniac."

"What?"

"Addicted to dick. Hugo's to be specific."

"I mean, I guess so." His cock was delicious, a tower of strength and pretty addictive. When erect, it had a soft glisten to the head that tasted sweet. If there was one part of him that I miss, that was it.

"So, remind me, dicksomaniac aside, why were you with him again?"

"For fun."

"Until it derailed."

"Anyway, I've not heard from him for two months," which can only be a blessing. "The hard thing now is to come up with a good reason not to bring him to the festival. I did my best to keep Cynthia away but failed with her friends who gave such a high review of him. She's determined to meet this 'fabulous' man of mine."

"Can you take someone else and pretend they're Hugo?"

"Like Mocktail? No. The Swizzles, mother's friends, know him too well." I sip my tea, remembering the last and only time I took Hugo to my parents' home.

※ ※ ※

The moment I had waited years for, to attend Jam-Fest with a boyfriend, specifically Hugo. I knew Cynthia would be disappointed not to set me up with random men but I didn't care, the timing was perfect. True, there was a high chance we were entering a baptism of fire, but he was man enough for the job. Hugo loves people, and people adore him.

The theme was 'A Country Fair'. Each year Cynthia selects a different theme to prevent boredom from setting in. Well, if she wanted to keep things fresh, I had just the thing in Hugo and couldn't wait to sign him up as my plus one. Only, he was still asleep after a night of partying. With a resemblance somewhere between a dusty ashtray and an empty bottle of own brand vodka he retained a unique allure. I climbed in to snuggle next to his naked body.

"Look," I waved the thick card in his face, "an invitation to Mother's summer festival. Shall I rsvp?"

"Anything for you, babes."

Before I could find a pen, I was pulled under the covers by his lean, powerful limbs. One hand held both my arms above my head, pinning me to the bed, the other worked its way to the buttons on my blouse. Butterfly kisses planted on my forehead, fluttering over the path to his goal. Hugo nibbled the side of my neck, sucking just enough to leave a mark. I should have been cross but I was intoxicated by his intense sweet charm and his hard cock pushing against the gusset of my panties. Pulling them to the side, he flexed his muscle pushing just enough to slide up to my clit teasing my pussy. I would've pushed him inside but I was still restrained by his strong grip. He was my nemesis and made me late for work again... and again... as I consumed shot after shot of climax.

Despite Hugo's positive reaction to the invite, when the day arrived, he was difficult to coerce. Yes, he'd been up all night partying and a little worse for wear, see previous description of Hugo the morning after and add a half-eaten cold kebab. Nevertheless, I'd expected him to be more enthusiastic about meeting my parents and making us official. The only way to persuade him to put on half-decent clean clothes and get into the car was the promise of a fast-food drive-through, and a good hour's kip whilst I drive.

"Before you sleep, I need to brief you."

"Babes, it will be fine, no sweat. Stay cool." Hugo's eyes closed as he slipped into a post-fast food coma.

"Hugo, they are not cool. They are anything but cool."

"Chill babes. No need to go on. I have it covered. Mums love me. And it's a festival, not a bloody funeral."

"Listen, this is serious. Cynthia loves to create the illusion of a festival, Jam-Fest, but in reality, we are entering the battlefield of the Women's Institute versus the University of the 3rd Age. Competition is serious amongst the Swizzles."

"The what?"

"Mother's friends. I call them Swizzles owing to their love of mixing up any calm situation. Especially where the blend of flavours clash."

"Bla bla bla." Hugo thrust one of those annoying hand puppet actions in my face that made me want to slap him. "Just wait and see. I'll be so popular with your mum's frenemies that she'll beg me to come back every year. The WI and U3A will be booking me in for regular experience events."

"No bla bla bla. This will be a challenge. If you think you can charm Cynthia into accepting you as a maternal son she never had, you're wrong. None of my boyfriends have made the grade."

"Babes, I'm not like any of your previous boyfriends."

Hugo was right. He was not like the last boy I introduced to Mother. If anyone could break Cynthia's icy resolve, it was Hugo. Destined to join the heroes of legends, my saviour, my superhero and now the one to reach the parts others never could, my mother.

Jam-Fest, not to be confused with Jamfest or JAMfest, both actual real-life high-quality events, is located in the back garden of my family home. There is always a buzz, even though the space is too small for an actual stage or fairground and there is definitely no camping allowed and the great unwashed are not welcome. When the theme requires, the event spills next door into the recreation ground, but Cynthia prefers to keep it bijou. Last year's theme, 'A Country Fair', fitted into the boundary of the back garden, the perfect size for Mother to tour, greeting her bespoke audience. Each ticket holder is individually selected to attend, in return for a sizable donation to the collection of Jam-Fest charities. In return for their generosity, Cynthia repaid her guests with a painted smile and a head tilt of condescension. That is until she saw Hugo. The smile shattered and it was clear he was an interruption to her plans.

Cynthia was assessing the finalists of the welly-wanging

farmer competition. Each year it's the same, she devises an inappropriate activity to highlight the most eligible bachelors and parade them in front of me. None of the 'volunteers' were ever farmers in any sense of the term although no doubt they'd be happy to plough me once Cynthia gave her approval.

We walked to the hay bale seating from where we could view the entire festival.

To my left was a miniature steam organ. Painted in primary colours, the engine puffed air through the pipes to shrill out a tune whilst tiny wooden Morris Dancers rotated. To my right, the premium bring-and-buy stall with a strict product code. Everything must be intact with original labels or show a receipt of professional cleaning. Next door was the craft tent, bursting with handmade goods. Slots were open for bite-size flower arranging tutorials, and while you waited you could guess the number of crochet hooks in the jar for a chance to win a yarn starter kit.

Beyond the sculpted flower border was the competition arena. The gazebo hosted baking, growing, brewing, and making and any traditional horticultural skill was allowed. The clash of scents from food both raw and cooked provided mouth-watering temptations for the second section of the arena, brimming with animals. Dogs, cats, guinea pigs, hamsters, and one fishbowl vying to win the happiest smiley pet. Happiest smelly pet is more like it.

Opposite us was clay shooting with a twist. The twist was the absence of live ammunition. This was sensible, considering the compact area and free flow of guests. A charge of accidental manslaughter would put pay to Cynthia's ambition to raise a million pounds from a single event. This was a laser shoot and the only empty activity.

I had a strange sense of dread that something bad was about to happen.

The bale tensed as Cynthia thrust her manicure into the stalks. Her gaze flashed across the lawn to a figure shoulder-rolling over the grass wielding a laser shooter. The perpetrator stopped on one knee and eliminated everyone in the line of sight. Dropping to the ground, they commando crawled into the dog agility course.

A crowd gathered. 'This is the best stunt yet', as the word DOG was removed with one swift wipe of a fist on the chalkboard. 'I heard a rumour the red arrows were booked, but this is much better.' Gun thrown to the ground the man of the moment ran on all fours over the first hurdle. To be fair, a chihuahua could handle that one. 'He is fantastic. Where did Cynthia book him?' The tunnel proved more challenging, and for a moment, it looked as though the racketeer would drag it around the rest of the course. 'Cynthia, I must have his name.'

The accolades did nothing to temper the heat growing in my mother.

"I... I will need to check my..." Pressure built, straining to be contained.

"That's Hugo. He's–" I tried to explain.

"Destroying my festival." Cynthia flashed me a warning that she was about to explode.

"He's–"

"Hilarious, Cynthia, this is the most diverting entertainment yet." At least someone appreciated him.

"No, he's–"

"Gone."

"What?" Fire flashed from my mother's eyes.

"Where did he go?"

Cynthia turned and there it was, a shot of Volcanic Blast hit hard. The flames blinded me and the world went black. Smoke choked my throat, reducing my voice to a whisper.

"Don't just sit there. Do something about it. Kat." Cynthia shook. "He's ruining my festival. Ruining!"

With eyes shut tight, I stood, legs unstable as the aftershock from the explosion hit.

"What are you waiting for?" Cynthia continued her reign of terror.

I grounded myself against the force of more blasts. The earth was solid beneath my feet, my calves rested on the bale for support. It had been a while since I'd had an attack this severe. I thought they were under control, but had not accounted for Hugo upsetting Cynthia.

"Kat. What are you doing? Stop him from doing any more damage to my reputation." Cynthia's tone sweetened as the flames receded, but the message was still there. I had shattered everything.

Opening my eyes, the world was framed in black and white squares with a hundred faces staring at me from in centre. All thinking the same. 'Stupid girl, she did it again' 'Her poor mother' 'They never should have let her out like this.' Being careful not to disturb the layers, I took one step forward, but it was too soon, and Mrs Abbott melted into the rhododendron bushes.

I needed help, and fast. I breathed in visualising a large shot glass for this Pousse-Café shooter and a steady hand to pour each layer. As I breathed out I added Kahlua, Cointreau, raspberry syrup, papaya juice, spiced rum, and overproof rum. Then I lit the mix and watch it burn. With a soft gaze focused on the lawn, I repeated once more whilst taking long slow breaths.

I managed to walk to the house, relieved to find it locked. At least Mother and Father were sensible enough to protect the silver. The posh hire toilets were empty and filled with brain-numbing panpipe music, the scent of blue flush overpowering any desire to pop back for a quicky once I found Hugo.

He could have been anywhere. From the top of the garden I worked through the attractions, checking every hiding place. Cynthia has been holding Jam-Fest, for like, forever. As a child I sought refuge when it was too boring, too noisy, too embarrassing, or when mother required me to parade around to prove I looked normal, ergo there was nothing wrong with me.

A couple of Swizzles from the next village walked past me up the lawn. They talked in low whispers with a giddy demeanour only obtained after being in the company of the hypnotic Hugo Edwards.

"Oh my, I had no idea it was like this." A Bourbon Swizzle exclaimed.

"Well, Ruby, I've heard it does wonders for rheumatoids,

and it works." The Apple Swizzle gyrated.

"I feel twenty years younger, Belinda. Lionel won't believe it when I get him home." Blushed the Bourbon Swizzle.

"I feel so alive." Giggled the Apple Swizzle.

Middle-aged women, high on dopamine, giggling like schoolgirls, empowered to conquer the world – or at least their middle-aged spread husbands, meant one thing. Hugo was playing shop in the summer house.

I was careful when opening the door to make sure it didn't slam in the breeze. The stained glazing was fitted by hand to a design by the ten-year-old Jeremy, and both the folly and its contents are as precious as their first-born and only son. The space was designed for solitude and reflection but was now furnished by Hugo smoking a spliff on my mother's antique chaise longue.

"Babes, where have you been?" Hugo's voice was as intoxicating as his drugs.

"Hugo, is there something you need to tell me?"

"Babes. Look at this amazing view."

"I grew up here, remember? I've seen it before."

"Sure, but not with me. Come and recline, it's really special." Hugo patted the tapestry.

"We don't have time for that."

"Babes, chill."

"Hugo, I don't need to chill." Not true. Never in my life had I needed to chill more. To get away from here, away from this disaster.

"Sure you do. You're doing that thing again, aren't you?"

"What thing?"

"Where your lips move but you make no sound, as though reciting some obsessive-compulsive list in your head like a freak. Try relaxing instead." Hugo removed himself from the prized sofa, offering me the joint which I extinguished in an empty glass.

Hugo was correct, I was silently repeating the Volcanic Blast rescue remedy. But I had never confided in him that this was my thing.

"How many others have you shared this view with today?"

With two hands-free he hooked one around my waist,

slipping the other up the hem of my dress.

"Well, not like how I share with you." His mouth was millimetres from mine.

"I should hope not! They're at least 30 years older than you."

"Babes, these older ladies are wild, let me tell you. They're gagging for it. Cougars need a second chance."

He was serious. He could have anyone he wanted of any age but he chose me, and I worked hard to keep it that way.

I let his hand feel the way into the top of my panties, his fingers confident and teasing. It was easier this way than to fight against the powerful grip of his other hand on my hip. Once he was happy I could persuade him to leave. As Hugo's hand slid further into my knickers I released a sigh of satisfaction, only my win-win descent into hedonism was not to be, as we were rudely halted by a tap at the door.

"Sorry to interrupt. I heard this is the place to be, and I see it lives up to its reputation." A Rum Swizzle true to her name stirred up the mood, and not in a good way.

Mrs Hughes poked her head around the door starving me of the amazing pleasure Hugo delivered.

"How do I get some of that euphoria?" Mrs Hughes chirped, spicy and bold.

Hugo slipped his hand from my pants and sniffed his fingers before tasting them, his tongue darting between his lips. Rather than display any level of revulsion at the scene before her, Mrs Hughes responded by sucking on her bottom lip, hand extended in greeting. I will never look her in the eye again.

"Penny Hughes." Ignorant to the importance of hygiene since becoming infected by Hugo's charm.

"Mrs Hughes, honoured to meet you." Hugo leaned in, took her hand pulling her close enough to kiss her cheek for just long enough to be socially unacceptable. "How may I be of service to you on this beautiful day?"

"Oh, please call me Penny." She flicked her hair, wafting a dry citrus scent.

I couldn't believe what I was hearing. Mrs Hughes, the headmistress at the local convent school was rumoured to give double detentions for the misuse of her name. Standards have gone downhill since the arrival of Hugo Edwards.

"Enchanted," Hugo displayed his winning grin. "Please, come... into my little paradise."

Penny bubbled like one of her pupils.

"Now, Penny. Are you here for what I think you are here for?"

"Oh!" Mrs Hughes gave a nervous sigh. "Well, the girls said I should come and see you. But I'm not sure I will enjoy what you do."

"Have no fear, Penny. Please handle and taste anything you see here. Only when you experience pleasure, can you be sure it is worth paying for."

"Oh, well, if that's okay." Penny took a step back, uncertain.

"Don't worry, babes." Hugo sparked up. "Just do this."

Watching the Swizzles try marijuana for the first time was a thing of nightmares. But there I was, complicit in the downfall of my mother's friends, along with her precious summer house.

"Ooh." Mrs Hughes giggled. "This is rather daring. I haven't so much as looked at a cigarette since my Ken died. And they were not home-grown ones like this. Have you considered exhibiting in the marquee? You would be very popular."

"These are very special, Penny. Nothing like the ones you buy over the counter. These chill you out and take the stresses away. Am I right?" Hugo whispered something in Mrs Hughes' ear, making her gush. Tension built in my throat, silencing my protests. Reaching into her bag, Penny exchanged crisp folded notes for Hugo's little package, accepting another lingering kiss on the cheek before she left.

Now I was the Volcanic Blast, ready to ignite.

"Hugo! How could you abuse my parents' hospitality, not to mention trust by dealing at their garden party? You've turned their prized summer house into a drug den, my mother's antique furniture smells of pot, but worst of all, you have led her closest friends astray."

"Babes, take a breath. It's all good."

"Take a breath? Take a breath? This has been a disaster. How can I face Cynthia again?"

"Cynthia? No, I don't think I have serviced her needs. Not yet anyway. I think you are safe." Hugo's muscular arms pull me close once again, and with one hand, he unhooked my bra through my clothes.

"Cynthia is my mother!"

"Babes, I know and believe me I've done it before, not your mum, but, well, forget that. I need to help you out of these as soon as possible." Hugo looped his fingers over the top of my pants and we were seconds away from them slipping to my ankles. I should have worn jeans. It would have given me some negotiating time before he dulled my senses with his heady musk.

Why did I think it was a good idea to bring Hugo? Of course, he would fail to impress my mother. Not even Gordon wears that medal. I was left with one option, to smuggle Hugo out and limit further damage and the sooner the better. Of course that was easier said than done. Easy would have been to let him take me from behind up against the leaded windows overlooking the water. A sated Hugo was no trouble to manipulate but sadly there was no time. Experience taught me that when he unhooked my bra and removed my knickers, he was in for a marathon. Knickers on for a quickie, the gusset supplying extra sensation to maintain the pace. Bra undone and knickers off for a long slow fuck.

The buzz had started and not just in my pants. Hugo was hot property. A wanted man. Cynthia James had a network of spies everywhere.

"Hugo, we need to be quick."

"Babes, chill. We had fun earlier, right? Now the old woman's gone, we can continue where we left off." Hugo took my hand, moving it to the front of his bulging jeans. "I hadn't even gotten started."

"No, I'm serious!" I dug deep into my reserves to stay strong but Hugo continued to ignore me, unzipping his straining jeans. As usual, he was commando and my mouth watered. Images of my knickers hung from the chandelier, chaise longue stained, and my virtuosity in tatters held my focus. "This is not the place. We can party the way you want, back at the club. I will even let you…" I whispered the rest in his ear as it was far too x-rated for public audibility. In an emergency, promising the taboo was the only guaranteed method of manipulating Hugo into doing what I needed.

Hugo relented. On a promise, he followed me into the field behind the garden and up the enclosed path to exit a few metres from the front of my parents' house. I'd successfully sprung Hugo out, without suffering the embarrassment of bumping into Mrs Hughes or any of the other ladies. More importantly, we escaped to freedom without the now-stoned Hugo meeting my mother. I could only hope Hugo's groupies didn't take their purchases back to the garden party to share out, transforming the whole gathering into a sixties-free love revival.

TWENTY ONE

Vodka

"Sounds tricky." Ethan drains his coffee.
"Too tricky. All I hear from Cynthia is how wonderful her friends think Hugo is, and asking when they'll see him again."

"I bet they do!"

"And if my mother's friends think he's wonderful, my mother thinks he's wonderful." I finish the tea. "But I can never bring him home again after what happened. Cynthia doesn't know the details. And that's how it must stay."

"So, what about the invitation?" Ethan wafts it under his nose again.

"All part of her obsession with meeting him. Perhaps if I take someone else, she'll forget about Hugo."

"Sounds like they need to be pretty fantastic to top his legendary performance."

"I know, right."

"Darling, when the option of being in a relationship with Hugo is preferable to telling Cynthia you have split up, there is something wrong. Your mum will understand." Ethan clears away the cups and wipes down the bar. The conversation is over. "Why don't you ask that guy?"

"Who?"

"The hot artist."

"Sid?"

"Yeh. He likes you."

"You don't even know him."

"I know him better than you think. He's a member of Tilly's

Retailer Guild, so I've known him for a while."

"And you talk about me?" This is out of order.

"Darling. No. What I mean is, there is a sort of chemistry when I see you together. And you have this glow about you when you talk about him. Not now of course. Not when you are cross with me."

"It's true, I do like him. I think. But he's a client, it's unethical." Until he pays me for the last assignment.

"That was a few weeks ago. Enough time has passed to make it legal. Stop hesidating and get on with it."

"I'm not hesidating! This is not even dating, so regardless of any hesitation, it is not hesidating. This is business. It's dangerous to mix business with pleasure."

"Well then, if you don't want to make it real with Sid, go with Grans."

"Maybe, but I don't have time to think about it now." Checking my watch. "I'm meeting a client."

"Glad to hear it." Ethan walks round the bar and gives me a bear hug by means of farewell. "Cute outfit, by the way."

Today is my first meeting with a new potential client. Grans has the car, so I'm walking which is good for both the environment and my expenses (zero risk of parking penalties). The cute outfit Ethan mentioned is a pair of wide-leg dungarees, a white shirt, and a round-necked cardigan. Add my vintage tote, white pumps, a low-side ponytail and I am ready to go.

The client, Stevie, has an invite to a school reunion. The support I bring will reduce the anxiety over the impending questions. 'Who is the most successful?' 'Who earns the most money?' 'Has the biggest house?' 'The most children?' 'The best job?'

I get it. If I were to go back to my old school, well, that would never happen.

I have archived that life. That was before.

The plan is to meet at Cioccolato on Oxford Street. Stevie wants to chat over a sundae. No doubt the choice of gelato will reveal the hidden depths of our personality and help us bond. Creating a cocktail is second nature to me, but not a sundae. So many flavours and combinations. It's not as easy as choosing a couple of scoops of vanilla and tucking in. A sundae is a full five-sensation stimulation. Imagine a spoon loaded with chilled chunks of chewy chocolate brownie dripping with hot fudge sauce. As you bite, the layers are woven with smooth whipped cream, contrasting with a crunch of toasted hazelnuts.

I could be a mint choc chip and flake type of girl, but this would be a disaster if Stevie wants to share a giant unicorn and rainbow flavour bowl of sugar. Pink, blue, yellow, red, layer after layer of candy cane, bubble gum and violet flavours with marshmallow layers, raspberry syrup and a fairy dust topping. Simultaneously taking a spoon, the popping candy fizzles on our tongues, exploding as we swallow in unison.

My phone blips. It's Stevie.

Running late b with you as soon as I can.

I should grab a table in the parlour and look at the menu. Plan what I want to ask Stevie and gather my paperwork. Or I could act on Ethan's words. It just so happens that Cioccolato is the ice cream parlour close to Sid's studio so I have time to see if he wants to be my date at Jam-fest. To take a chance and see if he feels the same.

Fate can decide. If the studio is open, I will walk into the showroom and ask how he is. Ask how he's feeling. And he will look just the same and will tell me he's been waiting for this moment to come. He's started a new piece and is deep in thought, hands dirty from sculpting. The interruption will surprise him, but he is pleased. I am his muse. Since we last met, he has worked day after day, night after night, creativity flowing. Feelings ignited. Embers glowing.

The blinds are up, and the door is unlocked, but no one is here. There is art, yes. But no Sid. I move closer to his private rooms at the back, creeping like a stalker.

There are voices. Sid has someone in there, a guest. A girlfriend. The woman with the slender arms from my dream, the one with radiant skin and perfect beach hair.

He has someone else. We were always pretending, and he

made it clear I was a hired girlfriend. There was never any more to it, not from Sid anyway. Of course he doesn't want to be with me. What was I thinking?

The voices get closer and louder. The conversation is most definitely heated, full of accusations and recrimination. The voice is familiar. It sounds like...

"Sidney!" Alexandria bursts into the studio. "I see the rebound is still on the scene. None of her stuff is here, so please explain why she is interrupting our conversation?"

This layer of the Pousse-Café, harsh and tasteless, cuts through the awkwardness. Shaking it up with added crispness. Potent and direct.

Sid follows, hands pulling on his hair. Could he be smoothing it down after sex with Lexie? There are no signs of lipstick on his cheek despite the obvious passion. His grey t-shirt and raspberry cargos look rumpled, but that could be normal.

This is not the relaxed creative perfection I imagined. Not a safe environment to share my feelings. I can't ask Sid on a date to meet my parents with her watching, I'm not that brave.

Sid's eyes meet mine and his face softens, his shoulders relaxing. He steps forward, his arms reaching out.

"Kat." Sid walks past Alexandria. His stubble has developed into a light beard framing his mouth. Teeth nibble his plump lips. "What a pleasant surprise. I wasn't expecting you until later."

Sid moves in close. Closer. Closer still. His eyes say he wants to kiss me and his lips mouth a word that looks like 'sorry'.

I nod, signalling my permission expecting a kiss on the cheek that you give someone you'd only met four times and spent a grand total of thirty-six hours with. But I was wrong, this is a full-on, hard-hitting, lip-to-lip kiss.

Moist, as a maraschino cherry, the liqueur oozes out at the first bite and lingers for just a moment before running down my chin. Then comes the thick clotted cream ice cream and my tongue slips easily to reach the amoretto cut with ribbons of cherry sauce wrapped. Condensation falls on my collarbone as he teases the dessert over my lips before kissing away the sweetness. I want it so much that saliva pools in my mouth as the aromatic scent hits the back of my nostrils and I dig deep, aching to capture each flavour as if this was my last chance. But I need to slow down, the brandy snap curl, fractures easily.

His soft lips are still on mine. He tastes the almond, the maraschino and the cherry too, soaking up the essence before it is too late. His beard is soft to the touch. Fingers sweep a stray hair away from my face, tucking it neatly behind my ear before stroking my neck.

That was not Sid. But it feels the same as it does now with him. I thought nothing could replace it. But I was wrong. That was another sundae, just as perfect as the first and it tastes just as good.

Each measure is a little different. Each sprinkle one or two grains more, the elements added in a different order. Sometimes the sauce lines the bottom of the glass, sometimes a cherry laced in liqueur.

Sid relaxes, slowly exhaling, his eyes bright.

I manage. "Uh, huh." It's all I have left after he took my breath away.

"We will continue this later, Sidney. I have not finished everything I came to say." Alexandria makes for the exit, but before she storms out she looks me up and down with dark murderous disdain. "Why ARE you here?"

I don't know. Something to do with ice cream and maraschino cherries. And his touch. His lips.

And then, whatever it was it was interrupted by a shot of vodka.

"Didn't you hear me, Karen? What the hell are you wearing?"

Only a person wearing a neutral, immaculately clean, triple distilled body sculpting couture suit with nude courts would want an answer as to why I'm dressed as a fourth member of an eighties pop group. But she doesn't wait for a response.

"Kat, I am so sorry." Sid steps away, hand over mouth. "Please forgive me. I never meant to impose. Honestly, I don't normally go around randomly kissing strangers... well... acquaintances, or well... you know." Sid Richmond is embarrassed. "I'm not sure what just happened, but it got rid of Lexie, so you're a complete lifesaver. She was doing my head in and I'm late in getting to the art fair."

I touch my lips, closing my mouth. Take two breaths in and one longer breath out behind my hand. I can't ask him out, not now it is clear he wants to be rid of me as soon as humanly possible after a moment so intimate.

Sid grabs a backpack from behind the desk.

"Anyway, why are you here?"

"No reason." For you. I came here for you. And then that happened. The kiss. The passion. Was it a reaction to pent-up frustration for Alexandria?

"Are you okay? Your eyes look a bit tipsy?"

From the kiss. The Amaretto. "Fine."

"What are you doing now?"

"I have a client meeting. In Cioccolato." Stevie.

"Will it take long?"

"About an hour. Why?" He is asking me out. Oh, thank God.

"No reason." Looking at his watch. "I need to get going. Maybe see you at the fair if you fancy looking around."

"The fair?"

"At the Riverside Centre. The art fair. Sorry, I thought you'd know all about it." Sid checks himself. "But then…" Back peddling. "I'm off to check out the progress of an exhibition I'm curating. You should come along."

"Today?"

"No! No. Not now. Not today. When it's open." Sid looks flustered. "I mean, you should come along when it is ready to be viewed."

Not a date, of course not. Why would he want to see me again?

The kiss was just for show. For Alexandria.

"You best get to your client." Sid ushers me out, locking the door behind us.

As he walks away, he pulls his phone out of his bag. "On my way, yep. Should have plenty of time. At least an hour."

TWENTY TWO

Snow White

Grans insists on a weekly Monday morning breakfast meeting to review the client base and address potential issues. She says all successful businesses have performance meetings, including mine. Only today, she is a no-show.

The next client profile is ready. Well, as ready as it will ever be considering the circumstances. The kiss with Sid put me off my game. The information about Stevie doesn't offer much more than what I knew from their email enquiry.

> MOCKTAIL CLIENT MENU
>
> NAME: Stevie
>
> EVENT: High School Reunion.
>
> BIO: Non-binary nursery nurse.
>
> IF YOU WERE A COCKTAIL WHAT WOULD YOU BE: Anything brightly coloured. All flavours, all styles.
>
> LOVES: To be my authentic self and be accepted for who I am.
>
> HATES: Bigots, Bollocks and Bananas

HOW DID YOU HEAR ABOUT MOCKTAIL: Internet Search

The whole kissing incident fuddled my brain. After Sid did what he did, I met Stevie, a Vespa, in a confused daze, surrounded by reminders of intense flavours and rich sauce. I barely touched my sundae. It felt like cheating. Even the thought of picking up the spoon felt like an act of betrayal.

I wait for Grans in the boardroom/library for another ten minutes before launching a one-person search party. It's not possible she has overslept, the breakfast meetings are at eleven o'clock in the morning, right after Grans completes her morning workout. In the whole time I've lived here, she's not missed a single session.

The dance studio is deserted. The vardo locked. The yoga retreat is empty. I search every room, one by one until the last possible option. Grans' bedroom.

The handle turns but the latch does not move, it is locked from the inside. Through the door, I hear voices, muffled but one of them is definitely Grans.

The door opens.

"Oh, my dear! It's you. Well of course it's you." Grans' face is flushed as the sing-song laughter blends into the words.

"You are late for the meeting, so I came to find you. I was worried."

Grans turns away, closing the door, leaving a finger's width of a crack. Her voice is low and serious. She does have someone in there! Someone she doesn't want me to see. She has a man in there.

"Grans, is something the matter?" I knock on the door, my knuckles barely making contact with the wood.

"No, no. Just finishing up here."

That is way too much information.

Grans opens the door fully.

"That was quick." I thought older men would take longer to finish. Or perhaps that's why she is late.

"I just needed to tidy up a little. I'm ready now." Grans steps out in a dirty smock covered in paint and clay.

"Is there someone else in there?"

"No, no. Just me. I was talking to my artwork. A little project with Oak Mews I'm near completing."

"But I thought I heard a man."

"Oh ho! I wish my dear. It has been a long time since I have gotten in this state thanks to a man." Grans takes me by the arm, leading me back to the boardroom. "You must have overheard a podcast I was listening to... on... vaginal cones." She does have a man in there and doesn't want me to see him leave.

"Grans."

"Yes, dear."

"Why would a man do a podcast on vaginal cones?"

"Oh, I know! It is about time we stopped the toxic patriarchy... but of course, this podcast was by a woman. Only you heard the man's voice because he... he... he was giving his personal review of his wife's vagina after she completed the thirty days of Kegel coning."

This is far-fetched even for Grans. Clearly, she wants to keep some things in her life private from me and that is fine.

"Grans."

"Yes, dear."

"Shall we get back to business?"

"Oh ho! Yes, dear. So, tell me, how was it?" Grans asks.

"What?"

"The meeting with Stevie."

"Awful. Worse than awful."

"Was the sundae not good?"

"So good. It was almost real." Only I am not talking about the sundae with Stevie, I'm still thinking about the kiss with Sid.

"Would you like to talk about it?"

"I think that door has closed."

"Doors can be opened. Even those we fear are locked. There is always a chance."

"Not always."

"Yes always. Stevie will go to their school reunion, with or without you. I can sense it. They have been honest with themself and listened. And if you do the same–"

"What? What will happen?"

"I've been thinking. It's unhealthy to hold such animosity towards your parents. You should make peace by going to your mother's festival this year. Tell her you have split from that shit of a boyfriend and you are an independent woman. Show off your new business. Build some bridges."

That's what this is about. One too many missed calls from Cynthia and she's called in reinforcements. Cynthia put me on the risk list. At risk of going missing. At risk of going off the rails (already happened). At risk of going mad at the thought of attending another one of my mother's events alone. That's why I went to see Sid yesterday, but I failed.

"I might be persuaded if you come with me."

Grans picks up a bottle of sloe gin on the drinks cabinet, fingering the label.

"A batch from Harold at Oak Mews, you should meet him. Very talented with his micro-brewery." Grans changes the subject. There is something she does not want to tell me.

"Grans...it's okay, I'm ready to hear it." I'm adopted. I knew it! That's why I am different from the rest of my family. Apart from Grans, I mean. Please say I'm right.

"Much as I'd love to be your guest at your mother's festival. I am not invited."

"But, last year, the Country Fair."

"Kat, I wasn't there."

"The Village Fete? I am sure I saw you there."

"Nope, I wasn't invited."

"Circus, Circus?"

"No, but that one sounds fun."

"What about the–"

"My dear, I'm a little concerned you think you saw me at one of your mother's festivals when I have not been since before you were born."

"Then who was that cheerleader at the top of the human pyramid?"

"I have no idea."

"The clown making all those balloon models for the kids when I was twelve?"

"Can't help you there, but I guarantee, I don't even attempt to sneak in. Not since…"

"What?"

"Oh ho. Nothing serious. Don't worry yourself. The last time I was there, something transpired. Your mother and father decreed I was not to be invited again."

"Why?"

Queue the familiar glassy-eyed stare that preludes one of Grans' infamous stories. I sense this is a good one, especially if she dishes the dirt on Cynthia and Gordon.

"Merely a case of an unruly cocktail. I'm sure you appreciate how that can be."

More than you perceive Grans.

"Who was it?"

"No one you are familiar with. A member of parliament with a grand vision, attempting to boost his rankings in the fundraising league and meet influential benefactors linked to your father's work. I took him as my guest because he was hot property. You appreciate I fall for the dashing young powerful types…" Grans drifts again. If I'm not mistaken, she has a slight blush on her cheeks.

"And?"

"Oh! Sorry, my dear, I was just recalling the details." This could be a long one. "The theme that year was Fairy Tales."

"Fairy Tales?"

"Yes, those were the days people used to dress up."

"Sounds fun. What did you go as?"

"Snow White of course."

The relevance is lost on me, but maybe it will become clear.

"So, what happened? Why were you banished?"

"Your mother didn't have the appetite for it after…" Grans rubs her eye and wipes away a tear.

Something bad must have happened for

        a) Cynthia to ban her own mother and

        b) Grans to find it so difficult to tell me.

"It's ok Grans. You don't have to tell me if you find it too difficult. I understand."

"It's not that." Grans looks up to the ceiling. "I think I got something in my eye earlier. Things got a little messy with the, um, art."

"You said it involved a member of parliament. A real MP?"

"Yes, but he will remain a nameless person for confidentiality. Need to protect his–"

"Anonymity, yes, yes. Carry on. You were dressed as Snow White."

"Yes, and the NPC was–"

"Wait, let me guess. Prince Charming?"

"No."

"Oh, but you went as a pair?"

"Are you asking for a clue?"

"Do I need it?"

"I already gave you one if you were listening."

Already gave me one?

Fairy Tale.

Snow White.

NPC.

"We were cocktails."

"Cocktails? Snow White." Vodka, White Crème de Cacao, coconut cream. What goes with that? A fairy tale character that's also a cocktail. "Umm, a Poison Apple?"

"No. But you are getting warmer." Grans enjoys the quiz.

"The Huntsman?"

"No. Shall I give you another clue? An ingredient perhaps?"

"Yes please." I must be miles off if I need a clue.

"Port."

"Oh, I know. A Foxhunter."

"Not part of a fairy tale."

"The Seven Dwarfs? That's quite hardcore." And involves more than one NPC. No wonder Grans was slapped with an ASBO.

"And I don't remember port being one of them. But you are getting warmer. Hot even. He put the Hi Ho in my Snow White." Grans waits no longer.

Hi Ho. Gin, white port, orange bitters and a lemon peel garnish.

"Nice. I can see how that could get out of hand."

"So much so. The bar was the busiest stand. Bottles were running dry, so I went to the cellar to retrieve a fresh bottle of port, stored on the bottom shelf. The NPC followed me and mistook my kneeling down as an invitation to show me his large Cockburns. Not an unpleasant proposition, hi ho! He was very attractive in those days and once you've seen what's on offer, it's hard to refuse. Even now, he's still a catch."

So, there was someone in Grans' room this morning.

"If it wasn't for his wife and mistress, I'd reconsider a relationship of sorts with him. But no one likes to play third fiddle."

"So how did it end with you being slapped with a Jam-Fest antisocial behaviour order?"

"Before I could assist him in putting it," Grans gives a small cough, "back where it belonged, your father came searching for Champagne. I'm sorry to say he walked in just as I was taken by surprise. From his angle, it looked like I was about to sample the tipple."

"Did you point out the mistake?"

"If only I had the chance, but the NPC put a stop to it before I opened my mouth. Offered your father to savour the goods first. His boundaries are fluid if you understand me."

"And you consider this man a catch?" Wife, mistress, threesomes. It is a democracy after all and he's just trying to win all the votes.

"Oh ho! I'm sure if your father agreed, things would be very different now. Sadly, it was the end of the party for me and the NPC. He still gets my vote, ahem, if I were his constituent that is. Such a charming man. So... you see now why I am no longer invited."

It was bad with Hugo, but at least he didn't ask my dad to suck his dick.

"Maybe I should tell them what Hugo did. And I will be lucky enough to be banned as well."

"I think you would need to do a lot more than introduce Hugo to the scene to get banned. Your mother, well she would never do that to you. You are too alike."

"But... we... I'm nothing like Cynthia. We don't see eye to eye. Nothing I do is good enough. When I see her, she talks about all the great things Jeremy and Zara are doing. Anything I share is inferior, but she insists on hearing about my failings. Then she parades man after man in front of me, always disguised as a competition at the festival"

"Kat, my dear. Cynthia loves you very much. She's overcompensating because of the guilt she carries over what happened."

"Guilt? But it wasn't her fault. She didn't do it. She tried to stop me going."

"And in her mind, she failed. She failed as a mother in protecting you from harm. From the pain. And when she couldn't take away your pain, she shoulders that burden and carries your pain as if it were her own. A mother's love for her child is the strongest bond."

"And how is this supposed to help? Am I to take responsibility for her suffering as well as my own?" The guilt is almost too heavy to carry, but I drag it behind me everywhere I go.

"Kat, a mother suffers if her children are in pain. She would do anything to fix things."

"I don't need fixing. Especially not to protect her image."

"My dear, it's not about how this looks. She feels guilty. Guilty, she could not help. She lives your trauma with you".

"Guilt that she got her wish no doubt." Believe me, no one can live my trauma. Not even close.

"That's a bit harsh. She may not have approved but would never wish for you to suffer in this way. She would never wish this outcome."

"She has a funny way of showing it."

"She thought you could do better but never interfered."

"Until after."

"Everything she does is an attempt to heal your pain. Yes, she tries too hard, but please give her a chance. A shared acknowledgement of the pain you both feel will help you heal."

The risk is too great. I've already tried to put myself out there with Sid. The rejection was tough, but not as damaging as if Mother rejects me again.

TWENTY THREE

Greedy Gobbler

J am-fest seems less scary now Grans has explained everything, but work comes first and with it a new client, Greg. At least I have a solid excuse when Cynthia calls. Grans says Mother will be proud of me when I tell her I'm building my business, even if she struggles to vocalise it.

    MOCKTAIL CLIENT MENU

    NAME: Greg Storm

    EVENT: The Guild of Young Business and Commerce luncheon awards at Lintuck Castle. Celebration of the most outstanding achievements to benefit the local area.

    BIO: Successful businessman. Youngest to become CEO in the local area.

    IF YOU WERE A COCKTAIL WHAT WOULD YOU BE: Strong and confident like an aged Whiskey.

    LOVES: Profits and results of my hard work. I put the customer first in mind and deliver every time. Networking.

    HATES: Timewasters. Dating.

> HOW DID YOU HEAR ABOUT MOCKTAIL: My mother gets her hair cut at this funny little community space in Tilly Minster. The hairdresser recommended your services.

After my failure with Stevie, Grans agrees to complete the pre-work on Greg, a tech start-up entrepreneur.

Greg's business is... well, I don't understand. Once he starts talking about metadata something and artificial intelligence thingamabobs everything becomes a blur. Turns out, the only intelligence that's artificial is mine. I hope his success will rub off and I'll join the prestigious group invited to next year's Young Business and Commerce awards, but first I need to establish a brand worthy of taking public, which means levelling up Mocktail. I have some ideas but not enough to leave the fake dating behind just yet.

The event is at Lintuck Castle, a castle in name only, sitting high on the hill overlooking Tilly Brook.

Unusually, I first meet Greg at the venue, but then he's not my usual Mocktail client. I'm getting strong Boilermaker vibes and I hope I am wrong. He is certainly swift, and hard-hitting and I drink him up in one gulp. Today I'm providing a higher quality Mocktail experience, the executive package. Greg has the confidence, guts and determination that goes hand in hand with the skills needed to make a success of your own business. We have this in common, integrity, professionalism and future insight.

We meet in the car park. "Remind me why I'm here." A sudden onset of nerves brought on by Gran's car dwarfed by Greg's enormous 4x4 on steroids. Electric, of course, one the first of its kind.

"Success is more than a profit line. It is a product of image and perception." Greg dominates with a techy geek style. The cut of his seductive tuxedo mirrors that of my own. I'm wearing Tallulah's tuxedo minus the ostrich skirt. Wendy upcycled the jacket into a jumpsuit with a deep neckline, almost to the bottom of my ribcage pairs. With matching fabric joined invisibly at the waist the wide-leg trousers are split at the side up to the knee. Some would say too provocative, but dedicated businessmen like Greg have one thing on their mind, and it's not women.

"The foundation of success is insight and penetration, which means presenting the complete package, including a beautiful woman on my arm."

He cannot be serious. Is that all I am to him, an accessory to business? Greg could have chosen a crocodile skin briefcase or a silver-plated fountain pen, but thinks a woman makes him look more successful. As if appearing attractive to women will give people the confidence he can make sound business decisions.

"Won't they wonder why we only have one date?"

"It's more efficient to dedicate time to my company than the opposite sex. In this industry, a date is often a one-off."

I am learning so much. According to Greg, I'm taking the right action with my future. There is no space for relationships. Family and social life can wait while I focus on priorities. It was right not to ask Sid to Jam-Fest and take this assignment instead.

"Once I'm in the highest league of richness, ladies will flock. It doesn't matter how old I am, women are attracted to money."

Yep, definitely a misogynist, but still a master class. Sometimes the greatest learnings come from what not to do, or how not to behave. If I've learnt this much from Greg in such a short time, imagine what I can learn from the rest of his colleagues today. More than from a bunch of stuffy Women's Institute members at Mummy's festival, that's certain. Once we're settled, I'll ditch Greg and work through the rest of the entrepreneurs gleaning as much wisdom as possible.

This is easier said than done, as it is impossible to escape Greg who has me locked on his arm like a garnish. None of his fellow entrepreneurs are interested in engaging in conversation with me. I lack the zest. Greg never tires of talking shop, and they never tire of asking him to share his secrets, whilst simultaneously staring down my cleavage. The question of how we met is never answered, Greg avoids talk of his private life. I am invisible in this world of male entrepreneurs.

The awards take place during an eight-course lunch. Each category and nominees are announced between the tastes. Greg oozes confidence that his project made the grade and tells everyone. The chat is so dull, that I lost track somewhere during the first palette cleanser. Listening to how artificial intelligence improved the quality of compost created by a superbreed of earthworms does little to wet my whistle.

Although the food is locally sourced, there is no drink alternative. A mocktail and smoothie bar in the corner would be a great talk point between courses. But as I am invisible, my ideas will not be shared with them.

I excuse myself by claiming to need the toilet. Even Greg can't deny me that basic human right. This may be the tamest assignment yet, but Grans will worry if I don't make contact.

A spiral staircase leads to the central courtyard. Just far enough away from the main hall without looking rude. Navigating the narrow void, I meet Vernon, Greg's business partner. It'd be easier to pass if he was not three stone overweight and sweaty from the climb.

I step right, into a fake doorway.

"So, little bird. Tell me about this arrangement with Gregory. Is it exclusive?" The sticky Vernon squeezes his bulky frame into my nook. "How do I, let me say, hire you for a similar position?"

Grans was wrong in assessing Greg's integrity and I fell for it too. He seems so professional and so respectful. But he is quite the opposite, as clearly he told Vernon I am an escort.

Unable to text, I hit the voice note button on my phone, "The Champagnes gone flat. We should leave this narrow stairwell." And can only hope it reaches Grans.

Vernon breathes out rich coffee essence. "Let me foam you up." Licking froth from his lips whilst rubbing his right nipple. He leans closer, hypnotised by my chest. "Oh," a shaft of sunlight from the slit window illuminates his wedding ring. "Ignore this, it's not a real marriage. Not anymore. The union is, shall we say, facing exit?"

"Is your wife here?" I lean back but the wall stands firm.

"Gregory was right, you are intelligent and intuitive to the needs of man, to my needs. I need someone like you. No, I need YOU to fill my void, the way you fill Greg's." Smooth as vanilla, his hands are wet enough to slide into my void given the chance. Instead, one slips between my tuxedo lapels. "Or both of us together? We are partners after all."

Once again, I have two choices. Fight him off, which could lead to him fighting back. Or a tried and tested method of appeasement and escape when the moment is right.

Vernon gobbles at my neck, his hot tongue licking my ear. "You are good enough to eat, like chocolate liqueur." His hot hand is on my breast, fumbling for my nipple. "I want to pour cream all over you and lick you up."

Before I push him away, his other hand glides down to my crutch. He looms in, tongue hanging out.

I should not be in this position, fighting off a Greedy Gobbler. It was such a mistake to think I was considered a revered date of a young millionaire, made more attractive by his money. To be respected as a human being. Even more stupid was dreaming of the day I'm honoured for services to business and applauded as a leading woman of enterprise. Instead, I am trapped in this narrow spiral stairwell being dripped on by Vernon who is living up to his name as a Greedy Gobbler. A mix of coffee liqueur, chocolate liqueur, vanilla liqueur and heavy cream. It forms a sickly stake once shaken up into a rich and frothy drink and can only be tolerated in small doses.

"Sorry to interrupt, could I ask you to move on, I've got equipment to squeeze through and it's quite tight."

Just when I thought it couldn't get worse, I was wrong. True, the voice belongs to a person. A person that could rescue me which is a good thing. The Greedy Gobbler will remove himself from my body, I can escape and find some dignity.

But no. The voice will not rescue me. The voice will ruin all hope I have. Once they see my face, it will be over. The voice is the last person I want to find me in this situation. Who must not think I am an escort. It's bad enough being felt up by a man assuming I put out for money, without another man watching.

The voice belongs to a client and the last man who kissed me.

Sid Richmond.

"My sentiments exactly. Nice and tight." The Greedy Gobbler is not moving. "Can you find another route? I'm in the midst of a tight gap with sizable equipment myself."

"Sure, but I'm running kinda late and this is the quickest way to the hall. I need to set up before they finish the awards."

If I push Vernon back down the stairs, Sid's view will be blocked, allowing a running escape and my reputation intact.

If Vernon backs off, leaving me alone in the alcove, Sid will recognise me and He will never see me in the same way again as he did at his studio, the day we kissed.

I shove Vernon away, and hope Sid is strong enough to catch him.

Back at the table, I'm too breathless to talk. I want to confront Greg and enlighten him on how dishonourable his friend is, but they could be in this together. He told the Greedy Gobbler Vernon, I was for sharing. Neither of them can be trusted.

The assignment with Stevie was a failure and this is turning into a disaster.

Greg looks over from a conversation about a new Android app for locating toilets. He sees me differently, I can tell from his eyes. He strokes his collar, nodding. He knows what happened. Greg points, then more collar stroking.

I text Grans a selfie to show her that everything is ok.

`Why is your nipple showing?`

This is mortifying. Bloody Greedy Gobbler pulled my top open and that's what Greg was trying to tell me. My boobs are hanging out. Maybe he is a good guy after all. I straighten my tuxedo.

"Caricature between courses?" Sid pops up with his easel.

"Yes please, one of me and my partner." Greg halts his conversation, waving Vernon over.

This is my time to leave. "Excuse me, I will make myself

scarce." I stand, but Greg stops me, his hand on my wrist, ignorant to my flinch.

"What are you doing? Sit still. People must see you are invested in my performance. My category is up next."

Vernon puts his arm around me, stretching over to Greg, making me the filling to their sandwich. Sid gestures towards Greg with his pencil, tilts his head and purses his lips before pointing to the Greedy Gobbler Vernon. Asking who I'm with. Wait, he's making his pencil meet his finger, joining them up in the middle, raising his eyebrows. He thinks I am with them both.

Greg relaxes his grip as the host returns to the podium.

"Gentleman, it is my great pleasure to announce the winner of this year's young entrepreneur."

Greg stands to accept his award, commanding every pair of eyes in the room. I stand too, this is my opportunity to leave while there is a diversion.

But first I need to explain to Sid. I can't let him think I was happy with what happened. I grab his sleeve pulling him to one side. Sketches fall from the clip, cascading to the floor. And I see it. Sid drew a hideous caricature of a faceless woman in a tuxedo being spit-roasted by Greg and fat sweaty Vernon. He saw the whole thing. This is what he thinks of me.

I grasp for the sketches, panic rising in my chest. If I look at Sid, the truth will come out. His disappointment. The horror. My shame. The spot at the top of my nose burns but now is not the time for crying. I look up to the ceiling to stop my feelings coming out. Sid must know this is a mistake, but what if I try to explain and he doesn't believe me. He saw me in action on the night of the stag.

I sweep up the sketches and drag Sid outside.

"Don't move." I command as my phone rings. "Mummy. Hi."

"Kat, what time do you plan to get here?" The festival. She thinks I'm going. But I told her I was working. "Mummy, I'm kind of in the middle of something at the moment." Not the best choice of words considering Sid's sketch.

"Hugo is already here. Will you be long?"

These are the last words I expected to hear. I thought

Hugo was a ghost but he's back, like a zombie feeding on my emotions. I won't allow him to mess with me again. If this nightmare with Vernon has taught me anything it is to stop letting men walk all over me once and for all.

TWENTY FOUR

Stinger

"Mummy! I'm on my way, but please keep it a surprise for Hugo. He's worked so hard for this and I don't want to distract him from his charitable work." I switch off the phone before she replies.

There is no time to explain to Greg, my client. I must leave now and stop Hugo from doing real damage at Jam-Fest. He could steal from Mummy and Daddy. Destroy the people closest to me. Yes, Mummy and Daddy have not been my favourite people recently, but Grans explained it all. They are doing their best and so am I.

Sid grabs the papers I thrust towards him. "Kat, is everything ok?"

"Yes. No. I need to leave. Emergency at home."

"What can I do to help?"

There is no time to reply. No time to text Greg. A bad review is the least of my concerns. He's lucky I don't sue him for assault. Technically I am working for him, therefore he is liable for his friend's unsavoury behaviour. If it weren't for Sid, who knows what would have happened? No. I mustn't think like that, I'm capable of looking after myself. I don't need rescuing.

On the drive over, I practice what I would say to Hugo. Rehearsing rebuttals to his grand gesture. No amount of charm can win me back. The mission today is to stop the destruction.

Hugo holds court with the Swizzles. Eyelids flutter as

he flirts three-sixty. The Rum Swizzle, AKA Penny Hughes nuzzles up to him whilst he rubs her left buttock.

Mummy swoops in. "Kat." Voice in auditorium mode, no mic needed. "Here so soon!" She kisses my cheek, which I accept, hugging her by way of a gentle squeeze. "Hugo is dreamy. Become so popular with the ladies I swear they are addicted. Penny wants to take him home and keep him as her plaything." Mummy laughs, eyes volcanic. "But we can't let that happen now, can we?" The pressure is building, only this time we are a team.

A gap opens in the harem. I step in as Mummy whisks Penny away to look at the floral tributes to Ruby's husband Lionel, who recently passed away.

Hugo is visibly stunned by the unexpected mother-daughter synchronisation.

"What? No 'babes'? No 'chill'? Hugo. Where is my money? What are you doing here at my parents' house? Selling your druggst?" I grit my teeth, not wanting to broadcast the fact.

"What are you saying?" Hugo acts the innocent.

"For fuck's sake Hugo." I keep my voice low as more people gather to pay respects to Lionel. "I returned to the flat... after losing my job, to find you'd trashed the lot, robbing me blind."

"Babes," here it comes, "it's all been a huge, and I mean like enormous misunderstanding. I came home that day, the same as you. It must have been those two skanks. They looked a bit dodgy."

"What skanks? The apartment was empty when I left for work." I distinctly remember as I searched every room. Each was as empty as Hugo's honesty. "Why were they there?"

Hugo reaches for my hand, dark eyes pleading. "Babes, it was so long ago. Everything's slightly hazy if you know what I mean." He thinks I'm a fool. "They must've been there for provisions. But it all turned a bit absinthe if you know what I mean, and the next I remember is waking up in a crack den. It must have been a few weeks later, as, by the time I found my way home, another dude was living there. Said he'd never heard of you. It was scary, phrough. I figured I imagined the whole thing."

"Hugo, which was it? The same day, or a few weeks?" I

won't fall for his shitty lies.

"Babes, chill. Don't cause a scene in front of your family. Some dude died, and they're holding a mini service for him." Hugo's attempt to deflect won't work.

"But why leave, and with two girls?" I lower my voice. For once Hugo is right, I don't want to cause a scene.

"They drugged me. And their overlord boss dragged me away or something. It was hell, I tell you. Maybe I owed them money. I don't know." His deep muddy eyes pool as though he's having an allergic reaction to honesty.

I move closer. Despite the bullshit, I am sensitive to the infinitesimally small chance his grief is genuine. But then again, he found his way here and clearly, he's put in loads of work building his business with the Swizzles. This is evidence he's capable of effort, just not when it comes to me.

"Why are you here?" I need more.

"Mrs Clay asked me to come. Believe me babes, I am as surprised as you are to discover this is your parents' house... but great to see you, and all that." Hugo reaches out, arms open.

"Surprised? Hugo, I know this is my parents' house. I grew up here!" I fold my arms. There is no comfort here.

"I mean, I must have amnesia or something from the shock of the whole kidnapping." He wipes a tear from his eye. Wow, he has really stepped up his game.

"We can't stay here." Aside from a blubbering boyfriend, oops I mean ex-boyfriend, the risk of Daddy finding drugs is too great. Any minute the remembrance service will conclude, and Gordon will do the rounds to present some awards.

Mummy pops up. The interlude must have finished. "Kat, Hugo, you must... oh my! Hugo, are you crying?"

Now is the perfect time to end the charade. "Mummy, we've broken up. I'm taking Hugo home."

"Oh, poor things. Such a shame. Probably best. No one wants to see a grown man cry." Mummy never understood the importance of mental health. More of the bury it deep and carry-on type. Hugo wipes his face with the back of his hand. "Best go before your true colours are revealed and you drag my daughter's reputation into the gutter with you."

Grans' is right. Mummy understands everything and sees through Hugo as clearly as vodka.

"Get rid of this one, you can do much better." Mummy kisses me on the cheek, wishing me a safe journey.

Hugo sleeps and I drive, the same old routine. I plan to drop him near enough to civilisation so he survives, but far enough from my parents' house to prevent return. I head for a part-time train station near Lintuck Castle. With any luck, he'll have a long wait in the cold, dark and hopefully rainy evening.

"This is you." I wake him with a prod.

"Babes. What is this place?"

"Where you disappear from my life, again. Forever this time. Unless you return my money." That was a stupid thing to say. No amount of cash could entice me to take him back.

Hugo releases his seatbelt. "Trains ain't my style babes. You know that." His breath is intoxicating.

The car feels small as Hugo and I inch back, my retreat blocked by the door. "In that case, you could hang around for some unsuspecting girl to pray on. Move into her flat, bring your skank whore friends around and then rob her blind. That's more your style, isn't it?"

Not dejected, Hugo leans in. After the dress rehearsal with Vernon, the Greedy Gobbler, I thought I'd be more skilled at rebutting advances. But this is Hugo. Sweet and intense, his charms wash over me, saturating my resilience.

"Babes, chill." His words are smooth, heavy and hypnotic. His hand moves to my leg, testing my dicksomania.

I reach for my seatbelt, but he connects first, smoothly unclicking it before grabbing my wrist. The dull clunk of the door lock confirms my captivity.

"No babes. No chill. No Hugo." The voice in my head telling me to resist gets further and further away.

Hugo lowers the seat back and slides on top of me, his dark brooding eyes real me in. "Babes, we're good together. Sure, I want you to chill, but no need to freeze up completely. I know I put you on ice for a while, but I'm back now. See how you melt to my touch."

Hugo's hand is not the first to fondle my nipple today. But he doesn't need to know this, it will only encourage him.

"Hugo, stop. Please." But he doesn't listen. I may as well be mute today.

He pulls at my jumpsuit. "What the fuck are you wearing? How am I supposed to… fuck it! I'll tear it off with my teeth, you like that I remember."

No, you like that. And I was wearing throwaway fashion, an easy to rip the seams number. This time my tuxedo jumpsuit is reinforced with Tallulah's stitching. Tough enough to remove a tooth with any luck.

Whilst Hugo grapples with my super strong high-quality crotch, I run through my options. I could scream, but my voice is not powerful enough to breach the collision-proof door. I could wriggle out from his clutches, but I'm getting used to being metaphorically fucked over by most men I meet these days. It's been a while since the actual physical act of sex. For sure Hugo is talented, so it would not be horrific. Complicity is not so terrible when there are guaranteed rewards.

"Babes, you're gonna have to take this off before I come in my pants. I need to taste you, and this chastity suit is a bit of a barrier." He dives in for another go, pulling roughly at my clothes.

But appeasement would be going back on my hard work. Every penny earned, gone, my independence and autonomy, sucked out of me the way only Hugo does.

Plus, any chance with Sid would be ruined. Sure, what he's seen today may ruin all chances, but I could make him see it's a huge mistake. The kiss we shared must mean something. One fleeting moment with Hugo is not worth risking that.

"Hugo. It won't work." Before I resort to violence, I try to appeal. But he expertly ties one of my wrists with the seatbelt.

"Babes, chill. Let me handle this. One last go, I'll rip it open from the top." He still has half of my crotch in his mouth, the fabric muffling his dicksomaniac potency.

"No. Hugo. We're never getting back together."

"I hear you babes, but this is just a bit of fun." For him maybe.

Trapped in the smallest car in the world, handbrake digging in is not for me. Even if I wanted a bit of fun, it would not be here. Not with him.

"Please stop. Stop. Stop! STOP!" I push back but it is useless.

Somehow, the driver's door opens and Hugo disappears. He has been dragged from the car. But he locked the doors. This is all very confusing, even if it helps me. Maybe I successfully opened the door earlier, enough to stop the locking mechanism from working.

The back of Hugo's head slams against the rear window and he slides to the ground. A hand reaches in to lift me out of the car, but I am much safer on my own. For all I know, I am about to be knocked out, robbed, and Grans' car stolen.

My rescuer / potential rapist untangles me and pulls me from the car despite my protests. I push against an attempted hug only to find that once again my breasts are swinging in the wind. Thankfully there is only one working streetlight and it is at the other end of the car park, but it is too late, the damage is done.

Hugo lies limp, head slumped, a bruise already forming on the ridge of his cheekbone. Next to him, is an easel, wooden, like artists use. Like Sid was carrying earlier today.

No. No. No. No. No. No!

It can't be. With shaky legs, I slide to the ground, my head held low. I don't want to look up.

"This is becoming a habit." Sid stands in the sepia light, tone superior.

"Sid, it's not what you think. I..." Explaining is pointless.

"Kat, you could have been hurt today. What if I'd not been there?" Warming tones, the brandy soothing my nerves. Sid is complex, that is why he worked so well with Alexandria.

"I can take care of myself, and besides, he's not a client." Pointing to the heap of Hugo on the gravel. "He's..."

"Your boyfriend?" Sid takes a step back, hands on hips his tone is frosty. He is annoyed.

"No! He's an NPC."

"A what? Kat, what are you talking about?" The words

sting, Sid is on the edge.

"A nameless–"

"Yes, I know what that is, but what do you mean?" He sounds cross.

"He's nothing, nobody. I had it under control." I still can't look at him.

"Control! He was attacking you! Kat, if…" Sid exhales. "Kat, this is not how it is meant to be… was never part of your plan… if I wasn't here…" Sid sweetens, his tone fresh.

"Thank you, but I don't need you to rescue me. He's," gesturing to Hugo, "a zombie from the past. Forgotten already and will not be back in my life if I have anything to do with it."

"And the other?" The white crème de menthe cuts through.

"Other?"

"The stairwell at Lintuck Castle. The rich, sickly, frothy man pouring over you." Sid is stirring.

"The Greedy Gobbler. A misunderstanding."

"A client?" Sid sighs.

"No. His asshole friend. You know how it is." He forgets Uncle Wilfred?

"Sure." The sharp tone endures.

"Sid, I'm telling the truth, believe me. Please, I've been humiliated enough for one day."

"Kat, I…" Sid hesitates. "I'm sorry. I thought Mocktail was a good thing, but now I worry it is compounding the problem."

"Problem?" He doesn't believe me and with good reason. It's simpler to imagine I'm the problem. "The problem is you are interfering in my life. I don't need you. Despite what you think, I'm not a–"

Sid cuts me off like a blunt force. "Kat, stop! I hear you." Reaching to recover his fallen easel, ignoring Hugo. "You don't need rescuing. I've interfered in your life enough and I'm sorry."

"Listen, we are miles from anywhere. Can I give you a lift home?" Despite my protests, Sid did actually save me. And his apology sounds genuine.

"Sure. I mean. No. I've done enough damage. I should have left well enough alone. I… I'll take the train." The stinger hits. A mix of calming brandy stirred with White Crème de Menthe, fresh enough to leave a mark, the medicinal brandy delivering hard love.

Even in his rejection of me, Sid stays smooth, calm and dare I say sweet. The denial to share a lift tinged with regret. Guilt I disappointed him.

He sees me the same as everyone else. I'm the problem. And the part I'm playing. It's not really me. I'm only pretending to be fixed.

The kiss from Sid felt real, the liqueur from the maraschino cherry seeping out, spilling over my lips. The sweetness, the aroma sweet but brittle. Broken now. Shattered so easily just as I feared.

The Greedy Gobbler Vernon was real. The rich cream, shaken with bitter coffee masking the chocolate liqueur which normally brings such pleasure. Frothy, sickly, overwhelming. Sid's rescue was real. And needed.

Hugo was real. Addictive, his power over me is still as strong as ever. Ethan is right. The fuel to my dicksomania. There is no cure. Even after today, it will not be enough. Not whilst I continue pretending I am okay.

With shaky arms, I reverse out of the space, taking care not to run Hugo over. I thought the car park was empty this whole time, but there is now a black Fiat parked next to the exit. What if they saw what happened? If Sid gets into trouble, it is all my fault. Everything that happens is my fault.

TWENTY FIVE

Playmaker Cocktail

"They are all NPC's, non-player characters in the story of your life." We are in Grans' dressing room. "I'm not trying to normalise their behaviour, but people always abuse trust, even when you intend to help them. That's human nature." She dips behind the screen, appearing in a knee-length skater dress. "What we need here is a course correct. If you were on a night out and a man propositioned you, you'd be flattered."

"That depends on the man." There is a fine line between seduction and assault and it all comes down to consent. The kiss with Sid is still a secret from Grans. To mention it would only encourage her.

"So, right now we are going to try something new." Grans lifts her arms, reaching for the sky followed by a slight bend backwards and then folds in half. "There," she says, rising back up. "Now I'm warmed up, you will join me for a healing release dance."

"Don't we need to go to the studio for this?"

"Too many mirrors for this mind-body experience. Just focus on your breath and allow the gentle free movement to release tension, thoughts and beliefs." Grans moves in a way unknown to humankind. "Feel the sensations, embrace your feelings and express your thoughts through the medium of movement. Plant your feet on the ground, they are your anchor. Unclench your hands and allow the release. And when we are done, we are going to the art fair. Oak Mews have an exhibit."

The Riverside Centre is a converted merchant building on the canal. In the evening, the streets buzz with life around the venues, the bars and clubs I used to work in. In daylight, live music spills out of the park and craft stalls line the wide pavements.

Grans walks into the concourse. "There are professional pieces here and loans from the big museum in the city. But the exhibit I want to see is from the art society at Oak Mews, they've opened up a new gallery for it. Although it is in the basement, which says a lot about what the curator thinks of the work of older artists."

"Anyone I know?" My friends at Oak Mews have not mentioned this work.

"Let's take a look and see."

A sign points us past the stairs which lead to the exhibition halls, through canary yellow doors, along a corridor, down a flight of stairs and through another set of yellow doors, accessed via a secret code printed in the guidebook. This really is the arse end of the building. We are faced with the art equivalent of choosing your own adventure: to the right *SELF REFLECTION* and to the left *LET'S PLAY*.

"The guide recommends we start with *SELF REFLECTION*. We may learn something."

Grans walks to the right, but I'd much rather have fun than examine my inner flaws. In the *LET'S PLAY* room I find one of those nine square grid games where the picture is all muddled. It shouldn't be too difficult, no doubt designed to improve old folk's hand dexterity to help prevent the plague of arthritis.

The picture has a sort of calico hue combined with fluffy purple, perfect to help those with ailing sight to still enjoy the pieces, fingering their way to success. The blocks slide easily to my touch. The joints are lubricated to enhance the pleasure of the game. As a child I was a whiz at this sort of thing and would always win in family competitions. I start to build pace. "Yes, that's it." I massage the bottom row in place. The ridges are symbolic of petals. The middle piece sticks before slotting into place. Yes, it is a bud in the centre. As the last two cubes find their home, I give a celebratory skip and a mini air punch.

"It is a flower." I declare to the room. "But quite unusual. What's this in the middle?"

"Clitoris." Grans creeps up from behind.

"Ha ha, Grans. I think you mean Clematis. Although I have never seen one like this before."

"Oh ho. No, dear." Grans plants her hands on my waist, a sing-song chuckle to her voice. "It is you who are mistaken. That is Olive Groves' labia majora. Or minora. And that nubbin in the middle looks very much like her clitoris. Although the piece is actually called *OLIVE'S GROVE*. A beautiful play on words."

"So, what you are telling me is I have been playing with Olive's lady parts." And expertly if I say so myself.

"Well, someone has to, my dear from what I hear it has been a while." Grans stifles her giggles behind her guidebook.

"How long has it been for Olive?" Not as long as me. A martini glass never sits unused for long.

"Does it matter? We all have desires and are all members of a sexually active human race." Grans has a cheeky tone to her voice.

She does have a lover, I was right.

"I suppose it doesn't matter that much. I just wanted to know out of interest seeing as I have been fondling her. Maybe we should start where the guide recommends. What was it called?" Before I hear more about Grans' love life.

"*SELF REFLECTION*. Subtitled *The parts we don't normally see*." Grans leads the way.

That sounds a whole lot better. An insight into the Oak Mews gang's minds, so I can learn a little more about them. Could be paintings of world sites, or portraits of the people they love. This is going to be good.

The section is laid out with tables and benches. On each table, sit display boxes in the shape of a mirror. The theme of reflection.

"Such detail. This one is truly stunning. Here, Kat, take a look." Grans moves out of the way so I can view the article.

"Grans?"

"Yes, dear."

"Is the whole of this exhibition going to be of grannies' oysters?"

"Don't be silly. Oak Mews has male residents too."

"What is this exhibit called?" I have been brought here under false pretences.

"*DOWN THERE*," referring to the guidebook, "subtitle *Labiart and Articocks*. So clever. And this little number is…" searching for the details. "*CORINNE'S COOCHIE*. That must be Corinne Bridges. Makes a wonderful Eton mess for the summer fete each year."

"Angled to look like we were using a hand mirror." I get it.

"Exactly. The reflection of the intimate self. The defining moment in your life when you see the object of desire for the first time. So magical. It would not have the same impact if hung on the wall."

"Hard-hitting as expected from Corinne." A shot glass delivered in one swift move.

I shuffle to the next table. Before I look, I'd like to know what I'm in for.

"This is *HAROLD'S HAEMORRHOIDS*." Grans takes the first look while I compose myself. "The moulding is exquisite."

"Was this a group activity?"

"Of sorts. They have a new art teacher, who is open to letting them explore any topic of interest."

"But how?"

"A little putty, some plaster of Paris and gentle fine tuning with a scalpel."

Well, not knowing Harold, his arsehole is of no interest to me, but Grans is correct in her anal analysis. It is visually pleasing. From an artistic point of view that is. The curator used the internal lighting of the display box to present the item as a sculpture.

"Poor Harold must be in pain. Look at the size of those piles." I wince at the sight.

"Wrong again dear. That's Harold's testicles. They have a habit of getting in the way in almost every situation." Grans bobs her head from side to side.

"What?!?! How? No." I do not need to know how Grans has

insight into Harold's ball sack.

"And as Harold clearly was not going to emasculate himself, even for art, no one else had the heart to chop them off." Grans moves over the piece cupping the balls in her hands. "See."

"He must be very attached to them." I watch as Grans smiles. Was it Harold who was in her room that day?

After viewing what feels like the contents of Oak Mews drawers, we move to the next section entitled 'Look me in the eye'. But something tells me we are not about to see any faces.

Seats indicate we must again sit for each viewing.

"Ahh, another immersive experience. The guidebook says being waist height to the display in this section is of utmost importance."

Each display is hidden behind a set of mini velvet curtains.

"The art group wanted this section to be behind fake trouser zips, but the local council said it negated the element of consent before we ogle the goods on display. So, curtains it is, along with little signs asking for you to open them." Grans gestures to the first set of cords.

With the ambience of a peep show, a tug reveals more plaster of Paris mouldings. Grans searches in the guidebook for the title of the piece.

"*TALLULAH'S TRANSITION*. Isn't it beautiful? Oak Mews provides such a supportive environment, that she felt confident enough to reveal her true self to the world. I feel honoured to be a part of this."

"Can any penis be described as beautiful?" Hugo's was both attractive to the eye, and velvety smooth to touch. My mouth waters just thinking about it, despite what happened at the railway station. Once a dicksomaniac, always a dicksomaniac I guess.

Next up, Eric.

"Careful!" Grans warns as I pull on the cord. "I've heard it's likely to take your eye out. Eric has a reputation for a permanent erection ever since he took one too many tablets at the Christmas party last year. The theme was 'orgy' which he took far too seriously. The investigation into how he acquired the pills is ongoing."

This exposé is intense. I was planning to grow (possibly the wrong word to use when staring at Eric's erection), my friendship with them. Only now, how will I look them in the eye? Err face I mean.

"Once again, such detail. The artist even included his Prince Albert. I wonder if that is one of his own, or if they purchased it for the event." Grans makes a note in the guidebook to ask him next time she visits.

The final entry in this section has a very wide curtain. Grans instructs me to "Open slowly from the right-hand side." Which I do with much trepidation. "This one is entitled *EVOLUTION* and is an anonymous piece."

Inch by inch, the curtain reveals mouldings of a 'member' of Oak Mews from inert to reactive.

"I'm not entirely convinced work of this quality belongs here." Grans has that far off wistful look.

"You took the words right out of my mouth, Grans."

"Such fine examples of equality and empowerment. A signal to the world that those who live in the communal residences are not dead and forgotten, but very much alive. Take this *EVOLUTION* as an example, I challenge everyone to really take in the majesty. To carry the message it protrudes with them. I would be mighty proud if that belonged to me."

With our fill of arti-cocks, we move on to the section entitled *WHOOPS*.

"No subtitle?" I ask.

"Not this time. But I heard it was all the take-outs. The outtakes I mean. The funny elements of the work." Grans chuckles at the anticipation.

There are some definite whoops moments here. Some of the mouldings bear no human resemblance whatsoever.

"Did someone attempt to mould their buttocks?" Although not very successfully, as it looks like two dents in a large tray.

"Yes, that was Charles." Grans rolls her eyes.

"And this one is an ear? Grans, why is there an ear?"

"Oh ho. Tom's todger was so... let's just say he had a substantial amount of putty left over after his moulding, so decided he would take a cast of his ear. Such fun."

"And are these photos?"

"Yes, a sort of docu-art of the work. Everything is captured now. They can use it for social media, and promotional material. Anything."

"Come on, let's finish off where I started." I quite fancy making a penis out of building blocks.

"Goody. I've been looking forward to this. Before the group settled on plaster of Paris, they experimented with other materials. Some of which made it into this section. I'm looking forward to giving Aggie a good feel. Her breasts that is. They have been immortalised in latex."

"Before we go home, I want to thank the poor curator of the Oak Mews exhibit. For shining a light on such important issues. Despite the location." The guidebook directs us back to the foyer and then up to the main hall of local artists.

"Grans wait." I can't go in there. What if Sid is here?

"What's the matter?" Grans hooks her hand in the crook of my elbow. "Come on, I won't be long."

That's not my concern. Grans could take as long as she wants to talk to the curator, praising their work, and thanking them for their coaching and representation. And I would be happy to join her if it meant not embarrassing myself. Not bumping into Sid.

He has his back to the room which makes me even more nervous. The pounding in my chest is so loud he is going to hear. Chunks of ice fall into the bottom of an old-fashioned glass. I fight the rising panic.

"Grans, I need the toilet."

"I won't be long." Grans' grip is steadfast.

Sid Richmond turns around and surveys the room. There is a sweetness about him, effervescent and zesty amongst the low buzz of activity. I was too cutting the last time I saw him, he was only trying to help, to offer protection and comfort like a measure of Cognac. And I repaid his kindness by shouting at him and ruining the thin slither of hope that there was a chance he feels the same as I do.

Yes, there is a spark of attraction, but it is not for me. A cranberry-haired, green-eyed, effortlessly slender woman glides into his booth, her skin so pure there's no need for makeup. Her hair gently tousled, reminiscent of post-beach paddle boarding, Sid pulls his Sex on the Beach into a hug and lifts her off her feet making her laugh.

A sharp, sour taste slaps my mouth as he kisses her on the lips before spinning her round. I touch my lips remembering the Cherry Bakewell sundae. Maybe they have another flavour, it certainly looks like they are devouring something delicious.

If this woman that he is currently holding hands with, oh no… I can't look, they're kissing again. If this woman is his girlfriend, then Sid should tell Alexandria. That would get her off his case.

I detangle my arm from Grans, mumbling "thirsty."

"Hold on a few more minutes. I want to introduce you to the artist who has been coaching us for the exhibit." Grans steps forward towards Sid's booth.

My throat does that heavy-blocked thing as I realise he is the curator of the exhibition from Oak Mews. I need to leave, he must not know I am related to Grans.

"Sorry, it's already too late." I pull free, but I am too slow. He sees me. Still entwined with his fruity partner, Sid gives a brief wave. I nod in acknowledgement.

"Do you know each other?" Grans asks, leaning on his table.

Sid looks uncomfortable, probably because he is ashamed of me. "Through Mocktail."

"What's Mocktail?" The girlfriend asks.

"Kat's incredible company. She came with me to Christian's wedding. I could not have done it without her." Sid makes no attempt to keep up the charade.

"Cool gig. If you have not realised already, this one is a keeper. I'm not sure I would have been able to restrain myself if I was pretending to be someone's girlfriend."

"That depends on who it is, right Kat?" Sid makes no effort to let go of her throughout this whole conversation.

This is payback for the incidents with Vernon and Hugo. I would not have thought him this cruel, but Sidney Richmond is a Playmaker.

TWENTY SIX

Recap

"How did I get here?"
"Here, as in the Vanilla Pod?" Ethan sounds nonplussed.
"No, I know that much. I walked. I walk nearly everywhere now, Grans insists." Much as I complain I quite like it.
"Pick up more shifts here. That will keep you on your feet more." Ethan asks me to help about once a week.
"It's not that. I think I'm losing my touch."
"With your clients? With Mocktail?"
Explaining is hard. "Sometimes I feel like none of this is happening to me. Like I'm going through the motions of life for so long with no plan. Just wandering." Life is hard.
"Do any of us have a life plan?" Says the man with a wife, baby and a bar that's packed out every night.
"Why are you answering me with a question every time? I'm having a moment here. Why me? Why not me?" It's useless even asking. No one understands.
"Just trying to help. To share that we all feel that way sometimes. Your feelings are normal considering what happened." Ethan tilts his head in the patronising, sympathetic way I hate. He corrects his error after I shoot him a look.
"Normal? Considering? That's exactly what I mean. I want to be normal. Whole. No longer broken." But it's too late.
"Darling. Why do you think you are broken?" Now Ethan sounds concerned.
"I don't work in the same way anymore. I've lost it." It's so

long ago that I felt anything.

"Lost what? We all feel like we are losing our minds sometimes." Ethan moves around to the customer-facing side of the bar, sitting next to me on a high stool.

"Ethan! I'm not losing my mind. I've lost my ability. Well, not with everyone. Just one." The one that matters.

"The artist?"

"How did you know?"

"You have that melancholy look about you that says things have not gone the way you planned." Ethan stands. "Keep talking, I have a rush of inspiration that cannot wait."

"Not another Fake Orgasm. Ethan, I am not here to provide you with fuel for a mocktail menu. I am here to gain some clarity." And the confidence of a friend.

"And that you will. Tell me more about why you think you are disconnected." He turns and gathers equipment and ingredients from the bar behind him.

"The night we met. Do you remember what drink I said he was?" I say this in a way to test Ethan, not to sound like I can't remember.

"Not exactly, but you did keep asking for a Black and Tan."

"That's right, a Black and Tan." I can see that now. He showed signs of this in the library after dancing with Alexandria. "The night we met, he had a cloud hanging over him for sure."

"That indeed is the way of the Black and Tan. The contrast of lager and stout. The fresh and the mysterious. A very attractive mix." Ethan always brings it back to the sex.

"That is not my point, and you know it." Even though I agree.

"Do I?"

"So then, the next time, at the planning meeting, he was a Perry." I move us on.

"Hold up. I still haven't heard about what happened after you left here that first night." Ethan is determined to stall the conversation.

"I know less than you do about that, and asking me again is not going to bring my memory back, I feel terrible not remembering." No doubt I made a fool of myself. Gave him a handjob, or was sick on his shoes.

"Kat James! I don't know why I didn't see this before."

"What?"

"You are literally the definition of katzenjammer." Ethan laughs. "All those bad decisions, multiple drinks and heart-wrenching regret. You live your life in one permanent hangover, and it is time to move on."

"You are not making me feel any better."

"Sorry darling. But I think this conversation will help clear the fuzziness and will be the best corpse reviver you will have ever experienced. Now, tell me more about Perry, was he fresh and fruity?"

"More like clear. He had a natural sweetness, sensitive but strong. Even though he was asking for my help, he was supportive." Like meeting an old friend after years apart, you fall back into where you left off as though time was not interrupted.

"So, what happened? From what you told me he lived up to his reputation. More so in fact." Ethan is not wrong.

"Yes, at the wedding he got promoted to a Poire Prisonniére. His behaviour was unflawed. Image intact. Prepared and presented in a delicate but pristine package." If only I had ended things there. Sid would still be unspoilt.

"The epitome of perfection. Perhaps you held him too highly." Ethan is still fussing but continues the conversation with the skill of a highly distilled bartender.

"True. The doubt set in the day after the wedding." I should have ripped off his towel and tasted his cocktail when he was fresh out of the shower.

"Ahh yes, the two-for-one deal." Classic Ethan. Teasing in the face of my disaster.

"Exactly. And he's still not paid me. Despite my seeing him three times since." Not that I've asked. I'm a business owner incapable of chasing outstanding debt.

"Sounds like an oversight. I am sure he didn't mean to forget." Ethan doesn't apply this philosophy to his own business debt?

"That will be his Angel Face. The sweetness from the apples masks the hard spirits behind the eyes. Ethan, clearly Sid plays tricks and you have fallen for them too by the sounds of it."

"That's not the Sid I know. I see only the brandy. The comforting healing properties. The sweetness of the apricot liqueur. The freshness of the gin. You act as though Angel Eyes is a bad thing. As though they are hiding something." Ethan knows more than he's letting on.

"Yes. Hiding my money, a hidden agenda and a new girlfriend." Saying the words makes it real.

"A new girlfriend? Really?" Ethan turns and frowns. His faith in me is unfounded.

"I will get to that after the kiss."

"What kiss? With Sid? Why have I not been told about this?" Ethan sets aside his project and leans over the bar.

"Because I have not told you yet." No one knows.

"Was it the day after the wedding?" Ethan gives me his full attention, eager for more.

"No. The day I got mummy's invite to Jam-Fest."

"The day you asked him to go with you? Sounds like a good thing to me." Ethan slaps the bar with a tea towel. "I knew he liked you. I could tell from the first night you met. Was it suitably messy?" Eyes wide, he wants details.

"Like a Cherry Bakewell sundae."

"Did you say Cherry Bakewell sundae? Like…" It's not often Ethan looks surprised.

"Yes. Just like that. Messy, intoxicating, all-consuming. And familiar. Every time he touches me, it's the same." I can taste it now, but it means nothing to Sid.

"Kat darling! That's amazing. What are you going to do about it?"

"Nothing."

"What? Why not? You of all people know those moments don't happen all the time. Not with Hugo. Not since…" Even Ethan knows not to say it.

"Because he had a girlfriend! Sid has a girlfriend. I was wrong. He's a playmaker."

"No. No. No. He could never." Ethan shakes his head. He has faith but he was not there.

"Ethan, you don't know him. I saw him kissing her with my

own eyes. I should have seen it coming."

"How?"

"I had a dream, after my assignment with Marshal. I was driving home and saw Sid with someone. This woman. Maybe he hadn't met her yet, maybe he has been with her all along, but it was the same one. I saw this happen. I made this happen." I manifested this. Me.

"But the Cherry Bakewell sundae? That means more than a dream. More than a kiss with a random." Ethan sounds convinced.

"I know what I saw."

"I refuse to believe it. Yes, the Cognac. But with the cranberry and lemonade and lemon. No matter how fancy the garnish. You are not being played." He seems so sure.

"You don't know him in that way."

"We had a good conversation the day he came into the bar looking for you. He seemed sound." Ethan presents a drink. Deep red with a garnish of dried vanilla flower. "I'm naming this one *The Recap*."

"You named a drink after my trauma? Is there no end to you monetising my grief?" I take a sip. "It is good. Almost as good as the real thing."

"So, now we have another Kat James inspired mocktail. Prove to me you've not lost your touch. Tell me what is in the recap."

I close my eyes and inhale. The words come slow and steady. "The base is grape juice. Deep and red it makes a good substitute for port. The light sparkle is club soda, adding sweetness and life. The herbal medicinal quality comes from rooibos. Cooled to room temperature. But not only that." Another slurp detects citrus. "A splash of orange juice. Perhaps zest. And then garnished with the vanilla flower and a curl of lemon. Wait... and muddled mint. Then something else... vanilla of course. Just a drop."

"See, you've not lost your touch. As accurate as ever. You can tell your katzenjammer to fuck off. You are Kat James and ready to conquer the world." Ethan attempts a high five, but his hand hangs in the air, unanswered.

"Ethan, sometimes I look in the mirror and don't recognise

myself. This is not me. I am not me. I don't know what I am, but it is not me. This life is happening to someone else. Each time I think I am getting it right I am proved wrong."

"Darling, people cannot be bottled as easily as drinks. What started as a natural talent has expanded into defining everyone in this way. Some people are not so easy to define."

"Like Alexandria."

"Who?" Ethan crinkles at the forehead.

"Sid Richmond's ex-girlfriend."

"And why are we interested in her? She is a nothing." Ethan is right as always, but this is not about Alexandria. Not really, this is about me and my failure to function normally.

"Because she is another person I find hard to read. I know she is a Pousse-Café, but I am not sure what. Each time we meet, another layer is added. How can anyone be so complex?"

"What do you have so far?"

"First at the wedding, sambuca. Then the next day Irish cream liqueur. At Sid's studio when he kissed me, vodka. But I am not sure of the order."

"You never said he kissed you in front of his ex-girlfriend. That really does mean something." Ethan looks justified in his prior assessment.

"And what about Sid kissing someone else in front of me? That also means something."

"Darling, you're buzzing." Ethan interrupts.

"It's probably Grans." The phone is deep in my bag on vibrate. It switches to voicemail.

"Who is it? By the look on your face, not Grans."

I look at the screen. "Sid."

"Maybe he has the money he owes you. Well, go on then, let's hear it. Play the message."

"I mean, that is naughty, but would be fun." Only I've not told Ethan about the Greedy Gobbler, Vernon. Or Hugo. Sid might mention it in the message. I'm not sure this is a good thing, but take a chance and switch it to speaker.

"Hi Kat, it's Sid. I've been thinking about Lintuck Hall."

No, no, no, no. Don't say it.

"Call me or come by the studio this week? I want to chat."

The call ends, thankfully before Sid says something regretful.

"Darling! What happened at Lintuck Hall? It must have been good if he wants to meet you again."

"I... I'm not sure."

"But you have feelings for him, don't you?"

"Unethical feelings. Like a doctor kissing a patient out of hours, contravening a Hippocratic oath." Despite the familiarity, I have a choice.

"Kat, he's not your client now. Not anymore. You are free to tell him how you feel."

"Not until I get my money." I must not forget, Sid is just another man that owes me. A Playmaker with Angel Eyes who's fooled me again.

"It's open," Sid calls, concentrating on his work.

"Hi."

"Oh, hi Kat. Sorry, I'm in the middle of something, I didn't mean for you to rush over. Any time would have been fine. Can you wait for me to finish this bit? The kettle's through there if you want a brew."

An open invitation to snoop for clues. Yes, please.

Behind the gallery is a small studio apartment, converted from a storeroom. Clothes folded on shelves muddled with food and books.

"Find everything?" Sid calls through the crack I leave open.

"Yes, thanks." Apart from any evidence to resolve my conflict. The accommodation is so small, there's barely room for one person, let alone two. Pousse-Café must have been nose to nose in here with Sid, shouting in his face, high on passion.

"Take a seat, I'll be ready in a minute."

Just enough time to snoop through the books on the shelf. Nope! The door opens. When Sid says a minute, he means a minute.

"Sorry, I was..." Fingering his periodicals.

"It's okay. I gave up keeping anything private long ago. I guess that's what life is like living with a control freak. What about you?"

"Me?"

"Yes, how are you?" Sid seems very calm about the intrusion into his privacy.

"How am I?" He is asking about my ordeal with the Greedy Gobbler Vernon. The incident with Hugo. Seeing him, Sid kiss someone else. In truth, I feel devastated but can't tell him that.

"Listen. Kat, I don't wish to know the details. I saw enough to understand." Sid makes no sense. "And I feel partly responsible."

"Sid, you have nothing to do with this. I make it clear to all my clients, as I did with you, that the relationship is completely professional. Not everyone respects this, the way you do or did." I place my cup next to the sink.

"Can we stop this?"

"What?"

"Mocktail. Can we stop pretending please, just for a moment." Sid's voice is earnest.

"What do you mean? You don't like what I do?"

"No, it's not that. You are very good at what you do, but this was never meant to go beyond us."

"Sid. This is a business. I made this clear from the outset. You are a client. I do have other clients."

"Kat, you misunderstand me." He pleads.

"In that case, let me clarify things. You have a bill outstanding. And then I will go."

Sid is prepared and hands me an envelope. "Kat, wait! Don't leave like this. I asked you here to talk."

"Okay." He has nothing to say that I want to hear. Not after I saw him kissing that girl.

"Do you remember my brother, Christian?"

"Yes."

"He and Jessica are due back from their honeymoon, travelling the world for a few months. A welcome back party is planned, and my mother specifically asked for you to be there."

"Your mother?" If only Sid liked me as much as Rebecca but it is to be expected after what he's seen. He should invite his girlfriend and tell his parents we've broken up. "Is that something you'd like? You seem sorted. I mean…" The pour is too heavy, I messed up.

"That came out wrong. What I meant to say was, I have a problem and need your help."

"Because your mum would like it?"

"Not at all. Obviously, I'd like it. We get on well and Lex is arranging it. She will hate it if I bring you."

"Ah, I see." I'm being used.

"That also sounded bad. I'm nervous. Please will you come with me?"

"But your new girlfriend? Won't she be upset?"

"Girlfriend?" Sid is determined to make me explain.

"At the Riverside Centre, the art exhibition. I should explain why I was there. Grans asked me to go, and I didn't know you would be there and…you were with a girl." I was right, he is a Playmaker.

"That… is nothing. Just another artist." Sid scratches his head. "We used to be close and have remained friends. But you must believe me when I say there is nothing between us."

"You were kissing."

"Just as friends, you understand, right?"

I have truly underestimated him.

"Well, no. I could never understand that. But I guess it's not that important. You're entitled to kiss whoever you choose as a young single attractive guy."

"Sure, but I don't want you to think I go around kissing just anyone." Sid throws the kiss back in my face. "We're old friends, that's all. She's not the relationship kind. There is honestly nothing there." He is protesting too much. "It seems to me there has been a misunderstanding on both sides. Can we start over? Will you be my date to the party?"

"A date?"

"Yes."

"You mean Mocktail?" It's much simpler that way.

"Mocktail." Sid examines the floor. "Back to that." He sighs. "Of course." He looks up, eyes screwed up as though he is confused.

"I'm not sure. I mean, I need to check my calendar. Message me the dates when you have time, you're busy with your painting. We'll meet a few days before the party to discuss the details?"

"Sure" Sid relaxes, and I taste Cherry Bakewell. "How about a week today? Meet here, and we'll go out somewhere."

"It's a date. Not a date. Not a date." But I wish it were. I wish he felt the same.

TWENTY SEVEN

The Artists Cocktail

"Kat, my dear. Before you go, I have a new client for you." Grans pumps hard with her foot at the kick wheel to bring it up to speed. "Can you stop at Oak Mews on your way and meet with Harold? He has some questions about launching his brand of sloe gin."

"Harold with the haemorrhoids?"

"Didn't you know? He had those done at the clinic last week." Grans lifts her arms into the air and launches a blob of clay at the wheel. "Given him a new lease of life. Now he's not dragging around that extra load, he's got the energy to take up a new hobby." A slither of clay flings off the wheel. "So sorry my dear. I've soiled your top."

"Please tell Harold I will see him tomorrow. Right now, I'm late for a client meeting and need to change." The mud smears across my breast as I try to remove the largest splat.

A quick change into my favourite mid-wash jeans, crisp white cotton shirt and espadrilles and I'm on my way into town for the appointment with Sid. Purely professional of course, the booking was made at the request of his mother, Rebecca. She doesn't know the relationship is fake, but this only cements the success of Mocktail as a prime venture. And no, I didn't tell Grans who I was meeting so no doubt she will ask questions later as there is no new client on the books.

Before I reach for the studio bell, the door opens.

"What are you doing here?"

I could ask the same question.

"Alexandria, hi. We're having a lunch date." Not that it's any of her business. She shuts the door behind her, blocking access.

"Sidney did not mention it to me. Clearly, you slipped his mind." Lexie routes around in her bag. "We have been going through the details of Jessica and Christian's welcome home party. No time for idle lunches."

"Okay, well, have a brilliant afternoon." I attempt to shut this down.

"Lex!" Sid flings open the door. "Oh, hi," his tone softens as he reaches out towards my arm. "You forgot this," holding out Alexandria's phone in his other hand, "for all your busyness and planning."

The Pousse-Café snatches the device and marches off up the street. Without a word of thank you or goodbye.

Sid bites his lip. "Sorry, I wasn't expecting her, she just showed up."

"No need to apologise." I keep my tone light on the outside, but inside I'm a concentrated mess of tortured feelings.

Alexandria has feelings for Sid. That's why she was here. She is always here. Sid is still in love with her and he asked me here to provoke a reaction. To see if she feels the same way. And she left her phone, so she had a reason to see him again. They are playing the same game.

"I thought, a trip to the beach." Sid breaks my flow.

"Like a...?" Date. "Sid, I thought this was business. And besides, we don't have time, being pretty much the furthest point from the beach in the whole country." I misread the situation. After all that happened with the Greedy Gobbler and Hugo, I should be better at this.

Sid laughs. "This is one hundred per cent business." He holds his hands out, palms open. "Although I have deceived you, it is true. Don't be mad, but this is not all about you. I have a new art installation to check, and I thought you would like to join me. We can complete the prerequisites for our next engagement at the same time. A double business date." Sid looks me up and down. "I see you have dressed for a walk."

"I walked here."

"All the way from Kingsgate? In those shoes?" His tone is spicy, like ginger, intent to tease.

"How do you know where I live?" Oh yes, Sid took me home.

"The night of Christian's Stag," Sid reads my mind. "I just assumed you walked from home."

"I have a pair of pumps in my bag." Stroking the soft brown leather. "I walked here in them." Now is not the time to delve into this. "Whilst we walk, let's fill in the gaps in our relationship. Fake relationship I mean."

Without a doubt, we would be intimately acquainted by now, sexually, and spiritually. The Cherry Bakewell Sundae just the tip of the ice cream, fantastically eating every meal off his toned body.

Instead, the reality is him kissing lots of girls, including me. And probably Alexandria.

"Nothing much has changed." Sid plays down his womanising, running the long game. "The last few weeks have been manic with the exhibition, coaching Oak Mews, and teaching at the local college. In fact, that's what we're looking at today. As you can see, I've been too busy to even get a haircut."

The unkempt look suits him, his mouth now framed by a short beard. Hair swept forward, choppy layers framing his face. A true Artist's Cocktail.

"So, you're saying we've not seen much of each other?"

"It makes sense to stay as close to the truth as possible. We've met up a few times. Nothing overly planned. I'm not suggesting it's been entirely coincidental, but this story must withstand scrutiny."

From Alexandria. He wants to keep things casual in our storyline to keep things open for her.

"I understand."

"But if we really were dating, boyfriend and girlfriend, you do know that would not be the case, right? Yes, I've been busy, but it would not have stopped us from seeing each other. I would make more time for you, Kat." He pauses and I find myself sucked in by his rich and clear deep blue eyes.

Sid tells the truth, only it's not me he's been seeing. It's the other girl.

"Here we are." Sid stops at a gate shielding the disused land next to Artisanal Delight. "It's not open to the public yet. But as curator, I can share it with you."

"The Arches? I thought you said we were going to the beach."

"You know it?"

"No, I mean, yes. I used to work around here." I look around as if haunted by the bad memories.

Sid opens the wooden gates to the courtyard where the lockups have been converted into pop-up bars and craft studios. The perfect example of toxic masculinity. This was my idea and Sid is showing it to me as if for the first time, just another man profiting from my creativity. Sid heads to a booth, a temporary structure acting as both storage and reception and I hear a familiar voice. I try to place where I have heard her before, she sounds too young to be one of Grans' friends, is not a regular in the Vanilla Pod and not from the club. Also not one of Hugo's ready mixes.

A flash of red curls slips into the sunlight. It is Monica. Maybe she will not recognise me, but if she does, it'll be a disaster.

"Sid! Lexie said you were popping in today. You are right on time. I was about to finish my shift."

If only Lexie had kept us talking longer, I would not be in this embarrassing position. If Sid was not ready to leave, we would have been here ten minutes later. Hold on. What did she just say? Monica knows Lexie. It must be a coincidence.

"I need to freshen up." This lame excuse has failed me in the past and once again is too little, too late. I lean in to give Sid this message but he steps up to the counter missing the cue and I end up air-kissing towards the flame-haired twin.

"Sweetie. Where have you been? I've been desperate to see you again." Monica steps out from the counter straight into my kissing zone, her moist lips stain my cheek. "Oops, let me clean that up."

"Hi. Err no, I got it." The grease smudges on my palm.

"You've still not accepted my offer of dessert." Her green eyes are drunk with desire.

Thank goodness it was just a dream! And yet it seemed so

real, the dress, the red silk panties. I also dreamt about Sid that night and that girl he was kissing at the art show. Was he there too? At Tossa? I search my memory for signs, but I cannot be sure. I was too intoxicated by Monica to notice anyone else.

"I'm on a diet."

"I can find something else for you to eat." She is relentless. "Completely calorie-free."

Monica says enough to arouse Sid's curiosity.

"Now this," Sid points to us, eyes fresh and zesty, "I need to know more."

"It's nothing of any consequence, boring business stuff. And confidential you understand."

"Why did I find you locked in an indecent position with that fat sweaty man and not Monica? Boring? No." Sid is not giving up.

"Boring. Yes."

"Never when Monica is involved." Sid persists. His eyes flash.

"What would fulfil your stereotypical male fantasy? To hear that Monica and I snuck off to the toilet and we kissed in secret?"

"And Kat teased my smooth waxed pussy with her fingers, before mercilessly leaving me unsatisfied. I masturbated three times when I got home, I was so turned on I had to break out the big vibrator." Monica calls as she leaves.

"Is that what you'd like to hear?" I look Sid in the eye to call his bluff.

"Kat, you give the impression you're joking, but you forget I know Monica." He points in her direction. "And your eyes look a little tipsy right now."

"Sid, you said it yourself. The pretending comes easy. I'm almost too good sometimes."

"Almost. Meaning you are so good, it can only be true. But it's okay." He notices my muddled state. "Kat, I get it. You are serious about Mocktail. But that's not why I asked you here. Not in the fake dating sense anyway." Sid stretches out his arms. "Welcome to the beach!"

It is a beach, albeit popup, sheltered by post-industrial

cliffs.

"The sand was imported a few days ago, along with the sculptures. I'd like to make it permanent, but that depends on Lex."

The repeated reference to Alexandria slaps me around the face like a mint garnish. My face asks the obvious question.

"She works for the planning department so it's good to keep her onside." He is using her too.

"So, what are we here for?" Certainly not to have their on / off relationship thrust in my face.

"You see those deckchairs?" Sid points to a stack of wood and canvas. "I need to lay them out to best present the artwork."

The walls of the space are empty. There is no artwork.

Sid slips off his flip-flops. Stepping over the sand to some rubbish.

"Here." He points.

"Probably blown in last night. Do you want me to get a rubbish bag?"

"No, this is the art." Sid laughs. "Come and take a look."

I slide off my pumps and join him, the warm grains of sand seep through my toes.

"The brief was to recycle the material that pollutes our beaches and turn them into art. This item is constructed from beer can rings." Sid strokes the item. "Feel the textures if you like. The installation is intended to be fully immersive."

I crouch down to something ribbed poking out of a drift.

"May I take your hand?"

"Okay." It depends on what he wants to do with it.

"Like this." Sid moves closer and rests his hand over mine. He guides my fingers over the piece. "Feel the texture. The ribs represent waves. Waves that wash up broken glass, plastic, driftwood. Things that pollute can be turned into something beautiful. Beautiful to touch and look at. Everything has value."

I close my eyes as I am guided over the ridges on the bottle. Waves of emotion wash over my polluted memories. Sid is wrong, some things contaminate indefinitely. There are forever chemicals in my body that are impossible to break down and release.

"Kat, are you ok?" Sid lets go of my hand. His voice, comforting like Cognac, is wasted on me.

I open my eyes and blink away the tears. "Sorry. I–"

"Art can be powerful at stirring up emotions. I didn't mean to upset you. Can I do anything?"

"Yes." I stand up, shaking off the embarrassment. I can't believe I cried in front of a client. Sid. He will never fancy me now. "You can tell me where I need to put these deckchairs."

"Of course." Sid moves to grab the first one, wrestling it into submission. "Try placing it to the left of the lobster."

I look around but see only crisp packets and beer cans.

"To the back. It's made of plastic bags and bits of kids plastic construction bricks."

"Whilst we work, update me on the party." I need a distraction.

"Lex booked the Victorian tea rooms at Marshford Country Park. Everyone's invited, although it's not catered, so we pay for our food and drinks. I booked us afternoon tea."

Very thoughtful. "What time does it start?"

"Saturday at three."

"Great, I'll pick you up at two and we can explore the gardens first. I've never been but heard it's nice."

"How about I pick you up this time?" Sid's intentions are sweet, but the question squeezes a sour taste over the celebrations.

"Oh. No. I. I'm working. And like to–" I can't tell him the real reason.

"Of course. Sorry. Sorry. I shouldn't have asked." Sid returns to the formal. "And I'll transfer the fee this afternoon if you're happy to continue. No pressure, it may be too soon after, well you know."

He means the Greedy Gobbler but I don't want to talk about that either. "Is there a dress code for the event, anything I can bring?"

"I trust you to look the part, you have never failed me yet. The dungarees were the best, retro suits you." Sid shakes up the mood again.

I wore them the day he kissed me.

Sid gives a nervous cough, his eyes say he wants to kiss me again.

"You're playing the Copacabana."

I answer my phone. "Hi… yes. Now is good… of course, I'm still ok to help… late? I hadn't… No, nothing like that… I lost track of time, that's all. Give me thirty minutes."

Trust Ethan to ruin the moment.

TWENTY EIGHT

Flash Point

On Saturday at two pm, Sid is ready and waiting on the pavement outside his studio. No naked body, no argumentative ex-girlfriend, just Sid in dark wash jeans and a white Oxford button-down. He seems, I don't know, more together with a neatly trimmed beard and shorter-styled hair. Part of me wants to ruffle it up and turn him back into the unkempt artisan, but that is also the look of the Playmaker, the Angel Face and I am yet to identify what cocktail he presents today.

The plans to explore the garden fade away quickly as we approach the glass-fronted pavilion. Alexandria waits on sentry duty, no doubt in pursuit of high-spirited work, one hand wielding an embroidered turquoise sun umbrella, the other threatens a clipboard as she fires jobs to unsuspecting souls.

"So much for relaxing." Sid says.

"Such a set-up!" I laugh, but Alexandria is no joke. "We could help for a bit, then sneak off before she gives us more?"

"Can I hold your hand?" Sid wishes to upload the fake relationship status.

I nod the answer and his hand is warm as it slips into mine. I like it a little too much and want to slip my other hand around his waist to pull him in for a kiss, but that would open up raw feelings again and I might not be able to stop.

Sid squeezes my hand to steady my footing as the gravel path morphs into cobbles.

"Sorry. Those stones are hell for anyone in heels." Sid hasn't clocked that I'm wearing flats today. "Come on. Whatever we do will annoy her, so we may as well slack off and come back later." Sid steers us towards a break in the walled garden but Alexandria is fast and swoops in to block our exit.

"Sidney. You move those tables to make space for the jazz band. Kathy, you go inside and fold napkins." She is in full potent mode.

"It's Kat" But before Sid can correct Alexandria, she is stalking her next victim. "Fuck it!" Being decisive suits him. "Let's just go. I'm not hanging around for this shit any more." Once we're out of sight the pace slackens, and although his grip relaxes, his hand stays in mine. "Is this okay?" The ground slips away as Sid steers us to a set of stone steps.

"Yes, no heels today."

"No, is holding hands okay? When we're not pretending, I mean." Sid retrieves his hand, there is no need for a charade here.

"I hadn't noticed. It felt so normal." For a moment I forgot all about my katzenjammer.

The steps lead to a grotto-type cave.

"Tell me about today's outfit. That is a unique design, is it not?" He pauses to photograph a Romanesque-style statue in a dark alcove.

Sid is not wrong. This is a Wendy original, a combination of batik and screen printing. The kimono is cut from one piece of silk, and the three-quarter length sleeves end in daisy geometric cuffs which contrast with the floral body. Underneath I'm wearing an inky silk satin column dress. I hug the kimono tighter thinking about Uncle Wilfred's spicy eyes once he sees how revealing my dress is.

"You don't like it?" I smooth the skirt, brushing forest dust off the hem, leaning forward just enough to flash my cleavage.

"It is perfect as usual. Like I said, you never fail to nail your wardrobe." Sid turns his attention to the next attraction. "This place makes great source material."

There is much less walking than I hoped, as the camera clicks a small stone circle enclosed by a ring of silver birches.

"But it's all artificial, yes?"

"The follies are art in themselves, but when taken in a post-industrial context of environmental concern, they form a strong narrative. A portrait of mother nature versus man. How we live in conflict and harmony." Sid creates an opening for me to open up a little.

"I'm struggling to find harmony, to be honest."

"Think about what I showed you at the beach, this is a natural progression."

"But that was all fake."

"Fake it till you make it, yes? Before it was built, the beach was a ruin of humanity's industrial dream. But before that, it was nature. The beach may be fake, but it is a path to harmony. Not the smoothest, but it leads somewhere and gets people outdoors. It shows what nature and humans are capable of when working together."

"But what if it doesn't work? What if the charade only masks a deeper problem and the beauty continues to erode until there is nothing left?" And it is too late.

"We won't allow that to happen." Sid sounds so confident his actions could be so influential on something so overwhelmingly enormous.

"We?"

"Acceptance comes first, that the current state is only temporary, that things can be different. You do have the power to make a change, to make a difference." Sid makes it sound so simple. But in all the years of trying, nothing has changed. "So, what is it you'd like to be doing?"

Of all the questions, this is the most offensive and it suggests I'm content with being nothing more than an escort, batting off advances as though other people have a right to touch my body.

"What do you mean?"

"If you weren't in this line of business." The lack of awareness of what he insinuates is shocking.

"This line of business?"

"Kat, it's a genuine question. Some lawyers dream of giving it all up to buy a chateau in France and open a bed and breakfast, despite never making a bed or cooking a meal in their whole life. What is Kat the entrepreneur's next move?"

I've not even talked to Ethan about my plans. Can I trust Sid?

"I want to launch a brand of organic drinks. Mocktails really, but for anytime, anywhere, not just night-time in the bar." To sell in the café bar community. That is where the big money is. "There's a real gap in the market for locally sourced bottled drinks that are free from preservatives. I've been working with Ethan on some new creations, but the plans are all in my head."

"Not anymore." Sid points. "You just accepted that things can be different. You sent it out into the world to manifest."

Back at the pavilion, Alexandria dashes this way and that whilst the Jazz band warms up. We head to the far side of the garden and a stone bench but are intercepted.

"My dears, how good to see you both again. You look lovely together." Nora, ever the Shady Lady, might be believed if it were not for her blindness to her husband's hobby.

Uncle Wilfred bounds over, no doubt fresh from a seedy liaison in the woods with his latest squeeze.

"Sid, my boy, looking great as always. I insist on dancing with your sweetheart again. A few spins with her once the music gets into full swing will get my blood pumping." Still spicy.

Ginger Rogers is such a legendary cocktail and far too good for him, but the muddling of mint with ginger and lemon clashes against the ice all the same.

"We're planning a quiet one today, Uncle. Feeling a bit delicate after a late one, if you get my meaning." Sid stands true to his promise.

"Keeping you up at night, hey? That's my lad. Takes after his uncle does this one." Wilfred threatens.

Nora removes Uncle Wilfred before her fake smile slips, or worse, I say something regretful.

"That man is such a leech." Sid reads my mind.

"You know? I mean, is there more to this than the wedding?"

"Sure. Everyone in the family knows. The current amusement is Imogen and before that some other young girl,

Diane, Dena, or both. It looks like he has you on his list of prospective candidates to replace Imogen when she gets too serious or tiresome."

"Is that likely to happen? I thought she was in a relationship with Frannie."

"Anything is possible with Uncle Wilfred. He targets unattainable women, but for some reason, they refuse to go easily when he breaks it off."

We try another move towards the bench but are stopped again.

"Kat. Delighted you're here, you are positively glowing, I trust Sidney is looking after you. Yes, yes, of course, he is, and you him. I have never seen him so relaxed, and it is all down to you."

"Keep calm, Mum. You're still giddy after the excitement of Christian's wedding."

"And they are so happy, so you cannot blame me." The band leaps into life, interrupting Rebecca. "Do come and dance, there's no one up there at the moment."

"Later, Mum. Just let us relax first."

Fortunately, Rebecca spies someone else and dashes off before making a formal application to the society of www.mothers-who-matchmake.com.

"Sorry about Mum. Now we've moved into a *proper relationship* there are higher expectations."

I make a solo dash for the bench as Sid peels off to grab a couple of drinks. The route looks clear until Jessica, fresh-faced and sun-kissed, halts my run.

"Kat! So stylish and fabulous as always." Jessica touches the cuff on my kimono. "Sorry to jump in as soon as Sid leaves. But I must tell you, I've never seen Sid so cheery. You guys are perfect, the real thing."

"No honestly Jessica, it's just casual, we have hardly seen each other since your wedding." People in this family are obsessed with interfering in Sid's happiness.

"Well, if that is true, it's even more obvious. Have you seen the way his eyes light up when he looks at you? He can't get enough," Jessica, the newlywed has love on the brain. "He was with Alexandria for a long time, years and years. But I never saw him so content as he is right now with you, and I say that as her best friend."

It feels like an eternity until Sid returns with the drinks, and he almost makes it until Christian bounds over complete with jazz hands.

"Come on love birds." Without warning, he grabs the glasses, downing both, and pulls us onto the lawn in some pressgang-enforced dancing regime. "Time to boogie."

Once Christian relinquishes his persuasive grip, I kick off my shoes. With hands on my hips, I lift each foot in turn feeling the grass between my toes. Christian and Sid share a joke, and Jessica pulls her husband into an embrace leaving me alone with Sid.

"Will you dance with me?" Sid's eyes spark with meaning.

I thought he would never ask. As the jazz flows. Each note defines us and this peculiar relationship. Haphazard and chaotic it holds harmonious predictable unpredictability. Erratic by nature, what we have is undefined, yet here is a band playing our tune. Sid leans in, stopping before our bodies touch.

The melody switches up to a swing and Sid moulds his stance to fit mine. The saxophone launches a tumultuous campaign on a skipped beat, raising the temperature. My hands lift higher, reflecting Sid's pose and we continue to mirror until the beat shifts and the pace slows to a standstill.

A horn shrills into the silence. A new melody in the pandemonium of disharmony and I itch to touch him, to pull him into me. Until this point, the notes have been short and erratic, but now there is an unceasing pitch and we drown in the note. The vibrations run through my body into my core and heat builds. My nipples pinch as my satin dress glides up against Sid's shirt and I want him to touch me, everywhere. I lift one leg, resting my thigh on his hip. I imagine his hand sweeping up, sliding into the slit of my dress, grabbing my ass and pulling me close.

A pause hangs in the air stirring up anticipation. Almost inaudible, the gentle swish on the snare drum marks the unheard beat and our breaths deepen to match the pace. I want to rip open his shirt to taste him.

Clock! The short wood sticks sound out, as the bartender lays down a shot glass on the bar. Clock! Another one and another lined up in a row. All the time, the low hum of the snare drum's circular rhythm mimics the hum of chatter. A long line of shot glasses waits, empty. The wooden rasp grinds out, steady like the hand that holds the bottle as it glides along the rims, careful not to spill a single drop. Heat grows between my thighs, as I think about slipping my hand into his jeans, to find Sid's cock bulging, ready to spill over. Desperate to taste. Lick. Suck. Swallow.

The snare drum builds to a light tap, the temperature building with each measure. The bartender sparks up a lighter and I am close enough to feel the heat from Sid's body. The flash point is where the danger lies. A flicker skims the shot glasses and the liquid bursts into life. If controlled it provides satisfaction, but too hasty and the flame mingles with the alcohol before it is even settled, rushing up into the bottle creating a back blow. A Molotov cocktail exploding in unqualified hands.

Our lips are too close to the flame. A crash of cymbals pulls me back to reality but a divot catches my foot sending me forward into his lips and the fire, the burn deep enough to scar.

"I need to freshen up. It's hot out here." My fake hand fanning fools no one.

"Sure. I'll get you that drink. To cool you down." Sid smooths his hair. Hair, I want to touch, tousle and twist between my fingers. To grip as he pushes inside of me.

I want him. All of him.

We didn't actually kiss but we got close enough to burn. I hold my wrists under cold water, as sweat runs down my brow. It got too hot for me. I crossed the line. No more Mocktail assignments. No visiting Sid's studio. No trips to exhibitions, beaches, or wooded parkland. These feelings put me at risk of ruining what I have worked hard for, he must understand after what happened with Vernon.

Back outside I keep to the shade to avoid Sid, the burn and the truth.

> Grans. The Champagne is flat.

The meaning is clear, she will understand.

On the far side of the lawn, Sid chats to Christian. A selfie captures the moment, both brothers relaxed and smiling. Sid checks out the shot, then beckons me over.

"Sid, it's time I went. There's been too much sun today." A solid excuse. After all, I am visibly glowing from the fire.

"Sure. This is all ending here, anyway. Are you okay? Listen, I've barely had one drink, let me..." His hand hovers in the small of my back. "Sorry. No. No. Of course, not."

My job is done, he needs me no more.

"Sid, you are needed here. Stay, please." But I must leave, alone.

"Kat, we're going to my parents house for food, you're welcome to join." Christian interjects. "Mother insists I persuade you."

"That is such a lovely offer, but..."

"Christian," Sid prevents me from making more pathetic excuses, eager to conclude our pretend romance. "Kat wants to ditch us. I'll walk her to the car."

"I really am sorry." And I am. It would be easy to give in and ruin everything.

"Well, I'll never hear the end of this from Mum. But we'll catch up soon, yes?" Christian shares his wife's enthusiasm for matchmaking.

I laugh nervously. The Richmond brothers are flirtatiously charming and it would be so easy to accept. Sid leads me to the carpark, escorting me out of his life. The break is almost complete.

"Guys, you look so loved up. I literally saw the sparks fly earlier like you were on fire. I miss the honeymoon period." Jessica leaps out from nowhere.

That was the flash point! She saw it, everyone saw it.

"Sure. But it's you and Christian who are technically honeymooners." Sid interjects. "Kat and I are..."

We are over. It was only ever fake. Nothing more than a charade. We played a big joke on everyone.

"Sid! We've been together for years, but you're just starting out. I remember what it was like. You could barely keep your hands off each other earlier, we all saw it."

"Babe, have you told them about the change of plans?" Christian, never far from his wife, puts his arm around Sid.

"No, not yet." Jessica skips on the spot.

"They caught Uncle Wilfred in a compromising position with a waitress in the secret folly behind the woods. Mum and Dad have ditched us, cancelled the dinner and called an intervention."

"Interventions are super dull, so we're having a secret after-party. You two must join us." Jessica waves her crossed fingers in the air.

"Kat's not feeling too good…" Sid holds strong.

It's over. He knows it too. He can tell I'm catching feelings so needs to get rid of me. This is not what we agreed.

"We're all tired but you will soon get a second wind." Jessica squeezes my hand excitedly.

"Sid wants…" But I have no excuse prepared.

"Please say you'll come. We will all be together without the formality of weddings and welcome-home garden parties." Jessica begs.

"What were you thinking, Bro?" Sid gives them hope. Unless he intends to go on his own.

"The club on the canal, do you know it?"

"The Lock Wheel?" I know it well.

"Yes. Straight there for drinks and a proper celebration once we're clear of the oldies." Christian has renewed energy already.

"Please say yes, Kat." Jessica is not giving up. Reluctantly, I nod to get them off my case.

"Amazing! See you later," Christian peels Jessica away.

"We need more people, come on babes." Jessica jogs off in the direction of the pavilion.

Sid waits for them to move out of hearing distance. "Kat, wait. Don't leave, I have something to say."

"Sid, no." Key in hand, I unlock the car.

"Kat." Sid persists. "Can we agree you're now officially finished for the day? No more Mocktail."

"Absolutely. Our business together is concluded." And I'm

leaving. This one-sided attraction hurts too much.

"So. No more pretence."

"No." I'm too close to caving in.

"The Lock Wheel, you don't have to come. But," Sid sucks on his bottom lip, "I'd really love it if you did."

"Sid…"

"Kat, I like you, and enjoy spending time with you."

Maybe this pretence is so perfectly planned out, that he's starting to believe it too.

"Just leave me a glowing review on the website instead."

"Listen, whatever happened earlier to upset you? If it's something I've done, I'm sorry. Come out tonight, it could be fun. I like you, and I thought you liked me too."

He just told me he likes me after thinking the way I feel about him is an act. This makes it hard to say no.

"Sid, I'm not sure."

"Off the clock, no more work and no more Mocktail. An opportunity to celebrate our success. A business agreement that went well."

"I would only be a drag."

"You're kidding. You are anything but boring." He knows nothing about the real me. "No more business I promise. And if it's hideous, you can leave."

I am not sure.

"Hurry love birds, we're leaving." Christian and Jessica jump into their car.

"Okay." The words tumble out before I can change my mind.

"What did you say?" He implores.

"Yes, I will come with you."

Sid smiles so hard his face is at risk of breaking.

TWENTY NINE

Grand Marnier

I park opposite Delight and the location of my untimely sacking. A nod to the doormen confirms no harm will come to Grans' Mini for the next twenty-four hours. I may not hold the respect of Dextra Dominica, but my peers and colleagues valued my efforts.

The entrance to the club is across an old lock on the canal. The Lock Wheel, a refurbished Dutch barge, sits partly in the water and the rest an extension on dry land.

"Kat, good to have you back. Keepin' well?" A Velvet Hammer greets us at the door.

"Always a pleasure Dom. How's the family?" I hug my kimono as the temperature fades.

"Grand thanks. The twins are at school now."

"No way! They grow up fast, don't they?"

Dom opens the door to the bar, welcoming us in.

Iain, the barman, otherwise known as a Sea Captain Special, has my drink prepared before we take two steps into the room. Dom must have radioed through.

"Not working tonight?" Iain hands me a glass.

"Thanks, Iain." The drink is clear and unlikely to be water. "No, off the clock for once."

A small sip confirms my suspicions, it is a double vodka and soda and the first alcoholic drink I've held in my hand for a few weeks. With the support from Grans and Ethan, I have been living the true mocktail life for a few weeks.

Sid orders a pint, reaching for his wallet.

"No charge for you guys." Iain waves away the offer.

"Thanks, Iain, you star. How's the studying?"

Iain took bar work to support his paramedic training. I don't know how he juggles studying, working nights and pulling shifts on the ambulance.

"Not bad, I qualify this year. Then I can kiss this place goodbye for good."

"Great news! Well, good luck."

Sid follows me into the main saloon bombarding me with silent questions.

"I worked in the Lock Wheel before I met Hugo. It was a great place, not that I remember much, too many of these." Gesturing to the liquid capable of sending me straight back to where this all started and the night I met Sid.

That could be a good thing if it helps me remember.

I pour my drink into the display foliage, but the minute I make the drop, Toni, the deputy manager and Southern Comfort, delivers a fresh drink, another double vodka and soda. This is not going well. Yes, I am officially off the clock, but Sid is still a client and if this afternoon is anything to go by, I need all my wits about me.

And so the evening continues. When I'm within spitting distance of a bar, they hand me another double vodka and soda. In return, I take one or two sips and leave them on tables, hand them to familiar-looking people, or pour them into empty Champagne buckets. I thought I was being discreet.

"How come you've palmed off your drinks all night?" Sid finds his voice.

"What do you mean?" Subterfuge is not my strength.

"And you know everyone here." Not an answer.

"I was the manager."

"You never drink more than two sips." Sid boomerangs back around.

"And what is wrong with that?" Two sips per drink times multiple drinks must add up to quite a few drinks for a person who's out of practice.

"Nothing. But I thought we agreed to no more Mocktail

today."

"I don't want things to get messy." That should be enough of an explanation.

"Messy?"

"Yes, messy."

"How so?"

"Like the night we met."

"That was fun." Sid laughs. "And gave birth to your new business. It was the start of something new, something good."

Now is not the time to tell him I don't remember.

"Look, I used to party hard, then one day, I lost pretty much everything. Alcohol makes bad decisions."

"Sure. But when the world falls apart, don't quit having fun. Call it a plot twist in the story of your life and carry on."

"And that's exactly what I've done. I was a mess that night." And will never go back there again.

"Okay. Forget the drinks, let's dance, have a laugh and see how the evening goes?"

"Define laugh?" I am such a bore and super scared by how close we got earlier. The flame has been lit. You don't actually need to touch to reach a flash point, so the question for me now is, do I let it burn or should I extinguish it before I get hurt?

"Silly dancing, random chat, relax a little. You be Kat and I will be Sid. No baggage, no work, no agenda."

I finish my drink. One can't hurt, but of course, another is immediately placed in my hand.

Sid says something amusing and makes me laugh in a way I'm not used to. I drink a bit more. Just a sip. He is charming, but not in a sleazy way. With Hugo, there was always an ulterior motive, usually something underhand.

Christian and Jessica are in the Flybridge, the disco room. Home of drunken dancing, shouty singing, and getting down and dirty. Sid gestures towards the deep beat sounds with a hypnotic hip wiggle and the end of his belt hangs free, teasing to be grabbed. I want to reel him in and slip my hand in the top of his jeans. To touch his toned stomach and slide my hand up his chest. To taste his lips. I finish my drink and follow him onto the dance floor.

The space fills up and we are pushed closer together. Pheromones spritz with every twerk as bodies clash and people mix. Jessica beams over from the corner where she is trapped with Christian and gives two thumbs up. I am nose to nose with Sid, each movement measured so as not to brush his lips. The risk of burning is too great. We breathe the same air, sweet and clear. I imagine being as free as the other dancers here. His hands rest on my hips, grinding to the beat of the music, lips tease, grazing up my neck. Damn those drinks, this is harder than I thought. I close my eyes like a child playing hide and seek. If I can't see this, it's not happening.

The energy shifts as his body tenses. The scent of orange is subtle, but not undetectable. Alexandria glides into the room bringing with her another layer to the Pousse-Café. Grand Marnier offers comfort like Cognac, only Alexandra harnesses its bitter origins. She is not alone and Sid's jaw pulsates, anger in his eyes.

"I'm too hot. Can we get some air?" I shout to be heard above the music and lead him through the bar and punch the code into a keypad leading onto the VIP deck. "We won't be disturbed here."

A slither of sunset hangs on the horizon, the moon faint, casting a light glow on the calm water that kisses the stern. We fling ourselves onto sofas reclining in the anonymity of the shadows,

"How did you do that? Make us disappear? Are we allowed up here?" More questions. Sid slumps next to me on the cushions.

"I remember the code, it's fine." I rub my arms to keep warm.

"You were amazing to work for. Or at least trustworthy if the codes are unchanged."

"Probably too soft and definitely too busy partying to assess if anyone was doing anything wrong. I was more interested in being their friend than a manager." Clearly not good enough or I'd still be employed. Not that I got the sack from the Lock Wheel. I was very successful here.

Goosebumps on my arms. Instinctively, Sid removes his blazer, "May I?" A nod and he tucks it over my shoulders. "Kat?"

"The answer's yes."

Gentle fingers under my chin, lifting my lips to meet his. The kiss is tender, with a garnish of tension wound into tight curls. Respectful, slow and measured, each taste, each flavour gently layered to preserve what's gone before.

The fairy lights surrounding the decking click on. Someone is coming.

Out of impulse, I slip my arms into the jacket and grab Sid's hand. Another door and a flight of stairs and I punch a number into the office keypad. Too fast and it fails. I try again and the lock clicks open.

Sid leans me up against the desk, "Is this okay?" his hands hovering, nerves exposed with a gentle shake. "Is this what you want?"

"You can stop asking now Sid." I run my hands down his chest reaching for his belt.

"I just want to make sure." He lifts me onto the desk with no effort, eyes still searching for approval, and I nod.

Sid's arm slips under the jacket, circling around, his fingers land lightly on my back. His kiss consumes all the layers at once, growing deeper, the flames ignited and taking hold. A hand moves to my waist, his eyes once again seeking approval, before moving down my thigh. I wiggle from side to side as he gently slides the silk up, freeing my legs to wrap around his waist.

Only now do I regret listening to Grans' advice about underwear. As usual, when I prepared for the assignment, she insisted on me wearing a full set of lingerie. "None of this modern stuff, dear. A proper bra, French knickers and stockings will be your armour."

All ladylike propriety has been shattered thanks to the vodka, Sid's hand rests on my knee, fingers caressing the crease behind. His other hand supports my head as he plants kisses up my neck, resting at my ear, each breath deepening.

"You feel amazing, like silk."

I have no answer for this.

His hand moves up my leg, slipping under my dress and I taste the liqueur on his lips getting drunk on his essence. Sid moves up my thigh reaching the lace on my silk stocking, mouths connected the entire time. I pull him closer, still searching for the belt buckle. My armour shattered. Protection gone. Sid is Sid and I want him.

His hand glides effortlessly over the lace, fingers meeting my skin. Now it is Sid's turn to pause, moving his hands to rest either side of me on the edge of the desk. A deep inhale precedes a slow exhale.

"Who? What? I mean, you're killing me here with these stockings." Desire spills from his eyes.

"It is my armour." The humour breaks the tension and an opportunity to pop open the fly buttons on his jeans slipping my hand in to feel him. I reach inside his shorts, fingers teasing the top of his erection. "I want to taste you."

Sid groans as his hand returns to my thigh, sliding up into my French knickers. "Wait your turn." My pelvis tilts, willing him to explore further as his fingers tease. I hold my breath. This is finally happening. His thumb slides closer.

"It feels so good. I want you now." I push down his jeans.

We are so frantic we rattle the furniture. I pause but the noise continues. Rattling. Rattling.

Sid is rattling?

No. Not Sid.

Oh no! I forgot to put the security lock on and the door opens too quickly for me to do anything but hide my face in Sid's shoulder.

"Shit, sorry Kat, I didn't know you were in here. Just like old times, eh?" Laughing, the person is gone as swiftly as they entered.

The crew are used to me using this room for escapades and think nothing of it, but Sid must wonder how many other men I have brought to this office for similar activities. In truth, he is one of many in a long line, but I don't care about the others, they were just fun, something to pass the time on a slow evening. This is different. He is my flash point and I've ruined it because I didn't stay in control. Because I let the moment run away with me. My legs loosen their grip on his waist. Sid's head hangs low, breath still quickened. He's ashamed. Regretful.

"Shit!" Not quite an apology, but all I can manage.

"Kat. I... We should get out of here. This was..." Sid's heart beats fast in his chest as I place my hand on his shirt. A stop sign.

"A mistake and should not have happened."

"No. I mean this is not normally how I do things. Can we–"

"Sid, stop. I let my feelings–"

"Feelings?" Sid questions the meaning of what we just did, his eyes searching. For him, feelings were never involved.

"I have to go. This is so unprofessional." My attempt at an apology is pitiful.

"Unprofessional? No, Kat," Sid moves aside as I straighten my clothes whilst making for the door. "Wait, it's not what you think–"

"Please apologise to your brother. You only need to make up one more lie when you tell them we split up. It shouldn't be too difficult for you."

The cool air on the deck is sobering and my brain whirls with what I just did.

I nearly had sex with Sid. A client!

I was so stupid and reckless. I condemned the behaviour of Fat Sweaty Vernon but allowed Sid to do the same. More than that. I encouraged him. I wanted him to touch me. It is immoral and beyond unprofessional.

I have a real problem. Ethan is right, I am a serial dicksomaniac. It was far too easy for Sid to cajole me into a free appointment under the illusion of a celebration, ply me with alcohol and seduce me. He knew it would be easy after everything he's witnessed up to this point. He was playing me the whole time, working up to this moment. A set-up from the start, well not quite the start.

I cannot trust him or anyone. Despite the humiliation, it's good we were interrupted.

The boat lurches sharply to the left, shaking up my stomach. I rush to the side, feeling my way to the exit.

"Kat, wait!" Sid calls. He followed me.

But I don't look back. I can't look back and risk getting burned again.

It is over.

THIRTY

Hot Chocolate Comfort

The evening events play on my mind.
"And then he shouted 'Kat! Wait. Don't leave like this.' As if that would stop me."
"How did he sound?" Grans presents an oversized mug piled high with whipped cream and shards of cacao nibs.
"Remorseful, I like to think, but it's all a calculated plan. From the start, he plotted for this to happen. He manipulated me, just like all the others." The cream glides into my mouth, melting away to leave the bitter raw crunch.
"I'm not sure he'd manipulate you into that." Grans defends the man she has never met.
"How do you mean?"
"He just doesn't seem the type, that's all." She cradles her mug.
"But Grans, you don't know him." Hold up, she met him at the Art Fair. But she doesn't know he is a client, my first client. Unless he told her.
"Yes, yes. You are right. So, what did you do? When he called out."
"Of course, I wondered if I had made a mistake but he didn't follow and I couldn't look back." He's never going to have serious feelings for me.
"My dear, a kiss sounds the complete opposite of a mistake." Grans holds her hand to her chest. "How was it? Cork popping good?"
"Flash point good."
"Even better." Grans licks the top of her cream.

It was possibly the best kiss I've ever had, but I can't admit that to Grans. And, she must never know I nearly fucked Sid on the desk. Yes, it was all in the heat of the moment, but given half a chance, I would do it again.

"No! Grans, he paid me to spend the afternoon with him. It doesn't matter if I was off the clock, he is a client. Technically it makes me a–"

"Person who is following their heart." Grans interrupts. Still defending the man she has only met in a professional art capacity.

"A person who can't tell the difference between fake and reality."

"And I suppose that's a fake jacket you're wearing."

"What?" In my panicked state, I hadn't noticed that I am still wearing his jacket.

A chirp sounds and we both hunt for our phones. But it's not for me, Sid will have found another girl in the club to replace me, maybe even Alexandria and it's all my fault. If he did want something serious, he should ask me on a proper date instead of trying to seduce me in the back room of a club.

Grans looks up from her phone. "How did you get home?" Still tapping the screen as I answer.

"Don't worry Grans, your car is safe. The security team at Artisan are watching it for the night. I walked as far as the Vanilla Pod, but Ethan had closed up. A city bike would be impossible in this dress, so I took an e/skooter for the first time and it was so easy to ride, I'm a natural. It zoomed up Castle Walk like there was no hill at all." I take a sip of the hot chocolate as Grans types away. "Is everything ok? Is someone hurt?" Someone at Oak Mews.

"No!" Putting the phone down. "Just a late-night booty call. Now drink up."

A late night booty call? I want to ask who from, but I'm not sure I am ready to hear the answer. So I sip my drink and pretend the conversation never happened.

The hot chocolate is rich and smooth. "Grans, this is amazing."

"Made with real chocolate. And a little something else."

Sounds like it takes a long time to make. "How did you know I would be back? I forgot to message in all the stress." The hot toddy was on the stove when I opened the door.

"A grandmother can sense when someone needs a Hot Chocolate Comfort."

"Southern Comfort, right?" A little too close to Grand Marnier for my liking, but it hits the spot.

I power down my phone. I can already feel myself spiralling so I need to minimise the katzenjammer as much as possible. If he feels the same as I do, he knows where to find me.

Grans changes the topic much to my relief. "Have you heard about the Centenary Ball?"

"I don't think so. Maybe Ethan mentioned something."

"It's taking place next month at the town hall." She lays the invitation on the table reading aloud. "*Come and celebrate 100 years of Tilly Minster and Newtown Tilly. Keynote speech and displays from The Tilly schools.* You get a formal meal followed by music through the generations. It is the event of the year, a century even! Sadly, I cannot attend. Your mother has booked a spa visit. For us to build some bridges."

"Yes," I remember. "Ethan has mentioned the ball. He's running a pop-up bar. Perfect to keep the Vanilla Pod on the map as he's outside the trendy Oxford Road district."

"Oh ho! But beautiful Castle Walk should be enough."

"Once people appreciate the heritage, they will see the value in walking a little further away from the sterile modern clean lines of the new clubs and bars."

"Will he need you to help? It's just I promised Alfred I would be his date, and with him not being well recently, I hoped you would take my place." Grans gets to the point.

"Of course, I will. Poor Alfred. Is he okay?"

"I am a little worried. He is going through so much at the moment, but nothing to worry about, just not up to driving. Needs someone with him. Hates being alone. You know how men can be."

"Not really, Grans. But maybe this will help."

THIRTY ONE

Kahlua

To prepare for the ball, I pop to Oak Mews to catch up with Alfred. This new style Mocktail will be free from letching, inappropriate touching and most of all, free from feeling.

A new banner hangs large and proud at the entrance. 'Rooms available. New residents welcome.'

This is never a good sign when it comes to a nursing home, sorry, community for older people. Availability means someone died and probably in the bed you are about to move into. This is truly terrible advertising.

"Are you here to say goodbye?" Sandy greets me at the door, same uniform, same indoor wellies squeak as she welcomes me in.

"I'm here for Alfred, I promised to partner with him at the Ball."

"Alfred would be glad to have known you were here. This is a big change for him, we thought we'd never get rid of him."

Alfred must know the deceased. How awful. He will be dreadfully upset.

Alfred's room is empty and I mean really empty. Something is wrong. There are no empty teacups. No plates strewn with biscuit crumbs. It's too ordered, too tidy. I check and yes, this is his room, his name is on the door. But he is not here.

Sandy said they thought they'd never get rid of him. What if he is the one who died?

Alfred is dead.

Grans said something about him not being well. I should

have come over straight away, this is all my fault. The stress of going to the ball alone was too much of a strain and he collapsed before I could reassure him. Maybe he was worried about the money, but I would have given a retired person's discount. Hopefully, he died peacefully in his sleep. A stroke, but still my fault, the stress of everything was too much for him.

I rush out of the room and collide with Anne carrying an empty bedpan. That was close! Imagine if I'd knocked her over going the other way when it was full. Eeeuw!

"Kat. How are you today?"

"Wondering where Alfred is. We had a meeting arranged and I can't find him anywhere."

"Oh, you've not heard? He's no longer with us." Anne sounds a little too jolly for such morbid news.

It is happening just as I feared. The Oak Mews gang are falling apart bit by bit, starting with Alfred.

"He's gone?"

"Yes, that's what happens when there's a death. But we didn't think it would happen like this. It was quicker than we hoped."

So it is true. Alfred is dead and there's not a shred of emotion in her eyes. In his room, I am the closest I can be to him now, surrounded by what is left of his things. The smell of disinfectant already doing its work. They move so fast. It's only money to them. Alfred was worth more than that, more to me anyway.

Sandy pops her head around the door.

"Just one more box and then we are free of this one. Doesn't normally happen this way. It was a bit of a shock."

"How did he die?"

"A car accident." Sandy removes Alfred's name from the clip on the door.

Then it is my fault. He tried to drive somewhere on his own, I could have stopped this from happening. I could have driven him anywhere he wanted. My eyes fill with tears, like an over-filled glass, a drop teeters on the rim.

"Don't worry. It was instantaneous, he didn't feel a thing. Best way really."

"That doesn't make it any easier."

"Well, Vera says we need to treat this as a celebration. They normally suffer before leaving us. This time it was one bang, and he was gone."

Her level of disconnection reaches new heights. When there is a bottom line involved, feelings are removed quicker than the deceased's possessions.

Now he is gone, I want to touch some of his things but all that is left is one box.

"Oh, Alfred. I can't believe you are going. Gone." I pretend he can hear me, wherever he is. "I have a friend. Will you give him a message if you see him?"

"I've not met anyone yet. How will I recognise him?" I didn't expect a response, but of course, it makes sense. It sounds just like him. If only everyone stayed as fresh in my mind.

"It's been a few years since I saw him." Smelt him, tasted him.

"How long?" Alfred's voice is soft and comforting. He sounds at peace.

"Almost ten years." But more like an eternity.

"Did you lose touch?"

"Well, yes, it's hard to speak to people there."

"Not even on socials?"

"Definitely not. Although I leave heaps of voice mails, he can't reply." It has been too long to hear his voice.

"That's a shame, I'm sure Vera said I'd still be able to use it. How else can I keep up with everyone at Oak Mews?" Alfred sounds a little worried death will be more peaceful than he hoped.

"Do people age in heaven?" I could describe him but he may not look the same.

"I don't know."

"Only time will tell." Every day is one day closer to being reunited.

"Kat, what happened to your friend?" Alfred feels right behind me.

"He died." With no one listening, it's ok to say this out loud.

"Is it him you are crying for?"

I look out the window. I never believed in ghosts but I guess the closer you are to someone, or the more you need the person, they will find a way to speak.

"Will you take this last box with you? I think the managers are keen to celebrate my departure. The quicker it's gone, the sooner they can get on with it." Even the voice of Alfred wants to clear out of here sharpish.

"Why are they so happy? The sign has gone up before we can grieve."

"So efficient considering the lack of notice. Of course, I need to make it up to them." Alfred laughs from his restful location.

"They made you pay for it?"

"Oh yes. Insisted. Said I should have a good many years here and now they would be out of pocket."

"I always took Oak Mews to be so caring." But to make money in such shocking circumstances. They are as heartless as the rest of the world.

"Oh, I don't mind. I don't need the money where I'm going." Alfred is resigned.

"I suppose not. Heaven doesn't cost anything."

"Haven. Haven Homes. That's what it's called. I've been waiting for ages to move in with Vera, but I'm allergic to her cat. Anyway, her cat died, nothing to do with me honestly. So now the path is clear, we can spend all our time together." Alfred takes my hand. "It's okay. I'm still here. Here for you if you need me."

Public speaking was never part of my portfolio. So a keynote speech at a funeral is a whole new experience for me and not just because of sobriety. Alfred insists it will help me grieve. What was said in his room has never been mentioned again, but he's making noises that he wants to help.

But it is all too late now. I'm the one that lives. Reminded every day. Nothing could fill the void, no funeral, no memorial service, no charitable activity. I missed them all. Not everyone comes back to life, like Alfred.

Grans holds up her black mini dress, the one I wore at the first Mocktail client meeting, with Sid. The fabric holds memories. Memories of hope in a time of despair. Today I pair it with black Argyle tights and leather Chelsea boots. Grans says, wearing something familiar has a 'calming effect', and 'frees up energy to concentrate on other, more important things', such as the eulogy.

The service is at the tithe barn, close to Vera's house at Haven Homes. It would be an understatement to say the room is chaotic. No more than eight meters wide, chairs buffer up against each other from one stone wall to the next, with a slender path down the centre. Seats are filled by humans and whiskered friends. It must have been on the invitation. One hundred cats in the same place at the same time is no coincidence.

If my funeral were tomorrow, who would I invite? Ethan, Mummy, Daddy, Jeremy my brother, Zara my sister, and Grans. It will be cheap at least. In the face of grief, they will have some solace.

The officiator calls my name and I rise with shaky legs. The lectern is sturdy, and I grip the sides before looking up. I can't see Vera, but she must be here. Although I know from personal experience, not everyone has the strength. I start with the front row. First, my empty seat. Then a fluffy ginger tom spills off the lap of a henna-haired owner. Next to him, a long scruffy ragdoll, asleep on a shaggy blond bob. Then a sort of hairless one, pink and wrinkly, standing on a multi-coloured headscarf. Then a short-haired marmalade tabby.

Oh no! She doesn't strike me as a caring, thoughtful and loving cat person. Alexandria's eyes narrow triumphant in her victory over Sid. She is sweet to the uninitiated, her richness fools everyone except me. This is hard enough without her cold clipped demeanour threatening my success.

The funeral director/pet burial person gives a little cough. I need to speak. Hopefully, people will attribute my silence to grief. I dab my eye, lowering my gaze to my notes. Searching for my voice.

"Well, what can I say?" The short-haired marmalade tabby jumps up onto my papers, purring into the microphone. After much wrestling, I'm not used to handling furry creatures, I remove it from the lectern and it settles on my shoulder. This can only make things worse.

"I guess my little friend here has said most of it for me." Queue perfectly timed laughter from the audience. Probably the wrong word for a group of grieving cat lovers.

> "Muddy paws, you never wiped your feet.
> Purring for your dinner and watching you eat.
> Leaping round the room, chasing the flies.
> The gifts from the hunt, a live mouse, the biggest surprise.
> Sleeping in my lap on a sunny afternoon.
> Tibbles. You are gone from me, far too soon.
>
> Kitty Heaven has four paws a new.
> But I stay down here at a loss for what to do.
> I miss you Tibbles, every minute, every hour.
> The house is empty, the milk has turned sour.
> What's it like up there? Are there lots of mice?
> There are bound to be, Heaven is supposed to be nice."

Okay, I'm no poet laureate, but the entire room full of cat mourners break into spontaneous applause before I even get to the last verse. It's clearly so sad they can take no more and want to hit the booze as soon as possible.

The prize for making it into the next room unscathed is a tray of sherry and a Champagne saucer of milk. Perfect as I'm still sporting the marmalade tabby as a scarf. I never realised how true the saying is that cats have a mind of their own. Each time I reach to extract my living stole, the claws bed in a little deeper.

"Kat, love." Vera greets me, resplendent in a black velvet trouser suit. "Let me introduce you to my granddaughter Alexandria. You already share her love of cats, so you will get on like a house on fire." Vera retreats, leaving me alone with Pousse-Café.

"Look who pops up to ruin every moment in my life." Alexandria's voice cuts through the crowd, smooth like vanilla but I sense the bitterness breaking through the cane spirit.

"Alexandria, what a pleasant surprise. May I extend my

sincerest sympathies for your loss? Tibbles will be–"

"You have the irritating ability to invade more parts of my life than you are welcome." Alexandria removes the fur collar from my dress, nuzzling and cooing. "I think you have proven your point." The bitterness contrasts with the sweetness of coffee. "First you take my boyfriend, but I will not let you steal my cat." She lowers her voice, leaning in. "Now kindly fuck off."

The choice is bob-cat fight or scaredy-cat flight. Flight means we all make it out unscathed, however Ethan tells me there is a risk of adrenal compromise. The coaching must be part of bartender training. He says the body recognises escape as the only way out of conflict if you never seek resolution. This means a fear of continued confrontation with Alexandria, presenting again and again. So, I pick the alternative which is to gain control back and clip her claws.

"Alexandria, I never considered myself a threat to you. There has been enough time and energy spent on this conflict you insist on promulgating. Sid and I, well, there is no Sid and I. I ended things at the Lock Wheel, but you know that, don't you? We are not friends and I am not yours to command. Once I have finished paying my respects, I will, as you so eloquently commanded, kindly fuck off and leave you to your wake. Please pass on my regards and deepest sympathy to your cat family."

Despite feeling shaky on the inside, I make it across the room to the furthest point, far, far away from Alexandria.

"Sherry."

Familiar green eyes offer comfort.

"Thanks." I take a gulp before returning the glass. "I'm driving, so I shouldn't have more than that."

"Monica! People are thirsty over here." Alexandria projects from the other side of the room the undertones of herbs complete the Kahlua.

"Don't mind her, she's just bossy." I apologise despite all she has done to me.

"Yes, she is." Monica agrees.

"Don't take it to heart. I'm sure she means well." Like hell I do.

"But then, that's what a boss is. Bossy." Monica ignores the orders.

"Alexandria is your boss?"

"Yep."

"And she has you working at a funeral. For a cat?"

"Yep. Have you noticed that only people with cats are invited? Apart from you and I that is." That must be why Sid is not here. "Serving Alexandria Smith-Richmond is a never-ending occupation. There are always more tasks to prevent escape." Monica sounds in good humour despite working for someone so unrelenting.

"She is married?" I trust Monica, even though I now know where her allegiance lies.

"That's not for me to say, but no."

"How can you be sure?"

"Because I did the paperwork. Even after they split, she insisted on keeping the name."

To show her dedication to him. To win him back. I like an idiot, I played him right into her hands, abandoning Sid at The Lock Wheel to leave him free for her to swoop back in.

"But you were not at the wedding, or the Victorian Pavilion."

"Alexandria had me work behind the scenes. The family must believe she is in control. Sid's family I mean. To add weight to her value. Alexandria always gets what she wants."

"It would appear so." I'm so stupid to think for one minute he would choose me above Alexandria. "But why is he not here now?"

"Sweetie, forget about Sid. You need to get under someone else to get over a broken heart."

"You mean Sid?" So, I'm right. He was using me.

"I mean, find someone yourself. To get under." Monica squeezes my hand. "Just don't overthink it."

Monica is telling me he has moved on or rather moved back. She is my friend and is trying to save my heart as much as she can. But it may be too late.

THIRTY TWO

Terminator

Olive and Harold scour the vintage shops for the perfect material for my outfit. Corinne sketched the design and Tallulah stitched the preloved fabrics to make a full-length amber gown in a mix of broderie and organza, tipped in silk velvet to coordinate with the waistcoat of Alfred's dinner suit.

The Town hall towers over Castle Walk on the edge of the park. The entrance, decorated with banners and lanterns, waves us in and we flow inside to canopies of white muslin and the soft glow of fairy lights. School children sing songs from yesteryear, welcome drinks, kiss lips and fingers pick at passing canapés. Fingers like those attached to the Boilermaker, Greg Storm. In between bites, he takes a photo with his heavy-set tech glasses. His hair is a few inches longer than the last time we met and swept back to the nape of his neck. Wearing the same black velvet jacket, black shirt and skinny tie, he recycles the outfit but refreshes with two student escorts, one on each side.

Alfred offers me his arm. "It's the only way for them to pay the extortionate university fees."

"No doubt he is offering them business advice." I should warn them about his ethics.

"They know what they are doing. More than him, I imagine. Success for them is extorting as much money out of their clients as possible." Alfred leans on me, he must be tired already. It's good I am here to support him. I can't bear for him to die on me a second time.

"Shall we find somewhere to sit?" Alfred rushes us through the photographic history of the town.

"There's an alcove near the pop-up Vanilla Pod. I could get us a couple of drinks?" But the risk of meeting Greg is too great. And where Greg is, Vernon will not be far behind. The delicate beading of my gown will spoil in his sweaty mitts.

"Follow me." Alfred lets go of my arm, darting to the right. "I designed this part of the building when it was remodelled. I bet you never knew I was an architect."

I hesitate and nearly miss where Alfred goes. A decal of Tilly Minster masks the invisible door leading to the main hall.

The tables are laid with Victorian tea, which Alfred consumes at an alarming rate. "I skipped lunch," he said, "worried I would not fit into these high-waisted trousers." Looking behind him, then to the left.

"Alfred. Is something the matter? You seem distracted. Are you in pain?"

"I could do with a drink, that's all."

"I don't want to be rude and leave you alone."

"Nonsense. I am fine. Now quick, before it gets too crowded." Alfred stretches his view behind me to a flash of red atop a Maidens Bush. Marshall, shoulder-length hair swept back to a half man bun, running seamlessly into a full beard, bright absinthe eyes light the room. If I'd known this was going to be an evening of avoidance, I would have turned down Grans' offer. But then Alfred would be alone in his fragile state.

"Use that door in the corner over there. It leads to the storage facility behind the pop-up bars."

"How do you know so much? I know you designed this part of the building, but–"

"I also had a hand in this event. The organiser pulled in everyone who played a part in the history of Tilly Minster and Newtown. To make it more authentic."

Unlike my job.

The pop-up Vanilla Pod buzzes with frantic excitement. Signature Vanilla candles glow on ledges, the atmosphere elevated by his regular jazz pianist. It turns out, the double date was not the first time I had met Miller but I was too absorbed in my own issues to give him more than a passing look.

The bar is rammed, but I'm close enough to catch Ethan's eye while he makes drinks. Sadly, it's too far for a welcoming bear hug, and worryingly, too close to a Vespa, another one of my clients. Stevie stands at the bar, in a sheer black blouse with an oversized pussycat bow, smokey eyes survey the crowd. I never heard from them after our meeting and failed to follow up. They wave before continuing their conversation with friends. Happy there's no animosity. The result was right for both of us.

Ethan reaches over the top of customers at the bar and hands me a Pomegranate Mojito Mocktail and a Scotch Mist for Alfred. I negotiate out of the crush with drinks in hand. I bump, sidestep, and then tread on someone's foot. 'Sorry, sorry'. In a spin, I close my eyes for just a second to get my bearings.

"Still getting those free drinks. What is it today?" There is a garnish of teasing behind his derision.

"One of the Vanilla Pods new mocktails. I've had enough minesweeping ex-clients tonight. I don't need alcohol to make it worse."

"Are you working?" Sid deflects the minesweeping comment.

"Yes." The air catches in my throat. It's not so easy to casually chat with the last man I allowed to caress the edge of my French knickers. Not to mention I held his throbbing cock in the same hand that I now hold the Pomegranate Mojito Mocktail. I know which one I would rather tease with my mouth.

"Kat." Sid is frosty.

"What brings you here?" I say awkwardly.

"I err helped with the curation of the art on display." Sid looks around, seeking a way out of the conversation. He must be here with someone, Lex.

"Of course." I try to sound as beige as possible.

"You're not going to run off again, are you?"

"Only to take these drinks back to Alfred."

"Can we talk?" Sid moves closer, the heat building.

"Sid, I need to get back to my client." This is not the time or the place.

"Listen, Kat. I need to tell you something. To explain."

There is nothing left to explain. I can't bear to hear the words confirm what I already know.

"There you are." The full terminator mode cuts across the room complete with what looks like a bulletproof black dress and zebra print kitten heels. It sounds tacky, being in leather, but Alexandria possesses an air of cold determined grace. This is what Sid was trying to tell me.

Finally. After all this time, I see her for who she really is, a layered Pousse-Café shot called the Terminator, with a mission to destroy any chance I have of happiness. First to add to the glass is half an ounce of Kahlua, the final flavour revealed at the funeral. Add half an ounce of Irish cream liqueur, the rich essence from the party at Sid's parents' house artfully poured to rest on top. Then another layer, half an ounce of sambuca, cutting and harsh like a bridesmaid scorned. More layers follow, half an ounce of Grand Marnier, the bitterness shining through as she swoops in to steal Sid back at the Lock Wheel, and finally, half an ounce of vodka, potent and clear, cutting through the memory of my first kiss with Sid.

And there it is. The spirit of Alexandria. The Terminator. So obvious now. Her destructive nature is cold, determined and focused.

"You're here with her?" I shake my head at Sid. "You're back together?"

What happened at the Lock Wheel meant nothing. The show at the Victorian Pavilion was just a game to make Alexandria jealous and get back together.

"Kat you..." Sid doesn't have space to locate his words as the Terminator looms closer.

"Kay. A coincidence, I hope." Alexandria interrupts before Sid can make his excuses. She takes Sid's arm, staking her claim. "Mummy has Alan Rainford, the Marquis of Shelby. It's about time you meet him, darling. He has heard much of your work and wants to commission a piece." Her voice is sharp and commanding. "Sidney, the vintage suit is a success! I told you Granny would help. This fits you like a glove." She runs her hand over Sid's chest, smoothing the lapel on his gunmetal tuxedo before reaching up to caress his cropped locks. "And the hair is a bonus. I've not seen you look this presentable in aeons."

"Well, good luck to you guys." Words are useless against the Terminator and I'm not wasting more time on this nauseating display of affection.

"WE do not need your luck." Alexandria's parting death stare hits me right between the eyes. She turns, intent to march out of the room with her obedient puppy but Alfred has other ideas.

"Miss Smith, how lovely to see you." It is a small world if he knows Alexandria. He said something about working for the Town Hall, but that was years ago so it must be through Vera, his girlfriend and her grandmother.

"Smith-Richmond." Lexie corrects him.

"You married? Congratulations." Alfred moves to shake Sid's hand but is interrupted before contact can be made.

"No. No." Alexandria waves away the felicitations. "How are you, Mr Turner? I want to thank you for your generous donation. Without it, this event," she gestured around her, "would not have been possible."

"Anything for the community. And you really must call me Alfred at least, and I will call you Alexandria. I am after all intimate with your grandmother, and I'm sure Alfred is preferable to calling me papa." Alfred takes his drink stifling a smile. "Thank you, Kat. Shall we get back to the main hall? The keynote speech is about to begin. Goodbye, Miss Smith, Alexandria. Well done on the ball. It is a fitting tribute to the town."

Sid is back with Alexandria. He didn't even put up a fight when she bossed him about. How could he be so devious? He planned this after she cheated on him and I was revenge to even the score so she would return and beg forgiveness. Not that I imagine Alexandria begging for anything.

I walk Alfred to his seat and then make my excuses. The air is so choked with clients, I cannot breathe. A few minutes in the cool night air should clear my head. I want to leave, like go home, but I'm committed to Alfred. Until I bumped into Sid the evening was going well enough, considering I was playing client Russian roulette. I did my best then boom up pops Sid, smelling so good and looking even better. The ground shifts as the pressure grows in my chest. I was so wrong about him. He flaunted his renewed love with Alexandria in my face, humiliating me.

"Where are you going?" Footsteps on the gravel, the voice unmistakable. He followed me out of the building. "Running away again?"

"I can't stay here." I don't need to explain myself to him.

"But your job? Did something happen?" He cannot be serious. He is so blind to my feelings and yet here he is, asking if I'm okay.

"It's not the job. My client is okay or will be. It's meeting other clients that hit me off guard."

"Clients? You mean me?" Sid sounds pained. "Am I still just a client to you?" But he doesn't care for me. Not really.

"What else is there?"

"Whatever you want." He stands with his hands thrust into his pockets.

"I want a business free from scandal. Where my clients respect me enough not to try to seduce me in the back office of a club." I wave my hands around, the energy swirling.

"If that's how you feel, then I guess I had it wrong between us." Sid catches one of my hands, pulling me off-centre.

I close my eyes and allow his grip to steady me. Only to ground me and nothing more, but it reminds me too much of what happened at The Lock Wheel. Sid's hand moving up my thigh, teasing my sex, thumb slipping inside. Citrus overwhelms my senses and I tilt my head up, searching for his mouth in the dark and it is happening again. The flash point. Our lips close enough to share one breath and I taste the liqueur from the maraschino cherry. But we don't kiss. It is only me that feels this way.

"Sid. I can't do this." Can't allow myself to get close again. I let go of his hand and take two steps back.

"I'm sorry Kat. I let things go too far at the Lock Wheel." Sid sounds emotional. But if he's here with Alexandria, he should be glad I'm leaving. "I thought, well felt we had something more than a working relationship. That's why I did this. Mocktail, I mean."

"Well, you have Alexandria back now, so my work is done."

"You know me better than that." Sid breathes deeply.

"But you are here with her. Yes?"

"Do you truly believe the charade she just put on? After all you know? Do you think I relapsed? Kat, you know everything about me, everything that's happened, and you still draw that conclusion."

"What other explanation can there be?"

"Kat. I have been seeing Lex, and yes, I didn't tell you, but it's only for-"

A shrill voice calls from the Town Hall building. Sid freezes at the full beam terminator death stare cutting through the darkness.

"You are being summoned."

"Kat, it's not like that. You don't understand."

"Don't I? Well, before you can mansplain, let me make it clear. My work is done and you were wrong about me. I am not too good at Mocktail, I am perfect at Mocktail. None of it was real." I am shaking now. "I let the pretence go too far and for that I am sorry. It was all a huge mistake."

"I admit, we went too far at the Lock Wheel, but it was never a mistake. Perhaps a dinner date would have been better. Kat, we know each other quite well now. I thought you felt the same."

"You know nothing about me."

"I know how your eyes look tipsy when you are turned on. How you were shocked the first time I kissed you, because it felt so right. And I know you are torn because you made me a client, but it doesn't have to be this way."

"It's all fake Sid. There was never anything there. There can never be anything there."

Sid looks up. "So the Champagne's gone flat?"

What did he say? I must have misheard.

He can't possibly know the code.

However, before I can challenge him, he is gone.

"Kat, are you okay?" A female voice.

"Monica? What are you doing here?" A hat trick of clients.

"I didn't mean to eavesdrop. I'm working here tonight and was fetching something for the event when I heard voices and wanted to check if everything was alright." She steps into the shaft of light from the lamppost. Red hair luminescent, tied up in a compact bun.

"How much did you hear?"

"Most of it. Kat, are you okay? I feel like you need a hug." For once Monica is not flirting as her arms pull me in. I rest my head on her shoulder as she pats my back gently. It is good to have a friend.

"Men are shits." Monica relaxes her hold. "If you ever need a friend, give me a call." She sweeps a stray hair off my face and rests her hand on the side of my head, thumb rubbing my cheek. "Bye, sweetie." She says and kisses me on the lips. Not a peck and not lingering but enough to taste the liquorice on her breath.

That's the Monica I know.

THIRTY THREE

Cock Sucking Cowboy

"Darling, what are your plans for Christmas this year?" Ethan is experimenting with a new cocktail at the bar, whilst I decorate the tree with lights.

"For the first time, since, well you know. I am single."

"Some might say available." Ethan always adds a positive spin.

"If you want to put it like that, yes. I am available. But why is everything about relationships?" I take out my frustration on the tinsel.

"Exactly my thinking. Any plans this year?"

Meeting Sid when I did, so soon after breaking up with Hugo was a fun distraction and it helped me move on but it's no foundation for a relationship. The Centenary Ball is proof of that. Discovering Sid is back with Alexandria makes everything worse like I've been betrayed all over again. I tried my best. But it didn't work out. Grans and Ethan think there is more to it but I know what happened. I was there. They were not. I did the right thing walking away at the Lock Wheel. If things had gone further, it would not be so easy.

"None. Well, only to focus on my new business plans. I hope to launch in the New Year. You?"

"The usual. Closing the bar for a week to spend it with the family, it's the little man's first Christmas and Laura wants it to be perfect."

"I could hold the fort here for you if you like."

"Now that is tempting. And you have everything here at your fingertips to finalise your product. Then you can ditch the fake dating for good."

"That's what I'm hoping. There's one last client booked for New Year which should be free from drama. People just want to party, with nothing more than a kiss when the clock strikes midnight." Plus I have a theory to test.

"Darling, I wouldn't kiss Peter if I were you, he can be a bit of a cocksucker. Maybe try a real date if you want some action."

My Mocktail swansong is a cowboy-themed fancy dress party. Grans' first costume suggestion is a can-can girl, all satin and frilly knickers which would definitely send the wrong message.

"Peter, my client, is dressing as a horse. No stallion jokes, please. And he trusts me to select a coordinating outfit."

"What about a cowgirl?" Grans routes in a box at the back of her wardrobe. "Here, I have a hat." Pink and glittery. "And must have a checked shirt somewhere. Lulah can add some fringe."

Tallulah completely remodelled the outfit to the extent that I don't recognise a single item from Grans' wardrobe in the final cut. Not an inch of check can be seen. Instead, I wear a cream chiffon blouse, heavily fringed at the chest and black sequin hotpants beneath brown leather chaps.

> MOCKTAIL CLIENT MENU
>
> NAME: Peter
>
> EVENT: New Year Party.
>
> BIO: Project Manager.
>
> IF YOU WERE A COCKTAIL WHAT WOULD YOU BE: Something you want to go back to again and again.
>
> LOVES: Party!!!

HATES: Killjoys

HOW DID YOU HEAR ABOUT MOCKTAIL: From Ethan at the Vanilla Pod and old friend from college.

Peter, already merry when I pick him up, started celebrating sometime last week. I'm used to handling slightly merry drunken men; a harmless, happy horse will be no problem. However Peter advances from tipsy to tanked within a few hours, and I lose him somewhere between the kitchen and toilet. The house is full of drunks as the party continues well past the chimes of midnight, with no breaks and no sign of my errant horse. The kitchen is a western bar, complete with swinging doors and saddles atop bar stools. A stage erected in the living room hosts girls clothed as dancers, doing their finest can-can, whilst guys lie on the floor desperate to up skirt. The dining room is a casino where real money exchanges hands. Outside, in the garden, you can freeze your butt off playing buckaroo before collecting your prize from a horse trough loaded with beer.

It is not as challenging as Ethan cautioned. Yes, it's tough staying up all night when sober, but I make it. Daylight eventually arrives just as the crowd thins out. The bar has run out of booze, the casino's bust and the can-can girls carried off by cowboys for an intimate showing of their legwork.

I find Peter sleeping in the horse trough, thankfully frozen solid, so I'm saved from the trauma of a Police investigation into why I let a client dressed as a horse drown. The costume is crispy from the frost, but he is warm enough inside the thick fur to stave off hypothermia. What is clear very quickly is that he's too large and too heavy for me to manage on my own.

The champagne is flat.

Of course, Grans cannot physically help me, but if my theory is correct, she will send someone, and I will find out the truth.

A trusty sheriff minds my hat whilst I tip Peter out of the trough. With no pocket-sized equine winch on my Christmas list, Peter falls to the floor. Success of a sort. I rescue my hat from the swaying sheriff about to use it as a sick bucket and try again.

The fall to the ground rouses Peter just enough to persuade him it's time to go home. On his feet, he's as wobbly as a newborn colt, mumbling something incomprehensible. I imagine he's thanking me for my efforts, but it sounds more like he's asking for a cock sucking from a cowgirl, or some sort of horseshit.

My hungover horse falters over discarded costumes and sleeping inebriates, the padding cushions his mishaps as much as possible but he's going to feel that when he comes round. Crowbarring Peter into Grans' car is impossible as he refuses to remove the oversized horse's head, he is starting to list, and it takes all my strength to hold him upright.

The chaps give a pathetic coverage of my legs, my shirt feels thinner by the second and even my padded bra does not mask how chilled I am. I look about for a bench to dump Peter on so I can do star jumps and anything to keep off the chill. If he takes much longer I'm going to get frostbite on my nipples. So, yes I am desperate but a taxi is out of the question.

"Good morning! Fancy seeing you here." About bloody time.

Torn between the joy of being rescued and the reality of the lies and manipulation I have suffered for the best part of a year I am speechless.

"Ahh ha ha ha! Looks messy." Sid chuckles, looking at me with that easy teasing sparkle in his eye. "Nice plaits, but why the long face on your friend?"

"What are you doing here?" I keep up the farce, to see how far he will take the deception. "This is, as you say, a little messy. My friend here is worse for wear and won't fit in my car with this costume. Plus, I can't risk horse vomit in Grans' mini."

"Sure." Sid looks like he's about to pop out another flirty one-liner. But no. "So, what are we going to do?"

"We?"

"Sure. You look like you need a hand and I agree there is no way you can transport Muffin the Mule in your tiny car."

"Actually, he's a Cock-Sucking Cowboy." I explain. "3/4 shot of butterscotch schnapps and ¼ shot of Irish cream liqueur floated on top. It's what all men dream a shot of cum tastes like, only they are wrong."

Sid pulls a face. "My van is around the corner. You can borrow that."

"No, really, I couldn't. It'll be fine. It's my mess."

"Sure, but I'm not leaving you here in the cold. So, you may as well agree." He rubs his arms as if to prove he is chilly, but with a thick scarf and padded jacket, he must be toasty warm.

His phone rings, and he answers straight away. Grans, no doubt checking if he found me. He looks me up and down, laughing at my expense.

Sid heaves the dead weight Peter off the bench and drags him to his van. I offer no help. This is payback time, not that it offsets the wrongdoings.

"Front or back?" He rests the horse against the side of the van, out of breath.

"Front, please. Client safety comes first." Plus, I want to see Sid struggle to lift Peter into the cab.

"Wait." I push past and step up into the van if only to give Sid a sight of my sequinned derrière. Moving to the middle, I offer no help in the lifting but do seatbelt Peter in.

"Scoot over." Sid waves his keys at me. "You drive."

"Oh, no, no, no." I have no intention of letting him drive but want to see if he will reveal what he knows. "I've never driven something this large." Lies. But I have a right to be dishonest after what he put me through. "And I'm not insured."

"I just rang my insurance, it's all set up. And besides I don't know where he lives." Sid jingles the keys teasingly. He knows.

I slide to the right, over Sid's lap, as he wriggles to the left, his hands staying firmly on the seat. Unable to even touch me, we are worlds away from the passion of the Lock Wheel. That is, until,

"I'm stuck."

"Just keep moving."

"But I'm caught on something. Your scarf?" As I move further right, Sid is pulled down with me, his head moving closer to my breasts.

"Stop. Stop. Let me see if I can unhook it. Is that okay?" Even now he asks for consent.

But he forgets I gave no consent to being his puppet.

"Just do it, without all the fake respect please."

"Kat, none of my respect for you has ever been fake. Now if you move forward a little, and lift your arse off the chair, I should be able to."

I grip the wheel and pull myself up as high as I can.

"Just a little more and," Sid has his hand right between my thighs, his head rammed against my left boob.

I can feel his breath through the sheer fabric.

"And we are free." Sid removes the scarf. "Here, you need this more than I do." Wrapping it around my neck.

Peter's house is relatively close which limits the time he can vomit and minimises awkward conversations with Sid. Now I know the truth, there is no need to pretend we are friends.

Sid wrestles the sleeping Peter out of the van as though he's a baby, disappearing into the house. Before I calm my nerves by making a Cock Sucking Cowboy, Sid returns.

"Peter is tucked up in bed, sleeping it off. What did he have?"

"Just booze, not that I was with him the whole time. I lost him pretty early on and found him this morning, asleep in a mock water trough."

"Well, you know what they say?" Sid has that cheeky teasing look again. "You can take a horse to water, you cannot make him drink, but he may fall asleep there." Sid laughs at his own joke, none the wiser at being found out. "So now you're done working, what are your plans?"

"A few hours admin, then catch up on sleep." I lean forward to turn out onto the main road, back to Grans' car. "Why were you just hanging around where I was?" Time to find out if he will tell the truth.

"Sadly, not stalking you." He's teasing, still flirting, even now he's been exposed. "You're not the only one working on New Year's Day. I was dropping off a commission piece early. So, I have the rest of the day to relax and get some work-life balance." The lies spill off his tongue too easily. "Listen, join me later? I want to apologise for what happened the last time we met. I'm afraid it wasn't a great situation for you to be part of."

"No thank you. And you don't need to explain yourself to me. You can date who you choose."

"Come on, Kat. You can remove the professional guard now. We know each other better than that. The whole thing with Lex was my mistake. Don't get the wrong idea. Nothing happened, she was just making it appear that way to wind you up because she can see I really like you. She knows," Sid stops. He is holding something back.

"She knows what?"

"Nothing."

"Sid!"

"She knows how I feel."

That Sid still loves her.

The road ahead is suddenly fascinating despite being empty so early on New Year's Day. Even if I could safely take my eyes off the road to look at him, I know he's lying. This is all part of his game. He said we were on the same page, but he never felt the same way I did. I almost believed him, he sounded so sincere.

"So, can we forget about the Centenary Ball?" Sid sounds apologetic.

"The Champagne is flat." There is no other response.

"What?"

"That's what you said. At the Centenary Ball. The Champagne is flat."

"I don't understand."

"Were you talking about Alexandria or me?"

"When?"

"At the ball. The code. You used it. I don't know how you figured it out, or when you felt justified to interfere with my life. Or what gives you the right."

"Kat, I..." Sid sighs.

"The more you protest, the less respect you hold. I know Sid, I know all about it. Every time I send the message to Grans, you show up to rescue me, pretending to be a knight in shining armour. Today was a test."

"Did I pass?" Sid makes no attempt to deny it.

"Passing a test in deceit is not a success. It is underhand and disrespectful."

"Kat there has been no deceit. You used me today when you were in trouble. I should say that is pretty deceptive."

"Don't turn the tables on me. I have always been honest with you."

"Have you?"

"What does that mean?"

"I had a great time at the Lock Wheel, and I think you enjoyed it too, right? There was a spark, yes?"

"It's called a flash point." And is only the biggest you can get. "But it means nothing. Not when you created this elaborate plan to trick me. Was Alexandria in on it too?"

"What? Kat, this has nothing to do with her. That first night I met you, in the Vanilla Pod, I saw you, the real you and that's when all this started."

"An easy target no doubt." He knows nothing about me. "And are you happy now, Sid?" Before he can answer, I pull the van over and step out. "Well, thanks for your help."

"Kat! Don't leave like this. Meet me later. Please."

"I can't. The Champagne is flat."

THIRTY FOUR

Back to the origin

"Kat, Wait! I can explain." Sid jumps out mid-slam of the van door. "Ouch!"

"Explain what?" I give no apology. He doesn't deserve one." It's clear you've been conning me this whole time and you dragged Grans into it as well."

"How could you think I would do such a thing? I would never take advantage of you, or anyone, especially an old lady."

Grans would never forgive him for that.

"Okay, answer me this. It was you in Grans' room that day, wasn't it? And you never paid for the appointments, it was Grans. That's why she acted so shocked when I made a second booking with you. And that's why you didn't have the money to pay me." How this equates to extortion I am not sure, as the money stayed in the family. "You were there at Tossa, weren't you? Spying on me after I messaged Grans. Did you hack her phone to stalk me?" Would that be any better? Probably not. "And the reason you were at Lintuck Castle, and how you knew to be at the station when I turned up with Hugo was..." Wait! "Was Cynthia in on this too? Just how far will you go to mess with my life?"

Sid looks pensive.

"Sid! Do you remember what you told me when we first met? About honesty?"

"That was the second time we met." Sid telling me I am wrong is not going to help.

"That's not the point. The point is you lied to me. Tricked

and deceived me whilst all the time pretending to be honest."

"Kat, do you remember what happened that first night we met?" Sid's tone is gentle. He already knows the answer.

"Christian's Stag do?" Nope, still nothing.

"Yes."

"Some of it is a little hazy." This is a massive understatement.

"Kat. I'm so sorry. I had no idea. I thought you knew everything. That you were playing a long game of pretending you didn't like me, acting the part or I would never have," Sid makes a slow exhalation.

"Why would I pretend to _not_ like you? I was just performing the part of a model girlfriend. None of it was real. That's the point of Mocktail. I was pretending _to_ like you."

Sid is deluded.

"Kat, do you remember taking me home with you?"

"That never happened. I would remember sleeping with you." Only I don't. "And besides, you told me I was not your type."

"Firstly, you were far too drunk to consent to anything like that. So, I could never. And secondly, why do you think you're not my type? How do you even know what my type is?"

"Because you told me. At the induction meeting in the Vanilla Pod. My looks were nothing to make Lex jealous." See I remember that much.

"Kat! I am not Lex. If a part of me can fall in love with you, when you are soaking wet, with a face like a thousand puppies had just been slaughtered, I," Sid just said he's in love with me. "I have nothing but respect for you. The way you planned a business at your lowest point showed me how to be the MC in my own life story."

"MC?"

"Main character. Kat, that night was the catalyst. The conception of Mocktail."

"The night Hugo left me, stole all my belongings and trashed my beautiful apartment. I was in a bad place." Not worth reliving the horror of my dismissal as well.

"And you lost your job." Sid does know everything.

"Well, you were in a bad place too."

"You don't remember anything?" Sid is still calm despite my arguing with him.

"Not after the shots came out."

"You don't remember insisting on being my fake date? Making me promise to do whatever you wanted." Despite the harsh words, Sid sounds earnest.

"And why would you agree to that?"

"Can we go somewhere warmer? Grab a drink. There must be a cocktail to go along with this."

There is. It's called Back to the Origin. But now is not the time to humour Sid with random chat. For the record, it is a good measure of the delicate situation we find ourselves in. The fragility of the coupe glass chilled almost as much as my ass. The rum, spiced with cacao and coffee, a mixture of bitter realisation intermingled with the hit of attraction. Yuzushu Liqueur adds freshness to the cool morning air. Claret, the notes of cherry reminiscent of the kiss we shared. Only it was just me that bathed in the addictive taste. I close my eyes and taste the sweet fresh elderflower liqueur and honey syrup. All shaken up in the icy air, the perfect cocktail for my origin story.

"You just did it again, didn't you? Selected the drink for this." Nothing gets past Sid.

"No! No, I don't want to go anywhere, I just want my origin story, I mean tell me what happened. Now." My chiffon shirt is so thin, I am naked save for Sid's scarf. But I can't go anywhere with him. I don't want to be with him for longer than I need to be.

"At least take my coat. I have a thick jumper on under here." He starts unzipping the puffer.

"Just tell me. Now!" I hold up my hand. A full stop to his fake kindness.

"Okay." Sid sighs. "Here goes. Ethan called last orders and then closing time. But not everyone was getting the message."

"You mean me? Was I that bad?" No wonder he didn't want to sleep with me.

"Never bad, just expressing your frustrations on a difficult day." Sid's eyes shift to the side, negating his compassion.

"Most of the stags were in the taxi, leaving you and me in the bar with Ethan."

"What was I doing?" I was supposed to be working.

"You were shouting 'There's no better way to get over a bastarding man than get over and under a bastarding man and under bastarding another man. They're all bastards, but this one is mine. He tastes of a Cherry Bakewell sundae, and I want to eat him. All. Up.'" Sid is enjoying my disgrace too much.

"Maybe just stick to the edited version. It would be quicker." And easier to stomach.

"No problem. Ethan seemed a little tense at this point."

"You knew him already?"

"Only from the local business community. You were slumped on my shoulder, half unconscious after polishing off some shots. He said, 'Kat, put him down now, he has places to be.' Your head slid down into my lap and we knew the fight was over."

"What about Christian?" I made Sid miss his brother's stag do. I am abhorrent.

"They told me to leave you, 'Ditch the bitch, let's get to the club,' they were a little fired up thanks to your hostess skills. You sat up and shouted, 'I would love to go to a club' then turned to sit on my lap shouting right in my face 'I will show you how to party Black and Tan.' Your eyes went into some crazy blinking state."

"Hypno-blinking."

"What's that?" Sid laughs.

"Something that clearly worked, or you would not be here now." A method of hypnotising someone into falling in love just by blinking. "Anyway, did you make it to the club?"

"No." He shakes his head.

"Sid, I'm sorry for ruining your night. Making you miss Christian's stag."

"Kat, believe me, you provided much entertainment, more than the boys got from what I heard." Sid's eyes crinkle at the corners.

"Are you saying it got worse?" Not possible, even by my standards.

"Never worse. More reckless and debauched maybe." Struggling to hold back the smile Sid continues. "Ethan presented me with two waterlogged bags. Man, they were heavy."

"You carried my bags home? Back to Grans', I mean."

"In a manner of speaking." Sid chuckles.

"Not a taxi. I would never."

"No! Of course not. Ethan told me what happened. About–"

"Stop! Don't say his name." It is not Sid's to own. Not his to speak. Not Ethan's to tell him.

"Kat, I didn't mean to upset you. What I'm trying to say is, we were respectful of your wishes. Ethan told me you never let anyone else drive you. He is a good friend to you. You came out of the Vanilla Pod and spotted those new e/skooters. I struggled to keep up with you, owing to the bags, and before I knew it, you were e/skooting off up the street. Until," He pauses.

"Until what?"

"You fell over. But it was ok, a bush cushioned your fall."

"So, we walked?"

"No, you got right back up and insisted we both take the e/skooter. Together. Getting to the end of Castle Walk took forever. The driving was touch and go at times. With you and two soaking wet bags to support, it was a little wobbly, but we made it in one piece. It took the best part of an hour to reach the gates at the top of the hill on Castle Walk. I thought I lost you when you hopped off and ran into the car park to wee in the bushes." Sid revels in the humiliation. "And then there was the stop at the end of the road so you could buy some ice cream. It would be sensible to stop and eat it, but somehow you managed to keep e/skooting leaning against me, spoon in one hand, tub in the other. After the ice cream stop, we made it halfway up to Kingsgate before you veered too much."

"And?"

"So, we stopped at a bench and sat for a rest."

"That was when it happened, wasn't it?"

Sid pauses, looking at the ground. Not for dramatic effect, but because he knows it too. All those times that he looked at me, touched me, he knew this was the origin story. His blue eyes hold the truth. Ethan didn't tell him. I did. "Kat, you force-fed me ice cream, then kissed me. It was like all your pain stopped for just a second. You smiled, not the professional Mocktail smile you put on, or the guard that goes up to protect yourself so no one sees the real you. You were in the moment, alive." Sid sounds so serious. The joke is over. "You told me it wasn't right for me to miss out on all the fun of the stag party." Back to teasing.

"Sounds messy."

"Fun. It was the same when I kissed you outside the studio, something lit up inside you. And again at the Lock Wheel." Back to being serious. "After you kissed me, you said that thing again about Cherry Bakewell sundae. I had my hand on your tattoo. The one on your leg. You told me there are eight. One for each year. The fact you confided something so meaningful to me, that you trusted me."

"Wait," ignoring the tattoo. There is no need to get into that now. I am not ready to speak of it to Sid. Even though he clearly knows everything. "You encouraged me to drink at the Lock Wheel. You did that on purpose."

"Kat, no. No! You must trust me by now to know there was nothing underhand going on. I wanted to spend time with you, outside of the pretence of Mocktail. Yes, I used Mocktail to see you again. You wouldn't agree to anything else. You insisted on Mocktail but you started drinking of your own accord. I had no idea things would end the way it did. How could I?"

"Because you plotted, went behind my back, influenced my friends and family to get closer to me, so you can groom me to get me drunk at the Lock Wheel and sleep with me."

"That's a bit harsh. I didn't buy you a single drink. And, if I wanted to sleep with you, I had plenty of opportunities the night of the stag. But I didn't because I'm not that guy." Sid stands, his hands on his hips.

"What guy? The one that underhandedly makes me fall for you under false pretences. The guy that cajoles my grandmother to message you when I am at my most vulnerable, so you can swoop in and pretend to save me."

"What false pretences? Kat, I didn't go behind your back. Yes, I've checked in with Grans because she asked me to, and Ethan is now a good mate, but any actions were to support what you wanted."

"How? How is any of this what I wanted?"

"After a few more challenges with the e/skooter, we made it to Grans. You were in no state to be left alone and I wanted to make sure you made it safely inside."

"But I know where the key is kept." Under the plant pot by the side door.

"On your person apparently."

"What?" No! Hugo and I would play a game, hunt the key. I would hide it, and he would search my whole person to see where it was, searching with his mouth in every possible hiding place. Never stopping until I revealed where it was, begging him to stop just so I could catch my breath. Clothes abandoned in the doorway, key still in my bag whilst he unlocked my passion. Surely, I didn't try this game with Sid.

"The next thing I know, you had slut dropped to the plant pot behind the bay tree, begging me to help you find it."

"No one slut drops anymore."

"I was being generous; it was more like a stumble and a mad fumble before I rescued you from falling into the holly hedge. Setting you back to vertical was easy. Even though you thought pulling me to the ground to wrestle in muddy puddles was more fun. You said the only way you could steady the world was by putting your hand down my jeans. To find something big and solid to hold onto."

"Don't flatter yourself."

"Don't flatter yourself! I was bent over, wrestling with a drunk downward dog when Grans opened the door wearing a flesh-coloured bodysuit."

"Pole dancing club. She says the one-piece looks more effective under the fluorescent lights in her dance studio."

"And quite translucent. I was not sure where to look, with Grans on one side, and you on the other." Sid blushes.

"So, was that it? You helped me inside before persuading Grans to establish a method of control for my life?" Such a bastard.

"I thought you wanted to know what happened?" Sid runs his hands through his hair. He is losing patience with me.

"I do." But it is painful.

"Then hear me out. There was no way I was leaving you alone with Grans in that state. It's not fair to just rock up and dump an insanely drunk granddaughter on a doorstep. Grans led us through to the living room for a drink, despite me explaining I was not your boyfriend, and I needed to get the e/skooter back."

"Drawing room."

"In the drawing-room, you leapt on a half-empty bottle of vodka and two shot glasses. Declaring, 'Perfect! Strip Twister,' forgetting Grans was there."

Ahh, strip Twister is amazing. Spin, take a shot, remove an item of clothing, and make a move. The fun begins after a few rounds when you are intertwined, a few layers down. One shaky move and boom, you fall over. Half-naked bodies sliding around.

"Grans seemed nonplussed. She owned up to it getting 'a little messy' the last time she had 'Vera and Alfred and Harold over for games night. The risk of another broken hip was too risky' so she took the game to the charity shop. I was quite relieved. The odds would not be favourable playing strip anything against a pensioner in a Lycra one-piece."

"Although she is very agile, so would probably win."

"Grans offered up chess, and Trivial Pursuit, but you said, 'strip chess is not sexy, and even if you strip whilst playing Triv, you either kill the mood by being too stupid, or stay fully clothed and look like a nerd'."

"Did everything involve stripping?"

"Pretty much. Apparently 'the clue is in the title. Bored Games'."

"Strip Jenga is the best, especially if you write forfeits on the blocks. It can go on for hours if you pick the right ones, if you have stamina that is." This was Hugo's favourite, snapping the best bits on my phone so he could masturbate to them later.

"And alcohol tolerance by the sounds of it." Sid is right. "Kat, you're distracting me from the events and confusing me at the same time. You say you don't want to meet me for a coffee but tease me with conversations about stripping."

It is about time Sid had a taste of his own medicine.

"Sorry. But you are taking a long time to summarise how you took what sounds like a fun evening and turned it into a life of deception and lies." Now we're back on track.

"Okay. Grans excused herself, returning to the studio to perfect her spinning chopper."

"Which she has by the way and is now working on Hercules. She has thighs of steel!"

"Yes. Although I'd rather not think of Grans' thighs. I thought you wanted to know more."

"Yes, sorry. Carry on."

"With Grans out of the picture, you picked up the vodka and a pack of playing cards and got very animated at the excitement of playing strip Snap, saying you would give me a head start."

"A head start?" To Hugo that meant a quick blowjob, usually topless. Me not him.

"Yes, so you took a huge swig of vodka. Opened the cards, threw them up in the air shouting 'shuffle' before attempting to remove your top."

"Attempting?"

"You have me to thank for a pair of perfectly intact ears. You caught your sleeve in your earring, flailing around like a lunatic in a straitjacket."

"Thank you." I am humbled.

"Well, I figured, you needed two. But it wasn't easy. Despite my good intentions, which were innocent, as I have already said. The release manoeuvre was conducted whilst you were wrestling with my belt buckle. Insisting it was caught in your bra."

"Messy."

"Fun."

"So, at this moment, I am standing in my underwear? Assuming you left my bralette on."

"You still had your jeans on. And so did I, much to your upset. You accused me of cheating, as I was straightening up the cards. When I asked you where the bedroom was, Grans reappeared, thankfully wearing a kimono. I attempted to carry you to your room, but you swung your arms around my neck, the bottle was still in your hand and cracked me on the head."

"Ouch, sorry."

"I recovered, enough to detangle myself from your octopus arms and legs, trapping you under the duvet. You have quite a grip when you put your mind to it."

"Messy."

"Fun."

"Was that it then? You left me in bed and went back to trick Grans with your controlling plan."

"Kat, hear me out. Then you will see there was no collusion. I only did what you wanted this whole time and I thought you remembered what happened."

"Fine."

"I was leaving the room when you shouted 'STOP!' Grans came running back, just to make sure I was not forcing myself upon you. You sat up, sober as you are now and said, 'I could go with you'."

"Where?"

"That's what I said. And you answered, 'to the wedding. I will be your fake date."

"You're saying it was my idea?"

"Those were your words. 'I'm serious. I could go with you to the wedding. A fake date.' When I repeated 'date', you said 'no. This is professional. No more drinking. No more sleeping with men'. You ordered Grans to take minutes for the first board meeting of your new company. You made me promise to be your first client but I was never to speak of this moment again. But I see now, that was a mistake."

Sid's recollection sounds like a mumbled offer to go with him to the wedding. Probably lots of rambling about Hugo never wanting to marry me, which is none of Sid's business. This is ridiculous.

"So, a drunken mumble about helping you at the wedding, and you plot this elaborate affair."

"There was no plotting from my side. Grans has the minutes. Feel free to check." Sid protests his innocence to the last.

"It doesn't sound like I was making a pitch to the dragon's den. I was vocalising some inner thoughts, which you interpreted as an invitation to meddle with my life."

"From the start, all we wanted was to help you. It was your idea. Your plan. Grans told me she would help."

"Anyway, where do you get off calling her Grans?"

"She asked me to call her Grans."

"Why would she trust you? A stranger who turned up at her house with her inebriated granddaughter."

"Because you trusted me, Kat."

"Trusted that you would take me home and fuck me into oblivion."

"Which I am still waiting to do, if only you would stop running away." Sid's eyes flash. "Kat, you trusted me enough to tell me everything. About Matty, about–"

"You lie. I never tell anyone." Never trust anyone.

"Then how do I know? About what happened that night. And how you felt so alone, despite everyone fussing round, desperate to help–"

"Why would I tell you all this?" He lies.

"Because you felt something when we met. I can't explain it. But the fact you never tell anyone what happened and you told me means something."

It was the Cherry Bakewell sundae. I lost track of who he was because he kisses like Matty. Not like Matty, but the same emotions, the same feeling. The maraschino cherry, the flash point, his touch. It felt real to me but it could never be the same again. Not now I know.

"So, you revealed all this to Grans and hatched a plan?"

"No. I only said enough for Grans to see you were in pain. Once you were settled, she showed me out and thanked me for taking care of you. Obviously, it was my pleasure, which I said along with recommending you stick to Mocktails from now on."

"You named my business?" Nothing is mine.

"Not intentionally."

"The last year has been a sham. And the joke is on me." I am shouting now. So angry I can't control myself. "My whole fucking life is a Mocktail. Fake. Invented and consumed by someone else."

"Kat, you're shaking. Please can we go somewhere and talk about this."

"I can't believe Grans was in on this from the start." I'm not cold anymore, but he's right, I am shaking. "The next day, you called me to plant this idea in my mind and claim it's mine after a night of drunken ramblings. Then you shared everything that happened with Grans and Ethan." If my suspicions are correct. "Manipulating me for, I don't know what? Pleasure? Fun?"

"Kat, I had no idea you couldn't remember. How could I? You seemed so together. Never once asked me what happened. All I did was help you."

"You call this help?"

Sid is partly right, he did save me from a few rather inconvenient moments. But only because Grans teamed up with him.

Grans' heart is in the right place. I could never be cross with her. But I don't know who Sid is anymore.

"Kat, please." Sid's remorse seems genuine.

"You took advantage of me at my lowest point."

"There were plenty of times I could have taken advantage of you and didn't. My only error was not checking if you remembered what happened the night of the stag do. But why would I? You acted as though you knew. I even checked if you were happy with how things were going. That it was what you wanted."

The cold reaches my core and I struggle to grip the car door. Sid leans in to help and I bat him off.

"I want you to stop interfering. I am fine on my own. If you know me so well, you know I don't need anybody. I never did." It is not worth the pain again.

THIRTY FIVE

Red over Heels

"How many is it now?" Ethan waits. "Kat, you have taken up the entire length of my bar."

"These are for Oak Mews. Every day the orders increase as word spreads." I place the lid on the final bottle. "Help me load these into the car?"

"Darling. Any dates lined up yet?" Ethan has his hands full, but his mouth is still free to quiz me on my love life.

"No, not yet. But I do have an offer."

"And?"

"I've not decided."

"Kat, you've been holding out for Sid for the best part of a year now and it's time to move on. Lots of men are nice. Try getting to know them before you reject them for not being him. What if, for once, you said yes? It doesn't have to get past an innocent drink in the bar, but at least you're giving them a proper chance."

"I suppose you are right."

"I know I'm right. Comes with the job title. Imagine how much fun you'll have on a proper date. And by that, I mean a date where you don't have to pretend to be someone you're not."

"Now you're making me sound fake."

"Not fake, my sensitive little one. I just want you to go out there and remember who Kat really is. Now you have moved onto the new phase of Mocktail," Ethan carefully rests the crate in the boot. "You have time to focus on yourself and have a little fun."

Fun. The words hang in the air. They remind me of Sid and the flash point, the Cherry Bakewell sundae and Back to the Origin. I want something that makes me feel desired. Something no one else can give me. So, I make the call.

Preparing for a real date is harder than I thought. Grans finds me in the middle of her dressing room scouting for an outfit that comfortably crosses over from bar employment to date night.

"My dear, are you working tonight? I thought you were helping Ethan at the Vanilla Pod. Can I help?"

"No thanks, Grans. Remember Mocktail has moved on. This is a real date and I want to do it all on my own."

"Oh ho! Marvellous!" Grans launches into a mock Irish gig. "I'm so pleased you finally sorted things out."

The perfect outfit that crosses over from the world of bar work into a date is as follows, satin sneakers for comfort, light-wash jeans with a rip at the knee and a white boyfriend shirt. Grans tucks some chunky jewellery in my bag to slip on once my shift has finished.

Tonight is going to be special. A first real date. The one with Sid at the Lock Wheel doesn't count as technically I was working. This moment is real. I've not organised, not arranged to pick anyone up, and not charged them money for my company.

Ethan offers pre-dinner drinks, so we meet at the bar. Part because it is a great place and part for emotional support.

We leave the Vanilla Pod in the direction of Oxford Street and dinner. My aims for the evening are simple, not too much to drink and not get carried away in the heat of the moment. To not lie, or pretend to be somebody I'm not and to stop at a simple goodnight kiss at the end. Easy.

The restaurant buzzes with excitement. Finally, I'm part of the dating community and it couldn't get better. The table overlooks Oxford Street, where twinkling lights contrast against the night sky. Now I'm in the swing of it, I will do more of this. Ethan says, until you both agree you're in an exclusive relationship it is acceptable to date as many people as you choose.

"I can't believe we're finally here."

"I know. I resisted for so long. But now it feels right." I smile over the top of my dessert menu.

"So why the change? I was beginning to think you didn't like me."

"I think, despite my resistance, you have been there for me when I needed you. When I least expected it. And it felt good." Caring, steady and reliable. Gratitude flows out of me around the restaurant. It is about time I admit the truth and stop protesting. "And there was a connection. Since the first kiss." Powerful, strong, and potent.

"If I remember correctly, you had your hand on my pussy at the time." Monica recalls, green eyes bright below her heavy red fringe. "I thought maybe I came on too strong, you left in such a hurry." She sweeps her long hair behind her shoulders, revealing a deep v on her emerald jumpsuit. Her neck is naked, providing silent drama as she licks her lips deciding what to eat.

"I was working. On a fake date with your brother, remember? It would be rude if I took you home."

"And now?"

"Let's wait and see." Must try to slow things down, even though I suspect where we will end up. Not a new start, just a slight adjustment in the right direction. "I've moved my business on. I don't do fake dates anymore."

"It's okay Kat, I believe this is real. Your hand hesitated on my clit that night before you removed it." The satin on her jumpsuit lifts as her nipples harden at the memory. "I knew you wanted more."

I close my eyes. "I had the biggest sex dream that night." My cheeks flush. "About you." I leave out the part about Sid and Marshall.

"You will have to show me sometime." Monica leans in. As she moves, her neckline drops lower revealing the curve of her breast. "But first, tell me about your upcycled business."

"The idea started about a year ago when I went to Ali's Salon, the one at the community space." I touch my hair, it gets easier to look in the mirror as time passes. "The drink, the mocktail I had was out of a bottle and I could taste all the preservatives. Nothing fresh like you get in a bar. And it got me thinking."

"So, you invented your own range?"

"Not as quick as that. It was more organic. Ideas gathered in my mind, one step at a time."

"One shot at a time." Monica is proud of herself.

"One sip at a time." I laugh. "I had some inspiration from friends and clients of Mocktail. And just like a dripping absinthe spoon," I will need to explain that to her later. "A range of drinks came together. All organic and freshly made. In recycled glass bottles, no plastic, no preservatives or additives."

"Kat. You should give this place a call." Monica routes around in her bag for a business card. "They've just opened a pop-up in The Arches. Your brand sounds perfect for them. I know the owner and I think they will love this."

Supportive and beautiful.

"So, which Mocktail am I." Monica's finished with business and back to the date.

"Red Silk Panties. Obviously." I can taste them now.

"Mmm." Monica closes her eyes. She is there too. "And what about your dream? No. Let me guess." She takes a long slow deep breath, holding the cleansing air inside. "You already gave it away earlier." Her laugh tinkles. "Absinthe. Am I right." Her eyes burn bright.

I stand. "We won't be having dessert. Not here." I pick up my bag. "This has been long overdue. We're going back to mine."

"It's a very long walk. And I have killer heels." Monica pulls on her denim Afghan coat. Not waiting to be asked twice.

"We can share an e/skooter. I believe they take two people easily."

The evening is cold and neither of us have gloves so we take turns covering each other's hands. The last time I shared this journey it was raining and my e/skooter partner was plotting ways to trick me. Tonight, it is different in every way. The air is crisp; the sky is so clear the stars compete with streetlights to light the way.

By the time we make it to the Vanilla Pod, Ethan is locking up. Curiosity is written all over his face, he smiles at us through the glass. Pleased I am making a fresh start.

Past the park and the bench where I spilled my heart out to Sid. We make it home without stopping. I want to do this.

"Grans!" I shout as she opens the door.

"Oh, my dear! There you are. I was worried sick you'd been abducted and killed. I was ringing and ringing your phone, but there's been no answer. I rang the Police but they said a couple of hours is not long enough to file a missing person's report. And as I didn't know who you were out with."

I must have left it on silent but when I look, my phone is not even in my bag. "Grans, I'm so sorry. I think I left my phone at the bar. Everything's okay, I promise."

Before I invite Monica in, Grans beckons us both through the door.

"The pot is still hot, no doubt you both need warming up after being out in the cold so long."

"Sounds too tempting to say no." Monica accepts the offer, although I can tell Grans being here has put a dampener on the excitement. "This is wonderful Kat's Gran, but Marshall will be making his own call to the police if I am not home soon."

"Life is too short to always be sensible my dear." Grans leaves us in the drawing room with the Hot Chocolate Comfort.

"Grans is right." I put down my drink and move closer to Monica. Seizing the moment, we kiss but it is conscious and awkward. Not like before. We left it too late and the passion has gone. I thought I was head over heels or Red over Heels, but I taste nothing. I lean in again looking for the spice like ginger-infused vodka. Hard-hitting and tangy. Her lips are sweet as honey syrup, I've been anticipating the taste all evening, but no. The lemon twist garnish is missing.

"You like him, don't you?" Monica sounds resigned.

"Who?"

"Sid. Sidney Richmond."

"I am finished with men. They are bad." I rest my hand on

her thigh.

"Bad?"

"I am a poor judge of character."

Monica envelops my wrist. "Sid Richmond is one of the nicest guys. If I was into men, he would be top of my list." Her laughter washes over me. "You really are a bad judge of character if you think that one is anything but well-intentioned."

"Listen, Monica. I am not here because of him. I like you."

"Kat, I know. And I like you."

"I mean sexually."

The laughter rings out again. "Obviously. And I like you sexually. But just to be clear what we mean. I want to peel those stale old bar job clothes off you, run a hot shower and wash off any trace of Sid Richmond." Monica moves her hands lightly over my clothes. "My hands will cleanse every inch of your skin, so there is no trace of anyone else. Once you are really good and wet, I will taste every part of your smooth skin, especially your pussy. Suck, lick, blow, rub. You will never think of bad men again." She sits back and roots in her bag. "I even have my lipstick vibrator. Small but powerful. Never leave home without it."

"Monica. There's something you need to understand. I was never Sid's girlfriend. It was all pretend. Part because I forced him to be a client, and part to make Alexandria jealous."

"But you know he likes you, right? He can't shut up talking about you."

I shake my head. "I don't want to talk about Sid. I want to hear more about that shower."

"Could you ever give him another chance?" Monica ignores me. "A real chance I mean. Remove the barrier you put up by making him a client. Unlock that imaginary chastity belt."

"Listen Monica. You don't understand–"

"I understand what I see when you are together." Monica smooths my hair back from my face. Her eyes pale. "And don't forget the part where you like each other."

"Okay, I admit I liked him but that is all in the past, he is back with Lexie now. And I'm here with you. Because I like you." I lean in for another kiss but Monica pulls away.

"And I like you. This is not easy for me, I would rather ignore it, believe me. As good as I am at masturbating, and I get plenty of practice after I see you, I would rather your tongue be licking me out for ten minutes than the hours I spend with my vibrator. But I can't risk starting something with you when you are in love with my friend."

"It doesn't matter anyway. He's moved on, or back to Alexandria."

This is not what I had planned for the evening. By this point, I imagined slipping the thin straps off her shoulders. Stroking the gentle curves of her naked breasts, watching her nipples harden in anticipation. Her back arches as I lick, suck, and flick to show her what's to come. I ache for her to touch me, to slide her hand over the top of my jeans, into my knickers. To feel the wetness growing as I fantasise.

"Kat, Alexandria is my boss, you know that. And I can promise there was never anything between Sid and Lexie. Not after they split up." Monica brings me back to reality.

"But the Centenary Ball. He was there with her."

She shakes her head. "Alexandria just wanted you to think that. Call it payback. Her sense of humour is often ill-placed."

"She was always at his studio. Every time I went to see him."

"They have lots of legal stuff to complete following their split. Kat, I know this because I know everything about her. Her dating history, her diaphragm size, and even when she ovulates. But I also know Sid. And he has moved on."

"I know! I saw him kissing another girl." Sid has moved on from anything real or unreal we had.

"So what? You kissed me, but that doesn't mean we're married. It doesn't mean you stopped fancying him."

"No, but it does mean he's like all other men."

"Kat, he's a free agent. Until you have that conversation, he can kiss a thousand girls and that will never make him a bad guy. I'm telling you, he lights up when he's with you in a way he never did when he was with Lexie. There were obvious sparks. I swear you could see the flames of passion. I would not let go of that, not for mistaken intentions, and not for pride because things didn't quite go to plan. He lights you up.

And you him."
　"The flash point."

THIRTY SIX

Sloely Does it

"Here's the last of them." Ethan makes room on the side for the crate of sterile bottles. "This is your biggest order yet, yes?"

"And I couldn't have done it without you." So far today, I've made thirty-six Mocktails comprising; Vanilla Iced Tea, Virgin Mary, Fake Orgasm, and Pomegranate Mockito. "It's for a new client. They're opening a gallery in The Arches that surrounds the beach installation. Monica put in a good word for me." Something good came out of our friendship for sure.

"What with this and Oak Mews, you're building up a good customer base."

"Thanks for letting me use your space, Ethan. And your recipes."

"Darling, they were inspired by you, so they're yours to take." Ethan added them to his own menu, so it is a win for both sides.

Oak Mews puts in daily orders, which grow each week as word spreads. The salon off London Road switched supply once they came to the end of their bland contract. This new deal with The Arches makes three regulars. Once news spreads even further I will negotiate franchise deals.

The heavy gate to The Arches kicks open with ease and I carry in the first crate of drinks.

"Mocktail delivery!" I call out to no one in particular. "Where do you want these?"

"There is a fridge behind the bar."

The contract for a new client is signed. Seventy-two bottled drinks were made this morning complete with bespoke, monogrammed labels. Magnetic signage is attached to the side of Grans' car. I thought I was prepared for everything. But I was wrong. I am not prepared for this.

"Let me take those from you." Sid reaches out for the crate.

"No. I can manage."

"Then at least let me get the rest." Sid takes in my uniform, a raglan t-shirt with red sleeves, branded front and back.

"Please, don't bother."

"Is that a new one?" He means my tattoo, which is on full display thanks to my denim shorts.

"Yes."

No doubt he knows all about it, after meddling in my life for so long.

"Sid, what are you even doing here?" I ask, hoping it's not another set-up.

"Are you parked out front?" Sid shuffles in his leather flip-flops.

As if things were not challenging enough, Alexandria walks out of the storeroom. "Kat, great to see you. Thank you so much for supplying your Mocktails, they are just what we need for this space."

"The gallery is called ASR." I say this aloud. ASR. Alexandria Smith-Richmond. They are back together. Monica was wrong.

"Is my husband helping you unload?" She walks out from behind the bar, dressed head to toe in black, save for a scarf wrapped around a baby bump. "Six months." She gives it a little rub. "It all happened so quickly."

Six months. "The Centenary Ball." My words come out weak. Barely audible.

"Yes, how clever of you to remember." Alexandria unpacks a crate.

How stupid of me to think for one minute, no one second that I may have been wrong about Sid. How could he do this to me? To her. To both of us. He made out he had feelings for me, but all this time was cheating on the mother of his child.

Sid returns carrying the final two crates.

"Lexie! Don't even think about lifting a finger. You remember what the midwife said." Sid places the crate down and removes the bottles from her hands.

"Sidney, you are early. You really did not need to help with that. Monica will be back soon." Alexandria has mellowed in her maternal haze. Now she's secured her man, or thinks she has, she no longer feels threatened.

"I'm here the exact time you asked me to be here. Not a minute too early and not one minute late. I know how much you value sticking to a plan." Sid helps Lexie down into a deck chair. "No doubt, you had an ulterior motive for summoning me here today."

"Sidney, you know Monica makes all the logistical decisions. If anyone is to blame, it is her. It is a shame my husband does not respect a critical path as much as you."

"Husband?" But I thought Sid was her husband. I look at Sid, silently questioning.

"Alan popped out for ice and hasn't come back yet."

"Alan?"

"My husband. Alan Smith-Rainford. ASR. It's his space. When he came up with the idea, I knew your product was just what we needed to add an individual touch." She smooths her hair, making sure her yellow diamond engagement ring flashes at just the right angle. "As a collector, my husband is useless at curating. So, I had to ask Sid here today. I only accept the best."

"Kat. You didn't …" Sid laughs, pointing at Alexandria's growing bump.

"What was I supposed to think?"

"How is it going with Monica?" Sid changes the subject.

"Sweetie." Right on queue Monica dashes through the gates. "So sorry I am late. I wanted to be here when you arrived." Monica kisses Sid on each cheek. I lean in to receive the same but get the full Monica experience. Soft liquorice lips, lingering with hope. "Nope, still no spark."

"Flash point." Sid and I say, both at the same time, locking eyes. The burn is still there.

"Kat. Listen… I never meant to hurt you…" Sid sounds earnest. "I only went along with Mocktail because you kept playing the part. If I could go back to the start, I would press stop at the planning meeting and tell you everything. That I don't want to pretend and I never did."

Another apology will not change the past. I know the truth now, thanks to Grans' meticulous note-taking.

It's time to put a stop to this once and for all.

"Yes." I interrupt.

"Yes?" Sid looks confused.

"Yes." I nod.

"Yes, what?" He smiles in anticipation.

"Yes, I will meet you for a drink."

"Are you sure? I mean, yes." Sid hides his grin behind his hands.

"But let's not get carried away. We got off to a confusing start." I take a deep breath and close my eyes. I can do this. "I read the notes. From the inaugural meeting of Mocktail." Not that it had a name at that point, but the facts are there. "You were telling the truth. I mean, you already know that, but now I know that too. In my desperation to move on and forget about the terrible day I was having, I made you swear to never mention what we talked about. And instead of thanking you for being true to your promise, I blamed you for everything."

It would have saved a world of confusion if I had known, but then I probably would not be in the place I am now. An entrepreneur with an expanding drinks company, a growing network of clients, and a chance to make things right with the man who I have been at cross purposes with for the last year.

Sid nods. He understands. "Kat, is this your last drop-off today?"

"Yes. No. Sorry. I have something." I have been practising being honest with myself. This should be easy. But of course it's not. "A café. A grief café. I have a grief café." I take a long slow breath out. "But you can pick me up after. It's at the Vanilla Pod. Maybe we start from there and see what happens."

When I arrive, Ethan greets me with a big bear hug. Even though this is not my first time, he still whispers good luck before letting me go. This is a big step, I am a bag of nerves and he knows it.

It is my turn to talk today. To tell my story.

"Some nights, I lie in bed. Awake. With overwhelming doom that it will happen again. That I will lose those closest to me." I reach for a drink of water, but my hand is shaking too much. "Only, I can't go through it again. I don't have the strength. The pain hurts too much. Even now. It is easier to be alone. Alone or with someone who means nothing so it doesn't hurt when they leave." I pause to see if anyone has any questions but it doesn't work that way. "So, I masked my pain with alcohol and sex. A short-lived, instant gratification to escape. I make sure the relationships self-destruct, so I can't fall in love. So it cannot happen again."

"Go on." The organiser encourages.

"I can't fall asleep because that is where it happens. When it happens. So, I took jobs working nights. But this only made room for guilt. The pain I brought to my family, my parents. I carry this with my own. They say there is nothing greater than a mother's love and I rewarded that with insufferable pain. Sometimes, when I am driving, I wonder if there is a way out. If I just nudge the car into the central reservation and end it all, end the darkness, the depression, the trauma, it would be better. It would be easier if I had died too."

It would have been easier. For me anyway. Saying it aloud is quite shocking for some, but I know it is the truth and it gives me pleasure. At last, I am being honest with myself. It would have been easier for me if I had died at the same time. I stifle the urge to laugh at the unexpected overwhelming joy. I cover my face with my hands, so others will think I am holding back sad emotions. There is a freedom of weightlessness to this path. A new beginning to imagine. Kat without the shame.

"Instead, I live and it is hard. I search for a way to get over the grief, like a magic pill. I suppose I try to accept it, even if sometimes it is half-hearted. Sure, I know this happened to me. Never do I deny it. Absolutely, I own the feelings and the mental scars, but I do not accept this is my life forever. Is it wrong to hope that one day I will wake up and not be tortured by what happened? To forget. Will it mean forgetting him if I can be like I was before?"

"Kat, would you like to say the person's name? Are you ready?"

"His name was Matthew Rose."

"Can you tell us what happened?"

"He was driving the car when it happened. My parents, mummy, didn't want me to go out. It was just before our A-levels and study was the number one priority. I felt like she never liked him and I told her. We had the biggest fight that day, there was so much shouting and threats to ground me but I ignored them and went with Matty. The argument made us late, but he was careful. He was a good driver and knew speeding was dangerous in the conditions. But somehow the car lost traction and skidded off the road. We crashed into a tree down by a river and that's all I remember. Somehow, I got out of the car but Matty didn't." The next words are the hardest to say. "And he died. They say it was instant but it doesn't change the fact he is gone. Doesn't change the fact I am still here. Alone. Without him."

"Can you talk to where you are now, Kat? How are you doing?"

"Yes, I got another flower added to my tattoo, there is one for every year since Matty has been gone. It represents my strength in getting here today. My resolve to keep going. Being here today, talking like this, seems strange like I am finally speaking my truth, allowing myself to listen. Ready to give myself the compassion I deserve. However, it is not easy. Because of what happened, I won't let anyone else drive me in a car. Won't tell anyone what happened. I would not let a friend suffer the way I have. Would not say the things to a friend that I've said to myself."

"And what do you have planned next?"

"To value my worth. And allow others to help me."

People around the group nod.

"My friends and family tried to help, but I would not listen. I flunked out of my A-levels. Left the exam room without completing the paper. Left home, so I didn't have to look at the pain on my parents' faces every day. Found a job here in Tilly, and coped the best way I knew how. I needed to get to this point in my own time, in my own way. There is even someone special. Not to replace Matty, but equal to him. Despite my efforts to push him away, he is still standing by me and if there is the chance of love again, I will do my best to give it the respect it deserves."

Sid waits at the bar until I am finished. "That was a brave thing you did tonight."

"Which part?" My legs shake so much, that I may collapse. That was harder than I thought.

"All of it. Speaking up here. Owning your truth. Meeting me."

I hold on to the bar for support. Sid is looking so hot tonight, I want to throw my arms around him and taste the Black and Tan, the Perry, the Poire Prisonnière, the Angel Face, the Stinger, The Playmaker and the Artist. And I don't forget the Cherry Bakewell sundae of course.

Ethan delivers two drinks which perfectly represent the journey to this point. A gentle sparkle to be savoured, the measure of sloe gin shaken with orgeat syrup. The sweet depth of fruit paired with sugary almonds topped up with Champagne.

"Thank you." I accept the praise even though it feels uncomfortable. I close my eyes and take a deep breath in, holding it for a few seconds, before breathing out and letting go of the imposter syndrome. My eyes feel tipsy as I look at Sid. "Sloely Does It."

"One step at a time."

"One sip at a time." This reminds me of Monica. And an unanswered question. "Sid. Can I ask you something?"

"Sure."

"In your efforts to help me with Mocktail. Did you set up Marshall as my client? I mean, did you tell Monica about me."

Sid looks a little shaken. I don't intend to stir things up so soon in our reconciliation but I am curious when it comes to Monica.

"I trust Monica completely. Although she works for Lex, she would never share anything that I didn't want her to. She saw you at the wedding and asked what you did. I mentioned you set up a new company."

"You told her I was a fake girlfriend?"

"Never. But I asked if she knew any potential clients."

"What did you say it was?"

"A relationship coach. I could not think of any other way to describe it and wanted to support you, without you falling for someone else."

"So, you set me up with her brother because you think he is not my type? Not a threat to you?"

"It was never about that. You were determined to make Mocktail a success and I trusted Monica to recommend a client who would respect you. I never considered you to be her type."

"She tends to go for what she likes." The real me makes no attempt to disguise my smile.

"You were telling the truth then? About the kiss in the toilets." Sid's eyes flash.

"And her smooth pussy." A missed opportunity. How different would things be today if I had not held back and fully tasted the Red Silk Panties? Would I still be here with Sid, or would it be Monica sitting opposite me celebrating this moment? I may never know.

"Should I be worried?" Sid holds my gaze, but I don't back down. "Okay. You posed one last unanswered question from our Mocktail dating. Now it's my turn."

"... Alright." I hesitate. The past doesn't matter now.

"You and me. Were you telling the truth at the ball when you said it was all fake? Was I always just a client to you?" Sid is humble and ready for the truth.

"You mean was any of it real?"

"Yes."

"What part exactly?" My flirty tone hits the spot.

Sid laughs. "You want me to go into detail?"

"Well, yes. It would be good to know which parts of the services I offered felt real to you and which parts felt fake." My heartbeat increases as the game begins.

"Sounds a bit like an appraisal. Shall I list them one by one so you can tick them off?"

"If you like." This could be fun.

"Perhaps we should play a drinking game. You like those." He remembers.

"I prefer stripping games, but as we're in public it will have to do."

"And when I get one right, you can take a shot."

"How will you tell I'm not lying?"

"Remember, I know your eyes look tipsy when you are turned on." Sid licks his lips.

"And your eyes flash when flirting."

"Like now." Sid smiles.

"You are very sure of yourself, Sid Richmond." This is a fun game already, made even more monumental by being first played with Sid.

"And you are not that good at bluffing, Kat James."

"Alright then, ask away." I take on the challenge, he can't be that good at this.

"Wait, I've changed my mind." Sid stalls. "For each one I get right, rather than a shot, you owe me another date. Deal?"

"And if you lose?"

"Oh, I don't think you want me to lose." Sid leans in, lips hovering close to mine, the flash point.

I close my eyes to hide that, yes, this turns me on. I can't give him the advantage before we start.

"Deal."

"So, we won't count the evening we met. The stag do. Because you have no memory of that." Sid reminds me of the one thing that held us back so long from getting to this point.

"Yep. Still got alcoholic amnesia."

"So, the second time we met. Here in the Vanilla Pod. You were pleasantly surprised that you liked me. True?"

"Is that a question or a guess?" I play hardball.

"A guess. True." Sid learns fast.

"Well yes, but I don't think that counts as date-worthy because it was an unfair situation. I knew you'd taken me home but as I couldn't remember anything, I spent the entire meeting imagining what we may or may not have done." Like his hands. I remember his hands, and imagining them peeling off my clothes, fingers tracing every inch of my body.

"Okay, so not a date, but definitely something to add to the list of fantasies to play out if we make it back to the bedroom." Sid's eyes flash brighter.

"Well, I think I won that round." I clear my throat. "What do you have for me next?"

"The wedding."

"Which part?"

"Which means there was more than one time your illusion was more cock than mock?"

"You tell me." I'm not giving anything away.

"Okay, but I'm not wasting time with foreplay. I'm going straight for the first dance."

"When I watched you schmooze with your ex? Hardly a turn-on."

"Ha! No."

"My torture with Uncle Wilfred?"

Sid is on a losing streak if he thinks that was pleasurable.

"Hell no! Before that, when I crept up behind you. Close enough to feel your body heat through your dress. I wanted to put my hands on your waist and pull you back. You had that one-sided hairstyle, exposing your neck here," Sid gestures to his own neck, "which was begging to be kissed. You leaned back into my hand and then brushed my cheek with your lips. That was cock, not mock."

"True." I remember. It was the first time I nearly kissed him.

"I knew it!" Sid gestures to Ethan. "That's one shot glass and one date for me."

When I wasn't looking, Ethan laid out a row of upturned shot glasses on the bar. Sid turns one over triumphant.

"Don't be too cocky, you got lucky that's all." Although luck has got nothing to do with it. I know there was no pretending with Sid.

"Let's see shall we? For my next guess, I am staying at the wedding. Do you remember the end of the night?"

"When your parents invited me over the next day?"

"No. Before that. The disco. That is what I'm talking about. That was cock and I don't just mean a semi. That was a full-on boner."

"For you maybe." That was the real spiritual turning point. But Sid is talking about raw sex. So, he is wrong on this one. "For me, it was not about the sex."

"What then?"

"More of a connection. That I didn't think I would feel again. Something in the core of my being. Here." I touch my heart. "And here." I touch my core."

"Real?"

"Yes."

Sid turned over another shot glass. That's two.

"And you held back because I was a client?"

"No." I look him in the eye, unafraid of looking tipsy this time. "Because of Matty."

"Oh, Kat. I would never attempt to replace him."

"That's not what I mean." I have talked enough about that today. This is not therapy. It is supposed to be flirting. "Let's carry on with the game. What's next on your list? The semi-naked just got out of the shower technique to trick me into taking that horrific painting?"

"So, you admit that turned you on?"

"You are not getting another free pass. It was a dirty move, so it doesn't count."

"The intention was to stop you from getting another parking violation, not to turn you on. Grans called me to let me know what had happened and there was no time to get dressed. It's not my fault you are so easily sidelined."

"And you are always in control?"

"Never, not when you are concerned. I want to kiss you all the time." Sid smiles. "Which brings me on to my next guess. The kiss at my studio."

"After you had the blowout with Alexandria. Why does that count? There was no assignment."

"Nevertheless, you persist in pretending to not like me. You turned up, all clean and casual in those dungarees, carrying that battered old leather bag. All fired up with that tipsy look. You wanted that kiss, there was nothing fake about it. You were there as Kat."

"True. It was a moment of weakness and you derailed my intentions with the kiss. Then I ran out so quickly I didn't have a chance to tell you why I was there."

"I was on a short deadline. To meet Grans whilst you were out. We were working on the plans for the art fair. So, why were you there?"

"To ask you out."

"And that is a double." Sid triumphantly turns over two glasses. "One for the kiss and one for the intent."

"A double entry is not my style."

"Ha! No. Poor wording on my account. But still, two more dates to add to the pile."

"Well, you can take one off for the kiss with that other girl. That was enough to shrink the balls off anyone."

"True, but when we take into account your tête-à-tête with Monica. They cancel each other out."

"Agreed." I sigh. "And before you get into it, you may as well turn over another shot glass for the Lock Wheel." No point reliving the humiliation of being interrupted.

"Ah yes, the scene of the ultimate pairing that never was." Sid flips over a fifth glass. "And what about the Jazz at the Victorian Pavilion? There was something there when we danced." His hand hovers over another glass.

"The flash point." My eyes burn with desire.

"Impossible to fake." Sid leans in.

"Almost."

"Let's see, shall we?"

Sid's mouth is on mine almost before he stops speaking. The heat burns deeper than any moment with Monica or Hugo or anyone since Matty. As I taste the Amaretto and cherry, the liqueur pools in my mouth. I wriggle closer and he lifts me up, my legs straddle his thighs, and grind against his growing desire.

"Definitely cock."

Sid pushes me back onto the bar and the shot glasses spin off.

"Wait." Sid pulls back laughing. "We're doing it again. We need a date first. How many did we get to?"

"Like a gazillion. But, there's no need to keep count. None of it was ever fake with you Sid. Not one kiss, or dance, or touch."

And we kiss again, the flash point burning bright. This is the real thing, it always was and always will be. There is no need to pretend ever again.

The End

ACKNOWLEDGEMENT

Thank you so much to every reader, your support means the world to me, and if you enjoyed reading Kat's story, please leave a review or some stars on platforms like Goodreads or Amazon - it makes a huge difference to independent authors and helps share the joy.

The fake dating trope is such fun, and Mocktail grew out of an overactive mind on a car journey listening to +1 by Martin Solveig on the radio. Thanks to my beta readers J, S, Y, D & F, who embraced my work, questioned plot holes and made me feel like a real author. A gift from D of The Ultimate Bar Book by Mittie Hellmich and some light spice from the Ann Summers Cock-tail books filled in the gaps.

Many rom-coms present characters with a history of trauma, and everything turns out all right in the end. In Kat, I tried to reflect the realism that there is no quick fix or magic pill. Trauma fills every cell of your body, and recovery is a journey supported by knowledge, professionals, family and friends. And for that, I thank K, J, H, C & G, who have helped me with my own Katzenjammer over the years, along with a couple of books, The Body Keeps the Score by Bessel van der Kolk and Why Has Nobody Told Me This Before by Dr Julie Smith.

Thank you to my husband for all your love and support. Never have you doubted me, asked when I will finish my book, or why I was doing another edit. You understand who Kat is and how important it was for me write as a creative outlet, motivating me to never give up.

Thank you to my boys, who have grown up with me writing in my spare time. Surprisingly you are not embarrassed with my social media posts, and without you I would know nothing about current trends and new slang. No cap.

Finally, thank you to my Mum, who waited patiently to read the finished book. Promise me that after you read all the rude bits, you will never mention them to me in conversation - ever (hiding behind my hands).

ABOUT THE AUTHOR

Eve Upshall

Eve Upshall lives on the south coast of England. Most of her writing happens when she should be doing something else. Should is not a kind word, so Eve prefers to do what feels good, which means using every spare moment (when not working) to create something. To crochet, write, read, listen to music and watch movies, or sometimes all of them at the same time.

Printed in Dunstable, United Kingdom